A Thousand Li:
The First War

A Cultivation Novel
Book 3 of A Thousand Li Series

By

Tao Wong

Copyright

A Thousand Li: The First War
Copyright © 2020 Tao Wong. All rights reserved.
Copyright © 2020. Sarah Anderson Cover Designer
Copyright © 2020 Felipe deBarros Cover Artist

A Starlit Publishing Book
Published by Starlit Publishing
PO Box 30035
High Park PO
Toronto, ON
M6P 3K0
Canada
www.starlitpublishing.com

Ebook ISBN: 9781989458402
Paperback ISBN: 9781989458419
Hardcover ISBN: 9781989458822 and 9781778550294

Books in the A Thousand Li series

The First Step

The First Stop

The First War

The Second Expedition

The Second Sect

The Second Storm

The Third Kingdom

The Third Realm

The Third Cut

Short Stories

The Favored Son

The Storming White Clouds Sect

On Gods and Demons

Clifftop Crisis and Transformation

Imperial March

Villages & Illnesses

Descent from the Mountain

The Divine Peak

Fish Ball Quest

Ten Thousand and One Fates

Table of Contents

What Happened Before

Two years ago, sixteen year old Long Wu Ying, a rice farmer in the state of Shen was conscripted into the army. Through a series of fortuitous encounters, Wu Ying gained the attention of an Elder of the Verdant Green Waters Sect and was admitted as an outer sect member, to begin his journey to immortality.

That year, he was forced to fight to keep his place in the sect where he defeated Yin Xue, the nobleman's son of his village in the final rounds of the competition. In doing so, he became an inner sect member with the attendant benefits and training. As an inner sect member, Wu Ying has progressed in his studies, growing in strength as a Body Cultivator – the lowest stage of cultivation – and gaining a secondary occupation as a Spirit Herb Gatherer.

Wu Ying is still in the early stages of his immortal journey, but has found fast friends in the sect in Tou He – an ex-monk turned cultivator – and Li Yao – a female cultivator who defies her noble parents to be a martial specialist. But the drums of war beat and Wu Ying must find strength, not only in his friends but within, to survive the encroaching armies.

Chapter 1

Cold winter air, humid and barely lit by the rising sun, was expelled from Wu Ying's mouth as he exhaled. Seated cross-legged in the central courtyard of his house in the Sect, he breathed in a slow, rhythmic manner. Chi—the energy of the world—entered his body and circulated through his still, muscular, lean form with each breath. As he drew in more chi to spiral through the twelve cleared meridians of his body, the chi pushed and strained against them, bringing with it pain and pressure. Again and again, it circulated, passing from meridians to just below his navel as it entered his lower dantian. There, the energy was packed tightly with the accumulation of the last five months' chi, energy gathered after his return from his expedition and throughout the winter months. Each breath brought more chi, his dantian a tight ball of energy that ached with the accumulation, one that sought a release.

Holding the energy tightly, Wu Ying opened his eyes. Dark brown eyes stared outward, fixing upon his friend who sat before him. Liu Tou He, the ex-Buddhist monk who still wore the orange robes of his order and kept his head shaved, sat before Wu Ying, watching over him. Beside the monk, Fairy Yang was seated on a nearby table, reading a scroll and casting occasional glances at Wu Ying. Tou He stared at his friend placidly, offering only a single nod of reassurance.

Wu Ying shut his eyes once more, drew another deep breath, and set to it. Chi gushed from his dantian, following his meridians, rushing forward at an ever faster rate. Each breath brought another circulation among the greater and smaller meridian paths, scouring them clean of minor refuse. With all twelve regular chi meridians cleared, Wu Ying was ready. He had been ready for months to take the next step.

Another exhalation as Wu Ying focused and pushed the distractions aside. Energy thrummed through his body, beckoning him to move, to make use of it. But all this energy, this accumulation of chi, was for another reason. For the next stage. Wu Ying directed the chi at the first of the Energy Storage meridians—the Conception Meridian, ren mai[1]. Breaking through the blocked Conception Meridian and freeing it for use was the first step in the Energy Storage stage. At least for the Yellow Emperor cultivation style that he practiced. From there, the cultivator would have to open and cleanse the other seven meridians as dictated by his style.

Each breath cycled the chi, bringing the accumulated energy to bear. Each circulation wore away at the blockage, an internal blow against the vessels that made up his body. Each circulation was a punch in his chest that started from within then reversed as the energy rebounded. With each rebound, Wu Ying had to take control of the rebounding chi and redirect it to join the normal flow of chi in his meridians, even as he pushed against the blocked barrier. The amount of chi he was channeling was greater than the amount his meridians could handle, increasing the pain ever further.

His dantian was the dam that had held back the flow of chi, forced to build up to dangerous levels and threaten the flood plains of his body. Now, Wu Ying had released the flow of water—of chi—into the drainage ditches that criss-crossed the fields of his body. But the flow of water was so great that some of it gushed out, spilling into the fields where they were not meant to be, while the rest broke against the dirty jam at the drainage ditch that led to the next field. Each time the chi flowed back, it spilled and was lost, wasting Wu Ying's months of careful husbanding. At the same time, the water damaged the fields.

Pain flowed through Wu Ying's body, making his breath hitch and his body tense. It mattered not, for Wu Ying's consciousness was concentrated within.

---

[1] Reminder. While the twelve meridians and eight extraordinary meridians (the energy meridians in my book) are actual meridians in traditional Chinese medicine, I am changing it for the sake of the story. Traditionally, the eight extraordinary meridians are already open.

At pushing and pushing at the blocked meridian. But no matter what he did, it would not give way. And in time, the gushing water subsided, the flow reduced. The impetus for his breakthrough receded. Even as his chi escaped, the pain faded, going from nerve-shattering, bone-breaking agony to the more subtle pressure of constant hurt.

A moment's hesitation, then Wu Ying began the slow process of reacquiring what chi still flowed in his body. He dragged the overflowing energy back to his dantian, wrapped it behind the dam of his will, and reduced the flow within until it reached a manageable level. When he was done, only then did Wu Ying open his eyes.

"I failed," Wu Ying admitted to his friend and Fairy Yang, though he knew they had sensed that already.

Tou He nodded placidly while Fairy Yang gave a simple curt nod before standing to leave. The most dangerous part of breaking through—or failing to break through—had passed. Though Wu Ying's body hurt, smaller blood vessels broken, the damage—for a failed breakthrough—was minimal.

Drawing another deep breath, Wu Ying pushed aside the feelings of failure and closed his eyes again. He might have failed, but he still had work to do. Work to recover what chi he could, to contain it for his next attempt.

***

Wu Ying stood in the middle of a courtyard much larger and more ornate than his own. Seated in front of him was his Master, Elder Cheng. Master cum sponsor for the Sect. Even seated, Elder Cheng looked to be taller than most men Wu Ying had met. Elder Cheng's oval face was framed with long, lustrous black hair, and like Fairy Yang, his disciple, he was dressed in the traditional green-and-black robes of an Elder of the Sect. By his side, Elder Cheng's jian rested against the wooden chair he sat upon.

"It seems that you failed," said Elder Cheng.

"Yes, Elder Cheng. I'm sorry," said Wu Ying.

"It is no matter. We all fail at some point," said Elder Cheng. "What is more important is that we learn from our failures. Now, what did you learn?"

Wu Ying hesitated as he considered his words. No use being dishonest with Elder Cheng. Wu Ying had been mulling over the failure for the last few hours, trying to work out what he had done wrong. "I did not have enough chi to break through to the next stage. My blockage must be harder than most."

"Incorrect," said Elder Cheng. "It was not that you had insufficient chi. It was that you had insufficient enlightenment. Cultivation is not just about an accumulation of energy. It is an accumulation of knowledge and experience. And you, you spent the entirety of winter in the Sect."

"I did take some assignments…"

"Some. But none of those assignments pushed you. None of them expanded your mindset, expanded the type of experiences you have had. And while your dalliance with Li Yao has given you something new, have you drawn upon that to expand your cultivation?" said Elder Cheng. "Have you achieved any enlightenment from being with her?"

Wu Ying flushed as Elder Cheng blatantly spoke of Wu Ying's budding romance with his fellow Inner Sect member.

"Don't think that I chastise you because I seek your embarrassment. I do so for your own good. At your age, there are many competing desires. The flush of youth is strong. But this is also the time to expand upon your cultivation. When one turns twenty or thereabouts, breaking into the Energy Storage stage becomes significantly more difficult. The blockages in each meridian harden. It is possible to break through afterward, but it requires herbs and spiritual treasures. Expensive spiritual treasures."

"As for Core Cultivation, after thirty, it is extremely difficult. Too many gifted students fall by the wayside, thinking they have time, indulging in fleshy pleasures and their ego."

Wu Ying blinked, never having had his teachers be so blatant about the difficulties of expanding one's cultivation. He knew that there were roadblocks as one aged beyond the normal lifespan of a mortal. Even though each level of cultivation expanded one's lifespan, the ease of ascending to the next level still favored the young. The additional lifespan that one gained from achieving a higher level of cultivation worked against the very laws of nature itself, or so it seemed.

"You should know that you are not one of those gifted sons of heaven. You have some skill. You have some ability. You have even achieved more enlightenment than most in the time I have known you. None of that truly matters if you do not seek to better yourself."

"I'm sorry, Master. I will do better." Wu Ying lowered his head.

"Good," said Elder Cheng. "That is all that I will speak of this to you. From here, it is your decision. That too is fate. Now, your Senior has told me that you have improved your swordsmanship. Show me."

Wu Ying nodded, walked to the center of the courtyard, and drew his sword. He paused, looking at Elder Cheng, and received a nod of acknowledgment. At first, Wu Ying started with basic forms of the Long family sword style. However, he soon diverged, adding in the movements of the Northern Shen and the Mountain Breaking Fist styles he had studied. Dragon sweeping the Branches turned into the Third mountain Fist which transformed into a sweep from the Northern Shen style before ending in the Dragon rises in the Morning. Motion to motion, form after form, he continued around the courtyard. It was fifteen minutes before he was done.

"Impressive," said Elder Cheng. "You've definitely improved and integrated the styles you have been studying. I have noticed that you are not touching upon the Dragon's Breath, your chi projection method."

"That is true, Master," said Wu Ying. "Because I have been trying to conserve my chi, I have not been practicing that form."

"That is your decision, but I would recommend you reconsider it."

Wu Ying waited for Elder Cheng to add to his statement, but he waited in vain. "Is there a particular reason I should be practising the Dragon's Breath?"

Elder Cheng looked concerned, stroking his chin. Eventually, he seemed to make up his mind and spoke. "The state of Wei has shown its aggressiveness over the winter. We have confirmed that they are purchasing large amounts of feed and other materials they will need for an extended campaign. As you know, the Six Jade Gates Sect have added to their Core Formation elders. It is because of this that we believe the state of Wei has chosen to escalate the war.

"While we do not expect, nor desire, our Sect members to take part in the war, it is not necessarily up to us."

"I see."

"Now, as for what you've been practicing, I have a few suggestions…"

***

Later that evening, after an exhausting afternoon of training with Elder Cheng, Wu Ying found himself at the inner sect dining hall with Tou He and Li Yao. With the year coming to a close, the Sect had opened up the stores and become more generous in the kinds of food that was served. It helped that the martial specialists had located a herd of white-tipped spirit deer, many of whom now graced the Sect's cooking pots. This uncommon bounty saw an increase in the hall's attendance, making the normally barren building busy with traffic. The sounds of people eating filled the room, the clatter of utensils, the tap of

14

wooden chopsticks on porcelain bowls, and the slurp of wet noodles a homey reminder.

"How did it go?" said Li Yao.

Wu Ying looked at his girlfriend, marveling once more that someone as beautiful and refined as her would deign to even pay attention to him, never mind being his girlfriend. Li Yao was smaller than him, standing barely five foot four, but she had the pale, smooth skin of a noble—and graceful demeanor of one too. But unlike most noble women, Li Yao was muscular and athletic due to her training as a martial specialist.

"It could be worse," said Wu Ying. "He did tell me that he is expecting this year's war to be worse than normal."

"I heard that too," said Tou He. "When I was out of the Sect, I noticed some movement among the peasants bordering the state of Wei. Many of them were sending their children and elderly to family farther from the borders."

"We do have it worse when a war breaks out." Wu Ying stabbed desultorily at his bowl of noodles, remembering when past wars had shaken his village. The worse the fighting got, the more the lords would take in terms of food, people, and money.

With a small smile, Li Yao watched the pair talk. "At least we won't be required to fight."

"Isn't that kind of what martial specialists do?" said Wu Ying.

"No, not really. We're the Sect's fist, but only when in contention against another Sect. We owe some loyalty to the kingdom, but we are cultivators. The Sect has already seen the passing of one kingdom and it still stands. We must have a longer view," said Li Yao.

"I'm surprised to hear you say that," said Tou He.

"Why? Because I'm a noble's daughter?"

"Yes."

Li Yao shook her head. "We are not all the same, you know. Some of us seek to be real cultivators. I know, I know, there are many here just to increase their strength. They are but an extension of their family. But you should know me better than that."

One thing struck Wu Ying about what she had said and he leaned forward, fixing Li Yao with his gaze. "You said the Sect had survived one kingdom?"

Li Yao nodded.

"Did the Sect abandon the previous kingdom?"

"In a way. This was three hundred years ago or so?" said Li Yao. "But if I recall my history right, the old kingdom insulted the Sect and the Sect Master chose to use the insult as an excuse to withdraw the Sect's support. Forced to fight cultivators and the invading army alone, the kingdom fell."

"Huh. That wasn't what I learned in school," said Wu Ying.

"I doubt the official curriculum would be as blunt," said Li Yao with a slight smirk.

"Well, let's just hope that they're all wrong." Tou He looked around the crowded dining hall then lowered his voice further. "We're not really trained to fight with an army. In fact, maybe it's something we should look into with the martial specialists."

"I'm not really interested," said Li Yao.

"Shirking knowledge for the sake of preference is not wise," cautioned Tou He.

Li Yao shrugged, a mulish look crossing her face. When Tou He looked to speak again, Wu Ying shook his head. He had learned to read Li Yao well. When she got into such a state, even logic would not dissuade her. In time, she would likely come around, but you had to let her come to that realization on her own.

"I do like that spring is coming," said Wu Ying, changing the topic. "I've seen some new assignments in the hall. Soon enough, I'll be out gathering again."

Li Yao brightened. "Definitely. I can't wait to see you fight for real. After all that practice with your sword by yourself, doing it together will be amazing."

Wu Ying kept a straight face, but Tou He could not help but choke off a laugh.

Grinning devilishly, Tou He leaned forward and said to Li Yao, "Tell me more about Wu Ying's sword. Have you taken a good look at it?"

Li Yao frowned at Tou He. "What you mean? You've played with his sword too."

This time around, Wu Ying could not help but laugh at Tou He's red face. Once they diverted Li Yao from asking about the blushing, the group turned their discussion back to the new assignments in the hall. And, of course, what they intended to buy with the contribution points they would earn.

Chapter 2

"You want to learn how to fight with an army?" said Chao Kun. The older martial specialist was in the late Energy stage of cultivation, rumored to be only a step away from reaching Core cultivation. Standing just under six feet, Chao Kun was handsome but not devastatingly so. His point of pride was his hair that reached his waist.

Tou He and Wu Ying were standing before the late stage Energy Storage martial specialist in the middle of the martial specialist training hall. Of course, the training hall wasn't a single building but a series of three buildings, a training yard with a dozen sparring arenas and the requisite exercise and training equipment. While technically not for the martial specialists' exclusive use, few who were not dedicated to martial arts dared to visit the martial hall. After all, the martial specialists just were not very good at not being competitive.

"Are you thinking about joining the war?" said Chao Kun.

"No," said Tou He.

"Maybe," said Wu Ying simultaneously. Tou He looked at Wu Ying with surprise, only to have his friend shrug. "I was supposed to fight in the war, you know? A part of me thinks that maybe I should go back and help."

"Well, you don't really need to worry about that. They only choose from martial specialists when they're looking for volunteers. You're not one, Gatherer," said Chao Kun. "Also, you are not even at Energy Storage. It would be foolish to allow an inner sect member who isn't a martial specialist to join the war. There are so many better options."

Wu Ying thought that Chao Kun was exaggerating a little but chose not to contradict his senior. There was nothing to be gained by making his senior lose face. In any case, he had a feeling his senior's comments were more to alleviate his guilt than about practical considerations. "It'd still be worth it for us to learn."

"Very well."

Chao Kun looked around the yard and spotted a few other martial specialists. He waved them over, gathering the group around him.

"Much of how a cultivator is used in a war will depend on the cultivator's abilities. A Core Formation elder is a very different individual from someone who has not reached the Energy Storage stage." Chao Kun looked directly at Wu Ying when he said that. "That being said, since we are mostly in the Energy Storage stage here, I will focus on our use there.

"Firstly, for those who have significant experience with qinggong techniques, they are often used as scouts and for flanking attackers. The ability to move quickly and silently across all kinds of terrain to attack resupply convoys, direct other scouting parties to hit un-fortified defenses, and in some cases, even take out their opposing army's officers are highly valued."

"But doesn't Elder Ko recommend we stay away from qinggong exercises?" Wu Ying asked with a frown.

"Only until you reach Energy Storage," one of the other cultivators said. "Also, Elder Ko is a bit of a traditionalist."

The group laughed, only to quiet from a glare by Chao Kun.

"Whatever he might be, Elder Ko is our Elder and should be respected. He only desires the best for each of us. And I'm sure his advice has helped everyone here at some point."

The group mutely nodded at Chao Kun's words.

"Good. Now, continuing. We have cultivator scouts who work alone for the most part, though they might work in pairs if they're working behind enemy lines. But not all cultivators have the skills or temperament to make good scouts. As such, most cultivators are grouped in small teams. Those teams can work independently of the main body, or in other cases, fight alongside the army itself. When working interdependently, very little additional training is required."

"Because we do that already?" Tou He asked.

"Yes. Exactly." Chao Kun gestured at the group, then made his gesture wider to encompass the mountain and Sect. "We already work in small groups all the time. And while the army raiding parties might be better equipped, most are not much better trained than your average bandit group."

"Some of them become bandits anyway," another martial specialist complained.

The group nodded. It was no secret that some soldiers, ill content to become farmers or to return to a life of drudgery, turned to banditry. And while the local lords were tasked with dealing with the groups, when the bandits were too well trained or numerous, the Sect was offered the chance to finish the job.

Chao Kun gestured for the group to focus. "Now, for the teams fighting with the army—which can make up most of the cultivators sent, depending on the needs and the ways the general uses us—the training is different. Standing in a line with soldiers in a pike wall would make poor use of our skills."

Wu Ying imagined his sword in a pike wall, the way he moved, and shuddered. All around, the other martial specialists did the same.

"So instead, most generals have us acting either as reinforcements, shock troops, or flanking strikers."

"Isn't that the same as fighting alone?" the noisy martial specialist said.

"No. Because not only will you have to learn to understand the flags and drums of the army, you might be tasked to act independently. Which means reading the flow of the battle. More"—Chao Kun held up a finger—"if you are reinforcing a line, you will have to not only rush to the broken line and beat the enemies, but also contain your style so that when the regular reinforcements arrive, you may leave."

Once again, the group tried to imagine that. There were more than a few grimaces as their imaginary scenarios played out. Big, swinging attacks, especially for those who wielded polearms, would be contraindicated. It might patch the hole fast, but then none of their reinforcements could take over. Same with big movements with the intention to reposition.

"For those acting as the vanguard or as shock troops to break a line, you'll need to learn how to do that. That means training against massed volleys of arrows and how to break a shield or pike wall," Chao Kun said. "Flanking is a little easier, though individual tactics there are somewhat different. Your goal will not be individual fatalities but disrupting the formation. In some cases, powerful and shocking attacks will be more important. The best flanking teams can break right through a formation, hopelessly disrupting an entire side. Again, you'll have to learn what works best for you, depending on your styles."

"We should learn that," Tou He said, elbowing Wu Ying.

"Yes, yes," Wu Ying muttered. It would certainly add to that experience Elder Cheng had spoken of.

"For the elite cultivators—those who have shown their ability—the generals often have another task for us. The most dangerous task." Chao Kun swept his gaze over the group, making sure he had their attention. "Cultivator hunting."

"Hunting?" another of the martial specialists muttered.

"If we are sending groups of cultivators to disrupt and bolster our men, don't you think the enemy will want to stop that?" Chao Kun said rhetorically. "Of course they will. And we will too, on our side. So we hunt their teams of cultivators, and they ours. Generals craft special teams and send them to fight or delay other hunting or disruptive teams."

Wu Ying nodded. That made sense. But… "What do Core cultivators do then?"

Chao Kun looked at Wu Ying before he shrugged. "It depends on the number of Core cultivators the enemy has."

Wu Ying raised an eyebrow in further query.

"If we have more, we send those who are in surplus to fight and disrupt," Chao Kun said. "In those cases, either their Core cultivators come out to fight and are beaten—or at least injured. Or they retreat until the numbers match. And we do the same."

Wu Ying nodded, recollecting the fights he had witnessed that involved Core cultivators. Alone, they could easily devastate an entire division. Even an Energy Storage cultivator could injure multiple soldiers with a single strike. But a Core cultivator not only had more chi, but also could expand the size and range of their attack. A single strike could consume an entire platoon. And while Core cultivators were still mortal, they were much harder to injure since their flesh and bone were strengthened by the chi within. A Core cultivator that studied Body Strengthening exercises would be a nightmare for an army.

Already, Wu Ying could see how a war could be—would be—fought between the armies. Keeping the number and presence of Core cultivators hidden in each army would be of vast importance. Intelligence—drawn from cultivators and spies—would play an important part in clashes.

"Any further questions?" Chao Kun said. "If it's nothing important, we'll begin. Some of you will need to play the soldiers. Others will take the part of the cultivators." When some grumbled, Chao Kun glared at all the martial specialists who had opened their mouths. "You'll all get the chance to play the hero."

Seeing that his last pronouncement had the group silenced, Chao Kun grinned and clapped his hands together. "Good. Then let's begin. Gao Fei. Lu Feng. Wu Ying. You can be the cultivators. Everyone else, grab a polearm."

***

Two hours later, Wu Ying was bouncing on the balls of his feet at the back of the line of "soldiers" as he waited for the signal. At first, there had been just over a dozen of them learning aspects of the fight. There had been a lot to learn, from the various flag signals and meaning of barked commands, to the most effective forms. The first hour had been a terrible mess, and within ten minutes, Chao Kun had made everyone slow down to reduce injuries.

Perhaps the clumsiness of their actions was what had attracted the first of the crowds. It was unusual to see the vaunted martial specialists failing at anything combat-related. At first, only a few inner sect members had come to watch. Then as word spread, more and more Sect members arrived. The group had grown nervous and self-conscious, making even more mistakes—which Chao Kun pounced upon and berated the group for in ever more creative language. Just before the entire group dispersed in disgust, Elder Hsu appeared.

The eccentric Elder, best known for studying a Northern snail-style grappling art, had been attracted by word of the training. Seeing the pitiful number of members on both sides, he had taken over from Chao Kun and proceeded to order the gawking crowd to join as new "soldiers." Freed from playing the soldiers, the martial specialists were split, with Chao Kun and Elder Hsu receiving equal numbers. Then the training had begun in earnest.

Wu Ying found himself grinning in a predatory fashion, his entire body poised forward as he waited. Waited for the flags to change. For the soldiers in front of him to part. Or for the drums—drums which had magically appeared in the last fifteen minutes—to signal another change. Behind, Chao Kun stood on a raised platform, focused on the lines.

A pink flag in the side of Wu Ying's vision moved. He turned, watching the flag holder's hands. Up-right, down-down, down and left. Wu Ying took off, closely followed by Tou He. The pair loped left and wide, passing behind their own soldiers at a distance even as Wu Ying counted the raised taps of the pink flag. One. Two. Three. Three cultivators looking to flank their party.

"Right two," Wu Ying called to Tou He.

"Heard."

And then they were around their own people and coming within sight of the enemy team. Wu Ying drew and exhaled, sending a flash of power—more a push of wind than a serious attack—at his targeted opponents. This was the Dragon's Breath attack Elder Cheng had told him to practice, though much reduced in strength. Tou He kept running, passing behind Wu Ying and going wide. His staff was ill-suited for fighting close to the soldiers, thus leaving Wu Ying to stay tight to the army and defend them.

The blast of chi-soaked air struck at the enemy. The closer of the two was more wary, bringing his dao[2] in a cut to destroy his portion of the attack in defense. His partner, less cautious, was caught out and stumbled back. Growling in frustration, the second martial specialist stopped running and moved warily off the field of battle, crossing behind the third member of the team, who was busy trading blows with Tou He. The pair paid little attention to the "dead" cultivator as they fought, wide sweeping attacks of staff against shield and mace.

Wu Ying had no time to focus on their battle, caught up in his own fight with the dao wielder. For once, Wu Ying had to admit, his favored weapon might be less than perfect. In a battle as fierce as this, with his movements restricted, the dao—whose only requirement was to cut—beat out the finesse of the jian. Frustrated and unable to move away, lest he open the soldiers to an attack, Wu Ying went on the defensive, blocking and throwing light cuts in return. Each blocked blow sent shocks down his arm.

A flicker of motion in the corner of his eyes. Wu Ying flicked his sword to intercept it but was too late. The sand-filled bag attached to the arrowhead smacked into Wu Ying's chest, leaving him with a bruise. Surprise filled Wu

---

[2] Remember, a dao is basically the Chinese sabre.

Ying for long enough that his opponent had to pull back a strike or risk injuring Wu Ying further.

"Arrows?" Wu Ying said, looking around. On the top of Elder Hsu's viewing platform, a semi-familiar cultivator stood, arrow nocked to bow and firing on the opposite end of the field now. "Bao Cong? That's not fair!"

"Off the field!" Wu Ying's former opponent snapped at him.

Realizing his mistake, Wu Ying scrambled off, idly noting the trio of arrows that littered the area around Tou He. It seemed that the ex-monk's defensive style—the Mountain Resides—could protect even against projectiles.

"I want archers on our side too," Wu Ying muttered as he reached the end of the field and rubbed his chest.

***

To Wu Ying's surprise, the mock battles became a mainstay of the training regime. Outer sect members were drawn into the mock wars, forced by their trainers to partake, while the martial specialists took the role of the opposing cultivators. As the training grew formalized, additional arms and armor appeared, partly to reduce injury for the outer sect members and also to allow the martial specialists to cut loose. Using a chi-filled air strike to blow apart a pike line at full and at half-strength were very different things.

In time, additional defensive options were added, with one-use talismans and special defensive equipment given out. Of course, it wasn't just the martial specialists who acted as the opposing cultivators, though they were the majority. After all, the hot-blooded youth of the Sect all enjoyed a little rumble once in a while.

What amused Wu Ying was the addition of the Elders, many of whom argued and fought for the right to be the commanders of the opposing teams.

It took the intervention of the Inner Sect Hall Master himself to sort out that growing issue. Now there was a sign-up sheet and rotation for the Elders.

Even more amusing to Wu Ying was the small, but persistent, betting ring that had formed around each battle. A couple of times, Wu Ying had tried his hand at gambling, but after losing a couple of Meridian Opening Pills, he had given up on that sin. Wasting resources, even if these resources were less useful to him now, was anathema to the peasant.

Scenario after scenario played out over the next month, with Elder Hsu seeming to take great delight in coming up with new potential battles. Sometimes the cultivators were sent in as the vanguard and had to deal with unbroken pike lines and flights of missiles. Other times, they were driven to the flanks, sent as reinforcements for fractured platoons, a stiffening agent for broken morale. Or they might fight between the opposing groups, dueling one another in support or in opposition of a winning side.

In short order, Wu Ying gained both an appreciation of the aid a cultivator could bring to an army and a realization of how limited their effects could be. Since most of society had received some cultivation training, most soldiers were in the early stages of Body Cleansing. As such, while Wu Ying was stronger and faster, he was not, in reality, a major factor in any fight.

However, those at the Energy Storage stage were able to project their chi in attacks that could shatter lines or reach behind guarding shields and kill archers or officers. Some cultivators with powerful qinggong skills were able to pass through packed lines to attack officers and other cultivators. The more powerful the cultivator, the more damage they could deal, their chi stores ample to deal out multiple strikes.

But for all that, cultivators were still human. Blades could wound, arrows could pierce, shields could bruise. Exhaustion, the press of bodies, the sheer mass of numbers of "normal" soldiers could wear down even the most powerful inner sect member. That was driven home in the sixth battle, when the cultivators were massed against a larger number of outer sect members. Forced to fight a delaying action, they did well. At first. But eventually, the cultivators fell. An errant blow. A missed parry. And one would fall. And then another. Wu Ying prided himself that at least he was not the first nor second to fall. He had managed to last for a while, using his skills and careful management of his chi and positioning to survive. Even if he did not manage to score as many kills, he had survived.

A failure, a lesson. It was all experience, as Elder Cheng had told him. And now, Wu Ying sat in his courtyard, meditating on the battles. Taking them in not only to analyze his martial forms to do better, but to study them for his own cultivation. His dao. What had he learned?

An image. Senior Ge, powerful and heroic, standing in the line. Beating aside poleaxe cuts, tearing weapons out of hands and striking raised shields. Each blow so powerful that he crumpled the wooden defenses and blew away his attackers. Striding forward into the middle of the battle line to be swallowed by the masses. Gone.

Tou He and himself, standing side by side as a rain of arrows dropped. Wu Ying pulling upon the Brilliant Woo Petal Bracer to charge his Dragon's Breath attack, slicing apart arrows that fell upon their team. Tou He striking the ground with his staff and forming a chi-empowered barrier. The flight of arrows was either cut apart or blocked, falling to shatter around them. Skipping past the defending pair, the rest of the team hit the side of the line.

Another memory. Of himself fighting a pair of Energy Storage cultivators as he tried to block them from approaching their rearguard. He was losing. Of course he was losing. The Long family style was not a defensive style. Nor could he win against two others—even if he was more skilled. But he didn't have to win. He just had to delay them, because in delaying them, the rest of his team could do their job.

Memories, learning, understanding. Each breath, he assimilated them. And then another memory rose, unbidden.

Crouched in a rice paddy with his family and the rest of the village. Working together to plant stalks of rice in the water, moving from rice field to rice field. Some tried to do it alone. But the work required to plant the rice stalks was backbreaking and tiring. You could work together or alone, but together was faster. More efficient. And more fun.

The same lesson.

It was all the same lesson. Perhaps Wu Ying was dumb. Perhaps he was slow. Or perhaps some lessons had multiple facets to them. Each bowl of knowledge consisted of multiple grains that had to be chewed upon and digested individually—even if it was the same bowl.

Chi swirled, gathered and formed, beckoned by the breakthrough. The world approved, once again, as a part of the Dao—the greater way—was understood. Wu Ying absorbed it, took in the chi even as it petered out. It was only a small lesson after all, and one he had once known. But still.

New experience. New enlightenment. Another step on his path.

Chapter 3

Letters from home were always a treat. Having to cross hundreds of li[3] to reach the Sect, letters had to be carried by local merchants or private postal couriers. Such individuals worked circular routes around the kingdom, only deigning to visit places like Wu Ying's village when sufficient time had passed. As such, the village had to rely on the trips by locals to the main city or the occasional merchants who were, for obvious reasons, less regular during the winter.

Seated in his study in mid-afternoon, Wu Ying caressed the side of the letter. It had arrived last night, but rather than waste candlelight to read the correspondence, Wu Ying had used it as a spur for today's training. Now, having finished early, Wu Ying broke the seal on the wrapped scroll and peered within.

In short order, Wu Ying had sorted the two letters into three components. First, set aside for later consideration, was more discussion about the Long family style. That would require time to puzzle out, since his father had taken to writing more and more cryptic statements as Wu Ying progressed. Second, was the actual letter from his father. The entirety of the contents fit on a single piece of paper. And lastly, the letter from his mother, which would contain the meat of the correspondence. That was the letter he read first.

Wu Ying greedily devoured the news from home, reading through her letter in one quick burst before returning to its start on the right[4]. Wu Ying read more slowly now, savoring the details.

…Chief Tan returned today from the city, having delivered our fall taxes and having sold the rest of our stores. We have more than enough for the winter, thanks to your generous donations. Chief Tan has made a deal to purchase a half dozen piglets in spring, when we

---

[3] Reminder. One li is half a kilometer roughly. Or somewhat less than a quarter of a mile.

[4] Traditional Chinese writing was written and read right to left, up to down. There is also little to no punctuation in this traditional style. Take that, Oxford comma!

have finished building the village pen. Three of those piglets will be ours, the Zhangs will own one, and the village will share the last two. I know you are concerned about us, but we must plan for all our futures.

He also brought back news that the others who left with the army will not be returning this winter. They are training very hard and expect to see fighting next year. He did bring back rumors that another conscription will occur, though I fear they will be disappointed by what they find if they choose to do so. There are few enough. But just the threat has the Pengs talking of bribing Chief Tan—their only son just turned fourteen.

Wu Ying's lips thinned. Fourteen. It seemed the kingdom was growing desperate if they were lowering the conscription age that far. He sighed, shaking his head. This was why war never saw a winner. Even if you won, your kingdom suffered for the next generation. If they took away all the farmers, who would grow the rice?

The money you sent for us to store for our travels arrived safely. Thank you for the herbs too—they have helped a lot with your father's leg. While Chief Tan continues to be resistant to the idea of leaving, many of the other villagers have agreed to consider it. We've begun preparations for the journey, though leaving so much of what we have built is hard for all of us. We pray that the army will hold and make all our preparations for naught.

Wu Ying breathed a sigh of relief. This was good. Ever since he had learned of the upcoming war, he had wanted his parents to come to the Sect's city. What had started as a goal to safeguard his parents had morphed into one to save the village, as his parents had refused to leave their long-time friends to suffer alone. Even convincing his parents to consider leaving had been a test of Wu Ying's scholarly skills. Even if most times, the peasants were left alone—unkilled, unenslaved—accidents happened. And in war, those accidents left behind broken bodies and empty homes.

It relieves my heart that you are part of the Sect. And working in as prestigious an occupation as a Spirit Herb Gatherer. I think—and your father agrees—that this suits you. You were always wandering around the fields when you were young, always curious about the world. And while it might be dangerous, I know that your father's lessons will keep you safe.

Wu Ying smiled, reading on as she turned to gossip. He shook his head at the litany of births, of the few deaths—much fewer with the fixed housing and surplus of food—that winter brought. He read about the travails of soil and drainage before his eyes fell onto the only portion that made him grimace.

…marriage was great. If the heavens are willing, they will sire a child soon.

While discussing marriages, I know you are enamored by this Li Yao. She sounds like a very nice young lady. But she is the daughter of a noble. When the time comes, duties and obligations will pull on her even more strongly. In that, she is even less free than you. We have no expectations of you, in terms of lineage. Your father has settled himself with your goal of immortality. In that way, the family name might continue for all eternity perhaps.

Remember. It is good to explore your feelings, but do not give too greatly. Some people are not meant to be together.

Wu Ying glared at the paper, almost wishing his mother was here for him to shout at. To explain. Of course, he would never do that. Still, it was a passing desire, an indolent, unfilial wish. Because what did his mother know of Li Yao? Of cultivator society? Why did she feel the need to meddle from so far away?

Exhaling, Wu Ying calmed himself and his mind. She was his parent, and all parents meddled. At least all she offered were words of advice, rather than commandants like Li Yao's parents.

Setting aside the letter to be filed with the rest of their letters, Wu Ying turned to his father's next. This one required only a single read-through.

Wu Ying,

I know what your mother has written to you. I will not say that she is wrong, nor will I recommend that you join the war. I will note that there is opportunity in conflict. You are my son, and I wish you the best. I know that whatever you choose to do, you will do it with forethought and caution.

On that note, I do wish that you take notice of the amount of funds you have been sending us. It is not seemly for our son to send so much to his parents, especially to a small village like ours. Save some of those funds for your own cultivation. Your mother and I have more than enough.

I have included additional notes from what you have spoken of when practicing the form. It sounds like the martial arts that you have learned can complement our own style. Continue to keep an open mind and make sure that you practice our form. While the Long family style has stagnated in the past couple of generations, it was once well renowned. There is more depth in the style than you will see at first glance. As you learn more, you will see that martial arts is a clouded and deep lake. I am only sorry to say that I do not have much additional advice I can offer. You will soon surpass me.

Your father

Wu Ying sighed after finishing the letter. His father was not a man of many words and certainly not one to express bountiful emotions. Still, Wu Ying preferred his short letter to his mother's. The heartfelt warmth and trust in Wu Ying's decision-making was heartening. His father hadn't even mentioned Li Yao.

Wu Ying tapped his lips, staring at the letters before he set them aside to be filed. He picked up his own stationary, dipped his brush in a nearby inkwell, and wrote.

Papa, Mama,

I have received your letters dated the nineteenth day of the tenth moon[5] of the year. Thank you for your thoughts and all your consideration. Papa, I have not had a chance to read your thoughts on our style, but I'm sure they will be enlightening as always. Not a lot of interest has happened in the last few months, as we have mostly spent our time studying.

I am glad to hear you are doing well with the funds I have sent. Please, let me know what you might need when you arrive. I have spoken with Elder Huang who runs the kitchens and he is willing to assign you multiple plots of land to the north of the Sect. The land will need to be cleared and drainage built, but I have assured him that this is something the village is well equipped to do. There is a nearby stream that feeds into the main river here, so it is decent farming land.

Wu Ying grimaced as he finished that part of the letter. That had taken quite a bit of convincing—and quite a few journeys up and down the mountain—to arrange. Still, with the agreement of Elder Huang and the magistrate in the city below, the village's arrival—if necessary—would be smooth. Even after all his work, Wu Ying knew that the villagers would refuse to leave unless things went bad. There had been too much sweat and bloodshed put into the development of their village to leave it so easily.

I continue to take lessons with Elder Li as well as reading further about the various herbs suitable for someone at my cultivation level. There is a lot to learn, and even if I have some experience at this, I still make mistakes regularly. Senior Goh continues to praise how

---

[5] The Chinese calendar is a lunar calendar with twenty-eight days and twelve months (normally). Leap years see the addition of an additional month and that happens every four years. Generally, the months are roughly one to two months displaced from the Georgian calendar (so New Year's is in January or February).

much I've accomplished, but I think he is more interested in the fact that I have decent martial skills and thus will allow him to work the gardens more. Still, the things he has taught me while encouraging my development are highly useful, so I am grateful for his attention.

In the winter months, I have other regular classes put on by the Sect. Much of this knowledge ranges from the classics to formations and spiritual equipment. I cannot say that I am the most brilliant student. As you know, there are many better suited to the scholarly lifestyle. Still, I do not think I shame our family. Certainly, compared to Tou He, I find many of the lessons easier. Tou He's previous life as a monk has created interesting gaps in his education.

Good news about Tou He too. He's managed to clear his fourth Energy Storage meridian. His Master is very happy with his progress, though I understand they intend to slow his breakthroughs now. At least for the next few months to consolidate his development.

Wu Ying looked at the letter and what he'd written. Tou He was, in many ways, the quintessential prodigy. A martial prodigy who had spent years of his life studying multiple styles. An incredibly quick cultivator. Except there was that unspoken issue with Tou He's chi cultivation. The ex-monk still had not revealed the details of it, but Wu Ying knew that Tou He's master was hard at work searching for a solution. If they could not find one, Tou He's rapid ascent could find itself bottlenecked at the Core Formation stage.

Admittedly, for many cultivators, that would be a problem they wished to have. But like Wu Ying, Tou He sought the furthest reaches of cultivation. To be bottlenecked before truly stepping on the road to immortality would truly be a shame.

Lip curling up, Wu Ying shook his head and returned to his writing.

I continue to practice the other martial styles that were taught to me. I believe I've managed to achieve a small breakthrough in combining the three styles. Fairy Yang has been particularly gracious about spending her time teaching me. Of course, she is very busy as the newest elder in the Sect, but she seems to make a little time every week to continue my training. It seems that unlike my Master, she is willing to be more hands-on. Elder Cheng continues to feel that too great a hand in my training will divert my fate.

Of the two cultivation exercises I have learned, I've achieved a greater understanding of the Aura Strengthening. I am unable to progress the technique further though, as I've sealed and compressed my aura as much as possible within my current cultivation level. Further progress will have to wait until I reach the next level.

There was no knock on the door as Ah Yee arrived, carrying a small, covered, clay drinking bowl on a serving tray. The older woman, his designated servant, set the bowl beside Wu Ying before lifting the lid with a flourish. Wu Ying choked at the smell from a mixture of months-old herbs, dirt, and other foul-smelling ingredients.

"Your daily supplement, Master Long," Ah Yee said. "Remember, don't leave it too long. It will lose potency if it grows cold."

"And taste worse," said Wu Ying.

Not that the sludge-coated oil taste could be much worse. The supplement was a requirement for Wu Ying's second level of his other cultivation exercise—the Reinforced Iron Bones technique. At this stage, it was insufficient to wait for damage and repair his body when it occurred. He had to induce the damage and the cleansing—which was where the sludge came in.

"Waiting won't make it better," Ah Yee said, tapping one foot.

"Fine!"

Wu Ying picked up the bowl and, holding his breath, drained it in one gulp. It was, as he remembered, terrible. A mixture of rotten food and herbs, with a weird texture and an oil-coated sludge taste. After he choked the drink down, he placed the clay bowl on the tray and reached for the cup of tea Ah Yee had poured in anticipation. Already, he felt the toxic sludge roil in his stomach, trying to come back out. In an hour or so, he would be in a dire situation with his guts. Until then, he could only hold on and distract himself.

"Good. We're nearly out of the autumn willow roots," Ah Yee said. "Seven-year roots are hard to find."

"I'll ask Master Li." If there was one good thing about the concoction, it was that Wu Ying had been able to find more effective and cheaper substitutes for the herbs within. Of course, part of the reason no one used the substitutes he did was because of the taste.

Ah Yee bowed and, after replacing the lid, took away the offending bowl, leaving Wu Ying to his silent torment. He stared at his paper, considering what else to write. More news about his cultivation exercises. Not about their recent martial training. His father would understand and approve—he always said the more one trained, the less one bled. His mother would be upset though, and while they might afford each other privacy, any letter he wrote would be read by both.

More news about Li Yao?

Wu Ying shook his head. No. His mother disapproved, and his father did not care. And, truth be told, his relationship with her was tenuous enough. All they had done was take long strolls and meals, the occasional assignment, and spar together. A lot of sparring. Discussions—deeper discussions—had been avoided.

Wu Ying sighed and gave up. There was not much more to write. He'd finish it later. Right now, he needed to meditate and channel his chi. It would not help a lot with the cultivation exercise, but any improvement was better than sitting here stewing.

Chapter 4

"You are back." The speaker was an elderly gentleman with an extremely deep voice, clad in the gray-and-green robes of a Sect Elder. Elder Ko, unlike most of the other Elders, wore the elaborate headdress that marked his elevated position in the Sect as Librarian and Scholar for the Inner and Outer Sect Libraries. He absently stroked his beard as he stared at Wu Ying, who had been wandering the stacks, pulling out occasional scrolls and manuscripts to browse through their contents before returning them.

"Yes, Elder," said Wu Ying. "I am still looking for a new cultivation exercise that would supplement my training."

"You're still blocked at Body Cleansing, correct?" When Wu Ying nodded, Elder Ko continued. "And you're looking to advance to Energy Storage soon, yes?"

Even though Wu Ying thought that this was very much a rhetorical question, he nodded yes. Elder Ko chuckled and gestured for Wu Ying to follow.

They walked half a dozen steps before Elder Ko looked back at Wu Ying. "You will pay the appropriate fee afterward."

He did not even spend time waiting for Wu Ying to acknowledge his words. Not as if Wu Ying intended to cross the Elder. Few individuals within the Sect would be more detrimental to cross than the Elder in charge of the Library. Maybe his own Master and the Sect Leader. Maybe.

"There are three types of cultivation exercises I believe could be of use to you. Firstly, we can increase the speed of flow of your chi. This will allow you to initiate energy projections and certain types of skills at a greater speed in the future. Of course, right now, none of this is particularly useful since you are at the Body Cleansing stage. Even your equipment will not benefit much from your work. However, this increased flow could be useful for you in breaking through to the Energy Storage stage."

When Elder Ko had finished speaking, he turned around and handed Wu Ying a small manual. The manual was more of a notebook than a full document, but by this point, Wu Ying had gotten used to the idea that many of the cultivation exercises recorded in the library were jotted down thoughts, well-constructed workarounds, or small techniques that his predecessors had created. Only a few were extended documents.

"Now for the second option, we can expand your dantian."

Wu Ying could not help but interrupt Elder Ko at this point. "I thought the Sect did not have any of these manuals?"

"We do not have many." Elder Ko glared at Wu Ying disapprovingly. "Especially compared to some other sects. But it does not mean we do not have any. We would not be the largest, most prestigious sect in the kingdom if we had none."

The scorn in Elder Ko's voice made the student quail and bow low while offering a profuse apology.

Seeing that Wu Ying had learned his lesson, Elder Ko moved on with his explanation. "In truth, there are many varieties of cultivation exercises that focus on the development of the dantian's size. As one of the most important areas in the first two stages of cultivation, it is an area of intense interest. As with most types of cultivation exercises, the various exercises are variations on a theme. Like cultivation styles, certain types of exercises work better for others. The majority will suit most of our Sect members who might need to expand their dantian a little. After all, you do not need to achieve full compatibility with the cultivation exercise when you are only going to be using it for a short term and for marginal improvements. It's only when a dantian is compromised or otherwise an issue that more variety or specific exercises are required.

"In this case, what we are looking at"—Elder Ko passed Wu Ying a bound scroll—"is a simple exercise that suits you." Wu Ying felt a chill as Elder Ko stared at him, a small smile on his face, almost hidden by his beard. "As you are studying the Reinforced Iron Bones technique, this will complement that exercise. Especially during your second stage. You only need to adjust your current concoction a little. The pain should not be significantly worse."

While Wu Ying was considering what Elder Ko meant, the head librarian had already moved on to the next row. When he came out this time, he was holding a much, much larger book. Instead of handing the book to Wu Ying, Elder Ko flipped through the pages until he'd located the section he desired.

Elder Ko pulled out a small strip of silk and slid it between those pages before he shut the book. "If you decide to go with this technique, you will need to copy out the instructions yourself."

"Yes, Elder."

"So, this exercise…"

"Elder?" Wu Ying held out his hand, ready to take the book.

Still, the Elder refused to hand the book over, looking reluctant and unsure for the first time that Wu Ying had ever seen. "I am uncertain if this is a good choice."

"May I ask why?" Wu Ying said. "It is dangerous?"

Not that that would necessarily stop Wu Ying, but he was not looking forward to practicing something that could cripple or kill him. There were, unfortunately, quite a few cultivation methods that walked that line much closer than they should. Cultivators were well known for taking risks for power.

"No. Well, no more than normal." Elder Ko shook his head. "It is the work itself. It came from a cultivator who walked one of the heretical paths. The exercise itself is not, in itself, heretical, in my judgment. But it is close."

"Oh." Wu Ying fell silent.

Heretical paths were, by nature, uncommon. Unlike Demonic daos, heretical paths were not in and of themselves wrong. They were just strange.

Deviant. Possibly dangerous to follow for many. That it suited a few special groups, a few heretical sects did not make them clean or widely accepted. For example, the famous heretical sect Seventh Plate, Third Serving, whose initiates all followed a single dao—the dao of gluttony.

"And the author's dao?"

Elder Ko said, "A shamanic path."

"Oh." Shamanic paths were strange to Wu Ying. Some of the smaller clans were rumored to still have them, groups of individuals who held to old religions. Old beliefs. More in the north and west, not so much in the civilized east. But… "What does the cultivation exercise actually do?"

"Regeneration. Again, it suits you. You tend to push yourself to the maximum," Elder Ko said. "And this will allow you to refill your dantian faster. But it requires you to consider the flow of the world in a way that is not normal to our current teachings of the five elements."

Wu Ying's eyes widened. Refilling his dantian, refilling the amount of chi he had was of utmost importance to him right now. He had to gain at least twice as much chi as he normally wielded if he wanted to again attempt a breakthrough. And that required the slow process of drawing in chi from the external world, purifying it, and storing it. It was not as if he was trying to restore himself to his normal levels—he was trying to achieve an overabundance. Which was always harder.

"Don't be too excited. It will do nothing for your current needs," Elder Ko said. "The process only works for your normal refinement. Everything above that, it will be of significantly less use. In fact, you'll have to discard the additional chi you now hold to practice this method."

That made Wu Ying frown. What he wanted was a way to speed up his cultivation, not another way to slow it down.

"Don't look like that. Read them over first," Elder Ko said. "There are notes about the efficiency within." When Wu Ying made to thank him, Elder Ko waved. "Go."

Wu Ying nodded and exited the stacks with the cultivation exercises. He quickly found an empty table and placed down the exercises, casting a glance around and spotting no others. In short order, Wu Ying delved into the works, reading them in detail. This level of scrutiny, the ability to read the actual documentation in depth was not something allowed with a cultivation manual or even a martial style.

Those kinds of details were often either locked away via a spiritual seal for rarer manuals. For the ones that Wu Ying had access to right now, the librarians just kept a close eye on the Sect members, ensuring they read no more than the first few stances and the principles. The details of cultivation manuals or martial styles were often so dense that a quick browse would be unlikely to garner the important, subtle details that made a martial style exemplary. A minute difference of an inch might not seem like much – until that inch was the distance to your heart.

In the end though, the advice of someone like Elder Ko was what would sway someone at Wu Ying's level to purchase a martial style or cultivation manual. Though Wu Ying had heard of more than one unhappy inner sect member who had purchased multiple manuals due to a lack of suitability.

Cultivation exercises were simpler by significant degrees. As such, reading through the documents was not particularly difficult or time consuming. Within a few bells, Wu Ying had finished analyzing the works and sat back, tapping on his lips in thought.

Speeding up the flow of his chi could be useful at the Energy Storage stage and the Core Cultivation stage. However, Wu Ying had noted several comments by those who had studied this work indicating that the progress they saw was insignificant when one advanced their cultivation. That, Wu Ying knew, was a matter of proper suitability and tiers. It was the problem with the various tiers of cultivation, especially once one had advanced past the Core Cultivation stage. Body Cleansing and Energy Storage cultivators were still within the mortal realm of strength. A particularly skilled Body Cleansing cultivator could beat an Energy Storage cultivator under the right circumstances. Unless the heavens themselves were looking down upon an Energy Storage cultivator, they stood no chance against a Core cultivator. This level of disparity continued through all the stages onward. As such, while increasing the flow of his chi now would help in the next stage, it was possible that the improvement and time spent would matter little at the Core Cultivation stage.

Expanding his dantian faced much the same issues. During the Core Development stage, the dantian was assimilated within the core—the gathered energy hardening and becoming the core itself. The various stages of Core cultivation included the hardening and layering of that newly developed Core. All the chi a cultivator had created became part of the core that a cultivator would use from then on. Of course, a larger dantian meant a larger core. That, theoretically, meant a more powerful cultivator. The difference in sizes of a Core, for most individuals, would not be a huge factor though—other issues like density, speed, and quality of the dao and chi mattered just as much in the Core Cultivation stage.

Just as important was the dao path that a cultivator was on during this period. Of course, it was not of the same level of importance as during the Nascent Soul stage. After all, during the Nascent Soul stage, a cultivator was beginning to embody the dao that cultivator studied. Only if he embodied it fully could he ascend.

Still, for all that, Wu Ying could not help but think that this was the most presently useful exercise. It would increase his strength and his chance of breaking through to the next stage, and it could provide benefits in the future.

The last cultivation exercise puzzled Wu Ying. After staring at the book once again, Wu Ying pulled it open and reread its contents and the notations made by the Elders. Once he was done, Wu Ying sighed. Like before, he was still uncertain about the exercise. He could not understand why Elder Ko had offered it to him.

Sure, the cultivation exercise allowed him to recharge his empty dantian faster. However, it was most effective when his dantian was empty. Regeneration rates would reduce as he grew fuller. And as Elder Ko had mentioned, it would be much less effective when he tried to overfill his dantian for breaking through to the next stage.

Of course, the most interesting thing about the cultivation exercise was the way it was built. Increasing his regeneration rates came in three forms. Firstly, he would pick the type of chi that entered his body during the acceptance stage from the world. It required an adjustment of his aura, allowing him to individually tease out the strands of chi that most closely suited his body. In this case, since he practiced the Yellow Emperor's cultivation method, it would be unaspected chi. The way the exercise required him to alter his view on the world, the way he sensed it, was the semi-heretical part. It didn't mean looking at the five elements but at much, much more, as each element that Wu Ying sensed had a "spirit" of its own. As such, even what he would consider "unaspected" chi might have spirits that required filtering out.

Next, he had to convert the chi within his body from unknown, unaspected chi to one that suited his body. It was like stamping his own mark on the energy. In normal cultivation, he would be converting aspected and unaspected chi types before he made it suitable for his body. Here too, the cultivation exercise was different as it taught Wu Ying a new method to imprint his own mark, his will on the chi at a greater pace.

Finally, the third aspect of the cultivation exercise created a small vortex flow within Wu Ying's dantian so that he drew in chi from the world faster. It was like a small whirlpool in Wu Ying's dantian, a complex flow of energy that was dictated by his level of mastery of the exercise. Of course, it looked nothing like a whirlpool, instead made up of multiple whirls and whorls.

The simple cultivation exercise had multiple aspects to it, all of which would force Wu Ying to stretch himself. And he had to admit, most of those exercises would probably be useful even if he ascended to a higher cultivation stage. Whether it was to strengthen his aura or being taught to process the chi of the world at a faster rate, it could not be harmful. At least in Wu Ying's mind.

Yet Wu Ying hesitated long and hard over his choices. Elder Ko's advice was generally extremely incisive. However, the Elder was also known to test cultivators. In that sense, blind faith in another could be harmful.

Cultivation, at its heart, was a lonely exercise. Finding one's dao was something that only an individual could do. A Master and Elder might provide a few signposts along the way, but it was a cultivator who had to walk the path. Knowing one's heart and knowing what one truly desired, and being willing to take the risk, was the only way a cultivator could truly ascend to the heavens.

Knowing all that, Wu Ying sat quietly with the cultivation exercise before him and considered his next step.

***

A week later, Wu Ying was in the gardens behind Elder Li's residence, hauling big baskets of compost into the greenhouse. As spring arrived, the entire gardening and gathering section of the Sect was thrown into high gear. That meant everyone, from inner sect members to outer sect servants, were forced to do the most menial of tasks. Unlike any of the other departments in the Sect, there were no complaints. Gardening or gathering, herbology at its base roots was about getting your hands dirty. Those who could not, would not, accept that simple truth were of no use to Elder Li and were discarded in short order.

That did not make hauling woven bamboo baskets full of compost back and forth a particularly agreeable task. Unfortunately, being both a martial specialist and specializing in external herbal gathering, Wu Ying was one of the more suited members to this task.

"Good job." Senior Goh slapped Wu Ying on the shoulder. "Two more runs and you should be done."

Wu Ying grunted, trotting into the warm greenhouse. The greenhouse was built with a large retaining wall along the backside, facing perpendicular to the movement of the sun. That allowed the heat from the sun to enter the greenhouse through the entire day, warming not just the main section within the greenhouse but the back retaining wall. Smaller sections within the back wall itself circulated heated air through the greenhouse, the fires being fed from the outside. Of course, living as far south as they did, the semi-transparent glass that made up the ceiling of the greenhouse and the embedded ritual wards were sufficient to keep the greenhouse warm during all but the coldest winters.

Within the building itself, soil was stacked three levels high on standing, movable shelves. Gardeners worked each shelf of plants, mixing soil and compost together with other, more specialized fertilizers to ensure the growth of the spirit herbs. Wu Ying had vivid memories of gathering some of that fertilizer—fire beetles, fruit bat dung, and the innards of golden koi were the least objectionable types. In addition, each gardener had a few bags of crushed demonic cores to disperse into the soil as they worked. More than once, Wu Ying felt the tremors of wood and earth aspected chi flow from a cultivator into the soil.

Every single cultivator worked with intense focus, driven even higher when Elder Li, with her wooden cane, strolled by, peering over their shoulders. At times, the old woman would provide words of encouragement or correction before moving on. Wu Ying quickly dumped his bag and trotted out, not wanting to engage the Elder at this time.

In short order, Wu Ying finished delivering the compost bins and trotted over to Senior Goh. He breathed deeply, clear of the burdensome containers, circulating his chi through his body as he tried to reenergize himself.

"You look tired," Senior Goh said, frowning. "The bags weren't that heavy."

"It's an exercise," Wu Ying replied.

Ever since he had made the decision to go with the regeneration exercise—amusingly entitled the Never Empty Wine Pot—Wu Ying had been training with his dantian as empty as he could. That required him to continually speed up the flow of his chi, an exercise that would also toughen up and train his meridians. If only marginally. More to the point, by setting up the first of the eight levels of chi vortexes within his dantian, he was working on improving his regeneration rate. At the same time—because, in theory, setting up the vortex was a one-off act which just needed to be continued—Wu Ying was adjusting his aura. Since he was "stuck" in the Aura Strengthening phase of his aura development, this would allow him to continue his progression in his studies there as well.

"Carrying bags of compost? At your cultivation level?" Senior Goh snorted.

"Cultivation exercise," Wu Ying said.

One of the disadvantages of having a mostly empty dantian was the exhaustion it engendered. Wu Ying felt as though he was constantly only a quarter-full, having only finished a single steamed bun every meal. Except this state persisted throughout the day until he woke, when his constant expenditure of chi stopped and his natural regeneration refilled him.

"Ah. Is it going well?" Senior Goh said, cocking his head curiously.

Discussions between cultivators, even those within the same Sect, were always tenuous. Cultivation secrets were common, because knowing what

46

another cultivator did gave you an advantage in battle. On the other hand, members of the same Sect were prone to practice the same cultivation forms and might be able to provide some degree of advice and support. And of course, being cultivators, most of their lives revolved around the progression of their immortality. Avoiding the topic entirely left one with few conversational topics.

"Not really," Wu Ying said. "It's… been a struggle."

Wu Ying had debated if he was trying too many things at the same time and pushing too hard. He could progress the vortex without being nearly empty. It was easier to notice the differences and its disappearance when he was so empty, but it made it harder on Wu Ying. On top of that, because he had blocked out—or was attempting to block out—the flow of chi to his body that was not properly aspected, the total amount of chi he was drawing was lower than normal. It was like supping on soup using a spoon meant for children while one was ravenous. Slow, painful, and frustrating.

"Huh." His Senior shrugged, having no more to say.

In truth, there wasn't much to discuss. Not without giving more information. And this was one exercise that Wu Ying decided to keep to himself.

"Well, keep working on it."

"I will," Wu Ying said. "What next?"

"For the garden?" When Wu Ying nodded, Ru Ping pursed his lips. "We have more than enough gardeners inside. And the weather sniffers say that there should be no more chills, so…" Ru Ping turned his head, his gaze landing on a series of standing stones in one corner of the expansive gardens.

"Oh no."

Ru Ping grinned. "Don't worry. We can move them after lunch. I'll show you all the map."

Wu Ying let out another groan and seriously debated letting his dantian fill for this. Elder Li's gardens were carefully adjusted according to the season. Between the chi gathering formation that surrounded the gardens themselves and the greater formation for the Sect, the chi density in the gardens was extremely high. But seasonal variations meant that the garden had to be constantly adjusted. In some cases, those adjustments were entirely natural—different types of plants that grew, bloomed, or faded during different seasons. But just as often, there were adjustments that had to be done manually—like the alteration of the rock formations, the pagodas, and the benches. It was backbreaking work. While it was done on a weekly—sometimes daily—basis, once a season, the major changes had to be made.

"Look at it this way. At least Elder Li isn't going to be quizzing you," Ru Ping said.

"At least." Wu Ying shuddered at that thought.

Ever since winter had arrived, not only had the Elder decided to make Wu Ying continue his apothecary classes to better understand and use the herbs he gathered, she had begun questioning him whenever they met. She prodded him to finish memorizing the documentation she had gathered and forced Wu Ying to begin his own encyclopedia. One that included locations of where and what he had picked.

Wu Ying saw the value of what she wanted done. Every herbology encyclopedia, every manual on plants and spiritual supplies he had found differed. Some in small areas, some in large amounts. But when you were talking about identifying potentially fatal and toxic plants, even a small difference could be considered dangerous.

It was not even a matter of incompetence, but individual idiosyncrasies. Drawings of plants that might work for one author might be insufficient for another. Regional variations on plants—especially spirit herbs—could be significant. At times, certain plants could be identified by identifying the plants that grew around them, rather than the actual physiology of the plant itself. But that required a knowledge set that might—or might not—be available to other readers. And lastly, there were complications that arose from cultivators who had specific cultivation skills like Thrice-Seeing Chi Sight or Nose of the Porcine.

And so, you created your own encyclopedia. You wrote what you knew, added to it the notes you found, and hoped that it worked out. Eventually, your own document might be added to others. And so, the circle of badly created encyclopedias went on.

"You're right," Wu Ying said, flashing his friend and Senior a smile. "But if I'm moving all that, I'm eating first."

Waving goodbye to his Senior, Wu Ying headed for the outer sect member he spotted carrying trays of food.

Chapter 5

Wu Ying groaned, staring at the slowly darkening sky as he leaned back and stretched the knotted muscles in his lower back. Sunset came fast in the mountains, which was why the gardening team had packed up once the sun started dipping. This time around, they'd managed to get everything finished on time, so Wu Ying found himself on the road down from the gardens, enjoying the smell of clean spring air. As he finished his stretch and continued his walk, the cultivator was surprised to see milling groups of sect members clustered together and chatting along the roadways, especially at the crossroads.

Wu Ying frowned, curiosity rising. Not enough to start a discussion with the others though, since he knew he'd eventually hear of it. The Sect was like his village in many ways. Any good gossip eventually made its way to his ears. And some not great gossip too.

He was nearly to his residence when his friends, Tou He, Li Yao, and Chao Kun found him. The pair of martial specialists and the monk were looking all too eager to discuss the latest gossip. Wu Ying stopped as they swarmed him.

"So are you excited?" Chao Kun said, his eyes gleaming.

"I'm not sure Wu Ying would be. Certainly not as much as you," Tou He said, shooting Chao Kun an amused glare.

"He's not dumb enough to get involved," said Li Yao.

"Excited about what? Involved in what?" Wu Ying said exasperatedly.

"What? You haven't heard?" Chao Kun said.

"Not yet."

"The war," Chao Kun said.

Wu Ying gave up and continued walking.

"You're supposed to reply when someone asks you a question," Li Yao said, rolling her eyes at Chao Kun. She skipped ahead and smiled at Wu Ying, falling in beside him with a welcoming, sweet smile.

"You haven't answered his question either," Tou He pointed out.

Li Yao pouted. "Neither have you!"

Wu Ying ignored the bickering group, strolling languidly and enjoying the walk in the fast cooling mountain. It would be nice to get home, to wash up. After a day of farming, a hot bath was perfect. And he knew that Ah Yee would have it ready for him. A luxury he felt guilty about sometimes, but one that he still indulged in. Was this the way nobles felt all the time?

"The king sent his envoy to talk to the Sect about the war," Chao Kun finally explained when the trio's argument ended. "He's here to discuss our involvement."

"They're going to ask us to send more help," Tou He said.

"The king always does this. He always asks for aid when things worsen. He should learn to wield his staff himself," Li Yao groused.

"You'd know," Chao Kun said.

Tou He frowned, cocking his head and looking at Wu Ying. Wu Ying mouthed "Lord," making the ex-monk nod in understanding.

"A king's envoy is a big thing, isn't it?" Wu Ying said to head off the argument. "Something like the king himself?"

"Not something like. Exactly as if. He has the king's seal," Chao Kun said. "This is big. The entire time I've been here, I've never seen an envoy before. This is big."

"You said that already," Li Yao said. "And of course it is. The Six Jade Gates Set has gained multiple peak Core practitioners. The kingdom will suffer greatly if we do not commit our own Core cultivators."

"Isn't that what the entire expedition was for?" Wu Ying said, shaking his head. "I'm sure Elder Po at the least would join. And both Elder Dong and Wei managed to ascend. They're in secluded cultivation now."

"All the good that'll do the kingdom," Chao Kun said. "Even Elder Li has spent much time reinforcing her cultivation. And you know she will not be at the forefront of the war. Only Elder Po would be ready to help right now."

"Kind of makes it seem as though everything we did on the expedition was a waste," said Wu Ying. "We suffered a lot for such a minimal increase to our strength."

Wu Ying looked at his friend, who had managed to heal for the most part. The ex-monk had never complained about the long hours he had spent healing after the expedition, but Wu Ying knew that the injuries still bothered him at times. It was only the progression in his cultivation stage that allowed Tou He to continue without any external effects. Of course, Wu Ying had to concede it could be that the experience and enforced rest had helped push his friend ahead too. Cultivation could be strange like that sometimes.

"In the short term, probably. But we are cultivators. We should not be thinking only in the short term," said Chao Kun. "Once the elders stabilize their cultivation, we will have a much stronger Sect."

"That does remind me," said Wu Ying. "Why do we dislike—no, not dislike—fight the Six Jade Gates Sect?"

"It is because certain cultivators who should know better keep interfering with the mortal world," said Li Yao. "Their Sect leader is the State of Wei's king's ancestor. It's why the Six Jade Gates Sect throws so much support behind them."

"I believe it is more complicated than that, Li Yao," said Chao Kun. "I have heard rumors that the Sect Elder of the Six Jade Gates' dao is that of conquests."

"I heard it was domination," said Tou He.

"Sounds the same to me," said Li Yao.

"Only to someone who isn't paying attention," said Chao Kun. "One requires you to constantly grow, to continually battle. The other only requires you to own."

"Own what?" said Wu Ying.

"Everything."

Chao Kun's pronouncement silenced the group. It also helped that they had finally arrived at Wu Ying's residence. Together, they retired to Wu Ying's greeting room, taking seats among all the wooden furniture inlaid with mother-of-pearl. After spending over a year in this residence, he had grown quite comfortable with it. Even if it was still the smallest, least ostentatious, and farthest inner sect residence, it suited him. He could have gotten something a bit larger, especially since the competition to add additional members to the sect had finished last fall, but he felt uncomfortable pushing himself forward that way. This was more than sufficient for him. Once the group settled, Ah Yee arrived with her usual efficiency and supplied the group with snacks and tea.

"I don't really care what his dao is," Li Yao said as she snacked on roasted sunflower seeds. "I just don't want to get involved in the war. I'm here to be a cultivator, not a soldier."

"So you're not interested in joining the expedition?" said Wu Ying. "I understand that the volunteers often receive a significant number of contribution points. I would think, with the king's envoy here, the rewards would be even greater."

In truth, that was one of the reasons Wu Ying was interested in the war. As a peasant, he did not have the riches many of his compatriots did. And while all inner sect members receive a stipend, no ambitious cultivator—and all cultivators were ambitious by definition—would suffer themselves to be slowed down by the minuscule amounts they received.

"You can't spend anything if you are dead." Li Yao took a deeper breath and added, "Not that I expect us to die, but it is a war. I can't help but think that taking part is probably a bad thing for one's dao, unless it was aligned to something like this."

"Li Yao is a well-known objector to the war," said Chao Kun.

"I just object to how much help we provide to the kingdom," said Li Yao. "The state of Wei is already overextended. If we let them fight our mortal armies, they will eventually tire themselves out. They cannot hold this much land. It is basic strategy."

"And how many mortals would die following this strategy?" Wu Ying frowned at his girlfriend and her callous dismissal of those who would have to fight.

"Well, that would really depend on the generals involved. General Jin has a tendency to fight losing battles, but General Zhen is much more prudent. He's more likely to pull back before things grow too damaging."

Wu Ying shook his head, once more remembering the things that stood between him and Li Yao. His village was one of those that would be taken, be sacrificed in her strategy. Li Yao, on the other hand, came from the north, her home safe behind the river that bisected the top third of the nation. Like Lord Yi, she and her family would never really have to deal with the armies of Wei. In fact, the rich silver-loaded mountains in the north made the entire region almost autonomous from the kingdom of Shen. There was probably more to the politics involved, but Wu Ying was still learning his way around these facts. As a former peasant, his local politics involved chickens, the occasional cow, and drainage. A lot of talks about drainage.

"Well, what do people think? How many core Elders will the Six Gates send? And did anyone hear how they did over the winter? Did they manage to promote anyone else?" Tou He said to return the conversation to their initial point.

Chao Kun pursed his lips. "I heard some rumors that the Six Gates might have had a few more fortuitous encounters. They managed to promote six new members to the first stage of Core development."

"Six!" exclaimed Tou He.

"Won't they need a long time to stabilize their cultivation?" Wu Ying said.

"It will be shorter. Depending on the individual, it could be as short as winter," Li Yao said. Of the group, she and Chao Kun were the closest to achieving Core cultivation and would have more information on the requirements. "After you form your Core, the initial period requires you to fill up your meridians and Core with chi. It is not—as my Master informs me— very hard. Other than that, they would need to gain an understanding of their new strength and learn a new, more suitable, martial technique."

"Which is easier on the battlefield," Chao Kun pointed out, waving his teacup.

"Only for those specializing in martial areas." Wu Ying chuckled. "I don't think Master Li sees any point in expanding her understanding of the martial arts."

"Har. No. Though with her skills…"

The talk turned to more speculation as the group threw out names of Elders, wondering if they would be added or subjected to the call for volunteers. The addition of Core experts to the force was a certainty. How many and who was the question.

And in between, Wu Ying was forced to wonder. Why did his fate-believing, karma-loving Master decide to join the war two years ago? It was very uncharacteristic of him.

***

Elder Li was the first to find Wu Ying a couple days later. The discussion with the king's envoy had continued in the upper levels of the sect and had, at first, been all that everyone discussed. But days after his arrival and with little word trickling down, the normal business of the Sect had reasserted itself. Elder Li thus found Wu Ying tending to a pair of early blooming magnolias, pruning branches and checking on the soil.

"You should not take part," Elder Li said.

"In the war?"

"No. Dinner. Of course the war." Elder Li thumped her cane on the ground to emphasize her point. "You are a Gatherer and my student. Not a stupid martial specialist."

"I—"

"Don't lie. I know you were thinking about it," Elder Li said, narrowing her eyes at Wu Ying. "I know all of you fools were."

Wu Ying shrugged. It was true that he had—he was—considering joining. However, unlike what she thought, he leaned toward not doing so. Not only because of Li Yao's displeasure and disapproval, but because the guilt he felt about abandoning his friends two years ago was a lie. His returning would not change their position in the army. It would only put him in more danger.

"You are a Spirit Herb Gatherer. You have skills and a base of knowledge that is rare. And your combination of martial skills along with that knowledge will allow you to go far," Elder Li said. "You have a future, one that does not have to include pointless violence. Or the risk of a war."

Having said her piece, Elder Li turned her attention to the plants. She sighed and whacked Wu Ying on the shoulder before pointing out mistakes he had made. Afterward, she questioned Wu Ying on his recent studies, laying her cane to his shoulders whenever he hesitated or gave the wrong answer.

***

Next to speak with Wu Ying was Liu Tsong, a half day later. The beautiful apothecary apprentice had been busy during the winter, first healing from her injuries and then spending more time waiting on her secluded Master while practicing her apothecary. The only time Wu Ying had met her was during her introductory classes that she continued to teach. It was she who had helped him adjust the herbal remedy. However, beyond that, she spent most of her time in solo practice, as during her Master's absences she had been given the run of her Master's various apothecary cauldrons. At least, those she could handle.

"Senior Li!" Wu Ying greeted Liu Tsong with a smile and bow.

All around, the various members of the gardening group glanced over, drinking in the beauty of the senior cultivator. While she was no Fairy Yang, she was still one of the more beautiful members of the Sect.

"Wu Ying. Thank you for coming out to speak with me." Liu Tsong tilted her head, eyeing the blooming plants with a critical eye. "I'm sorry I haven't been able to spend more time with you."

"It is fine, Senior. I have been busy too, trying to improve my cultivation."

"Yes." Left unsaid was Wu Ying's failure. "I wanted to ask about your intentions. For the war expedition."

"I am uncertain as yet."

"Pity. I had thought to work with you again," Liu Tsong said.

"You are participating?" Wu Ying exclaimed in surprise.

"I intend to. I have plans to put together a party myself." When Wu Ying looked puzzled, Liu Tsong explained. "If a group comes with a set team, they are often able to keep team members together. It improves the safety of the group, after all. And we did work well together."

An unbidden memory. A taotei throwing itself at Wu Ying, intent on eating his face. Sword in hand, ready for one last, final lunge. To make his mark before his death.

"Wu Ying?"

"It's nothing," said Wu Ying. "But I will have to disappoint you, Senior. I will not be taking part in the war, I believe."

"Very well. If you change your mind, let me know." Lit Tsong looked a bit sad but shook it off. "Now, tell me all about your remedy. How is it working for you? Is it as effective as we had hoped?"

"Very much so, I believe. You know how it is with these cultivation exercises," said Wu Ying. "It's not as if I can judge it on a numbered basis. It's just what I believe it feels like. And it does feel as though it is effective. Certainly, it seems to have found a number of impurities in my bones to replace."

"Good. I have been thinking though. The juju beans we had used. If we switch them out with the yellow and purple spotted mushrooms from the fourth peak…"

***

To Wu Ying's surprise, the next person to discuss with him the upcoming war was his own Master. Master Cheng, of course, did not come down to the gardens to visit him. Instead, he summoned Wu Ying to his residence. In the evening. It was after Wu Ying had completed demonstrating his progress in both cultivation and martial styles that Elder Cheng broke the topic.

"You're probably considering joining the war, are you not?"

"I am not, Master." By this time, Wu Ying was pretty sure he would not indulge in the war. Even if he could fight, he was not a martial specialist. While he enjoyed playing at the wargames, it was still a game. No one died. And Wu Ying was certain the Sect and its members could deal with the upcoming storm.

"Interesting."

Elder Cheng fell silent. Wu Ying waited to see what else the Elder had to say, or if he had anything more to say. It seemed to Wu Ying that Elder Cheng was debating something, the way his fingers tapped at the teacup. Rather than bother him, Wu Ying chose to stay silent.

"Are you not concerned about your parents?" Elder Cheng finally said.

"Somewhat. I worry about my village and my parents. But… I believe that the army will be able to guard them. They have managed to do so for so long already," Wu Ying said. "More so, I've already made arrangements with Elder Li and the city below. If things are truly dangerous, the village can evacuate here."

"Really?" Elder Cheng looked surprised. "That is quite ambitious of you. Adding an entire village to the Sect."

"There is ample land to sustain cultivation around the Sect. It is remote here, making it difficult for many to begin, but I have saved, the village has saved, enough, I believe."

"It is good that you have considered the matter." Elder Cheng sipped from the teacup he held before he gestured to the teapot. Wu Ying hurried to pour the drink for the waiting Elder. "I find that many of our brethren forget the ties that bind us, the karmic debts that formed between them and their mortal parents. I believe that our inability to tie off those debts properly is the reason so many of us fail to ascend. If we cut ties from what we were without fulfilling the needs of our destiny, are we not eating our own flesh?[6]"

"Yes, Master." Wu Ying bowed to Elder Cheng, then tilted his head as a thought struck him. When Elder Chang raised an eyebrow, he asked, "Are the gods not bound by the threads of karma then?"

"A good question. Perhaps they are bound even tighter than we are." Elder Cheng looked at Wu Ying then nodded to himself. "That is perhaps something only the immortals themselves can answer. But I believe so."

Wu Ying nodded. It made sense. The Dao encompassed all, and karma was but the threads of the Dao making itself known.

---

[6] Chinese equivalent of cutting your nose off to spite your face.

"I was not going to advise you on either cause of action. Nor will I advise you now. Your fate is yours, as it always has been. But I will speak to you of the potential within this war." Wu Ying made an inquiring noise, prompting his master to continue speaking. "It is simple really. There will be more Elders, some of them in the Core Formation stage, acting during this period than you will see in the next decade. Potentially more than in the next generation unless matters escalate. It is possible that some of our more illustrious Elders, those in the Nascent Soul stage, might even take part."

"But I am not certain what I would learn from them. I fear I am too far beneath them."

"That too is possible. But you will never know if you are not there to witness the matter, no?" Elder Cheng shook his head. "Sometimes, caution is good. At other times, a cultivator must be bold to progress on his path."

Wu Ying mentally grimaced. Those words sounded wise, but they were of little help to him or the actual making of a decision. In the end, he could only bank on his own beliefs and in that, Wu Ying felt he was not advanced enough. Not yet.

"I did have a question," said Wu Ying to his Master. "If I might ask it?"

"If it is not too important, you may do so."

"When we first met, you were taking part in the war. I do not understand why you and Senior Yang were doing so."

"Because of my dao?"

"Yes."

"This question touches upon more things than you need to know. An answer now might affect your destiny more than you know. Are you sure you wish this question to be answered?" Elder Cheng stared at Wu Ying, assessing his reaction.

Wu Ying debated what reason could be so impactful that Elder Cheng would change his usual stand on non-interference. Then again, his allowing

Wu Ying to choose the answer was his way of letting Wu Ying tie himself tighter to him. Or not. Why would Elder Cheng take part in a war, take part and tie himself to the world further, by acting on something on such grand a scale? Then again, on further consideration, Wu Ying had not seen either Senior Yang or Elder Cheng take action during the war. Were they just there to watch? That did not make much sense to Wu Ying either. Even their very presence could cause ripples, could alter destinies. Like his own.

In the end, Wu Ying shook his head and declined Elder Cheng's offer. Perhaps it was the wrong choice, but if his Master really felt he should know, Elder Cheng would tell him. Embroiling himself in further affairs would just make his own life more difficult. It was not as if Wu Ying had not enough matters to deal with.

When Wu Ying declined, he could almost swear he saw a trace of a smile on Elder Cheng's face. But if it had been there, it disappeared so fast that it had been but a mirage. Having said his piece, Elder Cheng dismissed Wu Ying.

As the cultivator strolled down the mountain in the cold air of the evening, passing by outer sect disciples who lit the pathways, he could not help but reflect on the discussion. His talk with Elder Cheng had left him with more questions than ever, but a less burdened heart. All that talk of opportunity and danger had left him with the realization that he had no desire to join the war. Even the vestiges of guilt blew away with the night's air.

His path, his journey was not in the war. Whatever gains there might be.

Chapter 6

Spring was well into bloom by this point in time, with the warmth of longer days and the abundance of newly bloomed plants. Wu Ying was seated in his courtyard, legs crossed, meditating and drawing in more chi. For the last month, he had been working on the chi regeneration exercise, improving it by inches. Over the last month, he'd realized he was not ready to try again for another breakthrough. Whatever that impetus was to drive him to the next level, he lacked it. Perhaps as Master Cheng said, he was lacking in experience.

Perhaps joining the war would have provided Wu Ying with that impetus. But joining the war, fighting in it, killing people he knew nothing of was not something he wanted. Experiences, good experiences, were what he needed to push himself onward. Things that would help him consolidate who and what he was. Not the horrors of the battlefield.

Of course, he could be wrong. He could have just had insufficient chi in his last breakthrough attempt. Last time he'd tried a breakthrough, he had used twice the amount as when he first began. Now, he could potentially begin the process with three times as much. After all, in the time he had spent training, he had increased his storage capacity in his dantian.

It did not matter. He had time. Even if this was the best time for him to be pushing ahead with his cultivation, he was still young. A small delay would not harm him, especially if the other option was death or the damage of his cultivation base.

Another breath in. Another out, and memories of goodbyes surfaced.

Chao Kun and Liu Tsong, in a team with a few other survivors from the expedition. Those who were willing to risk their lives. The envoy had finished the negotiations a week after he had arrived, and the Sect had agreed to triple its normal commitment to the war. That meant that there were at least two Core Elders with each army in the field. There were even rumors that one of the Sect Protectors had joined the army. At the Nascent Soul stage of cultivation, his presence could make a significant difference in the war. It was unlikely that he would directly intervene unless matters grew too perilous though. At his level of cultivation, it was difficult to justify meddling in the affairs of mortals unless it was part of one's dao beliefs. That was why Sect Protectors were rare and often taken from specific daos. Not only did one have to have the required strength but also the right dao.

Of more immediate concern, over twelve teams of inner sect members had joined the kingdom's armies. It was the largest gathering of martial specialists that Wu Ying had ever seen. And might ever see. It had taken nearly a quarter of all the martial specialists in the inner sect to make up those numbers. If you included the various members who were out experiencing the world, the Sect was understaffed. Especially as the slew of assignments requiring their particular expertise grew within the kingdom itself.

Wu Ying himself had just returned two days ago, having finished another assignment. All this activity had been boon for him and his store of contribution points. Wu Ying had his pick of assignments that allowed him to deal with physical threats and gather herbs at the same time. Of course, all those boons came with the added risk of injury due to insufficient numbers. Jobs that should have been carried out by Energy Storage cultivators were assigned to people like him.

"So. You're back." An arrogant, familiar voice.

Wu Ying's breath stilled before he exhaled and calmed his chi, sending it back to his dantian. As he opened his eyes, he gestured to Ah Yee who had rushed in after his visitor, profusely apologizing and explaining how his guest had pushed past her.

"Yin Xue." Wu Ying greeted the other, unfolding himself with easy grace and picking up his jian as he did so. He belted the weapon to his side, his gaze raking over the nobleman's son.

Yin Xue was dressed in inner sect robes, having made his way into the Sect last fall. Wu Ying had to admit, it suited the teenager's bearing and slim profile.

Yin Xue had a longer, narrower face than most which, combined with his pale skin, gave him a noble bearing. One that the young man had grown into in the past few years.

"What are you doing here?"

"Your village has been making plans to leave for the Sect," Yin Xue said.

"Maybe. What of it?" Wu Ying said, apprehension shooting through the cultivator.

"My father has learned of the matter and put a stop to it." Yin Xue's gaze dropped as Wu Ying clutched at the hilt of his jian. "Calm yourself. I had nothing to do with it."

"And why should I believe anything you say?" Wu Ying snapped.

Yin Xue tilted his head as he considered Wu Ying. Eventually, he spoke. "Did you know when I lost to you, my father was silent for months? Afterward, he sent me a single letter."

"Oh?"

"I'm to no longer concern myself with the family. Since I have begun my path as a cultivator, I should continue it." While Yin Xue tried to keep his voice calm, there was still a hint of bitterness in it. "My brother will take over my place. I am to find glory here."

"You were disowned?" Wu Ying said.

"No. I am to become a strong cultivator, to support my family," Yin Xue replied.

But Wu Ying saw the twitch in Yin Xue's lips, the way he raised his head to stare down his nose at Wu Ying. Those were words that had no real meaning, unless Yin Xue did manage to break into the Core Cultivation stage or higher. Then they would expect him to pay the family back, to offer his support.

"And you didn't tell them my plans to get a little revenge?" Wu Ying said, still distrustful.

"As if I paid that much attention to you." Yin Xue snorted. "I have better things to do. Like breaking into the Energy Storage stage. And gaining more contribution points."

Wu Ying frowned, then let his gaze roam over Yin Xue again. His eyes narrowed as he noted how the nobleman's son wore plain Sect robes, not the upscale robes sold in the armory. In addition, Yin Xue lacked the usual assortment of jewelry that many of the nobles wore. No jade amulets or bracelets, gold hair pieces, rings, or belts except for a single necklace that Wu Ying caught peeking out of Yin Xue's collar. More than that, as Wu Ying let his aura sense expand, he realized that Yin Xue had made a little dig at Wu Ying. For Yin Xue *was* in the beginning stages of Energy Storage, unlike him.

"Then why tell me?" Wu Ying said.

"My father has blocked all communication. By the time you learned of it, it would be too late," Yin Xue said.

"You want something."

"So distrustful. Can I not be sowing seeds of karma?"

Wu Ying pursed his lips but finally nodded thanks. "Do you have more details?"

Yin Xue shook his head. "It was a passing note in a letter from home."

"I see." Wu Ying grimaced. He wished he had more details. How had Lord Wen stopped their planned migration? Had he hurt anyone? How did he do it? Why would he do that?

"Are you that dumb?" Yin Xue said. Wu Ying blinked, realizing he had spoken the last question out loud. "What use is a lordship when there is no one taking care of the land? A village without villagers offers no tax. Of course he would stop them."

Wu Ying twitched. He had considered every aspect, every possible issue from the villager's perspective. He had checked with the Elders and the magistrate. He'd even set aside a store of funds so that he could pay for food during the first winter. It was expensive, but compared to the price of the spiritual herbs he sold, it was something he could afford. He'd even sent enough funds to purchase the travel passes for the entire village. But not once had he considered how his actions would be seen from Lord Wen's side.

"Can you guess what he would do?" Wu Ying said, subdued now. Worried.

"It would depend on how angry he is. But most likely? Confiscate the funds you sent and place restrictions on their travel. Without a pass, no ship will take them on," Yin Xue said. "He might punish your Chief though. It'd depend on how angry he was."

Wu Ying nodded, understanding the point. Initially, the travel pass would have been easy to acquire. After all, with Chief Tan coming too, he would use the seal provided with the village's huki[7] and stamp all the necessary passes from the village. After that, they only needed to receive a stamp at each city they entered—which was a formality so long as one had the funds. It was the first seal, with the approved travel destination, that was the hardest. As a Sect member, he bypassed all these restrictions, only having to flash his Sect seal—if his robes by themselves were not enough.

"Thank you."

If Yin Xue was correct, it relieved Wu Ying's mind a little. Hopefully Lord Wen had not been too angered. After all, many others would have taken steps to send away their most vulnerable. This was just a little more ambitious.

Having said his piece and answered the questions, Yin Xue turned and left. Wu Ying called out one last thanks, though the nobleman's son did not

---

[77] The huki (colloquially hokou—though that's actually the actual registration of an individual) is a system of household registration used in China. Pre-modern China had multiple variations of the registration system, ranging from a simple central registrar for the village and individual family registers to more complicated systems involving multiple households. Modern day China also has a much more complicated and political system in place for rural / city-based denizens. Obviously, we're using a simplified version here. The hokou was used mainly for conscription and taxation in pre-modern times.

acknowledge it, leaving Wu Ying to stare at the empty courtyard. He frowned pensively, debating what to do, what he could do, as the day grew dark.

***

Hours Wu Ying spent pondering his problem. What could he offer? What could he suggest to get his family to leave? The problem, as he saw it, was two-fold. Firstly, his family—the village—would refuse to leave if they did not have to. There was too much in their village to make leaving easy—from the graves of ancestors to farmlands painstakingly cared for over generations. Just getting the soil right would take decades, generations of work.

The second problem was more complex. When, and if, they decided to leave, Lord Wen would not let them go. How Wu Ying was to convince him otherwise, he did not know. What did nobles want? Other than their taxes. It was a different world from the Sect, where face and one's dao were most important. As different as his life as a peasant.

In time, Wu Ying walked out of his residence in search of knowledge. Knowing who to speak to was the start of the solution, and of those he could ask, one stood out in his mind.

"Senior Yang," Wu Ying greeted his senior sister when he was allowed into the moonlit courtyard of her residence.

Unlike his own residence, Yang Fa Yuan's had multiple buildings formed into the familiar multiple courtyard-style residence with walkways connecting each building. It created a sprawling mansion, one that had multiple larger, open-air gardens between each walkway. The gardens themselves followed a variety of themes that represented the four seasons. But it was the internal courtyard of the main building that Wu Ying was shown to where his Senior sat, surrounded by a pair of other Elders.

"Elder Shih. Elder Pang," Wu Ying said.

The male Elders glared at Wu Ying, but Fairy Yang smiled demurely. She quickly made excuses, sending the two Elders off as she "had to deal with her junior brother." Only when they had left and she had turned on the privacy formation did Fairy Yang flop back onto her chair and groan.

"Thank you for coming. If I had known it was that easy to get rid of them, I would have made you visit me more often," Fairy Yang said.

"Senior?"

"They will not stop courting me." Fairy Yang rolled her eyes. "As if I ever showed any interest in them."

Wu Ying prudently kept silent as his Senior groused about her suitors. He waited until she ran down her complaints, making sure to nod when necessary even as impatience gnawed at his control.

"Enough. You do not need to be hearing this about your Elders. Remember—do not repeat anything I said."

Wu Ying hastily agreed. He did not need to anger Elder Pang any further.

"Now, why have you visited me?"

Wu Ying quickly related what he had begun with his village and what Yin Xue had told him, ending with a simple question. "Can I trust what he said?"

"Of course not," Fa Yuan said. "Though I would be surprised if he had lied to you. Especially as he must have known you would tell others. Fights in the outer sect are expected. Some might even say encouraged." Fa Yuan's gaze shifted to where the two Elders had left. "There are arguments to be made that the competition makes for stronger inner sect disciples. But such underhandedness is expected to be set aside in the inner sect. At least for the most part. Competition is still encouraged of course, but there is too much to be done for that kind of distraction. In theory."

Wu Ying cocked an eyebrow at Fa Yuan, who shook her head, apparently disinclined to expand on her words. "Then what do you recommend I do?"

"You cannot leave this alone? Let your village, your parents, fate play out as it should?" Fa Yuan regarded Wu Ying as she spoke. Seeing his answer on his face, she continued. "A pity. Our Master would recommend that course of action. Your attempts are already being foiled, perhaps by fate itself. It could be argued that it is their destiny to be in their village."

"Could it not be argued that it is my destiny to change theirs? That I am meant to save them?" Wu Ying said.

"Maybe." Fa Yuan opened her hands wide. "Fate. Destiny. Karma. They are… difficult concepts to grasp. Still, if you are resolved, then you should speak with him directly."

"Him?"

"This Lord Wen," Fa Yuan clarified. "I cannot say what he wants. If you were older, stronger, more reputable, you could trade a favor in the future. Perhaps you still can. But nobles generally care for three things: their lineage, their land, and their wealth. Often in that order."

Wu Ying grunted. That didn't sound that different from a peasant. Family, land, and wealth—though the last two were the same for a peasant. If they even had land.

"Your Lord Wen has guaranteed his lineage by having Yin Xue stay in the Sect. He might even take further steps by sending his family to the capital. As such, what you can offer him is protection for his land or his wealth." Fa Yuan raked her gaze over Wu Ying's body. "Though…"

"I'm insufficient." Wu Ying understood that. He was one man. One Body cultivator. He could not destroy an army. He could barely even stop a platoon of normal soldiers by himself.

"Not alone."

Wu Ying stared as Fa Yuan gracefully picked up her teacup and sipped on it. He weighed her hint then bowed to her.

"Thank you, Senior."

"Little enough that I can offer. But…" Fa Yuan extended a single finger from her hand. "Be careful. You are at the most physically dangerous stage before your rebirth."

Wu Ying bowed to her again and retreated, leaving the young lady to her thoughts. Outside, he looked upward, spotting the half moon and the constellation of stars gathered around it, beseeching its company.

"Fitting."

***

"This is not a Sect assignment, is it?" Tou He asked Wu Ying.

The ex-monk was the first person Wu Ying had looked for. He found Tou He in his own residence, meditating. Unlike Wu Ying, Tou He had a much nicer home, though Wu Ying knew that Tou He had little use for the big building.

"No. Just mine," Wu Ying said. "I might not even need you. But…"

"But if you did, finding me afterward would be difficult." Tou He rubbed his bald head, feeling the coarse edges of stubble regrowing. "Very well."

"Very well?"

"I'll come, of course." Tou He smiled. "Sowing seeds of good karma is never wrong. And if I did not, who would watch your back?"

"Thank you," Wu Ying said. "I'll make sure to treat you to a meal when we're back."

Tou He grinned.

"What did I do to have a friend like you?"

Tou He looked at the sky, perhaps staring at the very same moon Wu Ying had stared at earlier. "Good karma in the past."

Wu Ying choked off a snort.

"Who else?"

"That's coming?" Wu Ying said. "I'll ask Li Yao, when she's back."

"Mission?"

"Yes." Wu Ying pursed his lips in concern before he shook aside the feeling. "Beyond that..." Wu Ying deliberately shrugged.

"We need more. If we want to do a job at this."

"Yes." Unfortunately, Wu Ying could not think of any others. Most of his friends were martial specialists, and they were all either caught up in the war already or busy with assignments and unlikely to run away for something that paid no contribution points. At least Li Yao would be—should be—back in a few days. He could count on her. Recollection of the martial specialists made Wu Ying remember a particular cultivator who wasn't a member of the group but still had some skills. "I might have one more."

"Good. I'll ask around too," Tou He said. "But..."

"Your friends are mostly not around," Wu Ying said. He could understand that.

"So anything I should know about this Lord Wen?" Tou He said.

Wu Ying shook his head. He had never met the man himself. At most, Lord Wen had been a distant figure seen when he arrived on his horse to pick up Yin Xue when he had been late. And that was early on, when Yin Xue was young. "My father never had bad things to say of him. He said that Lord Wen cared about us—his peasants. Better than most other lords. That he wanted his son—Yin Xue—to care about us too. It's why he was sent to learn with us, rather than receive a private tutor." Tou He nodded, gesturing for Wu Ying to continue. "Mother said that Lord Wen was just cheap and an unthinking traditionalist."

"Two different viewpoints."

"Just a little," Wu Ying said. "Sorry. I wish I could... but..." He shrugged again, feeling somewhat helpless.

"It will be fine. We'll talk to Li Yao when she's back, and you'll speak to your friend. And in the meantime, we'll get ready," Tou He assured his friend.

"For what?" Wu Ying shook his head. "We don't even know what we'll be asked to do."

"It doesn't matter. We'll keep your family safe."

If Wu Ying thought he could make his parents go without the rest of the village, he'd just ride in and drag them out. He was sure he could bully the guards into letting at least his family through. But he knew his parents. As stubborn as he was, his parents were worse. It left him with... well. Not no options. Just few good ones.

As Tou He picked up the wine pot his servant had delivered, Wu Ying regarded the alcohol. The relaxation it would offer. And he nodded. Not too much. But a drink would be consoling. Calming. There was little more he could do tonight. But tomorrow. Tomorrow was another matter.

Chapter 7

The next morning, Wu Ying began preparations for the expedition. The first thing he had to do was get the expedition trip permit from his Master. As a Body Cleansing cultivator, even though he was an inner sect member, Wu Ying was not allowed to leave the sect for extended periods of time without permission. After all, the Sect had spent a lot of resources developing him this far. Releasing him into the wild at his most dangerous and vulnerable time was foolhardy. Missions, close-by and carefully gauged were one thing. A long expedition into war torn regions was another thing entirely. Even his time with the expedition was uncommon, though of course his specialty and the presence of multiple Elders had mitigated the danger. Theoretically.

Luckily for Wu Ying, Elder Cheng was one of those elders who really didn't care about that particular rule. Once Wu Ying told him why he needed the leave permit, Elder Cheng only raised a single eyebrow before he took Wu Ying's sect seal and gave his permission. Wu Ying was glad that he did not receive a further lecture about the dangers, even if he was forced to listen to another of Master Cheng's lecture about fate.

Next in his preparations was the memorization of his martial styles and exercises. Not that Wu Ying had forgotten any of it. After all, one of the first things he had done was to memorize every inch of those books. Still, he often refreshed his memory and referred to the documents and his notes when he tried out another area or faced some problem. Better to be extra careful than risk chi deviation. So once again, Wu Ying went through his notes, making sure they were extensive and clear to him. At the same time, he ensured that they were obscure enough that he would be allowed to take the documents with him. He would not be allowed to take any of the actual manuals from the library out of the Sect, as that would risk the loss of them. Even copying the manuals would be considered theft and punished accordingly. But his own notes, as long as they weren't something a thief could understand, would be allowed to come with him.

That took him until the end of the evening, but Wu Ying knew that most of it was just a distraction. Wu Ying dreaded what came next, but after thinking of his parents, he strung up his courage and headed to the forge.

The inner sect forgers hall was one of the larger buildings. The sprawling single-story building was set a distance away from any other building due to the constant noise and fumes the forging process created. Within the forge, multiple stations were available for use, and even at this time of night, they were filled with cultivators. For a time, last year, Wu Ying had spent time training here. But he had learned that he had little talent for the forging of iron and steel. Blacksmithing was a powerful and important occupation, but it was not his path. It was, however, the path of the person he was here to speak with.

Wu Ying needed very little time to find Bao Cong. To Wu Ying's lack of surprise, Bao Cong was standing beside a forge, working a newly formed sword. In a pause between strokes, Bao Cong looked at Wu Ying and flicked his gaze to the bellows. Taking the unspoken hint, Wu Yang walked over and worked the bellows. In silence, they worked together for the next hour, Bao Cong focused on creating a couple more weapon blades while Wu Ying helped in the stoking of the fire, moving pieces around, and generally staying out of the way. It was work that Wu Ying fondly remembered.

In time, they were done, Bao Cong having finished his work. When Bao Cong gestured to Wu Ying to bank the fires, Wu Ying gratefully stopped working the bellows before wiping away the built-up sweat.

"What is it that you want?" said Bao Cong.

"What makes you think I want anything?" Wu Ying trotted over to the water flask and took a sip, feeling the blessed liquid flow down his throat. Even lukewarm, the water was heavenly after the oppressive heat.

"When was the last time you were here?"

Wu Ying bristled, angry because the comment was unfortunately true. He had not been back since he left the class. It was not because he disliked any of

76

the blacksmiths. He was just too busy to spend time socializing—especially in such an inhospitable location. "Fine. I have a request for you."

"Don't bother. I won't make you anything," said Bao Cong. The forger continued to put away his tools.

Wu Ying soon joined him, cleaning the forge and getting it ready for the next apprentice blacksmith. "I'm not asking you to forge me anything."

Wu Ying's gaze flipped over to the daos, ready to be sharpened tomorrow. They were decent work. Better than anything Wu Ying could make. But nowhere near the level of a master blacksmith or even a journeyman.

Bao Cong saw Wu Ying's gaze and shrugged angrily before returning to his cleaning. Working together, they soon had the forge in a condition that would be acceptable to hand over to another. When they finished, they walked out of the blacksmiths hall and stopped the moment the cold winter air hit their sweaty bodies. They shuddered in unison before Bao Cong turned to Wu Ying.

"If you're not here for me to make you something, what you want?" Bao Cong asked.

"I need to leave the Sect for an assignment. My own. It may be dangerous, and I might need some other hands. Hands that know how to handle themselves in a fight," said Wu Ying. "You are good with your bow, aren't you?"

"You know I am." Bao Cong smirked as they recalled the multiple times Bao Cong had managed to hit Wu Ying and other cultivators in the melees. Those had stopped ever since the martial specialists left. The Sect no longer had time or personnel to dedicate to that kind of training.

"Good." Wu Ying gave a brief explanation of what he intended and expected of Bao Cong. A trip near the front lines, but not to the war itself. Potential assignment by an anxious Lord. An unknown amount of time away from the Sect. And the potential for violent confrontations.

"Well, I can see why you need me. Can't take a Body cultivator out of the Sect, so you've only got me and a few others to choose from. No martial specialists would be allowed to go with you, not at this time. But I see no reason for me to join you."

"What do you want?"

Bao Cong looked back at the building they had left. He tapped his lips then dropped his hands to stroke the top of his sect seal, the one that recorded their contribution to the sect and gave them points for it. "Blacksmithing is very expensive in the beginning."

"Money?" Wu Ying grimaced. That was one of the few things he could not offer. Then his gaze slipped to the sect token. "You want contribution points."

In the sect, contribution points were just as good as taels. You could use them to buy manuals from the library, pills and herbs from the apothecarist shop, new weapons and armor from the Blacksmithing Hall, and materials from the general store.

"Contribution points or materials." Bao Cong's eyes narrowed at Wu Ying, then he clarified his statement. "Just make it contribution points."

"Five hundred contribution points now and a hundred a month every month for the next two years," said Wu Ying. That would allow Bao Cong to work in the forges rent free once a week every month.

"Nothing now. One hundred every month for three years."

Wu Ying's regarded Bao Cong, considering the counter. That was a lot better than a lump sum payment, since Wu Ying was rather low on points. He had a reserve of course, but that was for the village. On the other hand, three years...

"Why don't I buy you a drink and we can discuss this?" Wu Ying smiled at Bao Cong.

Wu Ying had seen the Chieftain do this many times. Drink with those he negotiated with to get a better deal. His father hadn't, but then again, his father had left most of those negotiations to his mother. Even if Wu Ying had never tried the drink-and-negotiate method, how hard could it be?

Bao Cong smiled widely at Wu Ying, clapping the cultivator on the shoulder and leading him up the path.

***

Wu Ying woke the next morning with the taste of dead frogs in his mouth. He rolled over while grimacing and only realized his mistake when he fell. He never managed to catch himself before he landed on the floor, bruising his shoulder. As he turned sideways on the marble, Wu Ying noticed the couch he had been sleeping on. It was a nice couch—and a familiar one too. Mother of pearl inlaid along rosewood furniture, depicting the local scenery around some village. It was the couch in his visiting room, the place where he would greet formal guests. It was not, obviously, his bed.

As he stood, Wu Ying took notice of the throbbing pain in his head. Ah Yee walked in with her serving tray containing his herbal supplement and a tea set. Wu Ying's stomach heaved at the small amounts of noxious fumes that arose from the herbal supplement.

"Not today," Wu Ying whined.

"What you are feeling will be extracted if you drink this. Short-term discomfort for a long-term benefit." Ah Yee placed the tray on the serving table and opened the clay bowl.

Wu Ying's stomach lurched again, and he held a hand to his face, turning green as he choked down vomit. "I don't think—"

"You faced down a taotei. Is a simple drink enough to send you running?" Ah Yee scolded Wu Ying.

Shamed by his servant, Wu Ying took hold of the concoction, then while holding his nose, he choked down the entire slurry. He gasped as he slammed the bowl down and grabbed the teacup Ah Yee offered him. As he poured the hot tea into his mouth, he burnt his tongue and throat a little, but thankfully, it washed away some of the taste. Tea didn't help with the pain, or his stomach, but at least he could focus a little.

Ah Yee picked up the tray and its contents, leaving behind the teapot and teacup as she exited. Wu Ying sat down and tried to meditate, forcing himself to ignore his roiling stomach and the pounding in his head, the glare from the sunlight. In minutes though, the feeling grew too large to be ignored and he rushed for the outhouse. At least, as Wu Ying bent over to expel the fluids, this would be good training for his Reinforced Iron Bones technique.

***

An hour later, cleaner and more alive, Wu Yang made his way out to discover if Li Yao had returned. Unfortunately, her house servant indicated that she had not, sniffing disapprovingly at Wu Ying as he usually did before sending the peasant away. Just to assure himself, Wu Ying stopped at the assignment hall and verified that Li Yao was meant to have returned already. Concern over her grew, mixing with the worry he had for his family and the future.

Since he was there, Wu Ying made sure to inform the Hall that he would be gone for an undetermined period. He made sure that they deducted the necessary contribution points he owed the Sect for a six-month period, while taking the contribution pills that they owed him for that period. At the end, all his hard work, all his savings over the last few months, even the rewards from the expedition, was gone. Almost.

Lastly, he added Bao Cong's name to the expedition group, fulfilling the bureaucracy required before he made his way to speak with Tou He. Unfortunately, the ex-monk indicated that he had had no luck in finding additional help. Not that they needed more. With Li Yao, there would be four of them and that should be sufficient. Or so he hoped at least.

Tou He chased Wu Ying out soon after, as he had a lot of work to complete for his Master before he would be allowed to leave. Once again, Wu Ying thanked his friend as he left, vowing to help find a solution for the monk's troubles.

***

As one of the most guarded locations in the Sect, the inner sect armory was large, isolated, and armed with multiple formations. With most of the martial specialists gone, Wu Ying knew the armory would see little traffic. Even at the best of times, the armory was never buzzing like the library, kitchens, or the blacksmiths hall. After all, most of the items within the armory were magical, higher tier equipment, not the common, mundane items made by the outer and inner set members for general use. These items were rare and expensive.

Wu Ying stared at the carved stone building for a short period, watching the small number of individuals moving in and out of the armory, before he walked in. Once he had announced himself and his intentions, he was taken to a small, private room. It was similar to the one he had been brought to last year, with its simple wooden table, plain chairs, and wall hangings. It was a place of business, not of comfort. While he waited, Wu Ying poured himself a cup of tea and mulled over what he could purchase.

"Long Wu Ying. I am surprised to see you here so soon." Elder Wen, the Elder in charge of the inner sect armory, looked at Wu Ying as she stepped in. Standing barely five feet tall, the tiny elder had a vibrant personality and energy. Even so, Wu Ying could sense that her aura was well contained and controlled, unlike her personality. What he sensed at least. For all that he knew, she wanted him to sense the control and hid something else.

Wu Ying stood and bowed in greeting, waiting for Elder Wen to sit before he joined her. "I had not expected to be back so soon. But I am going on an assignment soon, and I am hoping that you will be able to suggest some items for my use." Wu Ying fished out his sect seal and pushed it across the table so that the Elder could grasp his budget.

"Of course. Tell me about it." Elder Wen touched the sect seal while he talked.

In short order, Wu Ying had related his problems. He held nothing back, knowing that the more the Elder understood, the greater the aid she could offer. When he was done, Elder Wen questioned him about his cultivation and martial styles, verifying the information she had drawn from his sect seal and adding to it.

Afterward, the pair sat in silence as the Elder contemplated. Wu Ying took the opportunity to pour refreshments for them both and offer the refreshments to the Elder. Finally, Elder Wen turned to the waiting attendants and barked out a series of names. Wu Ying knew that they would journey into the armory itself and pull these items from whatever stores the sect had. Wu Ying had never seen the inside of the armory. No one, that he knew of, had. Even the attendants were sworn to secrecy about what happened within the armory and its contents, blood bound to keep their lips sealed.

"Now, tell me about your expedition. I've heard a little about it, but I want to know from you directly." Elder Wen leaned forward, her intense brown eyes on Wu Ying.

While they waited, Wu Ying regaled Elder Wen with the story about the expedition. He found himself going into detail about how the various equipment used among the various cultivators had worked, the Elder probing with insightful questions on the fit between the cultivators and their equipment. She was, of course, particularly interested in Wu Ying's Woo Petal

Bracer and his use of the equipment. Still, Wu Ying gained the sense that Elder Wen was just as interested in the gossip as the details of equipment.

Eventually, the attendants returned, bearing the equipment Elder Wen had requested. Wu Ying and Elder Wen walked to the table where the equipment had been artfully and efficiently arranged.

The first item Elder Wen picked up was a simple leather water bag. As Wu Ying took it from her and turned it around, he noted the gold inlaid stitching along the edges and across the bag's back. It made the bag look much more luxurious than its simple use, and while Wu Ying could sense the flow of chi around the bag and note the inscription on the stitching, he could not understand its use. The enchantment of items, with formations and chi energy, was not something he had studied in detail. Even the basic lessons he had taken were to understand the best use for various types of enchantments, rather than practical identification knowledge.

"The Bag of Never-Ending Water," said Elder Wen. "Of course, it is not never ending. It will refill itself to its brim once an hour. There's a secondary enchantment, like your storage ring, in it too, which allows it to hold even more water. And unlike the initial attempts, this is not a failed product. The enchantment that checks the volume is not broken." Elder Wen spoke the last sentence with slight smirk, almost enticing Wu Ying to ask about the story behind her comments.

But when he spotted one of the attendants turn red, he decided against it. Some questions were best not asked. "I am not sure the use of this."

Water was never really an issue, at least not during the spring. Not in the State of Shen. Between the constant rainfall of spring and the numerous streams, rivers, and canals that made up the country, it was more an issue of fighting an overflow of water. For a small group like theirs, finding sufficient water would not be an issue. In fact, with the various rest stops scattered throughout the kingdom and the river that they would likely use from the majority of their journey, Wu Ying did not expect they would ever need this bag.

"Ah, you youngsters. Always thinking short term. Did you not consider what taking your village will be like? Even if you leave behind the majority of your livestock, you will still need to water those you bring along. Do you think most rest stops will be able to take care of that many animals? How about if you continue moving through those stops? That's not even counting if you get caught in a siege."

They *did* intend to leave behind most of the livestock. Once they drove them to the nearest town, they'd probably sell what they could to the butchers and other merchants. Still, at the very least, they'd be bringing along the horses. A lot of work needed to be done, and such animals would be useful. They also made bringing along the children and elderly easier. Still, Wu Ying considered if he was willing to spend his precious contribution points on something so mundane.

He paused and scratched his nose. Perhaps he had grown a bit jaded. Even a year ago, Wu Ying would have marveled at the bag. Never having to go draw water from the well or the river? This was the kind of magical equipment he would have loved as a peasant.

"Next, we've got fasting pills. I don't think I need to explain the usefulness of these." Elder Wen tapped the simple clay bottle.

There was a group of five bottles, each containing a set of twenty pills. Of course, Wu Ying knew about fasting pills. Generally, they were not recommended for those who had yet to enter the Energy Storage stage at the least, if not Core Formation. The pills were concentrated foodstuff, but by themselves would not provide everything a body needed. Those at the Energy Storage or Core Formation stage drew much of their energy needs from the world itself, the chi that surrounded them. Still, the pills would stave off hunger and, in the short term, provide enough food so an individual could skip a meal or two.

"Large-scale Deception Formation." Elder Wen tapped the series of inscribed flags. She rolled out one of the flags to show him the simple inscriptions drawn on it before she packed it away again. "Usable three times. If you have someone with dual air and water aspect, they could recharge it once more before the enchantment fades entirely."

Wu Ying shook his head. Someone whose elemental aspects were dual aligned was rare. Not because the cultivation methods to achieve dual alignment were particularly secret but because aligning oneself to more than one element required the cultivator's personality to fit both elements. After all, cultivation was about finding the right path—or face a deadlock later on.

In addition, dual element cultivation was much, much slower. Like choosing one's dao, an elemental alignment was restrictive in what one could eventually achieve. Choosing to focus on two different alignments restricted one's eventual dao even further. It was because of that that most people did not dual align their chi element unless they had no choice.

"Understand that the Deception Formation will only work against those in the Body Cultivation stage and lower. This will, of course, include the equivalent strength Spirit and Demonic Beasts you might encounter. I know that you are very strong and have no fear of them yourself." Wu Ying's eyes narrowed at the hint of mocking in Elder Wen's tone, but it was so faint, he wasn't sure if it was his imagination. "However, such a large group is a concern. This entire formation will contain and protect a thirty-foot diameter."

Wu Ying made a mental note of the flags, knowing he would have to purchase them. Even if it wasn't useful for this assignment, having something like that would be useful in the future.

Elder Wen grabbed the next item on the table and showed it to him. It was highly familiar to Wu Ying, the talismans having been shown to him the previous round. Next was a thrice-enlarged storage satchel. Then enchanted bandages that would slow down bleeding and enhance healing.

None of the items Elder Wen showed was particularly impressive, almost mundane in form. Most barely qualified as Spirit level enchantments. However, Wu Ying saw that they were all quite useful, in the right circumstances.

The next item Elder Wen picked up and handed to him was a surprise. A simple scalemail undergarment. It was thin enough that Wu Ying could wear it underneath his robes, though no matter how he peered at it and checked it over, he could not find any indications of an enchantment.

"Is this…?"

"Enchanted? No. Not all good equipment need be enchanted." Elder Wen said. "I'd normally offer you the Azure Thunder Robes, but your refusal has been noted. This will work for your most vulnerable regions and is significantly cheaper."

Wu Ying winced as Elder Wen basically called him cheap. It wasn't really his fault… he just had a lot of demands on his contribution points.

"Now, who do you think will be your most likely enemy? Other cultivators or plain bandits?"

Wu Ying sighed as he realized the answer.

"Exactly." Elder Wen smirked. "And if you get caught in the war, most of those you'll be facing are just plain soldiers. When you are surrounded, no matter how well you wield your sword, you will be struck. This is just another line of protection."

Wu Ying turned the scalemail undershirt around, tapping the scales and hefting it again. It was well made, and he noted light felt at each of the edges, helping to keep the noise down. Worn under his robes, it would be mostly hidden.

After that, it was just a matter of making decisions of what else to purchase, keeping in mind his limited number of points left. Eventually, Wu Ying pointed out the items he wanted to purchase—among them, the Bag of Never-Ending Water.

With his equipment purchased and his bureaucratic duties taken care of, Wu Ying was done with his preparations. All he needed now was Li Yao to return. Soon, he hoped.

Chapter 8

Li Yao did not return the next day. That thread of concern within Wu Ying's chest grew. He started doing the math, trying to figure out how long he could afford to wait for her. There were two calculations he needed to do.

First was deducing when the first clash between the kingdoms would occur and from there, the time it would take for the armies to threaten his village. From Wu Ying's recollections of past years and the previous year, it would take the State of Wei nearly half the fighting season before they would near the village. But that was based on previous years, when the kingdoms had posed more than fought, when armies had maneuvered around one another and been hesitant to do battle. Depending on the general in charge and how aggressive the State of Wei intended to be, it could be as quick as a two-week forced march from the border to his village. Of course, it was unlikely they would send the entire army after his village, but the army wasn't the real threat anyway. The raiding parties that took from the villagers would be more dangerous than any actual army. They were the ones who stole all the goods, conducted the massacres, and captured children to be slaves.

Assuming the kingdoms were beginning the spring campaign as soon as possible, they would begin within the next week. If that was the case, Wu Ying needed to work out how long it would take for the armies to reach the border.

In short order, he had the map of the surrounding regions open and the locations of where the armies had gathered to train up new recruits and collect supplies for the campaign. The map was centered around the Sect, having been purchased from the Sect store itself.

From there, Wu Ying traced his finger east and south, down the river, then almost directly east again to reach his village. From his home, a straight line met the river Li, which created the natural border that the kingdoms had fought from over the last few hundred years. Of course, every few decades a few villages traded hands, but eventually, the natural impediment of the river reasserted itself.

Once Wu Ying had the map, it was a simple matter of using his abacus[8] to make some quick calculations. Thankfully, details like how fast an army moved on roads was part of the classic works that everyone had been forced to memorize, so the calculation was easy. In the end, he tapped his top lip with the end of his brush. Two weeks. Give or take a few days.

Assuming they did not have to fight and could cross the river that formed the natural barrier between the states, it would be another two weeks to his village for the army. That meant a month from now might see his village burn. Of course, that was an extremely pessimistic view and unlikely to come true. Then again, it would be the height of irony if Wu Ying did all this only to be too late. Better to be safe. Four weeks it was.

The next calculation was how long it would take him to reach his village and convince Lord Wen. Luckily, the lord was only a small rural nobleman, so his residence was close to the village. In fact, the distance between the lord's residence and his village was negligible, which was of course why Yin Xue had been able to study in their village. All in, Wu Ying figured it would take them about two weeks to arrive, using a mixture of ship and horse. Give or take three or four days, depending on the weather.

And that was the biggest question of all. It was still spring, which meant that spring rains and the resulting muddy roads were in play. On the other hand, if it was muddy and messy for them, it would be the same for the army. In theory. Barring strange weather patterns a few hundred li away.

---

[8] The abacus (known as a suanpan in China) is a wooden / bamboo rectangle with beads on sliding wires and split into two sections by a wooden beam—a two-bead top deck and a five-bead bottom deck. Counting is done by moving the beads up and down, with each bead set demarcating a single digit, tens, hundreds, etc. Learnt right, it improves mental math and can be faster than a calculator.

If he took all that into account, then Wu Ying could only afford to wait another day or two for Li Yao. He could only hope that she was fine and would return soon. If not, he would have to leave without her.

Sitting back, Wu Ying stared at the map, willing it to offer more clues, to make the harsh math of travel times different. When his wishes offered little succor, he put it all away and walked into his courtyard. If he had to leave soon, then it was time to focus on his cultivation and stop with the exercises. The middle of a war was not the time to be running low on chi.

***

Thankfully, Li Yao returned the next day. Wu Ying met her as she left the Assignment Hall, informed of her return via the speedy servant gossip network. Li Yao burst into a grin upon seeing him, the smile washing away the exhaustion he had glimpsed on her face. She skipped forward to meet him, but the smile disappeared as she noticed Wu Ying's unusually serious mien.

"What is it?" she said.

Wu Ying brought her up to speed on his current predicament. She frowned as he spoke, growing more obviously pensive with each word.

When he finished speaking, Li Yao gripped his hand tightly. "Of course I'll help. I'll contact my parents immediately. They will do the best they can to make Lord Wen let your parents go."

"No. That wasn't what I wanted to speak to you about. I'm going to speak to Lord Wen myself," Wu Ying said, squeezing back on her hand in reflex.

"That is not a good idea. If you come to him as you are, you have nothing to offer him. He'll have all the advantages. You need to think about this properly."

"Think about it? What do you think I've been doing all this time?" said Wu Ying, his tone brusque. "All I've been thinking of is my parents."

Li Yao winced. "I'm sorry. You know I didn't mean it that way."

"What way did you mean it?"

"I'm just trying to help you."

Wu Ying heard the contrition in her voice, but it didn't stop him from releasing her hand. "In what way did you mean it? All I asked of you was to help me on the expedition."

All that worry, all that concern Wu Ying had had for Li Yao and his parents, all that stress burst out of him as she questioned his judgment. What did she know? There was no time for her parents to talk to Lord Wen. Even if she could contact hers and they deigned to help her, it would be too late. It would take at least two weeks for her message to reach her parents and a similar amount of time for a reply to return. She just didn't understand the timelines.

"I know what I'm doing!" he said.

"Don't talk to me like that!" Li Yao said, her temper flaring as Wu Ying raised his voice at her.

"Then stop trying to put up obstacles. I don't need you to do that." Wu Ying threw up his hands in exasperation.

"Maybe you don't need me at all!" Li Yao crossed her arms and stepped away from him.

When she did so, she looked about and noticed how they had drawn the attention of the other Sect members. Relationship drama was not uncommon, but it was always good theatre.

Wu Ying followed her gaze, spotting the gawking crowd. His stern gaze landed on an outer sect member who was watching the pair. Wu Ying's lips curled up as he glared back, forcing the man to look away before scurrying down the path. Unfortunately, Wu Ying's actions made Li Yao even more self-conscious, her fists clenching by her body.

"Maybe I don't. Maybe you should just stay here. I'm sure I can handle it myself. He's just another noble," Wu Ying said.

"Like me?" Li Yao huffed. "Fine!"

She turned away and stalked off to her residence. Wu Ying watched her retreating back, already regretting the words he had said. All he wanted her to do was agree to come along. To help him. Not take over the assignment. Not to make suggestions over something she didn't understand. But maybe he could have done better in how he said it. He had just been so worried about her. About his family and the situation there.

He shook his head and turned around, heading back to his own residence. As he walked, he ignored the looks shot at him, the shock that adorned a number of faces. Let them stare. He had more important things to do. Like informing the rest of the team that it was time to go.

***

The group met the next day under the paifang that demarcated the line between the start of the sect interior and the rest of its lands. Underneath the joined columns that stood over the single path up the mountain, the gate guardian sat. Elder Lu rested with his eyes closed, head tilted toward the sky as his long pipe slowly burned. Each visitor to the Sect slowed down as they crossed the threshold and offered the silent Elder a bow or nod of recognition if they were known, or in some cases, checked in to gain his approval before they continued their journey. It was there that Wu Ying and his small team gathered as the sun was rising.

"You have everything?" Wu Ying said to the team.

He noted that both members carried nothing but weapons on their body. Bao Cong had a quiver of arrows slung behind his back but no unstrung bow in sight, a simple dao belted on the left of his body. Tou He had his staff in hand, though Wu Ying knew he used it as much as a walking stick as a weapon. As usual, the monk was dressed in his orange robes with no accoutrements other than a simple ring on one hand. The ring was not frivolous jewelry but a storage ring, just like Wu Ying's. It made travel much easier, though occasionally additional, non-spirit-tooled methods of baggage were required. After all, even the closet-sized storage ring Wu Ying owned cost thousands of taels.

The pair nodded in response to Wu Ying's question, gesturing to their rings. Happy to see they were ready, Wu Ying turned toward Elder Lu, ready to hand them his Sect leave permit, and was stopped by the sight of a familiar young lady. Coming from the Sect was Li Yao, the small martial specialist hurrying down the pathway while chivying along another. As surprised as Wu Ying was to see her, her company was the true marvel. Yin Xue followed beside her, hands clasped behind his back. Wu Ying frowned, wondering why he was there.

The female cultivator brushed right past Wu Ying, never bothering to greet him, though she did greet both Tou He and Bao Cong. The moment she was done, she added, "Come, let's get going. If we take too long, the ship will leave without us."

She followed her words with action, continuing to walk down the pathways, ignoring Wu Ying and Elder Lu. Yin Xue smirked at Wu Ying before he hurried after the fast-moving Li Yao, pausing only long enough to offer a nod to Elder Lu. That left Wu Ying watching all four of their departing backs under the slowly brightening sky.

"Never a good thing." Elder Lu's lazy voice interrupted Wu Ying's befuddlement.

"Sir?"

"Angering a woman. My mother used to say angering a woman and the heavens was equally foolish." Elder Lu cackled then added as he fixed Wu Ying with a firm gaze, "Or ignoring an Elder. None of them bothered to show me their leave permits."

94

Wu Ying gulped and hurried over to the Elder, bowing low and offering his own Sect seal and the permits he had procured for the other two. "Elder, I'm sure they did not mean to insult you—"

"Never you mind. I will deal with them when they return," Elder Lu said. "But you are going to help your parents, yes?"

"Yes, Elder." Wu Ying's eyes narrowed as he wondered if he was going to receive another speech about the dangers to his dao and his life. He would never admit that he was exhausted by the numerous times he'd been warned—from attendants to Sect Elders to Ah Yee—and he did not need another discussion about what he was doing wrong.

"The path of a guardian is difficult. It requires both the strength to protect and the wisdom to know what to protect. Sometimes, knowing when one must walk away is just as important as protecting those one loves."

Wu Ying's jaw dropped, but Elder Lu had already turned away to stare at the sky, enjoying the passing clouds. Wu Ying shook his head, getting over his surprise at receiving actual advice rather than another recrimination. Still, something in Elder Lu's voice spoke of an untold story, one that he probably would not relate. Still, Elder Lu's advice left Wu Ying troubled in a way the other admonishments had not.

A slight droop of the pipe as the Elder acknowledged another Sect member brought Wu Ying's attention back to himself. This was no time to be considering such things. His group had already left him behind. If he did not hurry, he could just imagine Li Yao urging the ship's captain to leave without him. Whatever ruminations he might have on the dao of being a guardian, or if he was doing the wrong thing, would have to wait. He had a team to catch up with.

***

It was on the fourth switchback that Wu Ying caught up with the group. He hurried to Li Yao and ducked his head to speak with her. "I'm sorry for what I said yesterday."

And he was. Even if he did not mean to take back the content of what he said, he certainly understood her position and could have said his side better.

Li Yao looked at Wu Ying, sniffed once, then sped up to leave Wu Ying behind. A flash of anger ran through him at his rebuffed apology. He was not the only one who was wrong. Still... he decided to leave it alone for now. She would cool down at some point. Probably.

In any case, he had someone else to speak to. He dropped back, waiting until his target arrived. "Yin Xue, what are you doing here?"

"Why don't you ask your girlfriend?" Yin Xue smirked. When Wu Ying's fists clenched, it only made Yin Xue's smirk grow even wider. Eventually, when Wu Ying felt as if he might boil over, Yin Xue relented. "Li Yao asked me, of course."

"To speak with your father? Would that even help?" Wu Ying said.

After all, at least from Yin Xue's perspective, he was the unwanted son. Of course, that might be a lie too. Or a misjudgment. Fairy Yang thought his banishment and presence here was now more a matter of hedging their bets.

"Better than an unnamed peasant who's trying to steal his villagers, I would think."

Wu Ying bristled but had to admit, that made some sense. He hoped they were right and that Yin Xu would be able to convince his father to let the village go.

As if Yin Xue had no desire to spend any more time with Wu Ying than he had to, he sped up and fell in line with the blacksmith apprentice. Wu Ying caught bits of their conversation as the pair introduced themselves. At least the group was larger, even if they had added personal drama to the entire thing. Safety in numbers. So long as they didn't kill one another.

***

"Good to see you here again," said the owner of the vessel the group had embarked on. He slapped Wu Ying's shoulder, his face—deeply tanned from being on the water all the time—breaking into a wide grin. Wu Ying had to smile, as they seemed destined to leave on the same ship he had arrived on so long ago. "Will you be working the oars with us again?"

Wu Ying glanced over at where the sailors were, some of them ready to help guide the ship out on the rowing benches, while others rigged up the sails. Since they were going downstream, they would not have a full bank of oars out. Not like when they had to come to the Sect, rowing upriver against the current.

"No, I don't think so." Wu Ying gestured to the drum that dictated the timing. "I don't think I would be able to match your tempo anymore."

The captain eyed Wu Ying again, more carefully, and nodded. "Pity, but I understand."

Having finished speaking to Wu Ying and having sent his vice captain to deal with the rest of the cultivators, the captain turned back to his men and the cargo he was loading. Wu Ying stood by as the captain disappeared, caught up in the work of their departure, before he walked to the prow of the ship. A trace of sadness was in him as he realized that he was pulling away from who he was and who he had been. Away from the mortal world. Even joining in on the oars would be difficult, requiring Wu Ying to match strength with those who were significantly weaker than him. Wu Ying couldn't be certain that he could do so, and if he failed, then the craft would veer off course.

More than that, he realized, his scope of worry had grown. Saving one's family was normal. Mortal. Saving an entire village was something only a cultivator could dream of. Something the boy he used to be could never dream of.

As Wu Ying waited for the ship to finish loading and for them to begin their journey, he could only hope for fair winds and smooth waters. If so, it would take them a week before they had to transfer from the ship and begin the overland portion of their journey.

Chapter 9

Wu Ying tossed and turned in the hammock, unable to fall asleep. Late at night, the ship was quiet, the creaking of old wood and the swish of sails the only sounds surrounding him. Giving up, he got off the hammock, making sure to move as quietly as possible as he left the common room, and went up to the deck. Below, the rest of the cultivators and the day crew slept. The deck itself was illuminated by lanterns to allow the night crew to work unimpeded. Up ahead, at the prow, a single lantern illuminated any upcoming obstacles. A lookout peered into the dark waters, doing his best to ensure that the ship would not run afoul of anything. It was only because the river flowed so quickly and was used regularly by other ships that the captain was willing to risk traveling at night. Unlike other waterways and canals that had less traffic, the main river that led from the Sect was always cleared of obstructions in short order.

To Wu Ying's surprise, seated in a cleared space near the bow of the ship was Tou He. The ex-monk had his legs crossed and his eyes closed as he meditated. Wu Ying stretched out his senses, feeling Tou He's aura and the ambient chi flows. He sensed the turbulence in the air as Tou He drew in the ambient energy of the world, a small vortex of chi that centered around his friend. Except there was also turbulence within Tou He himself. Wu Ying frowned. He had sensed his friend cultivate before, and it was nothing like this.

On consideration, Wu Ying chose to watch over his friend in silence, concern growing as Tou He's breathing grew more erratic and the monk sweated and twitched. Concerned as he was, Wu Ying knew better than to interrupt the cultivator. Doing so would be, could be, as bad as letting him continue. Maybe even worse. Chi deviation was something that every cultivator worried about. At the lower levels of cultivation, that meant the gathered energy within one's body stopped moving in the carefully prescribed patterns, creating a backflow into the wrong meridians, crossflows into overly burdened locations, and potentially, inflows to blocked locations. This would cause the chi to strike itself, creating turbulence within the body.

It was, in many ways, similar to the backlash Wu Ying had faced when he failed to break through to the next stage. It was why in the beginning, when one started cultivating, it was always recommended to be done in groups and under the watchful eyes of a teacher. The teacher would know the flow of chi within the students and block, divert, and fix the deviations before they became set in the student's body, requiring even further, more complicated solutions.

Even so, Wu Ying did not think that a chi deviation was what Tou He faced at the moment. After all, Tou He was in the mid-stages of Energy Storage and was not a beginner cultivator. He should be able to avoid the mistakes young cultivators would make. Furthermore, Wu Ying knew that Tou He was not pushing ahead, instead focusing on consolidating his cultivation, which meant repeating known patterns. As such, Wu Ying was forced to watch, though he stood ready to forcibly stop his friend's cultivation if necessary. Doing that would normally be dangerous, but the pair had shared their cultivation methods for such an eventuality.

Tou He continued to shake and shudder, beads of sweat rolling down his smooth face while Wu Ying watched. As suddenly as the shaking started, his friend stopped, jerked upright, and vomited a mouthful of black blood onto his robes. As Tou He slumped over, Wu Ying grabbed his friend and supported him with one hand while making a flask of water appear in his other. His friend took a swig of the water, leaned over, and spat out the remnant blood. He repeated the action twice more before grimacing at his robes. A quick wash with the water had the black blood flowing off, making Wu Ying twitch in envy. Even the monk's robes were more expensive than his own. Then again, those robes were often the only thing a monk would own—and would be worn all their lives. It was probably more economical to own a single good set than multiple cheap robes.

When his friend was finally ready, Wu Ying asked the question he had been dying to know. "What was that?"

"Thank you." Tou He wiped his face clean and mopped at the water with a conjured cloth, cleaning the deck and himself before returning the flask. Once Tou He was done, he began a series of stretches, still avoiding looking fully at his friend.

Frowning, Wu Ying sat on a nearby bench and waited.

"It was a cultivation exercise." Tou He sighed and sat beside Wu Ying, a corner of his lips twisting wryly before he finally met Wu Ying's gaze, the first flush of embarrassment fading. "It seems I still have not killed my ego."

"Idiot!" Wu Ying jabbed his friend in the knee with a finger. "You know you can always ask for help."

"I know. I thought I had a grasp of it already." Tou He sighed. "Should have listened to my Master. The exercise is to help increase the size of my dantian."

"Too small?"

"Yes."

"What does it do?" Wu Ying leaned forward, curious to hear what method the ex-monk had dug up.

"It's a simple exercise. In fact, it's not the most suitable for me, but it is the closest we can find. You overfill your dantian and push against its boundaries with your chi. At the same time, you set up a spiral to compress the dantian's edges. In doing so, you are meant to give it strength and flexibility. Every few days, I increase the amount of chi I use to achieve the next level. That was what you saw."

Wu Ying knew that the amount of energy one could contain within their dantian was set at birth, but it would also grow as one progressed in their cultivation. Just like a muscle. But not a big muscle. A small one, a muscle tucked away and supported by other larger, stronger muscles. Targeting it was like trying to water a single plant in a field of vegetables while using a washing bucket thrown from a distance. It was difficult and likely to overwater everything else unless one took great care.

Tou He fished in his pockets and drew out a small bottle, which he handed to Wu Ying. "My Master gave me these pills. They are Black Ice Chi absorption pills of the North Wen. If I go too far, I am to take this. Except I might not be able to do it myself."

"Just practice when I'm around then." Wu Ying took the pills and held the bottle before him, turning it around in his hand. Like any good cultivator, he asked a few more questions about the pills and what they were meant to do.

In short, the pills would absorb the rampant energy in an individual's body. It was part poison and part medicine, since it did not differentiate between good and bad chi. Instead it drew it all in, storing it in the pill before forcing its ingestee to expel the pill—and its contents—in a violent and explosive manner.

"Thank you for trusting me," Wu Ying said. "Is it at least helping?"

Tou He shrugged. "Not much. The entire winter I might have grown my dantian's size by an inch?"

Wu Ying winced. A good dantian and the compressed energy it contained should be half the size of a fist when one ascended to Core Formation. Initially, most body cultivators had a head-sized dantian made up of uncompressed, unrefined energy. A body cultivator's goal, along with the development of their meridians, was the compression and refinement of that energy, increasing its density. A cultivator would go through multiple stages of compression and refinement, the largest change occurring during the first half of Body Refinement.

However, just because the chi was compressed did not mean the amount of energy had changed. It was only by expanding the muscle—the base amount—that Tou He could draw more. If he did not, it would limit Tou He's ability to break through to the Core Cultivation stage. In fact, depending on the size of Tou He's dantian, he might even struggle to clear the final Energy Storage meridians.

"So are you going to try again?" said Wu Ying, noting that Tou He had regained his color.

"If you will watch over me."

Wu Ying nodded, and his friend flashed him a grin. They both made sure that they were comfortable before Tou He began his cultivation exercise. Wu Ying watched over him, splitting some of his attention so that he could work on his own cultivation exercise. Tou He had done this for him more than enough. Time for him to return the favor.

***

The next morning, Wu Ying found Li Yao practicing on the upper deck. He tentatively approached her, worried that she would rebuff his advances once again. However, this time she did not stalk away but kept her focus on her forms. For a time, he watched her wield her spear, enjoying the graceful loops and swirls of motion. Perhaps it was her previous training as a dancer, perhaps it was her natural grace, but she moved as if she were dancing. A very martial dance, for each pivot, each graceful sway of her body was punctuated by the crisp strike of a weapon. When she was done, Wu Ying was amused to note that he was not the only one watching the beautiful cultivator. All around, various lazing workers were eyeing the young lady.

When Li Yao put away her weapon, Wu Ying girded his loins and approached her with a pair of breakfast bowls. He offered her the simple bowl of congee that was their breakfast, the boiled rice porridge being seasoned with fresh chives, garlic, and just a touch of sesame oil. Layered on top of the bowl of porridge was a filet of freshwater fish. While Wu Ying could not tell which particular fish it was, the white flesh looked succulent and glossy. It was likely the same one they had eaten last night, a simple freshwater delicacy that had been caught as they left the city. One advantage of traveling by boat was the constant ability to add to the stores.

Li Yao looked at the bowls before she propped her spear over one shoulder and took the bowl with her now free hand. She offered Wu Ying a simple thanks and took a seat against the boat's edge, away from any of the sailors. After setting her weapon on her knees, Li Yao dug into her meal with gusto.

Wu Ying hesitated before he followed her and took a seat beside his girlfriend. Together, the pair consumed their breakfast, the second of the day. After all, they were both used to waking early and training. When they were done, Wu Ying took the bowl from Li Yao and stacked them together.

"I'm sorry. I should've chosen my words better. I'm just worried about my parents." Wu Ying tried apologizing again, hoping that this time she would accept it.

"You idiot." Li Yao didn't look at Wu Ying, tracing her fingers along the smooth wood of her spear. "You should work on where you put your mouth. That sweet tongue of yours won't always get you out of trouble."

"I understand," Wu Ying said. "I just had this image of what our conversation would be like. When my imagination was betrayed by the reality of our conversation, I could not handle it."

Li Yao nodded. "I know. I was just trying to help. If you go to Lord Wen without a plan and without any backing, he will take advantage of you. If he will listen to you at all. You're just a Body Cleansing cultivator after all."

Wu Ying reluctantly acknowledged her point. Body cultivators, even those at the peak, were common enough to be disregarded—by nobles at the least. In the world outside the Sect, someone at his level would be apprised as good, strong enough to be the personal bodyguard of an important noble. But he wouldn't be special. He wouldn't be considered a force that had to be

104

respected. There were still others, many others, who had broken into the Energy Storage stage. It was only because Wu Ying was so young that his achievements would be considered special. In the outer world at least. Obviously, in the Sect, he was at best middling.

"So what are you thinking about with Yin Xue?" Wu Ying asked, his brow furrowing now that their little tiff had been set aside.

"I'm not sure. He's his son. He should have insights about his father," Li Yao said. "Personally, I think using him directly might be difficult. It will depend on how Yin Xue is received by his father. We might need to verify that first."

"What do you mean?"

"Yin Xue was sent to the Sect to gain strength. Then he was abandoned after he lost to you. Maybe his father really meant to leave him in the Sect. Maybe he's there to ensure his safety. Both of those are different facts, different motives. Both will affect how Lord Wen treats us." Li Yao looked around and ensured that Yin Xue was nowhere near before she continued. "If he was left there to be safeguarded, his father will be angry with us for bringing him. But if we can tie him close to us, his father won't dare send us on anything too dangerous. It will force him to contain his desires."

"Dangerous?"

"Haven't you realized it? The only reason he'd make use of you, of us, is to send us to do something his guards can't do. Or aren't willing to do."

"I just thought…" Wu Ying had to admit his thoughts. "I thought he would force me to promise to guard his family or residence. Maybe move some of his things around or offer some herbs."

"Maybe. But I don't think will be that simple, do you?"

Wu Ying could only offer her a twisted half smile now that his vague hopes had been burst. Considering his experience thus far, ever since he left his village, smooth and easy was unlikely. He just hoped that whatever Lord Wen chose would not be that dangerous.

***

The remainder of the river journey was completed in relative peace. Yin Xue and Bao Cong spent the days over the side of the boat, Yin Xue being taught the finer points of fishing. When questioned, the blacksmith pointed out that it was impossible for him to work on his profession here. Neither of the nobles were as intense with their martial practice as Tou He and Li Yao, who spent their time either sparring, working forms, or cultivating. To punctuate the river trip, Wu Ying even managed to convince Tou He to join him on the oars on the opposite side at one point.

During the few moments of conversation Wu Ying had with Yin Xue, he learned that the noble had taken a secondary occupation as a Scholar. It was not the most glamorous of occupations, nor was it one that would earn a significant amount of spirit stones in the future, like a blacksmith or an apothecarist, but it was a safe and in-demand skill set.

Perhaps the one thing that Wu Ying was most grateful for was that the tension between himself and his girlfriend had faded. Some of it still lingered, a stain on a previously happy relationship, but overall, they were back to their happy selves. More than once, Wu Ying noted the jealous glances Yin Xue and Bao Cong shot them. Even the ship's captain was overheard muttering about sickeningly sweet couples.

When the ship finally reached their destination city, Wu Ying thanked the captain and the crew for the pleasant journey before hustling the team off. He brought his enlarged team to the local Sect branch and used the stables there to acquire horses for them all. Together, the group rode out of the city, headed to their final destination. Now that they were on their feet once again, Wu Ying felt that same urgency overtake him.

As much as Wu Ying wanted to set a hard pace, he reined in his emotions and his horse, ensuring that they set off at a measured trot. As they traveled the paved road, signs of the upcoming war were all around, from the increased traffic between the city's stores to the new, combined army bases dotted through the kingdom and the occasional sighting of deploying troops on the road itself. Wu Ying even spotted a familiar sight—a troop of conscript soldiers marching in roughshod formation, being yelled at by their platoon leader as they journeyed from one village to the next.

Only once did they run into any trouble, the Sect members forced into a confrontation with a group of bandits. By their dress, they were clearly deserters, their army uniforms dirty, ragged, and stained. The confrontation was over in the time required to take three breaths, so outclassed were the bandits that it could not even be considered a scuffle. Bao Cong strung, nocked, and fired his first arrow so quickly that he might as well have had his bow strung already. Li Yao charged the remaining members without hesitation, followed by the remaining cultivators. And while Wu Ying still worried about the morality of killing them off-hand, his companions—except Tou He—did not. None of the bandits lasted more than a single clash, and none of the cultivators bothered to use any higher-level techniques.

Whatever guilt Wu Ying felt was assuaged when they reported the bandits' deaths at the next village. The village chieftain regaled them of the bandits' most recent crimes, including the massacre at a nearby farm.

And the team continued on, under bright day and the occasional light spring rains that muddied the road and slowed travel. In the end, they arrived at their destination—a large mansion set a distance from the nearest city or village. This was the home of Lord Wen, and it was only a few hours from Wu Ying's own house. He ached to return and speak with his family. But it was better for him to finish this now, rather than see his parents with no news. By now, they would have known that their plans had been learned of and dealt with. Better to have some good news, hopefully, than to bring false hope.

Drawing a deep breath, he kicked his horse in the sides and felt it speed up. Time to talk to Lord Wen and see what fate had in store for Wu Ying.

Chapter 10

Lord Wen's residence was a large, sprawling estate protected by a single exterior wall ten feet high. Watchtowers on each corner of the wall allowed guards to track incoming guests, though from Wu Ying's recollection, they were often left unmanned except for the one over the main gate. The countryside was relatively peaceful, especially for a well-protected location like the lord's residence. No bandit leader would be stupid enough to launch an attack against the residence, for the eventual retaliation would guarantee their demise.

Through mostly empty fields, the group rode their horses toward the white-washed and ceramic-tiled walls of the estate. Unlike other times, Wu Ying noted the presence of multiple guards in the towers, watching the group's approach. More than one guard had a crossbow in hand, already cocked and lowered toward the group. All in all, Wu Ying could not help but feel somewhat intimidated.

"Good evening, cultivators. Who comes to speak with Lord Wen?" one of the guards from above called, his hand resting on the pommel of his sword. Clad in a simple lamellar plate suit and a helmet with a red crest upon it, the guard stared at the cultivators sternly. Still, his greeting was polite.

Before Wu Ying could reply, Yin Xue raised his voice. "It's me, Ah Chu. Open the gates. We're here to speak with my father."

"Master Wen?" The guard looked surprised, then snapped himself to attention and called commands to those below. "My apologies, Master Wen. We did not expect you to return!"

"That is fine. Just be quick about it. And tell my father my friends and I have come to speak with him," Yin Xue said.

Wu Ying shook his head, watching as the Lord's son stepped back into his role as the son of the master of the house. It suited him, Wu Ying had to admit, though there was also a change in the way Yin Xue carried himself. He lacked the arrogance of before, the edge of superiority that had set off the younger children in the village. His time in the Sect had done him some good, it seemed. Either that, or he had grown into his arrogance in the last two years.

Once the main gates were open, the group saw the marvelous, well-tended gardens that made up the interior of the walled residence. Ahead of them, the main mansion loomed, constructed in the typical siheyuan style of architecture. That consisted not of a single building but multiple connected buildings, halls, and courtyards, built in a rectangular layout with the main hall situated in the northernmost portion of the residence.

In short order, the group entered the first of the walled portions of the building, passing through the main gates of the residence, and the outer courtyard. There, they deposited their equine companions with servants before they were led through the second, inner gate into the building proper where they could see the first of the inner courtyards.

Wu Ying shook his head as they were led into the building. He wondered how many courtyards there were. His own residence in the Sect only had one, while Tou He's had two and the Elders had the typical three. It was rumored that the more prestigious members of the Sect had even more courtyards— and the resulting halls, ancillary storage, and servant rooms—but he had never witnessed it. Looking at the size and proportions of the buildings they passed, Wu Ying would not be surprised if there were at least four courtyards.

As interesting as the architecture and the well-manicured lawns were, the residents of the building were of more interest to Wu Ying. Obviously, there were servants—many who worked the hallways and courtyards, tending to the gardens, sweeping and cleaning, doing laundry, and the myriad of other tasks required to keep a building this big functioning. But on top of that, guards patrolled the inside of the building, watching over everyone with cautious and discreet gazes. Scattered among the commoners were the noble children and adults who lounged around the building, speaking to one another, doing embroidery, practicing martial arts, and advancing their cultivation or their studies.

Many of the lounging children and adults bore a close resemblance to Yin Xue, having the same long nose, tilt of the eyebrows, and thin cheekbones. More than once, when Yin Xue and the group swept past, guided along their walk by a guard, they left behind whispered conversations. Yet not a single member of Yin Xue's large family moved to greet him directly.

"Are all noble houses this... cold?" Wu Ying whispered to Li Yao.

"No. Or, sort of?" Li Yao said as she watched the ramrod-stiff bearing of Yin Xue, who led the group. "We're always competing to some extent. Even if lineage is fixed, sometimes people are disowned. Or sent away..." Li Yao shook her head. "Or if someone fails at cultivating properly..."

Wu Ying made a face. He did not understand that. Not really. In a peasant family, there was no great expectation on cultivation. Whether you achieved Body Cultivation 2 or 3, it did not matter that much while working the fields. Hard work and dedication made a bigger difference. An individual who cultivated and could do more was considered a blessing, but it was more important that they had the ability to manage the fields and relationships in the family. Even a large family often lived together in the same building. Only the very largest peasant family might need their second son to move to another field, another building. But in that case, that could be considered a blessing too—more fields, more wealth. If they could afford the land and the rent.

There were other options too. The army. Moving to the city to work as a day laborer. Even, at times, working for the local smithy or other artisans. More tragic alternatives often reared their heads in times of need—a family that had few or no sons would be happy to be gifted one from another family that had too many. Eventually, it all worked out in the village—through goodwill and the occasional brow-beating by Elder Ko.

"Yin Xue must be on the outs," Li Yao continued, flicking her gaze to a trio of glowering teenagers, the boys staring at their Sect-dressed cousin. "If that's the case, bringing him might be a bad idea."

"I know," Wu Ying said. When Li Yao made a face, he shrugged. "Still, maybe he can prove himself to his father by helping with whatever task he sets us on."

"If he sets us on anything," Li Yao said with a tone of caution. "He might not be willing to listen."

Wu Ying tossed his head, dismissing her concern. Not because he thought she was wrong, but because if he thought of it at all, then what was the point of him coming? Better to hope, to believe that there was a way forward.

After crossing through the second inner gate, they were led across a courtyard to the north-facing hallway. This was not the main hall, but it was not one of the first ones they had passed. It was clear, at least to Wu Ying, that their presence and their affiliation with the Verdant Green Waters Sect was being respected. It would, Wu Ying hoped, give them some leverage. Turning aside a single petitioner might be easy but doing so when a group of them had arrived from the Sect would be more difficult.

Once the group was inside, they were shown to seats where snacks and a pot of steaming tea awaited them. Small washing bowls and towels were placed on side tables, which the nobles went to immediately to wash off the grime of the road. Tou He and Wu Ying glanced at one another before they copied the actions of their friends, washing hands and dabbing at their faces with wet cloths before they took their seats.

For a time, the group waited, sipping on tea. Tou He and Bao Cong, after a short wait, started in on the snacks, unperturbed by their surroundings. Wu Ying on the other hand sat at the edge of his seat, his hands on his knees, tense and waiting. Yin Xue did not bother sitting, sipping on his tea as he strolled around the hall, peering at various pieces of artwork and stone carvings. He would occasionally stop and admire a piece. As for Li Yao, she sat primly on her seat with her teacup, neither tense nor lounging. Content to wait.

Long minutes ticked away and Tou He's slurping as he ate made Wu Ying grit his teeth in annoyance. He almost spoke up twice but clenched his jaw. The second time because Li Yao caught his eye and shook her head, forcing him to hold onto his patience. Wu Ying was so close but still so far as Lord Wen took his time showing up. Each minute was torture for Wu Ying, one that he tried to ignore by focusing on his breathing, the slide of cold air into his lungs and the way his aura teased at the various unaspected portions of chi that flowed through the hall.

It was nearly half an hour later before the doors leading further into the structure opened. Wu Ying shot to his feet and winced, realizing how eager he seemed. Li Yao stood up more languidly, followed by his friends all turning to stare at the newcomer.

Lord Wen was a large man, standing just over six feet, and big the way once muscular men who aged and stopped exercising were. There was still strength in his frame, but it was hidden underneath layers of fat. A slight graying in Lord Wen's hair and his imperial-styled beard showed the stress of the past few years. Lord Wen was dressed in the long, glittering robes that were his wont, golden thread and red on pale silk laid over his body. Numerous other accessories lay on his body, from jade bracelets and rings to a necklace that held the kingdom seal, the mark of his nobility.

"Lord Wen." Wu Ying bowed.

His companions mimicked his movements, even Yin Xue, much to Wu Ying's surprise. Though he noticed that Yin Xue did call his father by his paternal honorific.

"I've been expecting you," Lord Wen said, brushing past the bowing Wu Ying to take a seat. He flopped down, legs crossing as he stared at Wu Ying, unperturbed by the presence of the others. He did, however, fix his son with a reproachful gaze. "Not you."

"I came to speak with you about—"

Lord Wen cut off Wu Ying. "Stealing my villagers. I know. What makes you think I should even countenance a discussion?"

Wu Ying hesitated as Lord Wen went on the attack immediately.

"If you did not want to, you would not be speaking with us." Li Yao offered Lord Wen a smile, bowing again as she re-introduced herself. "I'm sure there is some agreement we could come to."

"For the loss of an entire village?" Lord Wen snorted. "Is the House Lee offering their support?"

Li Yao's eyes widened, and Wu Ying saw the growing smirk on Lord Wen's face. Lord Wen was playing with them.

Rather than let the others speak any further, Wu Ying stepped forward, drawing Lord Wen's sneering focus again. "This is between you and me. They are just here as my…" Wu Ying glanced at Yin Xue and then Bao Cong before changing the word he was going to use. "Companions."

Lord Wen snorted, his disdain clear. Yet Lord Wen flicked a gaze to the three nobles in quick order before stopping on Tou He, and he bit off whatever acerbic comment he might have voiced. "What do you offer then, Wu Ying?"

"Cultivator Long," Wu Ying quietly corrected Lord Wen.

He watched as the nobleman narrowed his eyes and smiled when Lord Wen grudgingly corrected his words. It was a minor victory, but it did assert Wu Ying's standing. He was no peasant, but a cultivator in a Sect that required respect. He was not bargaining as a peasant to his Lord and landholder, but one of near equals.

"At this time, you know what I want," Wu Ying said. "Perhaps it will be easier if you tell us what you desire."

"And why should I name my price when you are the one who wants to buy?"

"Most merchants do," Wu Ying said. When Lord Wen's eyes narrowed at the insult—comparing him to a lowly merchant[9]!—Wu Ying continued speaking. "But as you know, my means are limited. Even so, we are speaking. So there is something that you want from me. And my companions."

"What I want is for my village and lands to be unmolested. Can you do that? Can you stop the army?" Even as Wu Ying shook his head, Lord Wen continued. "Of course not. Even having you guard my lands from a raiding party is more than can be expected of the five of you."

Wu Ying inclined his head in acknowledgment of the point. While Lord Wen was not a prosperous nobleman, his lands were still large enough that the group would be unable to patrol all of it. Perhaps they might be able to stop one or two intruders, but if the army itself arrived, they would have to pull back.

"How bad is it? With the Wei army?" Yin Xue interrupted. "They've never done permanent harm."

Wu Ying pressed his lips together. Permanent. That was only from the view of a noble. Too often, they'd taken rice, seed, food. Slaughtered animals or stolen horses. It left the villagers bereft of everything but their houses and whatever rice they had managed to hide or had been left untouched. Still, there was truth to the words too. They rarely killed, took slaves, or burnt down residences.

"This time it's different," Lord Wen replied to his son. "This time, they are destroying what they cannot hold. They are taking slaves."

---

[9] So, one thing to note is that depending on time period, merchants were generally considered the lowest class in society. Very broadly speaking, in traditional Confucian society, it went from noble, scholar, peasant, artisans and craftsmen, then merchants and traders.

There was a joint hiss at his words. That was not entirely new news. Rumors had floated as far as the Sect itself of a change in policy. The closer they got, the more details had been offered. And slavery was not unknown, though it was not practiced in the State of Shen or, normally, the State of Wei. That it was happening now…

"Why?" Yin Xue asked.

"Money," Bao Cong answered for Lord Wen. "Wars are expensive. For us. For them. And the appetite of Cai has grown. They need more slaves every year as they expand eastward."

Wu Ying frowned and cudgeled his brain for information on the State of Cai. Farther east and north of Wei, it was blocked from expansion by a small mountain range and the river that flowed between the pair. So long as the state of Wei held both, it stymied the State of Cai's expansionist tendencies to the west. It helped that expanding to the north and east was easier too. But so long as the State of Cai expanded, it needed slaves.

"And you've confirmed they are taking slaves?" Tou He said, speaking up.

"We have," Lord Wen said. "Most of the villages close to the border have been emptied. Lord Yu is suffering. The king has indicated he will aid him, but there's only so much that can be done. His largesse will run out soon."

"Then why care if I take my family away?" Wu Ying said, eyes narrowing.

"Because it is not guaranteed the army will reach us. For your family—for the village—to leave in time, they will have to depart at least a few weeks before the army arrives. I am giving up my village for a risk. And even if the raiding parties come, not all of my villages will be hit. The tradeoff is poor."

"For you," Wu Ying said flatly.

"That is what matters."

Wu Ying bit his tongue as he stopped himself from retorting. He forced himself to draw a deep breath, to find calm before he spoke. "Then we come back to the question. What do you want?"

"From you?" Lord Wen stood. He walked to the door and only turned at the border of the room, offering the stunned group a taunting half-smile. "Coming?"

The group scrambled after the sauntering Lord. They went down one hallway then another, heading deeper into the building itself until they reached a new room. Within, multiple scrolls and books sat on bookshelves while the clear daylight streamed in from open windows. Dominating one side of the room was a wooden table, while the other side had lounging chairs for easy reading. It was to the table that Lord Wen walked. Wu Ying was surprised to note a map of the country and the State of Wei were laid out. On it were multiple markers—simple carvings of the words Wei and Shen.

It took little thought to realize that the map and figurines denoted the positions of the armies. Of as much interest to Wu Ying were smaller carvings of carriages and little boats placed along different trading routes. Those, Wu Ying estimated, were likely merchants Lord Wen had interest in—or maybe even the conveyances of a branch family.

"These are current?" Wu Ying said.

"As of yesterday," Lord Wen said.

The group crowded around the table, taking in their first clear view of the situation. One further addition that Wu Ying spotted was the use of a thin, light purple paper that was bunched and cut apart, to indicate areas the armies had traversed. In that way, a clearer history of the war was available.

"Not that close," Wu Ying said with relief. His gaze had been drawn to the only Wei army—one of three that had deployed—that might threaten the village. A quick glance showed that a second army was stalemated at a river crossing, and the last army was running unchecked before the city of Yu.

"What happened there?" Li Yao said and pointed at the last army carving. A short distance away, the marker for the army of Shen sat, but it was behind the army of Wei.

"A play on spies. The Wei general supplied us the wrong information, sending our army in the wrong location. By the time they learned better, it was too late," Lord Wen growled. "They will only catch them when they have begun besieging the city of Yu."

"Is that a bad thing?" Tou He asked. "Surely the city can hold?"

Lord Wen shrugged. "Maybe. There are rumors that the army holds a Nascent Soul cultivator within."

The group winced. If a Nascent Soul cultivator took action, the walls would not hold. No city could afford to build their walls with spiritual material, so the only reinforcement city walls received were from formations. Activating a formation was expensive and required a sacrifice of materials and spirit stones, so most cities never activated the ones they had in play. More than that, most cities did not invest in formations powerful enough to stop a Nascent Soul cultivator.

"But they couldn't hold it, could they?" Li Yao said worriedly. The little cultivator leaned forward and stared at the terrain. "They'd have to strike and move on, in fear of being caught out."

"Unless they entered the city and repaired the walls," Yin Xue corrected her. "Then they could hold within and force our army to besiege our own city. Then they could have their reserves come to relieve them." Yin Xue pointed at the fourth carving that sat behind Wei's borders, just waiting to reinforce.

While the group chatted about the problem of the second Wei army, Wu Ying looked farther south and spotted the marker of a fourth token from their kingdom. This one was across the border, heading deeper into the state of Wei, having already sacked one town on the border crossing, it seemed. An arrow pointing north east of the marker indicated its route of progress, direct toward the Wei city of Guitong. As Wu Ying peered at the maps, he noted the numerous mountains that dotted the region next to the city and the Li River that flowed right past Guitong. He frowned, trying to remember why the name seemed so familiar—beyond the rice grown in the region that was known to be nearly as good as their village's.

"They are attacking Guitong?" Yin Xue said, having spotted Wu Ying's perusal and turning to his father. His voice held a strange tone, one that set Wu Ying's senses on alert.

"Yes."

"You don't mean for us to…" Yin Xue stopped himself. "Of course you do."

Realization struck Wu Ying while Yin Xue talked to his father. Old lessons about their liege lord's upbringing. The Lord Wen and his family were not "true" members of the state of Shen, but branch members from a noble peerage in the state of Wei. The passing of some crucial information and an action during one of their intermittent wars—what action, Wu Ying could not recall—had seen to the grandfather of Lord Wen receiving his peerage in the state of Shen. It was why Lord Wen had such a small land allotment and why Lord Wen spent so much of his time currying favor in the court.

"You want us to take part in the army, don't you?" Wu Ying summarized.

"Not exactly." Lord Wen stopped talking to his son and turned fully to Wu Ying. "I want you to acquire something for me from the city."

"What?"

"The cultivation method for my family."

Wu Ying frowned. He had wondered why Yin Xue focused on the Yellow Emperor's method of cultivation just like the rest of them. After all, most nobles, like Li Yao, had their own cultivation methods. Most of those methods were developed specifically for their bloodline, suiting them better than something more generic. Or at least, the nobles insisted it was better.

"And this information is in the city?" Wu Ying asked.

"Yes. The Wen family estate is located in Guitong. While the main family spends most of its time in the capital, the family memorial is still located in the

119

city. By tradition, the family cultivation style and the lineage tablet must be kept in the city. Relocating it and the ancestors would bring bad luck." The last sentence was said with a sneer.

Wu Ying frowned, tapping his fingers on the side of his leg. "Even if we agree to do this, I don't know what your style is. Unless it's clearly marked, I could be easily led astray."

"Then it's a good thing you have my son. He will know what the true style looks like." Lord Wen chuckled. "And there is no if. If you want my agreement for your village to leave, you will take on this task."

Wu Ying stared at the marker for the fourth army. He had no desire to join the fight. He had no idea how the appearance of himself and his friends would even be taken. They might be powerful cultivators, but armies had a chain of command. Randomly adding in new people would be tricky. After all, spies were always trying to join armies.

Even so...

"Very well," Wu Ying said. "But I will have your oath to allow my village to leave. You will even guarantee their safety."

"If you promise to complete this task." Lord Wen stared at Wu Ying, daring him to turn away or look aside.

Wu Ying returned the gaze and offered a single nod, agreeing to the task. It was a simple thing after all. Join the army, lay siege to a city, break into the city, and steal a cultivation manual from the nobleman's home or burial grounds. All the while, not dying or losing any of his friends.

Simple.

Chapter 11

Of course, it wasn't that simple. There was more to discuss. Wu Ying received, as best as he could, the information that Lord Wen had about the main family's residence, the mausoleum, their numbers, and their security, as well as a map of the city itself. All of which was dated and liable to be inaccurate to some degree. Wu Ying was told where he should expect the documentation to be kept, and even given some brief overview of the cultivation style. Once all that was done, Lord Wen dismissed Wu Ying and his friends to the visiting hall they had come from. Only Yin Xue was left behind, to have a longer talk with his father in private.

It was nearly an hour later when Yin Xue came out. He refused to say anything about what had transpired behind closed doors, but he stared daggers at Wu Ying at every chance he could.

Their objective complete, Wu Ying took his friends over to his village. It would be a chance for him to show off to his friends where he came from, have the village thank them for their aid, and most of all, for him to see his parents.

In truth, Wu Ying felt an indescribable level of excitement and dread at the upcoming talk. He missed his parents, the village, the rice fields. But… he also dreaded introducing them to Li Yao. He dreaded what his mother might say. He dreaded what Li Yao might say. It was one thing to know he was a peasant. It was another to see it in all its mundane drabness.

In this mixed state of mind, Wu Ying led his friends to the village. The first signs of it were the terraced paddy fields, the gentle slope of the surroundings carved into flat fields to allow for production of rice. Next was the small cluster of buildings that denoted the village proper. Some families, like his, had their residences situated farther afield from the center of town. That offered them some privacy and space to grow their own vegetables in their gardens, but the longer-standing members of the village had their houses in the village square itself. They were the original inhabitants, the ones who had grouped together to begin the cultivation of rice here. And of course, the schoolhouse, the tavern, and the blacksmith were all located in the center of the town.

As it was approaching evening by the time the group arrived in the village, few people were in the fields, the last few stragglers in the process of putting away the equipment they had used over the day.

The sight of a group of cultivators on horses made the villagers tense. That was no surprise to Wu Ying. Groups of men on horses were never good news for the village. After all, only nobles or the army came in large numbers, astride horses. Or bandits.

Luckily, the Sect robes the group wore allayed some of those fears. Still, Wu Ying noticed that a small number of villagers had clustered around Elder Ko. Among them was his father, who was just arriving, a sword belted to his side. Even with the slight hitch in his stride, Long Yu Ri was an intimidating sight. There was a hardness to his father that Wu Ying could not replicate. It came from his time in the army, from his time working the fields, from pain and hardship, a life hard lived.

It was Elder Ko who first realized what the group meant. The elder was still sharp eyed, even at his age. Immediately, the elder barked out orders to the villagers. His father, hearing the cries, slowed down his approach, losing some of the intimidating air he had projected, but he did not stop, only turning to call out behind him.

Wu Ying watched all of this with a half smile. He had forgotten the kind of commotion his visit would likely cause. Or maybe had not forgotten but not considered it, since it was not as if he had ever been gone. In fact… when was the last time the village had had a cultivator return? Wu Ying had vague recollections of talk of a similar celebration a few generations ago? A long time at least.

"I'm sorry. I didn't realize it was going to be such a big deal," Wu Ying said to his friends as the villagers gathered into an appropriate greeting committee while others scurried around pulling tables into the village square, shouting for food and drink to be brought, for the fire pit to start.

"*Hua dan!*" Yin Xue swore at Wu Ying, shaking his head at the peasant's forgetfulness. His return would obviously create a commotion, one that would throw off all kinds of plans.

Tou He just offered his friend the placid calm he always projected, though Wu Ying heard a muttered prayer when he turned away.

Wu Ying took a deep breath before facing the oncoming villagers. He plastered on a smile, readying himself to greet them and explain matters. What would come would come. And really, this wasn't so bad. They were his friends, his family, people he had grown up with. He could sit through their celebration, give them the hope of making their way out.

And if he found some of the conversations boring, a little prosaic, Wu Ying kept it to himself.

***

The celebration lasted well into the night, ending only because the village ran out of food and wine to supply their esteemed guests. Tou He, Li Yao, and Bao Cong were highly popular at the celebration, their easy familiarity with everyone making them favored guests. Yin Xue held himself aloof, as was his wont. Still, Wu Ying noticed a few of the younger girls clustering around the noble Lord, offering him smiles and hints of further pleasure. More than one parent kept an eye on Yin Xue and the young girls, ready to head off any unfortunate incidents. Ambition was good, but unchecked ambition without hope of achievement only led to disappointment and grief.

As for Wu Ying, he was of course the proud returning son, the honored guest. It was only late in the night, when most of the villagers had stumbled off to sleep off the alcohol, that he found time to speak with his parents. Seated in the warm and familiar surroundings of their small hut, Wu Ying regarded his parents.

"The village looks prosperous," said Wu Ying. It was an obvious comment, but face to face with them, he was not sure what else to say.

"It is. Thanks to you. And Li Yao is a very lovely girl." Wu Ying's mother offered him a smile. "She will make a fine cultivator. And wife."

Wu Ying narrowed his eyes, trying to discern the meaning of her words. But he could not find the barbs within them, so he could only nod and smile in return.

"I am very happy you have so many friends, so many willing to help you with this foolishness of yours. Even if I'm surprised that one of them is Lord Xue," his mother said.

"He's not a friend," Wu Ying said.

"But what you're doing is foolish," Yu Ri said. Wu Ying's father glowered at his son, rubbing his aching knee in reflex. "Joining the army, but not officially with your Sect? Journeying into the State of Wei? What made you choose such idiocy?"

"Need. It's the only way Lord Wen was willing to let you all go. And they're taking slaves now," Wu Ying said. "There's no way I am allowing you to become a slave."

"No need to worry about that. Your father's too broken to become a slave. They'd just kill me first," Yu Ri said wryly.

Unsurprisingly, his mother smacked his father on the shoulder.

"It's okay, I would kill you first," his father told his wife.

That received a much harder blow.

"Putting aside your father's black humor, you are doing too much for us. Filial piety can only go so far," Fa Rong, Wu Ying's mother, said.

Wu Ying set his jaw. "It will go as far as I need it to go. I will not abandon you."

124

His parents shared a sad look before they clasped Wu Ying's hands.

"Your path is different from ours now. You might not see it yet, but we do. Do not let the past hold you back from your future," Fa Rong said.

"My future will have no meaning without my past," Wu Ying said firmly.

To those confident words, his parents only shared a smile. Turning away from more serious topics, the family spoke about the other, more important portions of their lives, the everyday occurrences that wove together a person's existence.

***

The group left late the next morning, saying goodbye to a much smaller crowd. Unlike the villagers, the higher cultivation levels among the Sect members meant they recovered faster after drinking. Of course, faster did not mean entirely untouched; but the group had watched their intake. Even so, the group was subdued as they rode their horses away, intent on making up the distance between them and the army.

"They are a nice group," said Bao Cong.

"Thank you," Wu Ying replied with a smile. He turned around, regarding his friends. "They liked you all too."

"I know." Tou He shook his head. "Some of the younger girls were…"

"Aggressive," finished Bao Cong.

"As were their mothers," Li Yao said with a laugh. "Both ways."

"That'd be Auntie Qiu," Wu Ying said with a half-smile. "I thought Bao Cong almost fell for Qiu Er."

"She is quite lovely…" Bao Cong's voice grew remote, his eyes dreamy. Tou He smacked Bao Cong's leg with his hand. "What? She was."

"I noticed her shooting glares at Li Yao," Tou He said. "Did you insult her somehow?"

"I did nothing!"

"She had a crush on Wu Ying," Yin Xue said, speaking up from behind. "Though he was always oblivious to it."

"I was not!" Wu Ying scratched his head. "I just didn't want to get involved with her. And you. And Fa Hui."

"Fa Hui?" Li Yao said.

"My friend. My best friend from the village." Wu Ying quieted as he recalled his friend. His friend who had not answered a single letter. Who had not written to him. Not a single letter in two years.

"Har. Yes, we did fight over her back then, did we not?" Yin Xue's voice was amused.

"I noticed she avoided you," Wu Ying said.

"We talked."

"And?" Wu Ying probed.

Rather than answer, Yin Xue kicked his heels into his horse and sped up, leaving the group behind. Wu Ying exchanged a glance with Li Yao, who shook her head, dissuading her boyfriend from bothering Yin Xue further.

The group rode together for a time, stopping at a village when it was time for lunch. Seated together, Wu Ying extracted a map to allow everyone to see it. He traced the route they would have to take, first down the roads and across before they stopped at the town of Xin Ming. He tapped the town.

"We have a decision to make here." Wu Ying traced his fingers down the map along the river, stopping and tracing it further east as it met a canal. He then returned his finger back to the starting point and did the same with the southeasterly road. "These are two routes we can choose. The first might be faster. If there are no obstructions and we can find a boat to take us, sailing will be faster. Of course, that requires us to pay for the boat, or potentially buy one.

"The other option is technically shorter, but slower as we will be going over land. It is a direct route though, and we won't be at the mercy of blockages. In either case, I expect it will take us about two weeks to get close to the army."

"And how do you expect us to sneak by the border guards?" Bao Cong asked.

"Simple. We buy some new clothing and disguise ourselves as scholars," Wu Ying said.

"Scholars in a war zone?" Yin Xue said. "Flimsy disguise."

"What would you suggest then?" Wu Ying said.

"Li Yao or I could play nobles," Yin Xue said. "The rest of you could play guards. Maybe even Li Yao and I could be husband and wife on our first journey around, perhaps visiting the ancestral shrine. It would give us a good reason for being there. And for having so many guards."

Bao Cong nodded. "That will allow us to keep our weapons. And it's better than playing a merchant. We don't have the money to buy the goods."

"Why are you and Li Yao husband and wife?" Wu Ying said huffily. "Bao Cong is a noble too."

"He doesn't look like much of one. No offense meant," Yin Xue said.

"None taken. Working the forge has given me a strong tan."

"Aren't we forgetting someone?" Li Yao said, interrupting the burgeoning argument between Wu Ying and Yin Xue. She fixed her gaze on the quiet Tou He, tracking her eyes upward to rest on his bald pate. "Even if we all disguised ourselves, our monk here can't disguise his hair style."

"I can go alone." Tou He shrugged. "No one ever looks twice at a monk on a pilgrimage."

"That means you can't have any meat on you," Wu Ying teased.

Tou He made a face but nodded.

"I don't think we should have anyone travel alone," said Bao Cong.

"Then what do you suggest?" said Yin Xue.

The group fell silent as they contemplated their options. Wu Ying grinned and leaned forward, inspiration striking him like a thunderstorm on clay roofing tiles.

***

In the end, the group chose to wait to decide on the route until they arrived at the town. There, they would be able to learn how things fared on the river and canal. The merchants would certainly know better than they did. They did, however, choose to adopt Wu Ying's disguise plan when they left the tavern.

The group split, with Wu Ying and Tou He in one group, acting as fellow wanderers. Wu Ying would be what he was—a herb gatherer for mundane herbs, supplying apothecarists and other medical professionals. His knowledge of herbs and plants would be the perfect disguise and would explain his presence. After all, a wandering gatherer without his own herb garden needed to travel to ply his trade. Tou He would be a monk on a pilgrimage to the temple in the capital of Wei. Together, the pair had banded together for mutual protection in these turbulent times. They would be the ones at the forefront. In this way, the group behind would have a scout for potential issues, especially as the nobles were the "juicier" targets.

Li Yao and the other two nobles would act as a noblewoman and her guards. She would be a dutiful and tragic widow sent to a convent after the death of her husband as her new family had little use for her. That the convent in the State of Wei was well-known for accepting the widows of nobles and peasants and for safeguarding them all bolstered Li Yao's cover story.

For all their precautions, they were still far behind the front lines of the war. Even bandits, like the ones they had met before, were rare. Chaos would arrive soon enough, but it was still a dark rain cloud on the horizon, threatening a deluge but only sending threats so far. It was at the gates of the town of Lipu, after a long period of traveling, that Wu Ying realized his first mistake with their disguise.

"Passes?" the guard said to Wu Ying and Tou He, his tone bored from the hours spent asking the same question.

Tou He reached into his robes and pulled out a simple token. The guard scanned it, glancing at the name of the temple then at Tou He, before he returned the token without further questions. He turned to Wu Ying, who hid his surprise at his friend's resourcefulness and started his own excuse.

"I'm sorry, honored sir. I was waylaid by bandits. My pack and most of my belongings, including my pass, were taken." Wu Ying bowed his head low. "I was hoping to speak to the magistrate to reacquire my travel pass and my merchant license."

"With what money?" The guard sneered at Wu Ying. "If you have no pass, you will not be allowed entry into the city. In fact, we should take you into custody to ensure that you are not a runaway."

Wu Ying lowered his voice and leaned forward, passing his hands over his storage ring and extracting a palm-sized root of ginseng. In addition, he extracted a small number of coins. "They took most of what I had, but not all. I keep some things hidden on me." Wu Ying extended his hands and the guard automatically palmed the ginseng and coins. "I understand that there is an entrance fee. I am not attempting to avoid that. But I'm sure there are better things we can do with our time than waste it on more paperwork for both of us. Don't you think so?"

The guard glanced at the ginseng and frowned in consternation.

"It's only fifty years old," said Wu Ying, acting as if the ginseng's age was something to be ashamed of.

"Fifty years old…" The guard looked Wu Ying over once again, taking in his dusty clothing and worn fingers, his cracked fingernails still caked with dirt. He glanced at his fellow guard, who was still busy with his own line, before he waved Wu Ying through. "Make sure you get your permit dealt with immediately. Speak to Junior Magistrate Khoo. He is my cousin. Tell him I sent you."

"Thank you, benefactor," Wu Ying said, bowing slightly before hurrying off after Tou He.

The ex–monk had continued to walk on, not wanting to mess with Wu Ying's deception. They turned the street and walked a couple of blocks farther before they felt comfortable enough to break the silence.

"I didn't realize you still had your old temple seal." We Ying shot a glance at his friend, amusement in his eyes. It seemed that Tou He was more of a rebel than he looked.

"And I didn't realize you were so knowledgeable about bribing," said Tou He.

"It's a fact of life. Even in the towns we sold our goods at, we occasionally had to bribe the guards. So long as we are circumspect about our actions and are not asking for too much, they will look the other way." Wu Ying sighed then rubbed his storage ring. "But the next bribe will be expensive."

Tou He shrugged. He had no experience in this matter. Bribing the magistrate was something Wu Ying would have to handle directly.

"I do hope that Li Yao and the others will manage…"

***

They met later that night at an inn Yin Xue knew of, in a private room at the top of the building. Wu Ying and Tou He sneaked into the room after the servants had delivered the evening's meal for them all. Wu Ying carried his usual travel bag filled with purchased herbs and other materials he had scavenged along the way and kept within his storage ring, as well as the newly written permits. All that, of course, meant Wu Ying had used even more coins, leaving him significantly bare of purse.

"How did you get in?" asked Wu Ying.

"I showed them my family seal," Li Yao said matter-of-factly. She looked somewhat surprised at Wu Ying's question. "Why? Did you have trouble?"

Wu Ying sighed and shook his head. Of course they'd had no issues. No one questioned nobles about where they went or why. The restrictions on travel were only for those who weren't nobles or cultivators. Already, Wu Ying missed being able to enter cities without having to pay or show documentation.

"Did you learn anything?" said Yin Xue.

"No." Wu Ying winced. The time he'd needed to fortify his disguise meant that he was unable to do the necessary research on their potential routes.

"Then why—"

Tou He interrupted Yin Xue. "The river route is still open. There is no indication that there are any blockades on the river itself. But the canals might be troublesome."

"Troublesome?" said Bao Cong.

"The canals are narrow and easy to guard. The captains were speaking of a lot of bandits working them during the last war. Many refused to go on them any longer. I don't know if we could find passage when we needed it."

Wu Ying imagined the map, thinking of the route they would need. The nearest canal took them farther south than they wanted to go. They'd have to cross the ground on horseback if there was no transportation, adding at least a few days to their trip. Any time they saved by taking a ship south would be eaten up by the additional distance. And then they would still have to head slightly north to catch up to the army from there. If they could find another ship, they could save up to a week. If.

"It looks like we will be going over land then," Yin Xue said, stating what they all thought.

"Yes! I get to ride more," Li Yao exclaimed. "I've really come to like Qiufeng. He's big and strong and lets me ride him without complaint, all day long."

"Qiufeng?" said Wu Ying.

"My horse."

"Of course." Wu Ying shook his head, hiding his mouth behind a raised teacup. "Then we are agreed. We go by land."

***

Travel by land had one advantage, at least for Wu Ying. Even on the horse he rode, he could cultivate. His training on learning to cultivate while running allowed him to optimize his time. Cultivating in this way was not as efficient, especially for his cultivation exercises, but considering they were traveling for hours at a time, he could still progress.

In terms of his actual cultivation—his progress with the Yellow Emperor's style—he was stymied by the same blocks. To break through, he needed to collect a large amount of chi and force the breakthrough—unless he managed to achieve a moment of enlightenment—and that was too dangerous to do out here. Better for him to wear away at the edges of the blocks, decreasing their effectiveness. If he did it right, his next attempt at a breakthrough would be easier.

But mostly, all that was a by-product of his other training. While they traveled, he focused on his aura cultivation exercises, working on suppressing his aura while at the same time making it semi-permeable. Working on the new cultivation technique to increase the speed of his cultivation, of his recharge rates.

At first, he failed. Continuously. It was one thing to learn to use it while sitting still, another thing to do so when he was walking—then it was a matter

132

of control of his own movement. But it was another thing entirely to work on the cultivation exercise while trying—badly—to ride a horse, keep a lookout for potential dangers, and talk to one's friend.

Again and again Wu Ying failed, his aura growing fully permissive without him realizing it. But eventually, Wu Ying managed to increase the amount of time between his failures. He increased the flow of chi in his dantian, the whirlpool of the cultivation technique, while hardening his aura at the same time. He managed to pick out unaspected chi, draw it into his body and in the areas where he failed; he stripped the aspected chi of its properties and made it his own.

In the process, he learned something new.

Unaspected chi was significantly faster to "own" than aspected chi. After discussion with Tou He and having his friend compare his own process of cultivation and his own intake of fire chi, Wu Ying realized one advantage of the Yellow Emperor's cultivation method. Unaspected chi was not as prevalent as aspected chi, but it was easier and faster to subsume. Even though Wu Ying had less chi to draw upon, the little that he did could be controlled and made his own faster than the fire chi Tou He used. After all, unaspected chi was just that—without seal, without ownership. But fire chi—or any other aspected chi—was drawn from the elements of the world, given form, and so Tou He would need to forcibly remove it and add his own flame to it.

After their talk, Tou He grew contemplative, focusing within. He soon pointed out an even worse issue for one like him, who was aspected to flame and heat. Water chi was incredibly difficult and slow for Tou He to strip and utilize. It took Tou He almost thrice as long as any other chi and five times for his own aspect. When he revealed that, he had Wu Ying explain what he had been doing in the cultivation exercise, enough that Tou He could grasp the plan. And then the ex-monk grew silent, experimenting with his own aura.

It was days later, when Tou He's aura shifted and grew hotter, that Wu Ying understood what his friend had done. Instead of hardening his aura and blocking out chi he did not use, Tou He actually projected a small amount of fire chi into his. In this way, he "burnt" and repelled water chi, leaving him with fire chi that was drawn to his aura and other, less inimical energy forms. It was a different type of utilization than Wu Ying's technique, though Tou He had derived some aspects from it. It was also grossly inefficient in the beginning, but Tou He was focused on increasing its efficiency.

In the meantime, Wu Ying kept at his own cultivation exercises during the day, refining and making them more intuitive.

In the evenings, he and Tou He sparred, training their martial styles. Wu Ying tried to combine his cultivation exercises with the duels, intent on keeping his energy regeneration ongoing. It allowed him to last longer, to keep going even when he should be tired out. If Wu Ying could not beat his friend with skill or talent, then he would have to be stubborner and endure longer.

Chapter 12

"Hold it right there!"

The voice commanded the pair of cultivators to stop, leaving them standing in the middle of the road in surprise. Wu Ying carefully moved his hands away from his sword as he looked around. Now that the strangers had revealed themselves, Wu Ying could sense their auras. It seemed at least one of the strangers had the ability to suppress his friends' and his own aura signature.

The strange cultivators exited the sides of the roads, exposing themselves from the foliage they had hidden in, wearing the yellow-and-brown robes of the Six Jade Gates sect. There were five members of the intercepting party. One who wielded a crossbow stood the farthest away at fifty yards down the path, at the top of the slight rise they had been traversing. The other four clustered around Wu Ying and Tou He, weapons already drawn. Two wielded daos, while the third carried a long trident and the last a simple spear. Wu Ying absently noted that the trident-wielder was a female who stood even taller than him. The men, on the other hand, looked very similar, their long hair tied up into buns, with the narrow features of the people of Wei.

On command, Wu Ying and Tou He carefully got off their horses, making sure to make no aggressive motions. They stepped away from their rides, standing with their arms by their sides as Wu Ying gauged their opponents' strengths. The weakest of them—the spear-wielder—was in the high Body Cleansing stage like Wu Ying. The others were in early or middle Energy Storage. Not easy opponents, but not too dangerous either.

"My brothers, why have you stopped us?" Tou He said.

"We are looking for spies, and you two are very suspicious." The leader of the group pointed his dao at Tou He. "What are you doing in our country?"

It had taken Wu Ying and his friends over a week and a half to make it this far. Luckily, the border guard post had been simple enough to pass through. The guards stationed there were lazy, barely even paying attention. They were more intent on harassing a local fisherman and his daughter than the pair of them.

Since then, for the last few days, the pair had been making their way deeper into the country. To Wu Ying's surprise, he'd seen few signs of a war being fought in the state of Wei. Oh, the farmers looked a little leaner, a little hungrier. There were few more vagrants on the road. But nonetheless, there were few signs of rampant destruction. In the end, the language was the same—with minor regional accented variations. The writing was the same, thanks to the Yellow Emperor, and the people… well, people were people.

So Wu Ying was surprised that they had been located so quickly by the cultivators of the Six Jade Gates Sect. As Tou He related their backstory to the group, Wu Ying watched them all carefully. He was grateful he had learned to suppress his aura, letting only a little of it leak. He even ensured that he was using the heretical chi gathering method, so that he would seem somewhat different, feel different, as befitted an independent cultivator. As for Tou He, his Energy Storage level was less of a concern. Everyone knew the monks had their own paths of cultivation and immortality.

"You are a wandering cultivator," stated the leader of the guard team. "Prove it."

"I-I don't know how to prove what I am." Wu Ying shook his head, wondering if they had deliberately demanded what would be impossible for him to prove. How do you prove you are not part of a sect?

"Show me your cultivation manual."

Wu Ying hesitated. Anyone, even a wandering cultivator, would hesitate. The notes of a cultivator were private. Asking to see a cultivation manual was like asking to see a man's small clothes. Unseemly and intensely invasive. Who wanted to show the holes and stains that resulted from life? Yet, understandable or not, his hesitation resulted in the opposing cultivators raising their weapons and pointing them at the pair. Wu Ying let his gaze track over the group, assessing them all.

"You are quite strong for a wandering cultivator. Body cleansing eight, is it?" the spear-wielder said.

"I've had a few fortunate encounters," said Wu Ying.

"Like?" the leader asked suspiciously.

"I met another wandering cultivator, Elder Dun Yuan Rang, when I was early on in my cultivation. He helped me out of a difficult spot," said Wu Ying. "I practiced with him and learned a little."

"I have met Elder Dun myself." The leader smirked, gloating at the fact that he had, he assumed, caught Wu Ying in the lie. "Describe him to me. Prove that you studied with him."

Wu Ying hesitated then did his best to describe the wandering Elder. It had been nearly two years since they had met, since the Elder had saved Wu Ying from the bandits at the waterfall. When Wu Ying was done speaking, the leader of the other group was not smirking any longer.

"I was still—I still am—vastly inferior in cultivation to the Senior. I could not learn much from him, but I did spend time studying his form," Wu Ying said.

"Show me." The leader walked a distance away, taking station on the road itself. He raised his dao, touching it to his forehead as he readied himself.

"Senior Cai! You cannot do this," the girl protested.

"Junior Ren, I am the senior here. I can do what I want." Senior Cai looked away from her and gestured at Wu Ying. "Come then. Or die as a spy."

Wu Ying grimaced but walked to the center of the road. He drew his sword and saluted his opponent. Inside, he was grateful for the arrogant Senior Cai. This was a method he could prove. His manual had too many notes, especially notes for a cultivation level that was much higher than what he showed.

Wu Ying took a deep breath, thinking back to the moment before Elder Dun had struck that last time. That single form, that simple motion that became a focused point in his attack. It had been many moons since he had considered that event. He thought he had taken all he could from that encounter, but now that he was thinking of it with his higher cultivation level, with his better understanding of the sword, Wu Ying realized that there was more to learn.

He could almost see Elder Dun, feel the way his legs bunched, his arms shifted, the way he positioned himself and the energy he had gathered. Imperceptible to Wu Ying back then, impressions that he had discarded came back. He copied those motions, integrated them with his own understanding of the sword and his own style, and crouched low.

"The Sword's Truth," Wu Ying whispered a moment before he threw himself forward.

It was his best lunge ever. He crossed the five feet that separated him from Senior Cai in moments, his sword aimed directly at Senior Cai's heart. Wu Ying's arm was extended, his body braced behind it, his legs flowing together in a single extended line into the earth. Everything he had learned from his father, from that image of Elder Dun, he used.

Senior Cai was caught by surprise by the explosiveness of Wu Ying's attack. He hesitated for only a fraction of a second, but that fraction brought the weapon inches closer. A hasty block came too late, the strike pausing a half-inch from plunging into Senior Cai's throat as Wu Ying's momentum ended. The Sect member flinched and glared at Wu Ying, his posturing come to an end.

Senior Cai gulped before he stepped back. "That... that wasn't Elder Dun's attack."

"No, it wasn't. I am not his disciple. I just spent a little time with him. I took what I could learn and integrated it with my style." Wu Ying stepped back and sheathed his sword, looking the man in his eyes. "But I'm sure you can see what I learned."

"I did," another of the dao-wielders said. "It's a poor imitation, but it is an imitation. And it's not something someone could gain from just watching."

Senior Cai glared but eventually sheathed his sword and gestured for the group to go. Wu Ying exhaled, relieved as the cultivators took off, heading down the same road Wu Ying and Tou He were journeying on.

Neither of the friends spoke for long minutes as they got back on their horses and rode, letting the tension and adrenaline fade in silence. Only when they felt safe, a couple of hours later, did the pair speak.

"That was close," Wu Ying said.

"Yes," Tou He agreed.

Wu Ying sighed. Perhaps they might have to reconsider their travel plans. If they'd had to fight, they would have lost for sure. But… part of the reason for doing what they did was to avoid a fight. Mulling over their options, the pair rode on in silence.

***

That evening, Wu Ying made his way to the group at the rest stop's only remaining table. The stop itself was no more than a small, ramshackle two-story structure that had seen better days. It was manned by a single merchant, one who was both portly and slow with his service while having the hangdog expression of one who had been set upon by the world repeatedly.

"What did you learn?" said Yin Xue when Wu Ying took his seat.

"The owner explained that our dinner is a result of the despicable army of Shen coming by a few days ago and taking all his provisions." Wu Ying picked up his curved spoon and dipped it into the watery rice porridge that had been served as dinner.

Supplemented by thin strips of pork that had been steamed over the boiling porridge and flavored with dried, salted fish, the meal was only barely sustaining. The three nobles turned up their noses at the meal, but Wu Ying had eaten similar repass before. Droughts and an overabundance of water could impact a harvest, leaving peasants with little to eat. Still, Wu Ying wished that the innkeeper had used some of the fresh spring onions and wild ginger Wu Ying had traded to him for his night's accommodation. It would give the porridge a little more body.

"At least the wine isn't bad," commented Bao Cong. He raised a small teacup that he was using and swirled the wine before he sipped it.

"Peasants are very good at hiding the important things," sneered Yin Xue.

Wu Ying bristled but kept his mouth shut.

They had been careful to introduce themselves to each other when they arrived at the rest stop, still putting on the pretense that they didn't know one another. Even if the innkeeper had doubts, he was only one man, but it was still good to practice.

"I told him about our encounter earlier today, Brother Long," Tou He said. "I believe the noble lady would be willing to journey with us for mutual assurance. We are all concerned that there might be even more bandits or army groups. It would only take a single misunderstanding for tragedy to strike."

Wu Ying raised an eyebrow at Li Yao, surprised to see that the group had discussed and made a decision on this while he was speaking with the innkeeper. Still, he had been considering joining up again. It would not be too surprising for a number of small groups to travel together for safety. Even if there was the threat of betrayal, Li Yao's group was larger.

"That is good," Wu Ying agreed then supped on his meager dinner.

The group followed his actions, holding off on talking until they had finished their meal.

"Did the innkeeper mention anything about the army? Maybe where they're located? Or where they are headed?" Yin Xue said, leaning forward. "We want to avoid them if possible."

"No such luck. The men they sent were not very talkative," Wu Ying said.

"Then we will have to play it by ear," said Bao Cong.

Having said all they needed to, the group broke up, heading to their quarters for the night. In this case, it was a sparsely furnished bedroom for Li Yao and the main common room for the others. As Li Yao walked up the stairs, Wu Ying could not help but send a longing look after her. It had been many days since they had had a chance to talk, and he had to admit, he missed her company.

***

The next morning, the group left early, none of them particularly interested in the breakfast the shop owner would try to press upon them. They all had better and more filling foodstuff in their storage rings. Once they were sufficiently distant from the rest stop, they spoke more freely, though they kept a lookout for additional ambushes.

"How much farther, do you think?" Li Yao asked. "I'm quite sore from riding all day."

"If it was a small raiding party, then ordinary military doctrine would have the main army within a few hours' ride," Tou He said confidently.

Wu Ying also recalled that lecture on the practicality of resupply for the raiding party and the return of acquired goods to the army. Small groups would travel in the close countryside, pulling whatever forage they could locate for the main army and adding to the army's supplies. After all, a single cartload gained of the enemy's provisions was worth twenty of their own. The larger groups, those that consisted of entire platoons with a large number of wagons and carts, would forage further. It was a dangerous job and often resulted in losses to the foraging groups if they were defeated by their opponents.

"So only a few days then?" Bao Cong said rhetorically.

With little else to speak of for now, Wu Ying rode ahead of the group slightly. He continued to scan the surrounding vegetation, hoping to acquire some additional herbs and resources. While the roadside was likely picked over, there was still hope of finding some better herbs and vegetation. Especially those that were more easily mistaken. Whenever he did locate a new item, Wu Ying dismounted and extracted the herb, storing it in his bag before returning and catching up with the team. At times, when a herb or vegetable was more valuable, he'd store it in his ring. Doing so would decrease the value of the item, since it would die and fail to regrow, but it was better than leaving them to be stolen or rot.

Traveling in a group as they were, Wu Ying was not as worried about demon beasts. After all, with most of his friends being unable or unwilling to suppress or hide their auras, most demon beasts would avoid their group. Really, only the injured or sapient races would chance attacking creatures more powerful than them.

In the meantime, Wu Ying watched for herbs and turned over their upcoming introduction to the state of Shen's army. He dreaded it, to some extent, knowing they would have to tread a careful line. They had their own objectives, and one that they did not, could not, allow the army's to conflict with. Yet at the same time, they did not have any real bargaining strength. Not as low-leveled as they were—relatively speaking.

***

A day and a half later, the group crested a barren hill, stripped of its timber in recent days, and were greeted by the picturesque sight of the riverside town of

Guitong. Short, gently sloping hills rose up all around the town, bracketing in the town as it sat by the river, protected by its high walls and guard towers. On some of the farther hills, terraced rice fields had been cut into their surroundings, locations for farmers to feed the city. Now, they lay barren and untended by the farmers who hid behind the walls.

Around the city, the Shen army sat before the walls, siege engines being built from the wood that had been brought and the forests that had been cut down around the city. All along the front of the walls stood the beginnings of long trenches that were to encircle the town and ensure the defenders could not escape. With Body cultivators in play, the trenches were already a couple of feet deep and stretched toward the river's edge. Of course, the sodden ground threatened to disrupt the work, making this particular siege tactic more difficult to complete.

The town of Guitong was laid out in the usual manner for a riverside town. A small dock allowed ships to land and deposit their goods, while a wall that reached the edges of the river and a little past it covered the rest of the town. In the center of the town itself, with roads leading from the docks and the three main gates, was the magistrate's office. Wu Ying knew, from his studies in the second year, that the state of Wei had few large noble houses, most of those being relatives of their king. Instead, they used bureaucrats—magistrates—to oversee major cities and collect taxes for the government. Small noble houses, like Lord Wen's, had been subsumed into the official kingdom lineage, leaving them related to the Emperor by marriage, however distantly. That was why the ancestral home of Lord Wen was left mostly empty in Guitong, and the main branch family now lived in the capital when they were not fighting and joining the imperial army or serving as magistrates.

As for the besieging army, Wu Ying noted the straight lines and orderly set up for the various units of the besieging force. He could now see, with his greater understanding and training, the order in the chaos that he had first

143

experienced as a peasant arriving in the milling throng of the army. He saw how each unit was set up, read the unit flags that indicated the unit's locations, and spotted where the generals and other commanding officers' tents were.

Before the group could continue their journey, Bao Cong pointed out the incoming platoon of soldier scouts. Leading them was a familiar face, seated with casual ease on a horse that stood half a hand taller than the soldiers' own. Wu Ying sighed and shook his head, wondering whether it was destiny or luck that saw him meeting those he knew. Sometimes, it seemed destiny placed too heavy a hand on his actions.

Chapter 13

On Wu Ying's command, the group rode down to the approaching soldiers from the state of Shen. With friends and allies so close, Wu Ying's group found themselves relaxing, some of the tension from the past few days draining away. Traveling behind enemy lines, even disguised as they had been, had been stressful. Thankfully, the army of the State of Wei was mostly deployed outside the country, leaving the Wei countryside bereft of their protection but for a few roving patrols of guards and cultivators.

"I thought you didn't want anything to do with the war," Liu Tsong called the moment they were close enough to speak. A flick of a gaze at his companions had her adding, "I'm also surprised to see the company you are keeping."

"It's a long story." Wu Ying had to shrug a little at what probably was a strange sight. At least to those who knew him and his friends.

"Cultivator Li, do you know these people?" one of the soldiers, a red crest on his helmet flaring high to indicate his rank as a unit leader, said to Liu Tsong while he eyed the group before him.

"Yes. Even if they look the way they do, they are my Sect members. Though"—Liu Tsong swept her gaze over the group—"I'm sure they will be willing to show their Sect seals."

After prompting, the group pulled their Sect seals from their storage rings and showed them to the suspicious guards. Liu Tsong crooked her finger and the seals flew to her hand, manipulated by her control of the flow of ambient chi. She touched them, one after the other, infusing a little chi into the seals to verify their authenticity. When she and the guard were satisfied, Liu Tsong sent the seals back to the group with a half smile.

"I need to continue my patrol. But we will send an escort with you to greet the general. I'll speak to you all later tonight." Liu Tsong gestured to the guard, who proceeded to designate two of his men to lead the group back to the army.

With a wave, Liu Tsong continued their patrol while Wu Ying and his team rode down the foothills. At least this part was going well so far.

***

"Unacceptable."

Wu Ying winced as the lieutenant general stated his opinion without hesitation. Their meeting had started out well—until Wu Ying had detailed his needs. Obviously, Wu Ying had volunteered their group to help the army, to join them in their siege of the city. But he had also asked that they be allowed to enter the city when the time came to retrieve the manual.

"With respect, Lieutenant General, I—" Wu Ying began, only to be interrupted again.

"This is a military operation. Even if you are cultivators, you must abide by our rules. We will not allow you to flounce around, doing what you please, and causing havoc. Nor do you get to the make additional requests from us," Lieutenant General Hao said. As he spoke, the edges of his large, luxurious mustache quivered. He leaned forward, the top of the crest of his helmet that he wore even now in the command tent almost touching Wu Ying's face. He glowered at the cultivator. Scattered documents sat upon his table, forgotten after Wu Ying's interruption. "You can either agree to work for us or you can leave."

Wu Ying crossed his arms and glared at the lieutenant general only for the other to sneer at him. Wu Ying tried again. "At the least, I want an assurance that we will be allowed to look for the cultivation style when it is safe to do so."

"Impossible. You will do as I say or not take part at all."

Wu Ying sighed. "Then I think there is nothing more to say." He turned around slowly, moving toward the exit.

"Where are you going?" Lieutenant General Hao snapped.

"Away. There is nothing here for us."

"You can't do that. This is a military encampment. You are under military law!" Enraged that his bluff had been called, the lieutenant general raised his voice and called, "Guards!"

The guards who stood outside walked in, their spears leveled at Wu Ying. Through the opened flap, Wu Ying caught a glimpse of the other guards that had been watching his friends level their weapons as well.

"We are cultivators from the Verdant Green Waters Sect. We are not military personnel. We have not joined, nor do we intend to join your army if our demands are not met. You have no authority over us," Wu Ying said.

He ignored the guards and the spear points that glinted so close to his throat, doing his best to keep his voice calm and borrowing some of the arrogance that he had seen his noble friends carry unconsciously. In truth, they were both correct on some level. This was a military encampment, and by coming here, they were subject to military law. But they were also not in the State of Shen anymore, and as cultivators in another country, the reach of the laws was debatable. In addition, Wu Ying was from a respected ally. How far the lieutenant general was willing to push matters would depend on his arrogance and temper.

"We will see how long you are willing to be stubborn after spending time in our prison," sneered the lieutenant general. At his gesture, the guards grabbed Wu Ying's arms and escorted the cultivator out.

The guards outside noticed what was happening and gestured at the other members of the group to raise their hands too. Tou He raised an eyebrow at Wu Ying, who quickly shook his head. Already, Bao Cong and Li Yao had their arms in the air.

"What did you do, Wu Ying!" Yin Xue exclaimed.

"I refuse to make us a part of the army," Wu Ying explained.

One of his captors shifted his hand as if he wanted to strike Wu Ying then thought better of it. Even if Wu Ying was a prisoner, he was also a cultivator.

"I knew one of us should have come with you to speak with him," Yin Xue complained as the group was led away, spears leveled at their backs.

Not that the group was worried about the small number of guards watching over them. It was the larger number of soldiers all about that might be an issue. And of course, the repercussions when they got home.

Wu Ying had no reply to that accusation, because a part of him wondered as well if his friends could have done a better job at negotiating. After all, he was not a noble. He was just a peasant who cultivated. On the other hand, Lieutenant General Hao had seemed extremely set in getting his way.

Before Yin Xue could continue complaining, Tou He spoke up. "*Amitoufo*[10]."

Yin Xue gritted his teeth but still fell silent. The rest of the group also held off on commenting, knowing there was little they could do now. They could only hope that Liu Tsong and whoever was leading the Sect members in the army could smooth things out.

***

To Wu Ying's surprise, they were not thrown into an actual prison but instead restricted to the tents they had been given. They were separated, left to stew in their thoughts. With nothing better to do, Wu Ying found himself seated cross-legged, meditating and working on his cultivation that evening. He did his best to remove the negative thoughts and the worries of the day, intent on

---

[10] Amitoufo is the transliteration of the Sanskrit words Amithaba Buddha. It calls upon the Buddha of Infinite Light to help calm the mind and come from a compassionate place. In this case, Tien Huo is using it as a reminder to Yien Xue to let this go.

progressing his cultivation exercise. Unfortunately, his progress in drawing in unaspected chi and working the chi circulation exercise had slowed ever since he had filled his dantian. It was unfortunate, but he would rather be slow in his progress than dead because he had insufficient chi during a battle.

Late in the evening, the food delivered for supper grown cold before him, another familiar presence intruded upon Wu Ying's awareness. He cracked an eye open, surprised to see the Elder in his tent—especially considering Wu Ying did not notice his presence until he had moved the tent flap aside. In an encampment like this, the Elder should have lit up his surroundings like a bonfire to Wu Ying's senses.

Wu Ying scrambled to his feet, bowing low. "Elder Po! I did not know that you are part of this army."

"The Sect felt I should accompany this army as I have the most experience in the State of Wei. But it is not this matter that we are speaking about. What have you done?" The bare-fisted metal-aspected Elder glared at Wu Ying.

They had traveled together on the expedition—the one which had seen the Elder progress in his cultivation after his long years of being bottlenecked—and as such, they had some familiarity with one another. However, none of that familiarity could be seen on Elder Po's face at this time.

"I have a small assignment that coincides with yours…" Wu Ying quickly explained to Elder Po what had transpired.

Elder Po shook his head after Wu Ying had done speaking. "Bad luck. Lieutenant General Hao is extremely strict about the rule of law. Military law. He is particularly angry that the army must rely on us. Like many of his compatriots, he feels that the army should have the right to enforce recruitment first, before the Sects."

"Then… Elder?" Wu Ying let a little bit of hope into his voice.

"I will do what I can. But you'll have to accept military law when you are here," Elder Po warned Wu Ying.

"Of course."

Warning given, Elder Po swept out of the room, leaving Wu Ying to his cold dinner and his cultivation.

***

Even after Elder Po's assurances, nothing happened for days. Wu Ying was left confined to his tent, only able to cultivate. His days were only broken by the arrival of meals, for he did not receive additional visitors, forcing the cultivator to sit and stew by himself. All around, he heard the sounds of the army going on with its day, the talk of idling soldiers, the neigh of horses as they were led past, and the constant strikes of stones against the city wall as the trebuchets fired. If not for the years of training at cultivation; from school to Sect, at being forced to do nothing but sit still and focus within, Wu Ying would have gone insane.

Instead, he threw himself at the task of cultivating. At this point, he was not harnessing the chi from the world except as a secondary by-product for constantly cleansing his body and meridians, sending the cleaned chi to brush against the blockages in his Energy Storage meridians like a water stream against rock before filtering out the new impurities and discarding them. His primary purpose now was meditating—focusing upon the experiences he had gained, his memories.

He saw, once again, Elder Dun as he struck. As the Elder curled himself and launched his attack at Wu Ying, the way the blade targeted his heart, the flow of power through his body and within the blade itself. Wu Ying mined that memory for all the knowledge it could gift, turning it around in his mind's eye again and again, taking in flashes of reflection on the water. In time, he no longer focused on the flow of chi or the Elder's body, but the look in Elder Dun's eyes. That coldness, that implacability. That focus.

150

Another moment, another memory. A bandit, one that Li Yao and he had killed last year. Wu Ying's blade plunging through the man's neck. The widening in the pupils, that moment of clarity and release. When the bandit had realized he was dead. When all that struggle was done. The giving up on life.

The taotei jumping at Wu Ying, seen past the guard of his sword. That last sliver of time before it would land on his weapon. Resolved to make the taotei pay, to injure it at the cost of his life, Wu Ying would not, could not, stop fighting. And rage—rage reflected in the taotei's never-ending hunger. Anger at the pain its own existence created.

Another memory, floating alongside the others. A newer one. The rest stop keeper from before, angry and sad, his hard work stolen by the army. Left with nothing but the little he had managed to hide, the few coins and goods he had managed to keep for himself. All that he had managed to secret away to rebuild his life. Refusing to leave, give up, or despair. Serving subpar food and the same within, knowing it for what it was. But refusing to leave.

Stubbornness. Resolution. Will.

Elder, bandit, monster, and peasant.

Reflections of one another. Neither good nor bad—but a facet. Imposing one's will upon the heavens, demanding it change. Sometimes failing, sometimes succeeding. But trying. Always trying.

It was not enlightenment. There was no greater Dao involved in this. But a knot within Wu Ying's heart, one that had grown when he failed to breakthrough, eased.

Failure happened. Destruction happened. But starting over, going on. That too was part of the Dao. That too was human.

***

The curtain of his tent was drawn aside, leaving Wu Ying to blink into the early morning sunlight. Wu Ying stood, brushing down his robes as he stared at Chao Kun.

"It's time."

The serious and grim expression on Chao Kun's face made Wu Ying decide not to ask any further questions. At least, not just yet. When Wu Ying took a step forward, Chao Kun shook his head.

"Change first." He tossed Wu Ying a set of clothing and armor similar to that worn by the regular members of the army. "And make sure you have all your equipment. We will be fighting."

Wu Ying nodded. He took the armor and clothing and retreated behind a privacy screen to change. In short order, he walked out, clad in black-and-grey lamellated armor like all the other soldiers—if not for the jian by his side. As for his own clothing and armor, he had placed it in his storage ring.

"Ah, I forgot. You are still using your jian."

Wu Ying touched the weapon at his side, raising an eyebrow. "I did not bring another weapon." Well, he had a couple of other swords in his storage ring, but they were of the same type.

"You know how to use a dao, yes?"

"Obviously," Wu Ying replied.

Even if he did not specialize in using a dao, the Long family-style had forms and passages devoted to the weapon. He had also practiced with the weapon in his village. It just was not his preferred weapon. After all, the Long family weapon style focused on the jian, but a sword was a sword and things like distance, timing, muscular chain activation were the same.

"Then we shall get you one."

Chao Kun gestured, and together, the pair exited the tent. They walked along the pathway between tents, the army personnel dodging around Chao Kun and Wu Ying as they hurried to their stations. Finally, they crested the slope of a hill and spotted where the hubbub that had grown around them was focused. Sprawled below them in formed ranks was the majority of the army. In the morning sun, spearheads pointed toward the sky glittered, bathing the waiting army in shifting beams of sunlight as they faced the city.

Arrayed before the walls, between the army and the city, were the siege weapons, many of them still leaking sap from being cut down and built. They had stopped firing last night, allowing more rocks to be placed near them for this morning's assault. Assault covers—mostly simple rolling, covered carts—were the majority of the siege weapons, though Wu Ying spotted a few more elaborate assault covers. Behind the initial assault covers was the mixed group of archers and infantry who would hide beneath the covers as they rolled close to the walls. Directly behind the initial wave of siege weaponry were the sky carts, mobile siege ladders with a hinged, folding ladder that would be deployed when they were in place.

As for the city itself, its wall were beaten, fractured in the front. Targeted attacks had knocked down or damaged the guard towers, but the walls still stood. None of them had been destroyed or shattered. No gaping holes faced the waiting army. For all intents and purposes, in spite of the damage done to the walls, they were intact.

"Are we starting now?" asked Wu Ying.

"Yes."

Chapter 14

Chao Kun let Wu Ying marvel at the sight for a long minute before he gestured for him to hurry along. Together, the pair headed for the army's blacksmith, where weapons were being fixed and sharpened. Chao Kun spoke rapidly to one of the guards before he made his way to one of the racks and searched through the repaired daos before finding one to his satisfaction. He tossed it to Wu Ying, who caught it and the scabbard that followed, testing the weapon in his hand.

It was serviceable. The weight was slightly off, a bit farther toward the pommel than Wu Ying would have preferred. It made the sabre's weight a little more unwieldly, made cutting a little harder. The metal itself was of low quality, adequate but likely to chip after vigorous use. And it had no sense of style at all, looking similar to the hundreds of daos that lay around the encampment. Even if most soldiers used the spear as their primary weapon, the dao was the preferred secondary weapon since its single cutting edge and heavier blade design required less training and could be used more effectively in a shield wall. The jian, once popular as the main side-weapon of the army, had decreased in popularity as closed ranks and more formal shield walls had been adopted.

Those cultivators and martial artists like his family who stayed loyal to the jian were growing rarer each year. Even if the lighter weapon had been the more popular weapon to begin with, the dao's adoption by the army had seen the jian's slow decrease in popularity—at least among soldiers and the general populace. On the other hand, while martial styles for the dao were increasing in number, for the highest tier sword arts, it was said that one needed to study the jian. But...

"Good enough?" Chao Kun asked.

"Yes. In the end, a sword is a sword," Wu Ying said, belting the scabbard to his body as he replaced his own weapon. It was both an ultimate truth and lie, depending on the circumstances. As any true sword stylist would tell you. For what came next, this would do. "What is my role?"

"You'll be part of the first wave," Chao Kun said. He puckered his face as he had eaten something sour before leading Wu Ying away from the blacksmith's to where the army waited, talking all the while. "You, your friends, and a small number of other cultivators—mercenaries and other Sect members mostly—will be held back in reserve but near the front of the line. When our army reaches the walls with their ladders, you will be sent to scale the wall."

Wu Ying's eyes widened. Assaulting the walled city, even if it had been softened up with the fire from the numerous trebuchets, was no easy feat. And on their first assault, it was unlikely the army would succeed.

"There aren't any holes yet," Wu Ying said as he tried to recall how many sky cloud ladders he had seen. Not enough. Not without more holes in the walls to split the army's attention.

"The general believes that using cultivators in the initial breech might surprise the defenders," Chao Kun said.

His tone was entirely neutral, but Wu Ying could not help but glance at his friend. Finding his friend's face entirely still, Wu Ying sighed. In the end, whatever they thought, they were still under military law. They had orders to follow. And that was it.

"Where will you be?" Wu Ying asked.

"We will be watching for retaliation by other cultivators." Chao Kun gestured down the line to the left. "My team will be deployed with Elder Po." Chao Kun paused then added, "Do not expect us to take action unless a Core cultivator or worse shows up. Pray that we don't have to reinforce you."

Wu Ying nodded, trying to relax. At least the Core cultivators would be dealt with. If the city used them. Now, all he had to do was survive the arrows, spears, and swords of their opponents as they assaulted the wall.

***

"About time you got here," Li Yao said to Wu Ying, punctuating her greeting with a hug.

They had regrouped under the awning of an assault wagon, hidden from the prying eyes of their enemy. Chao Kun had dropped Wu Ying off with his team before marching off to inspect a few other wagons.

"I came as soon as Chao Kun got me." Wu Ying eyed the group, noting how they were all dressed like him in the standard army uniform. It was probably so they weren't targeted by archers. Yet as he let his gaze rake over the group of familiar and unfamiliar faces, he stopped on one unexpected addition. "Senior Liu?"

"Wu Ying." Liu Tsong nodded to Wu Ying.

"What are you doing here?" Wu Ying said. From what he gathered from Chao Kun—more between the lines than directly—this was a punishment. Surely his Senior had not done anything that deserved her presence here.

"There are more contribution points here." Liu Tsong shrugged. "I'll be providing us cover during the last stages." She smiled as she tapped her ring, drawing Wu Ying's gaze toward it. "I have a few tricks that should help."

Wu Ying frowned but nodded. He was quickly drawn into greeting the rest of his friends.

When Wu Ying got to Tou He, his friend pulled him close to whisper, "Senior Li's being modest. She was sent here because she demanded our release from the lieutetant general."

Wu Ying's eyes widened, then glanced at the junior apothecarist. It was obvious that her actions had resulted in failure, but still, he was grateful for the attempt. Finding friends who were willing to risk their standing was rare. Or so he was told.

Because as Wu Ying looked around the small enclosure, his gaze falling on his friends in turn, he realized he was lucky. Lucky to find people willing to risk so much for him. Lives. Standing. Time.

"Thank you," Wu Ying said.

The words caught the attention of a few, with Yin Xue sneering and Bao Cong shrugging. Li Yao just offered him a grin and hugged his arm quickly before she released it to point at the unfamiliar faces.

"This is Yan Bai Hu, Xu Gong, and Huang Zu from the White Tiger Sect in the lower Ru province," Li Yao said.

The three members had ruddy, dark faces, looking more like peasants or bandits than the noble sect members Wu Ying was used to. Certainly, the daos and thick axe-blade polearms they held suited their coarse appearance. They offered him curt greetings, which Wu Ying returned before Li Yao continued.

"Lady Pan is an itinerant cultivator who will be joining us," Li Yao's curt introductions grew a little softer when she reached the woman.

Lady Pan was well shaped, reminding Wu Ying of a wine gourd even under the formless wear of the army. When Lady Pan caught Wu Ying's wandering gaze, she raised a single eyebrow and smirked, making the peasant blush.

Li Yao glanced between the pair then punched Wu Ying in the arm, though her smile continued to stay on her lips. "And this is her companion, Yan Qing."

Yan Qing, on the other hand, was a handsome youth, six feet tall with red lips, thick eyebrows, and broad shoulders. The youth looked to be in good spirits and sported a straight sword, though its hilt and blade were longer than the traditional form, allowing him to wield it two-handed. Near his side, a beautiful, unstrung bow rested.

"You'll watch over us, right, Brother Long?" Lady Pan asked. She blinked her clear brown eyes at him.

When Wu Ying stuttered, Li Yao laughed and elbowed him in the side. "Stop it, Sister Lian. Wu Ying is quite innocent and won't be able to take your jokes. He'll be too distracted."

"Oh, we wouldn't want our brave hero to be distracted," Pan Jin Lian said, her eyes twinkling.

Yan Qing rolled his eyes as he checked over his bow and arrows.

Her introductions done, Li Yao leaned in to continue her chat with Jin Lian inside the siege weapon.

Released from their teasing, Wu Ying escaped to the other side of the small enclosure. Outside of the cultivators, the enclosure contained a few soldiers who stood silently, waiting patiently for the signal under the watchful eyes of their unit leader. At first, they seemed calm and still, but on closer inspection, Wu Ying noticed the shifting feet, the hesitant words the soldiers passed between one another. Rather than witness their discomfort, he turned away to stare out the back, where he saw the remaining members of the army waiting patiently, and the clouds.

"Hopefully we start soon," Wu Ying muttered.

"Oh?" Li Yao said, cocking her head. "You see something?"

"Rain," Wu Ying said, nodding to the sky.

Li Yao frowned, eyeing the few clouds and the occasional gusting wind. "I don't see it."

"It's coming."

"Not according to the general's soothsayers," Yin Xue, who was lounging near the exit, said.

"It's coming," Wu Ying insisted.

Yin Xue looked at Wu Ying and nodded. Perhaps he recalled Wu Ying's previous occupation. But he then studied the ground in more detail. Wu Ying could already tell him what it was like. The lush grass beneath their feet hid dark brown river soil. Of course, the river itself no longer overflowed as often, as canals and dykes helped pull it from the banks, so the alluvial soil beneath their feet was old and settled. None of the gray soil from often-flooding rivers, perfect for growing, with touches of nearly black soil from the mountains farther upstream. All of which meant that when rain came, it'd soak into the soil and run off the grass without any issue. For the grass. Not so much for their footing.

Now that that discussion was over, Wu Ying turned to Li Yao, who'd made her way back to him, and dropped his voice to ask, "That's all?"

"All?"

"Us cultivators."

"Oh!" Li Yao shook her head. "No. There are more cultivators in the other assault covers. But the general decided to split our attack in hopes that one of us will break through."

"And once we do?" Wu Ying said.

"We hold the wall until reinforcements arrive. Widen the gap when we can and link up with the next cultivator group. The more sky ladders fix to the wall, the more soldiers will arrive, so providing aid to neighboring ladders will be nearly as important as holding our own," Li Yao said.

Wu Ying nodded slowly, then whispered, "What are our chances?"

Li Yao shrugged.

He could only hope that they had not been sent to die without any hope of success or retreat. It was unlikely. No matter how much the vice-general disliked him, wasting their lives would cause more problems than the man could bear. In that sense, being part of a powerful Sect was protection in itself.

***

The start of the true attack began without fanfare. For a half hour after Wu Ying had arrived, the trebuchets had fired on the walls, hammering at portions of the obstruction and the towers that guarded the defense. But as the morning sun finally rose a quarter of the way to its zenith, the signal drums beat a new rhythm.

160

Wu Ying cocked his head, watching the signal flags echo the commands of the drum. Even if he did not have significant experience with the army or the drums, this command was easily recognizable.

Advance.

The creak of wooden wheels being pushed forward broke Wu Ying from his reverie, making the cultivator turn forward. To his initial surprise, their assault cover was not moving—until he realized that they had to wait. Ahead of them, the initial assault cover wave had to approach, reach their positions under fire, and deploy their men. Only then would the next wave, including the sky ladders, begin their approach. Only once those were close would Wu Ying's cover move forward. No point sending them until then, to stand under fire with nowhere to go.

Realizing his foolishness, Wu Ying pushed forward to peer through the small gaps at the front of the wagon. He had to elbow aside Bai Hu as he did so and received a silent glower in return. But Wu Ying was a little too excited to pay proper attention to the man's displeasure as he tried to catch a glimpse of what was happening outside.

"You there. Soldier. Let him take your place," Bai Hu growled. He dropped a hand on the soldier who was meant to be steering and watching from the front and yanked him back, creating space for Wu Ying. "If he wants to push, then let him."

"Honored cultivator, I…" the soldier stuttered, caught between duty and the displeasure of the glowering cultivator. One could see his head lopped off for disobedience. The other might see his limbs broken, from the way Bai Hu's fist rose.

"It's fine," Wu Ying said, stepping into the gap. "I wanted to see." He flashed the soldier a grin then gave Bai Hu a narrowed eye look. "Better view here. And I have no problem pushing a wagon. Better work than pushing a plow behind an ox."

"Definitely less shitty," the other soldier beside Wu Ying muttered under his breath. He probably thought Wu Ying could not hear, not realizing how sharp cultivator senses grew.

Wu Ying decided to dissuade him of that notion by leaning over and murmuring, "Definitely."

He watched the soldier flush, stutter an apology, before Wu Ying turned his attention back to what he could see in the gap. Luckily, their assault cover had been set on a slight rise in the surroundings, giving them both a rolling start when needed and a slightly better view of the battle going forth before them.

In the time he had been speaking with the soldiers, the first wave of assault covers had covered a hundred yards under the insistent beat of the drums. Wu Ying saw, already, how the formation had grown a little ragged. Wagons that had better terrain, stronger teams, or were just better put together took the lead while others lagged behind. As much as their superiors might desire the first wave to arrive at the same time, reality ensured that it was not possible.

A change in the beat of the drums had the second wave—the sky ladders— begin their slow journey forward. They would take longer to arrive, so their staggered approach was required. Wu Ying knew that soon, they too would begin the advance. But in the meantime...

A harsh snap and whistle, as if someone had cracked a single, large string, broke through the hubbub. As if the first wave had passed an invisible line, the defenders on the wall acted, sending the first of many volleys of arrows at the assault covers. Rising high above, so high that Wu Ying lost sight of the glinting arrowheads, the arrows rose.

And fell.

The actual strike of the arrows as they landed was muted by the all-encompassing noise of the army on march. It only sounded, to his ears, as though a cloud had broken open in the distance, dismissing its wet attendants to the earth. Dozens of light drops, all rolled together such that a single one could not be picked out. The fall of rocks as defending trebuchets released their own payloads was louder and more insistent in being heard.

If the noise of the battle was less than astounding, the sight was eye opening. Wu Ying watched the arrows land, striking at assault covers and bouncing off or raining upon the ground, creating wooden sprouts in the field. Impediments for the oncoming army. And if one wave of arrows finished landing, others arrived soon after. The rocks from the trebuchet were majestic, striking the ground and bouncing. Wu Ying watched one particular rock land almost directly ahead of their route, skipping off the ground and ploughing into an assault cover. It crushed a wagon wheel, leaving the siege weapon to list to the side.

Moments later, soldiers spilled out of the damaged assault cover, holding shields above their head as they ran forward to their assigned position. One caught an arrow in the neck, dropping to the ground as an improperly raised shield failed to save him. The others ran, ignoring the fallen body as infantry paired together with archers in a mad dash to their position across the no-man's land of arrows.

"Push!" the soldier beside Wu Ying barked at the cultivator.

Wu Ying blinked, then realized he had missed the signal. He hastily gripped the handy wooden divot ahead of him and added his strength to the effort. The covered wagon rolled forward, at first at a snail's pace but picking up speed when the simple cloth brake holding them still released.

"Not too fast! We have to wait for the sky ladders," warned the soldier. He was already breathing hard, though whether it was due to fear or effort, Wu Ying could not tell.

Wu Ying slowed down as requested, making sure to not add too much strength. Before him, the war raged, arrows and cast stones landing amongst the assault covers and the newly arrived sky ladders. Already, Wu Ying saw the bodies of soldiers littering the ground, some still moving as they writhed in pain and attempted to crawl back to the safety of their lines. Protective cover or not, the occasional arrow managed to make its way through gaps in the protection or—when used by a powerful cultivator—through the protective coverings directly.

As the assault covers grew ever closer, more and more soldiers were forced to disembark damaged vehicles and risk the fire of the walls under cover of shield and armor. Still, the covers had allowed a good portion of the first wave to arrive unscathed and get into position. Already, some of the archers were returning fire, helping suppress the attacks raining down on them.

A new sound arose—the start of drumming, fainter and deeper than the drums of their own army. Wu Ying frowned, inadvertently slowing. He noticed a slight pause in the arrow fire as the drums signaled a change. Even as the cold thread of dread grew in his stomach, Wu Ying saw a new flight of arrows rise up from the walls.

"That doesn't look right," commented Lady Pan. Somehow along the way, the female cultivator had managed to join them at the front of the assault cover.

"I don't see it." Wu Ying tried to gauge what it was that Lin Jian had seen before the arrows disappeared from his view. He was still trying to figure it out when they started landing, bringing with them flaming fury.

The arrow storm was much smaller in size, the attack concentrated on the covers themselves rather than spread out across the siege engines and soldiers on foot. Each arrow, upon striking, released a small explosion. Not all the arrows exploded, but a large majority did so, and soon the dried and clay-coated roofs of the siege weapons caught fire, along with portions of their walls.

"What was that?" the soldier beside Wu Ying exclaimed. He released his grip on the wagon, stumbling to a halt only to be pushed forward by the passengers behind. Reminded of his task, the soldier found himself taking hold of the wagon and pushing with Wu Ying once more.

"I…"

Taking pity on Wu Ying as he hesitated, Lady Pan said, "Talisman arrows. Expensive to wrap each arrow with a talisman, but they're extremely useful for war. If you want to set fire to siege weapons, it's the easiest method—unless they're by the walls. Then, of course, there's oil. They'll probably fire on the siege ladders soon."

Wu Ying's eyes widened, realizing that they too would likely come under fire when they got within range. Luckily, each of those talismans did not look powerful enough to destroy the covers themselves—just set them alight. Even so, the first wave had stalled, many of the soldiers abandoning their vehicles to escape a fiery death only to be targeted by the arrows of the defenders. More and more of the first wave fell, only a few groups managing to form protective shield walls and return fire now that they were within range.

"Are we still going in?" came the deep voice of Huang Zu from behind, highly disapproving of the idea.

None of the cultivators answered him, for the decision was out of their hands. The general and drums would tell them of their fate. In the silence that encompassed their small, cramped, and suddenly too fragile siege weapon, they rolled forward under the relentless beat of the drums.

***

A change in drum signal and a tapped warning had Wu Ying and the soldier apply the brakes. They stopped just outside of bow range and watched the ongoing struggle before them. As expected, the moment the sky ladders had made their way halfway through the fields to the wall, they came under fire from the talisman arrows.

To Wu Ying's surprise, the army had an answer to the talisman arrows. Around each of the siege weapons, a wall of sand and air kicked up as talismans that had been placed on the siege weapons activated. Each of the talismans lived briefly before they expired, releasing their stored energy into the wind and conjuring soil ahead of them, sending arrows targeted at the sky ladders swinging aside and falling away. The attack had the added benefit of throwing up a significant amount of dust and dirt, obscuring the view of the engines as they rolled forward. When Wu Ying managed to glimpse the battlefield again, he was surprised to note that brave soldiers were climbing the ladders, buckets of water in hand as they doused the fires that had managed to light up the ladders. Even as Wu Ying rejoiced at the successful tactic, another wave of arrows was fired.

"How much is this costing them?" he asked, mentally gauging the cost of each flight of arrows.

Lady Pan chuckled. "When it comes to battle at this level, it is more a matter of taels than skill. Whoever has more wins."

Bai Hu added his own two coins. "It is a complete waste of resources. Each of those talismans is at least an hour's worth of work by an apprentice. These enchantments are not particularly hard, but they shot a small Sect's entire month's production in a single volley. Only kingdoms can afford this kind of waste." The disgust that filled Bai Hu's voice made Wu Ying take a closer look at the man.

"Just be grateful we can afford to do it too," Lady Pan said.

As Wu Ying watched the third volley of arrows land, to some minor result, he could only agree with Bai Hu. It really was a waste. Not only of resources, but of the bodies that littered the field. At least now that the majority of the fire was targeted at the siege ladders in an attempt to slow them, the individual soldiers who had disembarked from the first wave had been relieved of the pressure placed upon them. Having set up their positions and with shields in front of them, the crouching infantryman who once wielded the propped-up shields were digging into the dirt before the walls.

"What are they doing?" Wu Ying said.

"Digging trenches. It'll give them better cover," said the soldier beside Wu Ying. "The deeper they dig, the more places they create, the easier it will be for the next fight."

"Next fight?"

"Yes. The ladders won't make it. Not enough of them at least," the soldier said, shaking his head.

"How many would be enough?"

"At least half. The general is being too impatient."

"Isn't that a dangerous thing to say?" Wu Ying said, cocking his head and looking at the soldier.

"It is. Why do you think I'm out here?" The soldier grinned wryly. "Too many opinions for someone who crawls in the dirt."

Bai Hu laughed and clapped the soldier on his shoulder. "Good man. One should live free from the strictures and worries about the fools above us. If you survive this, find me and my sworn brothers. A man with such bravery should not consign himself to a life of following orders."

The soldier let his gaze roam over Bai Hu and his brothers before he said slowly, "I don't think your life is much better than mine. Going from war to war, being mercenaries. At least I know where my dinner is coming from here."

Bai Hu glowered at the soldier before he laughed again. "Good man. Keep telling truth to the world. Maybe in the next life, your obstinance will pay off."

The soldier shook his head, deciding not to answer. Adrenaline and fear could only make him open his mouth for that long. A few seconds later, the whispered message from those at the back of the assault cover, those who could see the flags, came. It was the same old message.

Advance.

"I thought this assault had failed?" Wu Ying said to the soldier.

"The assault covers and the sky ladders are too far forward to pull back. They need to be used. The general will continue the assault. Pulling back now will lose him face and the spent resources for little gain. Better to spend it all properly. And who knows, maybe we'll pull off a miracle," Lady Pan said wryly.

"Hun dan!" Bai Hu swore.

Chapter 15

Under the cover of the siege weapon, Wu Ying and his team moved forward. This time around, there was no reason to hold back, so they moved as quickly as they could. They still had a lot of ground to cover, and the siege ladders were nearly at the walls. The last push before the ladders met the walls would only happen when the cultivators were close. Otherwise, they risked the ladders being destroyed well before anyone could ascend. Still, the ladders were close enough to the walls that the trebuchets—which had been firing incessantly—were unable to adjust their angle to attack them. Now, the only risks the ladders faced were talisman arrows and the occasional pot of boiling oil.

As the cultivators pushed forward, the defenders targeted the assault covers. Even if they did not need to hold back too much, Wu Ying cautioned the soldier beside him to slow down a little.

"Why are we slowing down?" Bai Hu asked.

"We don't want to let them know that cultivators are in here." Wu Ying drew a deep breath and concentrated, letting his senses feel the auras of those around them. "Start suppressing your auras. All of you. You're too strong!"

There were more than a few grumbles, but when Li Yao, the titular leader of the group as designated by the general, repeated Wu Ying's assertion, they complied. As arrows fell like hail and the smell of spilled blood permeated the assault cover, along with the rank stench of fear, Wu Ying continued to sense the auras of his companions.

It was no surprise that most of them were bad at hiding their auras. Luckily, there was a significant distance to the walls. And even if they could not suppress their auras all the way, they didn't need to. An assault cover with no occupants would be more suspicious than one which had a series of slightly-stronger-than-normal occupants. Still, Wu Ying was grateful that Elder Li had made him practice the aura suppression technique. It was highly useful and continually made its presence known.

The group had initially stopped five hundred yards away, well outside most bow ranges. At least any shot fired with any type of accuracy. Even cultivators had to contend with the vagaries of wind, humidity, and materials. Of course, spirit weapons provided both greater accuracy and range, but those individual attacks were of little consequence in a war. A single arrow would make little difference—not yet at least. And highlighting oneself with that great skill and weapon made oneself a target for future attacks.

Crossing the final distance to the walls was a slog, one that had Wu Ying breathing hard from suppressed fear and nervousness. Arrows rained upon them, like the staccato beat of a child playing with a pot. Except the danger here was more to life than sanity. With each step, the wagon rolled forward at all too slow a pace.

The cultivators were a hundred yards away before the first of the trebuchets targeted them. At first the stones thrown at them were not particularly accurate, landing around and past their assault cover. To Wu Ying's surprise, a stone fired shortly after the others crashed within ten feet of them. Only a fortunate depression in the ground sent the stone skipping to their left. The noise from the near miss was sufficient to make the occupants behind Wu Ying cry out with questions. The cultivators were, after all, still mortal, and being struck by a siege weapon would likely kill them. They were no Core cultivators, who could shrug off such attacks with a smile.

"Speed up!" Li Yao barked from behind.

Wu Ying put more muscle into the activity, driving the assault cover forward. The soldier beside him had difficulty keeping up, stumbling and making the entire assault cover turn. They shifted from heading straight ahead to swerving sideways and eliciting a set of curses by Bai Hu and his sworn brothers. Realizing that if they kept this up, they'd turn all the way around, Wu Ying slowed down and stopped pushing as hard. A second later, the car lurched forward faster as others provided aid to the soldier.

The drunken, weaving journey of the assault cover did have one advantage. The defenders shooting arrows and stones at them could not forecast where they were going, missing the assault cover and landing all around them.

As the siege weapon lurched forward at a faster clip, the soldier cried out, "We need to go for the left! There is a—"

"Broken assault cover. I see it," said Wu Ying.

The wrecked assault cover sat before them, obstructing their conveyance's path and forcing them to swing around.

As more arrows targeted their transport, some exploding with flame, Li Yao cried out from behind, "They know. Don't stop."

As a group pushed, a new and foreboding noise rose above them. The explosions of talisman arrows striking the rooftop shook the assault cover and mixed with the crisp crackle of flames that caught, the fiery explosions occasionally licking across the small gap that allowed Wu Ying and the soldier to see ahead. To Wu Ying's surprise, the assault cover burned but slowly, the heat not reaching them below. Somehow the cover stood up to the attacks with aplomb.

"Second stage energy cultivators! Pitiful apprentices who think they are any good. Hah!" Bai Hu cried out in triumph.

Wu Ying looked back, spotting Bai Hu slapping glowing talismans on the roof of the assault cover, providing it with increased durability and protection.

"Push, push, you handsome young man. You do it well, I'll do some pushing myself later," Lady Pan teased Wu Ying. Her cheeks were flushed, her eyes glittering in the occasional flash of flame and light.

A moment later, Lady Pan let out a girlish yelp as Li Yao extracted her retribution. As for Wu Ying, he was too busy pushing and hoping that none of those arrows made their way through the gap to pay attention to lewd suggestions.

At least, that was what he was going to tell Li Yao. Even if his cheeks were flushed red.

***

Each step of the way, the assault cover was attacked. Arrows, talismans, and more struck at them. Wu Ying noticed the volume of fire increase as the lack of damage to their assault cover was a dead giveaway about those within. As if the group had agreed to his unspoken thoughts, they released their auras, no longer bothering to suppress them. At the least the numerous soldiers from the first and second waves had relief from being targeted by a portion of the defenders.

A dozen yards from their cover, the sky ladder was being pushed forward to lock onto the wall. Moments from now, they'd be ready to launch their attack. A sixth sense made Wu Ying turn and look up. At the edges of his vision, on top of the wall, a cultivator in yellow-and-brown robes stood with a guandao in hand. He lifted the large polearm weapon, its curved, edged blade glinting in the sunlight as he swung at them.

"Cultivator!" Wu Ying roared. He reached for his ring, recalling the defensive talismans he had stored but doubting they could stop the attack.

A crescent blade of visible energy flew from the edge of the guandao, formed from the attack. As it flew, a rough sketch of a phoenix appeared on the trailing back corners of the crescent attack. A disinterested portion of Wu Ying's mind noted the Energy Stage cultivator must have been in the early stages—Minor Achievement—of his energy attack.

"Move!"

Wu Ying and the soldier were shouldered aside as Huang Zu made his way to the front. Huang Zu crossed his arms, leaning forward and bracing himself even as the image of a golden bell formed around himself and the front of the assault cover. Not a moment too soon did Huang Zu trigger his defensive skill.

The opposing cultivator's attack struck. Like a bell rung, the noise caught the attention of those around. An explosion of chi, released energy from both styles, pressured Wu Ying's chest, making it hard to breathe for a second. The low cultivation soldier beside him had it worse, reeling back and spitting blood.

"Out!" Li Yao shouted even as Bai Hu slapped a few more talismans on the assault cover.

Taking the lead, Tou He ducked out the back of the cover, his staff spinning to block the approaching arrows. Liu Tsong held up a hand for a second, conjuring an apothecarist cauldron with its integrated brazier. A flick of her fingers saw the lighting of the cauldron, and a follow-up gesture threw in a series of herbs. Moments later, she sent the entire cauldron spinning out and trailing smoke, opposite of the direction Tou He had taken.

"I'll cover us," Liu Tsong said, walking out behind the cover as she pulled out her staff as well.

Bao Cong sprinted out, his bow now strung and a quiver by his side. He held three arrows in one hand, a fourth already on the string as he joined Tou He on the non-smoky side. Yin Xue, Lady Pan, and her companion chose the safer route and followed Liu Tsong and her cauldrons.

"Move!" Li Yao snapped at Wu Ying when he bent to check on the soldier.

The man shook his head when Wu Ying dragged him toward the exit.

"Leave me. Safer... in here..." he said around broken ribs.

Wu Ying frowned, hesitating, but knew the longer the cultivators stayed where they were, the more likely they would be targeted. Giving up, he followed the exiting cultivators, joined by Li Yao.

Wu Ying was surprised by the efficacy of Liu Tsong's cauldron. Already, the apothecarist's mixture had filled their surroundings with thick, unnatural smoke. He spotted the cauldron spinning in circles around their wagon, slowly layering more and more smoke as it moved farther from their location. Liu Tsong frowned in concentration as she controlled the spinning metal object, though she used her weapon to bat aside the occasional arrow that came too close to her.

"To the ladders!" Li Yao shouted at the group, commanding them to rush ahead.

Wu Ying reoriented himself, then led the way to where the sky ladder should be. Together, the group charged forward, their weapons drawn as arrows suddenly appeared from the smoke and fell toward them. An arrow glanced off Wu Ying's helmet, sending sparks to live brief, fiery lives in front of his eyes before they disappeared. His breathing grew harsh, the familiar churned earth smell of torn ground mixing with the tang of spilled blood, crushed bones, and ruptured organs. Fires brought whiffs of green wood and the smell of Liu Tsong's herbal mixture, all making breathing harder than ever.

"We need cover," said Wu Ying.

Even if they were not targeted, they could still be hit by blind chance. He frowned and eyed the wall. Even through the slowly-thickening smoke, he saw the crenellations at the top. Bao Chong had stopped shooting, unable to make out the figures who fired down on then. Most of the arrows that were fired were not targeted, but the volume of fire coming from the vicinity of the sky ladder meant that they were in danger.

Drawing a deep breath, Wu Ying focused his strength through his bracer and swung his sword, sending the arc of energy straight at the wall. Even if he missed hurting anyone, it would keep some heads down.

Wu Ying ran toward the ladder and the gathering of soldiers who had formed around their blockade of shields. Already, soldiers were climbing the ladder, doing their best to rise up under cover of the smoke. But most only made it halfway up the ladder before they were struck off by arcing arrows.

Whether the light wind that had arisen from the river was dispersing the smoke or another cultivator was controlling the wind, Wu Ying noticed that their cover was fast disappearing. Liu Tsong had altered the movement of the cauldron, sending it to work its magic farther upwind. That reduced the fire from that side of the ladder, but by the time the smoke reached them, it had reduced significantly.

Now that he could see, Bao Cong returned fire, though he stayed close to Tou He as the opposing archers targeted him as well. Even as the cultivators grouped up to charge up the ladder, Wu Ying could not help but worry that their attack had failed. Only two other ladders had managed to make their way to the walls, with cultivators attempting to ascend as well.

Before Wu Ying could take his position on the ladder, the sworn brothers charged ahead. Xu Gong, who had been silent thus far, and Huang Zu led the attack. Somewhere along the way, Huang Zu had put away the axe-bladed polearm they had carried and was now wielding a pair of swords while he ran up the sloped ladder. His feet barely touched the swaying, bouncing wooden contraption as he charged ahead, showing a surprising degree of agility. Wu Ying could only marvel at their qinggong skills. The occasional arrow that targeted Huang Zu was struck aside while Bai Hu, at the bottom of the trio, cast an array of talismans at the wall. The yellow papers flew as if they were rocks, striking the wall and flaring brightly with light.

When Xu Gong reached the top of the ladder, instead of stepping off it, he threw himself into a graceful jump. He struck out as he reached the apex of his jump, using his daos on the pair of defenders at the top. One of the soldiers who held the wall wheeled away, clutching at his throat, while the second managed to deflect the heavy attack. Even then, he staggered aside, leaving Xu Gong uncontested on the top of the wall. Immediately, Xu Gong widened the gap, lashing out with his swords at those soldiers who tried to close in on them.

In short order, Bai Hu and Huang Zu joined him on the wall, weapons and skills making short work of the soldiers.

"Come on!" Li Yao shouted encouragement at the group, excited at the advance they had made.

She pushed past Wu Ying, taking her place on the ladder and crawling upward. Realizing that he had just been watching, Wu Ying joined Li Yao and Lady Pan as they scrambled up the ladder. Beside the ladder, Yan Qing and Liu Tsong kept the defending soldiers busy, harassing them with arrows and smoke.

Li Yao was nearly to the top of the ladder when screams interrupted their desperate scramble. Looking up, Wu Ying saw an unexpected sight.

Rather than the three White Tiger Sect fighters, there were only two remaining – Bai Hu and Huang Zu. Of Xu Gong, there was no sight to be seen.

Facing the pair was a giant of a man. Nearly seven feet tall, clad in an unusual set of armor that covered his face, his neck, and his body in overlapping steel and iron, the armed and armored cultivator wielded a six-foot-long blade. The sword was nearly as thick as two of Wu Ying's wrists. The weapon was so long and heavy that it should have been unwieldy for anyone but a cultivator to use. Each of his strikes was so heavy, held such great sword intent that the pair of brothers could not handle them. They reeled back after each engagement, new wounds appearing on their bodies as the wind pressure and remainder sword intent injured them.

Even as Wu Ying marveled at the man's virtuosity with his unusual weapon, Huang Zu was struck across his chest. Huang Zu's armor provided him some protection, but even so, it did nothing for the force behind the attack. As the sword crushed his chest, it also sent Huang Zu flying off the wall into the inner portion of the besieged city. His scream echoed before it ended abruptly, leaving only Bai Hu to fight. By this time, Li Yao had reached the top of the wall, but she was forced to engage the soldiers coming in from the other side, exposing her back to potential danger. Wu Ying scrambled up only to find that Lady Pan had frozen, refusing to move farther up from the three-quarter position she had reached.

"Move!" Wu Ying shouted at Lady Pan.

Still, her form was static. Only slight movements in her hands made him consider that she might be doing something more. Before he could demand again that she continue her ascent, blossom petals fell from the sky, surrounding the unknown armored cultivator. They swarmed him, a stark contrast of pink against the gray-and-black metal, each blossom creeping into the cultivator's armor. Their enemy let out a cry of pain even as Lady Pan clapped her hands together. The petals converged then exploded outward from his metallic form, leaving behind a trail of blood as the conjured material disappeared. From his vantage point, Wu Ying could see the attack had hurt the armored cultivator, driving him to his knees but not much more.

"Your turn." After saying that, Lady Pan threw herself off the sky ladder, allowing herself to fall to the ground and leaving the way open for Wu Ying.

Wu Ying scrambled up the ladder as quickly as he could, while Bai Hu struck the stone of the wall with a pair of talismans. When the opponent took another step forward, he froze; energetic light released from the talismans wrapped around the enemy combatant. Seeing an opportunity, Wu Ying got ready to launch a strike against the frozen enemy.

"Don't touch him. If you do, the talismans will stop working," Bai Hu warned.

Wu Ying grimaced then finished climbing over the walls and drew his sword, setting himself before the huge man. Wu Ying could only hope that the other cultivators would be on their way soon, for he wasn't certain he could deal with this monster of a man himself. Bai Hu was certainly not going to be of much use. Wu Ying could tell that Bai Hu was gravely injured, his face pale from blood loss, his side bleeding from one big wound and numerous smaller cuts along his form.

The only good news was it seemed there was only this single defending cultivator here, the others somewhere else. Wu Ying had seconds to contemplate, to take in the field of battle. Now that he could see inside the city proper, he noted clusters of shops and residences, the gap between the city walls and the beginnings of blockades along the streets. And then…

The drums changed.

***

"Do you have any more of those talismans?" Wu Ying shouted at Bai Hu. When the man looked at him, puzzled by the sudden change of topic and his blood loss, Wu Ying clarified. "That's the sound of the retreat."

Rather than answering Wu Ying, Bai Hu scrambled for the ladder. He slid down, almost knocking aside one of the ascending soldiers. Wu Ying cursed— for a moment later, the lines of power that had surrounded the enemy cultivator broke, freeing the man to swing his sword at Wu Ying. A hasty block sent Wu Ying crashing into the wall, barely holding onto his dao and allowing it to clip his body. The dao he wielded shrieked, sparks flying as the enemy cultivator threw another series of cuts that Wu Ying blocked.

"Go!" Wu Ying shouted, hoping Li Yao heard.

Wu Ying had no time to look behind him as he fought for his life. His opponent had the Sense of the Sword, a grasp of the weapon in a way few martial artists had. If Wu Ying had not reached that same level of understanding himself, this fight would have been over already.

A part of the issue was the fact that Wu Ying was wielding a dao, the weapon limiting his options, as did the narrow footing of the wall's battlements. On the other hand, he was also grateful, for the heavy-handed strikes the enemy cultivator used were already chipping away at the heavier, thicker sword. Focused on defense, Wu Ying gave up ground unwillingly, eking out each inch that he was forced back. Too far back, and he would be forced away from the ladder, unable to escape.

A flash of green in his peripheral vision as a familiar sword's aura came skittering along the edge of his senses, then a flash of green as it struck his opponent's gauntleted arm. Li Yao perched precariously on the wall, leaning around Wu Ying as she struck at the enemy. Her attack had done no damage, at least not visibly, though the armored cultivator stepped back, allowing Wu Ying to regain the tempo.

"I'm going first!" Li Yao cried out, scrambling down the ladder, trusting her boyfriend to save himself.

Even as she ran, Wu Ying threw himself at the enemy cultivator, unleashing a flurry of blows. Dragon in a Tempest was a series of strikes Wu Ying rarely used, especially not with a jian. Building up the momentum on the lighter weapon was tough. It was well suited to the dao though, especially when used correctly.

For once inside the enemy cultivator's range, Wu Ying was able to force the larger, stronger enemy to change grips, to fight holding the weapon halfway up the blade. Even as Wu Ying thought that he might have a chance, an arrow bounced off his shoulder pauldron, throwing off his timing a little. In a fight like this, even a small advantage would turn the tide.

That fraction of a pause forced back Wu Ying again, a shoulder strike sending Wu Ying stumbling away. As his opponent shifted grips, ready to swing again, Wu Ying flicked his gaze about and found himself alone on the battlements.

Surrounded by enemies, death imminent, Wu Ying took the better option—throwing his weapon at the enemy cultivator and himself off the battlement. Wind rushed past his face as he reached sideways to grip the edge of the ladder, twisting his trajectory and feeling the strain on his muscles. He reoriented himself, feet tucked close as he hit the wall before he kicked off, throwing himself clear of the attacks above and the ladder below. As he fell, Wu Ying hoped that he was right and his reinforced, sturdier body could take the damage.

If not, his hasty escape would mean a hastier death.

Chapter 16

The retreat from the front lines was a hurried affair. Thankfully, after they reached about fifty yards from the wall, the defenders no longer shot at them. Wu Ying could not tell whether or not it was because they felt no need to or because the enemy general was conserving his ammunition. In either case, Wu Ying was thankful, as he limped back to camp, helped along by Tou He, who carried his friend and a shield.

The fall itself had, predictably, done a little damage to him. A twisted ankle, shocked knees and hips, and a throb in his back where he had rolled into the fall. All that time reinforcing his body, increasing his cultivation, had increased Wu Ying's sturdiness, his ability to take a fall. He wasn't Lady Pan, who had used her qinggong skills to avoid any damage, but he had managed to roll with the fall, absorbing some of the shock. Even as he scrambled away, keeping an eye out for another arrow attack, Wu Ying knew that all of this would help him progress his body cultivation.

As he limped along, returning in ignominious defeat with the rest of his army, Wu Ying could not help but stare at the corpses littering the ground. Some brave soldiers were hurrying into the no-man's-land and carrying the injured back to their lines. It was a dangerous task as no moment of parley had been called, no guarantee that they would not be shot while doing so. Still, the soldiers risked their lives for their friends, helping the few who had survived. To live another day. Perhaps.

By some of the screams, the way blood bubbled from pierced chests or around wounded limbs, they might not either. Inflammation, infection, diseases of the lung and blood all held hidden dangers for the wounded.

As Wu Ying limped back, he listened to the cries of pain, smelled the refuse of voided bowels and the stink of iron from spilt blood. He heard sobs and whimpers, soldiers calling for parents who were not present, and saw others staring numbly at the fallen. He saw a soldier who crouched on the ground, wounded not in body but broken in his soul, unable to move. Wu Ying could understand that. Even the chi of the battlefield felt strange, transformed by the mixture of death and loss that surrounded them all. He noticed the energy that had spread around them all, building upon their bodies and sending surges of unwanted ecstasy and energy.

In the end, Wu Ying could only hope that their army had gained something from this debacle. What it could be, what could be worth the loss of so many men, he did not know. Then again, he was no general. He was just a simple peasant cultivator.

***

Tou He and Wu Ying made their way to the medical tents. Having found a little energy while they walked back, Wu Ying had insisted they help some of the other wounded soldiers. He did not need to convince Tou He much, and soon even the other cultivators joined them, each of them helping one of the wounded.

The medical tents were the most familiar aspect of the army to Wu Ying. After all, during his tenure in the army, he'd spent most of it in those same tents. The smell of spilled and drying blood, the cloying tang of herbs and poultices, and the retching of soldiers brought back less-than-pleasant memories. Even so, that experience allowed him to quickly pick out the location of the appropriate triage spot.

"Do you need help?" one of the medics asked Wu Ying, looking over his bruised and limping form.

"No. Take care of them. I'll heal myself," Wu Ying replied.

The medic's lips curled up but he did not protest, already hurrying to help the wounded. Wu Ying turned to find that Tou He was hurrying off, headed to the no-man's-land. As Wu Ying took a step to join him, a hand landed on his arm.

182

"Don't be silly. You're injured. It will be more of a hindrance than a help for you to go," Li Yao said to Wu Ying.

"I can still help."

"Then help me. I need to report in," said Li Yao.

She inclined her head toward the center of the camp, where the vice-general probably awaited her. For a moment, she looked uncertain, her usual bouncy demeanor disappearing. She had been in charge of the cultivator team after all. Wu Ying nodded at his girlfriend, following her to the tent where the commanders waited.

What followed was not as bad as he had expected, for the commanders had had a view of the entire proceedings and, considering the cultivators had at least made it to the walls, had little to complain about. The commanders had numerous other issues to deal with as well, so they were quickly dismissed.

Along the way, Wu Ying learned that Li Yao and the rest of the team had been released days before him, leaving them free to take on assignments for the army. The assignments had earned them a number of contribution points, which Li Yao had been quite happy to showcase to Wu Ying, leading him to the army commissary. Along the way, she made sure that he received his own army token to register his participation in the attack.

"Four thousand contribution points?" Wu Ying asked the commissary officer. It sounded like a high number, but he had no comparison.

"Regular soldiers get between ten and twenty contribution points for participating in the attack itself. As cultivators, we have a higher base number, but even our other assignments were only worth a few hundred at most." Li Yao frowned, turning the military token around in her hand before she looked at the army personnel in charge of the assignments. "Why is this so high?"

"Because you survived." The officer smirked at the pair of cultivators. "Base rate is a thousand points for a first wave, first attack. Then we have your contribution because you're from the Verdant Green Waters. Then you get a contribution increase due to your cultivation base, then a survival bonus for those who returned, which almost doubles your return."

"What can I buy with these contribution points?" Wu Ying asked. He vaguely recalled the contribution points mechanism from before, but he hadn't thought it was so elaborate. Then again, he hadn't exactly been in the army for long. Or contributed to anything.

"The usual. Better food, better weapons, some martial styles. Training by some of our elite members. There are even cultivation manuals, though I doubt you lot will want that." The officer flicked his gaze up and down the pair of cultivators. "Nothing we have would suit you people. Of course, you could change it for coin or hang on to the contribution amounts and trade in at headquarters. There's a lot more there."

Wu Ying raised an eyebrow, but it made sense. All those wandering cultivators, they joined not just for coin but the opportunity to find martial styles and cultivation manuals. It was an opportunity for them to improve themselves, something that did not come along often for those who did not join a sect. Still, they had a level of freedom that sect members did not.

"And what would four thousand contribution points get me?" Wu Ying asked.

"We have some protective talismans for sale at that price. Some low-grade martial styles. Access to the officers' mess hall." When Wu Ying looked less than impressed, the man shrugged. "It's only four thousand points. Any equipment of value is in the tens of thousands of points, especially when we're in the field. You might be able to find something more when we're back, but it's not as if we carry the armory with us."

Having been disappointed, Wu Ying and Li Yao left to find their friends. They checked back at the medical center first, only to be thrown out. Since neither of them were physicians, they had little to offer other than a warm body. Even the wounded had stopped being brought in by this point—only corpses being moved off the field to be buried in a different location. No one wanted a high accumulation of yin chi to form. That was how you got jiangshi and ghosts, even maybe formed gates to the demonic plane. The priests would be working all night, purifying the corpses and laying them to rest. While the losses were still few, the army would do their best to honor their dead. Later on, Wu Ying knew, that option might disappear and mass cremation would be chosen.

With nothing much left to do, Wu Ying returned to his tent to rest his wounded body. He would need to cultivate and work the Iron Bones technique, making the best use of the damage to reinforce his body. After all, he was certain that he had more injuries to look forward to.

***

To Wu Ying's surprise, when he woke the next day, rumors were already spreading that another attack was imminent. All through the night, sappers had been working on extending the pits and other lines of cover, offering the next wave additional safety to attack the defenders from. Siege weapons continued to throw rocks at the walls, damaging the archery towers and slowly breaking apart the reinforced wooden gates and their support structures. In the meantime, workmen were making even more assault covers and sky ladders, the necessary siege weapons to ensure that they could mount the walls.

Of course, Wu Ying wondered why they had not assaulted the gates on the first attack but was quickly dissuaded of that notion. It seemed that the gates were often the most reinforced position in a wall, with many reinforced with multiple formations to stop, harm, and destroy attackers. While the army would continue to batter the gates, it was easier and better to go over the walls. At least for now.

When Li Yao appeared, Wu Ying broke away from his conversation from the wandering cultivators and asked, "Are we joining the attack?"

Li Yao shook her head, a wry smile twisting her lips. "We are joining the fifth wave. Because of our previous involvement, we are unlikely to get called upon unless they do manage a breakthrough."

Wu Ying raised an eyebrow, but it was Yin Xue who spoke first. "Are they likely to break through? They didn't even activate their defensive formations last time."

"Unlikely," Liu Tsong said, appearing from behind the cultivators. They turned to the older woman, waiting for her to explain. "This is all to soften them up. The real assault will come later."

"A lot of wasted lives for little gain," Tou He said disapprovingly.

"He has little choice there," Li Yao said. "The general needs to learn what formations and what cultivators are inside. The only way to do so is to push them. I do not think he has any spies in there. And even if he did, I do not know how much he could rely on them."

Liu Tsong nodded, smiling approvingly at Li Yao. She let her gaze rake over the group before she spoke again. "I will not be with you all for now. I have my own duties with Chao Kun. Watch yourselves." As the group all nodded, Liu Tsong added, "And stop taking so many risks."

She stared at Wu Ying at her last words, as if she knew it was him who needed that warning the most. He snorted but accepted her well wishes and sent her off with thanks. Together, the group headed to their assigned position, where they stood in line, forced to wait.

"I still don't think we have the full picture," Yin Xue complained. "There's no need to throw away so many lives."

"You think they're rushing this for another reason?" Bao Cong asked.

"Yes. What worries me is that there might be a second army, one coming for us." Yin Xue looked away, eyes raking over the looming mountains surrounding them. If they were caught in here…

"There are no armies coming," Li Yao said. "I've checked with the scouts. No signs at all. Anyway, you remember your father's map. The closest army was the Wei reserve, and that was nearly a month away."

Yin Xue nodded, but that pensive frown did not leave his face.

Wu Ying glanced at Tou He, who offered him a shrug and mouthed, "*Amitabha.*"

It was true. What would be would be.

***

A rock soared through the air, banking gracefully before it smashed into the wall. Stone crumbled, and the rock itself bounced off, landing a short distance away from where the siege ladders were rolling forward. As if the artillerymen foretold the distances, no additional fire appeared. Instead, soldiers from both sides exchanged fire, crossbow bolts and the occasional arrow winging between both armies.

Like the previous battle, a wave of assault covers had approached first, allowing infantry and crossbowmen to near the city. This time, the second wave of assault covers had approached as well, bringing with them a larger number of fighters while the assault covers were drawn back. In turn, the defenders sent fewer volleys of talisman arrows, leaving a larger number of the assault covers intact to make it back to the lines.

All this, Wu Ying watched from the safety of the fifth wave. The constant creak of ropes twisting, the twang of bows, and the shrieks of falling men resounded through the air. He watched as the brave and foolhardy threw themselves forward, attacking intact walls, firing arrows and killing the occasional defender. Infantrymen, crouched in their holes, dug furiously as they extended and built up their defenses, propping up shields while the crossbowmen and archers exchanged fire with the defenders.

The sky ladders had moved forward, but this time, they held back just outside the range of the trebuchets, just outside retaliation, as if the general taunted the defenders. Daring them to sally forth and destroy the ladders. Instead, the trebuchets fired, wearing away at the walls.

For long hours, the army stood, baking in the heat of the midday sun. Others ran back and forth, offering liquid refreshment and later on, chewed hardtack for meals. The soldiers in the army began to rotate, each wave moving forward to take the vanguard position.

During the fourth hour after noon, as the sun slowly banked toward the horizon, the battle changed. Already, the soldiers who had been attacking had wearied, many having pulled back under cover of the assault covers as replacements arrived. As the assault covers returned with the latest wave of weary soldiers, the cultivators came.

The Six Jade Gates Sect members dropped from the walls, some kicking off in midair, others using ropes to help break their fall, while a small number—like Wu Ying the day before—just dropped and absorbed the fall. They rushed forward, launching chi-filled attacks at nearby assault covers, flames and earth erupting and tearing apart the siege weapons. A rotating whirlwind of metal and air flashed over to a cover vehicle and wood shrieked as it was torn apart, exposing the soldiers within to the metallic storm.

Their attacks destroyed some of the covers, wrecked roofs and shattered wheels. Other attacks were more obtuse, still green wood warping and growing, twisting as they drew upon the remaining nutrients in their forms and the chi infused in the attacks to trap and tear apart their occupants.

Those with less destructive elements and styles assaulted the remaining soldiers directly. They rushed toward fixed defenses, jumped into foxholes, and killed without remorse.

Horns blew, drumbeats changed, and flags rose and fell, signaling their own army's response. Cultivators from the State of Shen threw themselves from behind their lines to meet their enemies in combat. They charged across the open ground, riding horses or dashing across no-man's-land with barely a tap of their feet. Even so, hidden enemy archers who had been waiting rose from the walls, leveling bows and crossbows at the charging cultivators. They fired, some of those attacks bursting into flame, others gleaming and wrapped in other elemental chi methods.

Wu Ying's breath caught as he noticed a pair of familiar figures riding alongside other cultivators from the State of Shen. Chao Kun ignored the arrows for the most part, only acting to catch one as it moved to strike his face before tossing it aside with a casual motion, impervious to the chi imbued into the attack. On the other hand, Liu Tsong took a more active role in her defense, using a trio of apothecarist's cauldrons, each smaller than the one she had showcased yesterday, and wielding the cauldrons with her chi to block attacks. The cauldrons had a strange gravitational effect, where arrows that seemed to be about to miss them would swerve, attracted to strike the cauldrons. As he watched, Wu Ying noted how Liu Tsong had taken much of her recent fighting techniques from her master. Still, as they neared the first of the cultivators, Liu Tsong drew her staff from her storage ring and swung it, warding off a few of the more dangerous attacks.

An elbow to his side made Wu Ying turn to look at Li Yao, who gestured at the walls. There, a familiar armored figure stood, staring down at the cultivators who fought. Wu Ying frowned, curious to see if the man would jump down, but the armored cultivator just watched. All around the front of the city wall, the cultivators from different sects battled, clashing in explosions of elemental chi. Water and fire turned to steam that was blown aside or collected into ice by another cultivator and thrust at an enemy. Earth rose from the ground, formed into a grasping fist that clutched at a cultivator, only to be shattered apart by a kick. And these were all the low-level, almost mundane attacks.

More exotic attacks were showcased occasionally. Chao Kun's Star-Spangled Fist, now having reached Greater Achievement, made the light around him congregate into pinpoints of energy, his fist moving so fast that the defending cultivators couldn't block them. Each strike shattered armor, weapons, and bodies, the energy within the attacks blasting through the defensive auras conjured to protect the others.

On the other side of the battlefield, a roaring turtle head formed, its body made of chi, its legs drawn into its shell. A gesture and it went spinning, head withdrawn as it bowled over the Verdant Green Waters Sect fighters who opposed the powerful Energy Stage cultivator. Spotting the difficulty his sect members were having, Chao Kun turned and ran forward, only to be stopped by an ominous door. As it opened, tentacles sprouted from the door, attacking Chao Kun.

A flash of light tore Wu Ying's gaze to the side, where formations appeared, locking down a half dozen cultivators on both sides, pressing them into the earth without care of side. The weakest of that group screamed, his bones shattering under the pressure.

All around, chaos reigned and bodies fell. Wandering cultivators, Verdant Green Waters Sect, and Jade Gates Sect members fought, while smaller sects clashed against one another on the edges.

"We need to help them," said Wu Ying to Li Yao.

"Don't be an idiot!" said Yin Xue. "We have our orders. We stay until we are ordered to do otherwise."

Wu Ying shifted angrily, but Li Yao placed a hand on his arm. "He's right. I know you don't want to hear this, but that's what they teach us as martial specialists. We follow orders, because otherwise plans will be disrupted. I want to go too, but we cannot."

Wu Ying's lip twitched, but motion to his side made him spot Tou He moving unopposed through the ranks. The soldiers glanced at the ex-monk, some calling for him to stop or questioning his actions, but none tried to stop him.

"Tou He!" Li Yao shouted.

"I'll get him," Wu Ying said. He pushed ahead, brushing off Li Yao's hand as she tried to hold him back. He was not going to let his friend go out alone.

Wu Ying caught up with his friend at the edge of the first wave, grouping up near a sky ladder that waited for orders. Beside them, an assault cover made its way back, a pair of soldiers holding up the axle of one set of wheels and trotting alongside the cover to bring it back. Wu Ying laid a hand on his friend's shoulder as he looked to enter the fray. Ahead of them, the chaos of clashing cultivators continued.

"Are you here to stop me?" Tou He looked unhappily at his friend.

"Stop you. Join you. All the same thing," Wu Ying said. "But you do know that they're not going to be happy with us."

"People are dying."

Having said his piece, Tou He took off, his staff appearing in his hands. He angled himself toward the nearest group while keeping a close eye for arrows that might attack him.

Wu Ying chased his friend, drawing his own weapon. "You could have at least warned me before running off."

They made it about three quarters of the way to the nearest group before the enemy archers spotted them. At first, only a few arrows, unenchanted and unskilled, targeted the pair. But soon enough, the cultivators who had chosen

191

the bow as their weapon of choice fired on the pair. After all, these two were not engaged with their friends in combat. There was little chance of them hurting a friendly face.

A single arrow exploded into flames, creating multiple fire sparrows that flew in an arc toward the pair. Tou He stopped for a moment, his staff spinning, enacting the Sixth form of the Mountain Resides style. The chi of the world responded to his cultivation, the earth itself forming into an image of the cliff face that he'd conjured from within. The fire sparrows struck, flared, and died upon this unyielding wall of chi.

Wu Ying stepped around his friend, trusting that Tou He would stop any additional attacks, and cut. Once. The arrow, hidden almost to all sight and only sensed by Wu Ying due to a shift in the environmental chi that he had been drawing upon, was cut apart. As it broke, the skill-formed chi formation around the arrow shattered. Wu Ying grunted and ran, knowing that if they stayed still, they would continue to be attacked. At least this way, the attackers would avoid attacking the rest of his Sect mates and focus on them.

"Thank you," Tou He said to Wu Ying as he caught up with his friend, striking at arrows.

Now that he had been alerted, Tou He paid a much closer eye to his surroundings, picking out the hard-to-spot attacks from the defenders on the wall. The pair ran on, hopping over a rise in the ground and finally reaching their targets. By this point, only a single one of the initial four Verdant Green Waters Sect cultivators was still standing. Even as Wu Ying watched, one of the opposing cultivators thrust his spear into a prone form, pulling one last groan from the cultivator before he died.

"You twice-cooked rotten egg," Wu Ying cursed as he drew upon the chi within his Woo Petal bracer.

He unleashed it, along with his own chi, in a single crescent of power, the Dragon's Breath attack sending green-and-white metal chi arcing forward. His opponent managed to raise his spear to block the attack, suffering only minor injuries as the attack dispersed around the solidified aura his opponent formed.

In the meantime, Tou He skipped past Wu Ying, his weapons striking out, only to be blocked by the cultivators he was fighting. However, the distraction helped the lone standing cultivator, buying him time to recover and fall back to Wu Ying and Tou He's impromptu defensive line.

For a moment, both parties stood facing one another, hesitant to launch another attack. It was at that point that Wu Ying and an enemy cultivator shouted at the same time.

"You!"

To Wu Ying's surprise, he recognized these opposing cultivators. They were not random enemies, but the same individuals who had accosted him and Tou He on the road.

"Lying cultivator dog. You're no gatherer!" the cultivator accused Wu Ying. "I should have known. You people have no honor."

"What do Six Jade Gates scum know of honor? These people killed my friends," the surviving cultivator snarled back, taking advantage of Wu Ying's and Tou He's presence to launch himself at his opponents with renewed vigor.

Not to be left behind, the pair followed. As if they had an unspoken agreement, Wu Ying and Senior Cai paired up to fight.

But in short order, Wu Ying found himself retreating constantly from the barrage of attacks he faced. He had a better grasp of his weapon, especially now that he was wielding his own jian, but his opponent was of a higher cultivation level. That meant he was faster and stronger than Wu Ying, able to react more quickly to changes in position. The difference was not much, but a small amount could make a big difference when one was fighting for his life. Fighting was always about inches, the millimeters of difference that made a successful dodge, a good parry, a lethal strike. Worse for Wu Ying was the fact that the enemy cultivator still had a lot of chi in his body, being able to release

193

energy-filled attacks at Wu Ying constantly. More than once, Wu Ying had to reinforce his aura with his own chi, only to feel his aura shatter under the pressure and the attacks dig into his armor, his clothing, his skin.

Not being in the Energy Storage stage, Wu Ying was projecting energy out of his body in a manner that was unnatural for him at his cultivation level. Even if he had experience doing so, training from his aura control exercises, this method of defense was wasteful. The Energy Storage meridians not only stored energy but also allowed one more control over the chi they wielded.

Again and again, the pair clashed. A high block turn into a low cut, the lunge and sidestep twisting into a disengage, then a swift cut toward an offending leg. Wu Ying tried all his tricks, ranging from the Dragon's Whiskers to Paws snatching Claws. None of it worked. Even the minor strikes he managed barely did more than leave scratches on his opponent. Still, as they danced across the ground, Wu Ying could not help noticing his opponent was holding back.

A twist, a disengage, and Wu Ying jumped, sending a kick at his opponent's face. To his surprise, the attack landed, sending the cultivator to the ground. Unfortunately, Senior Cai rolled and came up onto his feet, a wave of energy reaching out. Wu Ying jumped back, dodging the attack as realization arrived as well.

His opponent was wary of Wu Ying. He probably thought Wu Ying was an Energy Storage cultivator too. Wu Ying's initial attack with the Woo Petal Bracer had likely convinced his opponent Wu Ying was holding back, waiting for an opportune time to release his attack. In truth, that was a part of Wu Ying's plan, though the conjuration of energy from the bracer required more concentration than he would care to use in such a frantic battle.

In the gap of time offered to him as his opponent rolled away and recovered, Wu Ying looked around, taking in the battle. Tou He was in the process of beating down his opponent. That he had not one but two archers

194

targeting him was the only reason Tou He had not finished his own opponent. On the other hand, the cultivator they had come to rescue was in a deadly struggle, grappling his opponent and rolling on the ground like barbarians.

As for the larger view, Wu Ying had no time to check as his opponent finished recovering, sending another arc of energy at him. Wu Ying dodged, getting ready to lunge in.

As the pair readied to reengage, a new series of notes rang out from the city. Senior Cai hesitated, then glared at Wu Ying before he turned and ran. As Wu Ying gave chase, a glint in the ground made him hesitate, just before it exploded into flames. He hopped back, wiping his face, as the trapped ground continued to expand, forcing him to retreat again and again.

As he angled away, Wu Ying did his best to move toward where the grappling cultivator was, but he failed to get there in time. Through the flames, Wu Ying glimpsed as the cultivator choked on his own blood, his throat crushed by an elbow as his opponent stumbled away. A glance to the side saw Tou He being the only successful member of their group as he deflected an arrow aimed at his leg before he finished his opponent with a strike to the head with his staff.

Another change in drumbeats, this time from their own lines.

All around them, the cultivators were leaving, breaking away to return to either the defensive walls or the army's lines. Wu Ying checked over the fallen bodies around them, but none breathed. To his surprise, Wu Ying noticed that Tou He had lifted the body of the cultivator he had been fighting.

When Wu Ying raised an eyebrow, his friend clarified. "He is still alive."

A quick nod, then Wu Ying turned to pick up the weapons of those left behind, sliding them into his storage ring. None looked particularly special, but decent was decent. Once he had looted the fallen weapons, he took hold of a pair of corpses and set them on his shoulders before taking off for the safety of their lines. He left Tou He to watch their backs as he bounded away from the fight.

Luckily, it seemed that the opposing cultivators had stopped targeting the pair of them. Whether it was because they had better targets now or because they had been told to stop firing, Wu Ying was uncertain. Either way, he was glad to not be shot at anymore.

Together, they retreated, bearing their prisoner and the corpses of their sect members. When Wu Ying reached their lines, he saw one extremely upset female angling her way to him. He could only wince, knowing that he was in for it. Especially when he saw the pair of soldiers standing right behind her, hands on their swords and glaring at them.

Actions had consequences. And worse, they'd managed to do nothing actually useful. Not a single life saved. Cursing himself and Tou He, Wu Ying continued to run.

Chapter 17

"You know, all things considered, we got off quite easy," Tou He said this as if to the air as the pair of them stood on guard, watching over the soldiers beside the riverbank.

They were a couple of li from the city walls, safely away from any likely attack and, of course, any excitement. All of them, the entire cultivator group, had been relegated to this posting since Tou He and Wu Ying's escapade.

"You mean there's something worse than being sent to babysit soldiers washing their clothing and cleaning pots?" Yin Xue said sarcastically.

"Well, they could have made us do it for soldiers dealing with the latrines," Tou He said.

"Don't forget they also took your contribution points," said Bao Cong.

"Our contribution points," Li Yao said disapprovingly as she sat on her horse a distance away from the group.

For the most part, the group was spread out to ensure they could keep an eye on the river and any approach. Along the route back to the army, other mortal soldiers patrolled, travelling back and forth between the route and along the river edge. All to keep an eye out for potential attackers. Stationed as they were, Wu Ying's group could spot any ships approaching from the city, and Wu Ying knew that more patrols roamed the hills and the riverbank, ensuring the security of their supply line.

"Well—"

"What Bao Cong means is that we are sorry," Wu Ying interrupted Bao Cong before he could spill the beans that he had threatened to leave if Wu Ying did not make good the lost contribution points. It was why, after both the penalty and Bao Cong's threat, Wu Ying was currently sitting at only a few hundred points.

"Being sorry is not good enough. Just because you don't want to follow the rules doesn't mean they don't apply to you." Li Yao crossed her arms, speaking to Tou He. But Wu Ying knew she really was speaking to him.

"Amitabha."

In opposite of its intended effect, Tou He's words managed to make the group sullener. Wu Ying gave up on trying to lighten the mood, choosing instead to watch the soldiers and the flowing water. At this point, a never-ending stream of soldiers was arriving, some coming by to fill their pots and water skins, others loading up the water wagons that traveled back and forth between the army encampment and the river. Others stopped by to wash their bodies and clothing at the same time. Pots and pans were cleaned by another group, while clothing was washed farther down the river. The entire process took up a good amount of space, forcing the group to watch over a wide area.

"Boat," Bao Cong called, gesturing at the river.

The group turned to eye the large flat-bottomed barge that made its way down the river, oars banked. It was the fifth time in the last couple of hours that a boat had left the city. Without boats of their own, the army was unable to blockade the city, allowing it to continue its merchant activities and to resupply the city with food. It was perhaps one of the reasons why the general was so focused on taking the city quickly—there was no point in trying to starve them out.

Of course, it meant that the team was wary of any ship that arrived or left the city. Each time, they had to send one of the soldiers that waited beside the group off with a message. Once the message was received, additional teams of cultivators would ride along the riverbank, keeping close attention on the ship and ensuring it did not stop and release enemies into the backcountry. Not that the army didn't have enough harassers as it was.

Still, while this type of work was boring, Wu Ying could not help but be grateful that it was also not dangerous. They might not be earning any contribution points, but like coin, neither could be spent if one was dead. And the number of corpses was slowly increasing as the army continued its assault on the walls.

198

"We just going to wait here then? My family's style is inside the wall, not here," Yin Xue said, once the boat they had been watching had passed by.

"If you have a better idea, I'm open to hearing it." Wu Ying shot Yin Xue a glare.

Until the army breached the walls, there was no point in the discussion. He couldn't sneak in, they couldn't break in—they couldn't even participate any longer. All they could do was wait and hope that they could get in before the home or tomb was looted.

"How about through the water? If the walls are too sturdy, can we go by the water?" Bao Cong asked. He had been watching the water, scratching his cheek while waiting.

"The water?" Li Yao shook her head, pointing farther up to where the city hid behind the curve of the river and low-lying hills. Only the edges of the wall could be seen from their current position. "They check every ship that comes in. Every single person. If they don't know you, they leave a bunch of cultivators to watch you unload. The same thing we do. Only trusted ships are even allowed to get close before they are searched."

"Oh." Bao Cong shrugged, obviously unconcerned with the process. After all, he was being paid no matter what happened.

Silence enveloped the group as they considered the reality of the situation. Until further notice, all they could do was wait.

***

It was later that evening, when the team was done, that Li Yao guided her horse over to Wu Ying with a deft touch of her knees. Her brows were drawn, her lips pursed, making him realize that the talk that had been brewing for the last few days could no longer be avoided. Wu Ying dreaded it, but he had known he could only avoid it for so long.

"We need to talk." Li Yao gestured for the rest of the team to go ahead without Wu Ying and her.

As they rode away, Wu Ying could not help but notice the smirk on Yin Xue's face, though Wu Ying wasn't entirely certain it was unjustified. He and Li Yao rode for some time in uncomfortable silence. Twice, Wu Ying tried to speak, but she had raised her hand each time, stalling him from doing so. It was only when they were a distance away from the group, when even the straggling soldiers who were busy running their errands were gone, that she spoke. Even so, she refused to look at him.

"I was given the role of the leader in this group." When Wu Ying moved to agree with her, she sped up what she was saying, overriding his words. "I'm supposed to lead. I'm supposed to be in charge, dictating everyone's moves, their depositions, their places. If you don't listen, then it creates problems for all of us. No one will listen to me if you don't."

Silence stretched between the pair before Wu Ying realized she was waiting for him to say something. "I know. I'm sorry. I just—"

"You just what? You just chose to stick your sword in, even after I told you not to," Li Yao's said, her voice rising a little. "You could have chosen to listen. You could have chosen to stop. You didn't. You chose to follow your friend. To defy me. To put the rest of us in an awkward position."

"I'm sorry. When I see something like that, I... I can't help but get involved. I can't look away." Wu Ying tried to explain his position, tried to explain why he'd done what he had. "I just... I didn't want to not listen to you. I couldn't help myself."

"It doesn't matter what you wanted to do. It's what you did. You chose to ignore me. You chose to ignore what I asked of you. You went right ahead." Li Yao finally turned, only now looking at Wu Ying. She saw the look of pain, the look of doubt on his face. He had not really meant to put her in a position like that. She knew it but... "Would you do that again?"

"Charge in and save others?" Wu Ying searched his conscience, trying to determine why he'd gone. He had stopped after all, when she asked him to. Then Tou He had gone. "I don't know. I did stop. But Tou He kept going..."

"I've talked to him," Li Yao said sternly, shaking her head. "I expected it from the monk. And I've worked out what to do with him. So has the vice-general. But you? You're no monk."

"That doesn't mean I can't have a conscience."

"You didn't go because of your conscience. You went because your friend went. And you thought you could get away with it."

Wu Ying's eyes narrowed. "That's not fair."

"You said it yourself. You went because Tou He went. You didn't have the courage, you didn't have the conscience to do it because it was right."

Wu Ying felt a flash of anger, his back straightening on the horse, tightening around his body. The signal sent the horse cantering forward, forcing Wu Ying to yank on the reins. The conflicting orders made the horse slow down and toss its head, hot-stepping a little, forcing the somewhat inexperienced rider to battle it before the creature settled. None of that helped to settle Wu Ying's temper. By the time the horse was settled, Li Yao had caught up to him again.

"That—"

"Was not fair. It was not true," Wu Ying snapped before he shook his head. "Don't worry. I will listen to your orders next time."

Li Yao opened her mouth to try apologizing and snapped it shut. She wasn't wrong. Blunt maybe, but not wrong.

"Is that all?" Wu Ying asked.

When Li Yao nodded, he kicked his heels again, sending the horse cantering and leaving the young lady behind. How dare she say that to him. That he lacked courage! Lacked morality! Everyone did compared to those monks. At least he'd acted. Tried. Rather than just follow orders.

He found himself snarling and, in a fit of pique, kicked the horse into a gallop.

***

For all his anger, Wu Ying made sure to verify that Li Yao had made her way back safely later that evening. Once he spotted her horse and her, he made sure to avoid her. He still smarted from her words and chose to spend the night manning a secondary watch for additional contribution points. Even with some of the cultivators on watch, the military never had enough of them for their peace of mind. Rather than create additional problems by enforcing extra watches, they chose instead to incentivise cultivators to take additional watches.

It was only mildly successful. Few cultivators wanted to do something as boring as standing watch, so the army had to compromise between having as many as they wished and keeping their most powerful members happy.

As Wu Ying stalked the periphery of the camp, searching for trouble, he chewed over Li Yao's words again and again. In time, his temper cooled. He had to admit, she had a point. He had decided to not go because she'd asked him to. He did see the point of military orders. He understood them and even valued them to some extent. The military, like a farming village, was not comprised of a single person. Taking care of the drainage, fixing up the riverbanks, dealing with water flow and planting, those were tasks no single person could do. No single person should do. Refusing to work with the village, doing things themselves, or choosing to do things out of order only disrupted the work of others. Sometimes it forced the villages to redo the same work again and again, wasting time and effort. Releasing water to flood one's fields when the rest of the fields were planted not only angered the rest of the farmers but also wasted time.

He could understand that. He could see how his actions had affected her standing with his friends. With the army around.

But when others died, when he could help, he wanted to help. And even if he had stopped, Tou He had gone. So maybe Wu Ying had taken the opportunity to go to. He wasn't going to allow his friend to rush out alone and without protection. Maybe that was the reason why Wu Ying had gone. Not because his conscience had said he should protect others, but because it had said he should protect Tou He.

His friend.

Or maybe he was a coward. He valued one life over others, valued the life of one he knew over those he didn't. He did not have the expanse of mercy, the heart to sympathize with strangers.

And if that was not cowardice of the heart, what was it? To choose to not hurt, to choose to safeguard one's heart, one's body, from the pain and death of others.

Wu Ying kicked a stone, sending it spiraling off into the darkness, soon lost to sight beyond the light of the camps. He continued his patrol, turning as he heard the shuffle of feet behind them. To his surprise, Tou He was there, walking up to him with his staff over his shoulder.

"Did you choose to take the night assignment too?" asked Wu Ying.

"No."

Tou He continued the patrol without waiting for Wu Ying to follow. Wu Ying cocked his head before hurrying to catch up with his friend. Unfortunately for his curiosity, Tou He chose not to say anything further.

Eventually, Wu Ying threw his hands in the air and said, "What are you doing here?"

"Joining you."

Rather than continue this charade of question-and-answer, Wu Ying punched his friend in the shoulder. Tou He danced aside, though he took a glancing blow from the sudden attack.

"Okay, okay. I want to say thank you."

"For what?" Of course, Wu Ying knew for what. But he kind of wanted Tou He to say it.

"Having my back."

Wu Ying smiled at his friend. It was what it was. But it was nice to be thanked anyway.

They continued walking together for a time before Tou He added, "I'm sorry about you and Li Yao."

"It's fine. Couples are supposed to have fights," Wu Ying said. Right? He really didn't know.

He still resented the things Li Yao had said to him. He resented that she felt she could see into him, see what he had done. That she thought to judge his intentions as much as his actions. And he wasn't sure he would choose differently if things changed. This fight between them, it was one of clashing positions. They both thought they were right. It was not like their first one, where he had insulted her with what he had said.

Did it mean they were done? How did you move on when neither party thought they were wrong? At least, not entirely.

Under that glum thought, the pair continued their patrol through the night, along the outer portion of the army that faced the walls, down to the river, and back. Walking, enjoying the humid and cool night air as thoughts churned and the world turned.

Chapter 18

Days passed with nary a change of circumstances. The walls around the city continued to be destroyed, the siege weapons continuing their assault through day and night. After all, it was not as if the walls were going anywhere. The biggest issue facing the trebuchets was keeping sufficient projectiles in stock. A constant stream of wagons and haulers traveled between the army and the nearby hills, picking up and dropping off rocks. The rocks came in a variety of shapes and sizes. A few cultivators gifted in earth and metal shaping worked the rocks, hardening and combining them to useable shapes. After all, quarrying the right shape and size was a difficult process. Much simpler to have cultivators rework them.

Even so, not all cultivators with an Earth aspect could do the work. It required both an understanding of their own chi as well as the external, environmental chi and an appropriate cultivation exercise. Thankfully, these types of exercises were common and easily purchased from the army—for obvious reasons. In fact, some cultivators even volunteered to work these shifts as it improved their control.

None of that mattered to Wu Ying. The constant, daily attacks on the walls of the city, the occasional raids against supply lines, and the battle against the soldiers from the city. Even the army supply teams that went and acquired additional supplies. None of those had anything to do with Wu Ying and his team. Instead, they continued to watch the water, the least likely location for an attack. In time, Yin Xue and Bao Cong managed to trade favors and end up working more comfortable jobs within the army encampment itself. In turn, other cultivators joined Wu Ying's group, people like Lady Pan, Yan Qing, and Bai Hu.

At the top of a hill, astride their horses, the cultivators surveyed the empty ground before them. From there, they could see the launch of another futile attack against the city, hear the crack of stone as it struck, and smell the sweet fragrance of the field of flowers before them. The midday sun beat upon them, and Wu Ying took a swig from his water bottle. The enchanted one. Because he might as well use it.

"I'm surprised to see you here," said Wu Ying to Bai Hu, who sat astride his own spotted mare.

"Did you expect me to run? Do you think me that much of a coward to run over the loss of my friends? You think we did not know what would happen?" Bai Hu glared at Wu Ying, his arms crossing beneath his swarthy chest.

"The opposite actually." Wu Ying gestured to where the edges of the city met the water. Because of their angle on top of the hill, they could look into the docks, watch the ships being loaded and unloaded. A boring job, but one that allowed them to keep an eye for potential new problems that might be dropped off—or taken away. "I thought you'd be at the walls again."

"Oh!" Bai Hu seemed mollified by Wu Ying's words. "Brave doesn't mean stupid. The death benefits from my brothers are enough for me to purchase what I want. Safe now is good. I have to survive long enough to pick out the style, after all."

"Death benefits?"

"Yes." Bai Hu smirked at Wu Ying. "Don't worry, you're not missing out on anything. Your Sect takes it all for those of you who die. They make sure they aren't missing anything."

Wu Ying blinked. That did make sense. The Sect would want the resources it had expended on the slain returned to it. He wondered if that was what the Emperor's envoy had been negotiating, then shook his head at his own naivete. As much the Sect valued them, they were also still just bodies—until they became Core cultivators. The Sect had hundreds of members in the same stage, and all too many geniuses who never managed to make it further than Energy Storage.

Still, Wu Ying felt less treasured now.

"I'm glad to hear that you've gotten something out of this," said Wu Ying. The moment he said it, he realized how callous it sounded.

But this time around, Bai Hu didn't seem to mind. "Yes. The martial style I will purchase will help. There are a number of demon beasts that were impossible for us to hunt. Now, I will be able to do it. I will honor my brothers and progress further. I will become a Core cultivator."

Wu Ying turned to Lady Pan and her companion, the pair watching over the river and busy with their own activities. To Wu Ying's amusement, Lady Pan was embroidering a silk scarf while Yan Qing was playing his erhu while balancing perfectly on his equine companion. The two-stringed bowed instrument cried and moaned under his skilled hands, the tune a sad accompaniment to the thrum of war in the background.

"Us?" Lady Pan shared a glance with Yan Qing before she shrugged. "We never intended to take part in the main assaults. Unfortunately, circumstances dictated otherwise."

"Circumstances? That vice-general just didn't know how to take no like a gentleman," Yan Qing said, his hands stopping. Even though his words were aggressive, and his tone was neutral.

"The vice-general?" Wu Ying's voice sounded troubled, the implications somewhat staggering to him. He did have to admit, Lady Pan had a certain way to her. The way she teased people, the way she acted and drew the attention of everyone who saw her. The few times he'd glimpsed her in the encampment, she had been surrounded by admirers. Mostly male, many wanting to spend time with her. But still, the vice-general…

"You get used to it," she confided to Wu Ying. "It's one of the disadvantages of my cultivation method."

Wu Ying slowly nodded. That would explain a lot, including his attraction to the Lady. Not that she wasn't beautiful in her own right, but he was with Li Yao. Sort of. Maybe. Maybe not anymore. He shook his head, discarding the thoughts that threatened to make him spiral into self-doubt again. Instead, he fixed his gaze upon the city's docks as the enemy cultivators left another ship, along with the customs guards, to row on their own boat over to the next ship.

"Why do they stop some and not others?" Wu Ying said.

"Stop what?" Bai Hu asked.

"It depends on the boat. Those with higher status, those with captains and crew who can be trusted will be allowed through," Lady Pan clarified. "The rest of them will be tested more thoroughly."

Wu Ying noted, letting his gaze roam over a couple of individuals, tiny dots that walked along in the river. Jade Gates cultivators. Probably sensing for auras, checking to make sure there weren't hidden dangers.

"Hmmm." Wu Ying rubbed his chin, trying to work out how he'd break in through the water.

Unfortunately, every idea he had come up with in the last few days had failed on further review and discussion. Swim underwater? Tried and failed. The cultivators who worked the docks were specially picked for their aura sensitivity. Also, Bao Cong had pointed out one evening, there were at least a couple of Core cultivators in the city who were close enough to the docks that they would pick out anyone trying to sneak in even if the guards missed them. So long as they were present, sneaking into the city was impossible.

Not to mention anyone who managed to make their way in had to leave again—or open the gates. Which, considering how reinforced the gates were, would require a significant force.

"I don't understand," Wu Ying said. "How are we supposed to get in?"

"We probably aren't," Yan Qing said. Having said his piece, he was playing his instrument again, hands slowly moving the bow across the strings.

"What do you mean?" Wu Ying said.

"We were probably never meant to take the city," Bai Hu said.

"Definitely not. How would the kingdom care for it? We are too far from the border. No, I think we've done all that we were meant to," Lady Pan said.

Wu Ying frowned, and the lady looked him over, considering. After some thought, she conjured a jian from her ring, replacing her needles and embroidery with the weapon, which she used to draw on the ground. She never actually touched the ground, instead instilling a small amount of metal chi into the blade and using the weapon to form the map. Wu Ying quickly understood the simple lines for the river and the city they were watching. Quick stabs added nearby cities, and he assumed the Xs were the armies. When he questioned Lady Pan, she acknowledged his guesses.

"Now here we are." Lady Pan gestured. "And here is the reserve of the army of Wei. They are moving toward us now, making sure that we do not take and hold the city."

"Yes." All of that was public information now, among even the soldiers.

"Now, what would happen if we hadn't been here?" Before Wu Ying could answer, Lady Pan continued. "Their reserve would have been free to reinforce the others. But instead, we're here, fighting on their soil, allowing us to destroy their crops, damage their city, eat their food. Even if they come, they have no chance to trap us. We will be able to leave in good time. Maybe we'll fight them farther down the road. Or maybe we will avoid them. But either way, their army within the city is of no use to them."

"What if we were ignored?" Wu Ying said.

"Then we have a new city." Lady Pan shook her head. "War is not just about what you see, nor the objective that you might see. No general chooses a single path to victory. The smart ones, and we do have smart generals, always make sure there is more than one path."

Wu Ying nodded, then looked over the map again. If they were never meant to take the city and just serve as a distraction, then...

"What the hell am I doing here?" Wu Ying said softly.

Perhaps not that softly, for Lady Pan shot him a sympathetic gaze. Even Bai Hu ended up offering Wu Ying a condescending smile.

***

Late that evening, Wu Ying was seated cross-legged in his tent. He breathed slowly, churning his chi and parsing the energy that was unaspected, that was empty of influence. Yin fire chi, Yang fire chi, metal aspected and earth aspected, it all flowed around him. As it met his aura, the selectively permeable barrier that he had formed around his body bounced them off, leaving him with just the unaspected chi he needed. In the churning morass of chi from the battle, the cultivators who drew and expelled chi around him, Wu Ying found himself rejecting more than nine parts in ten of the chi that tried to reach him.

At the same time, his body churned, the whirlpool in his dantian pulling at the chi around him, allowing him to keep his cultivation speed, his intake of energy, at a higher level. It was difficult training. Aspected chi slipped in constantly, polluting his meridians and requiring him to cleanse them of their aspects, requiring him to expel them into the air. Yet that too was training.

Each moment, each second of training added to his progress as each drop of energy, of effort, wore away at the barrier that kept him from advancing. Each indrawn portion of chi added to the core that was his dantian, allowing him to compress it further and refine the energy. Each breath built the foundation that he needed to progress. And always, he felt the blockages that stopped him from advancing, a light pressure, an ache deep in his body, in his soul that refused to budge.

He pushed on. Through the pain. Through the failure.

For failure was failure. But it was not permanent. Not so long as one continued to try.

Walls could be worn away. Water, time, energy. Lives. The barriers between one stage to the next might be as impenetrable as the walls that stood before them, but they could be split. Could be forced open.

If one persisted.

Through loss, failure, and pain.

A memory of Bai Hu staggering back to their lines, bleeding. Tears running down his face, his brothers slain and left behind for the worms. Of ordinary soldiers running back to camp to take position in the lines. A soldier late at night, clutching the stump of his hand, chi swirling around his body as enlightenment came in the midst of loss.

Persist.

Through danger, injury, and loss.

One breath, one ounce of chi at a time. Whispered words of remembrance, of promises to return favors and to greet others in the next life. Failure—only when one gave up. For the cycle repeated, rebirth and death, over and over, until one broke it.

By becoming an immortal. Or achieving nirvana.

So you kept training, second after second, moment after moment. Until you died. And started it again.

***

Days later, Wu Ying and the team stumbled back from another attack. They had been sent in as the fourth wave, a commitment of forces twice the number they had done before as another wave had arrived right after them. They had pushed against the walls, clustering under the eaves, attempting to climb to the top while the siege ladders were destroyed via talismans and chi strikes all around them. But rather than give up, the general had ordered hand-held ladders, unused thus far, to be brought and thrown up at various walls. Twice,

Wu Ying had had to throw himself off a falling ladder and hit the ground hard, bruising feet and body. Still, it was better than falling still wrapped in the ladder.

For half a day, the army had pushed against the wall, sacrificing numerous bodies and gaining no ground. Thrice, they had taken a portion of the walls just long enough to bring on a few more people before they lost them. Once, they had even had a Core cultivator, a member of the Sect Wu Ying had never met before, standing on the wall. Unfortunately, it seemed that the city had been waiting, for they sent two of their own to do battle. The fight between the three had been enough to clear the wall, destroying portions of the walkway and killing the Elder and one of the other enemy cultivators.

It was not a good trade. Not at all.

Whether the general had decided not to waste any more of his precious Core cultivators or because he felt the attempts to bait out the opposing defenders had been unsuccessful, he had never sent another major power to attack. And so, it was Energy Storage cultivators and regular soldiers who had fought, bled, and died. But that was the way of it. Those who had the most to lose would be put the most at risk.

And it really did not matter. In the end, the general called them back, leaving the walls damaged, the defenders bloodied, but the city untouched. The cheers that roared from the city, the catcalls and the horns had been uncharacteristic of the usually disciplined army of defenders. But Wu Ying could understand their jubilation. Rumors had already spread amongst the State of Shen's own ranks that the State of Wei's reserve army was only a week away. The siege was likely to be lifted, for no general would risk his army getting caught between the city, a river, and another army.

Later that night, under the cover of darkness, the siege weapons were rolled closer to the city. Then burning talismans, grouped flasks of oil, and flaming rocks had been tossed into the city, to damage, destroy, and otherwise wreck what they could.

212

Wu Ying and his team had a good view of all this, for they had been designated to sneak closer to the city ahead of the siege engines. There, under the cover of the assault trenches, his team had hidden. Waiting for the obvious retaliation. The State of Wei could not just let them send rocks and fire into their own city. So while archers imbued arrows and artillery in the city fired back, the gates of the city opened for the first time.

Wu Ying was tempted to dash in, but he knew they were likely looking for some foolhardy attack like that. Also, he wasn't exactly sure that Yin Xue would have followed him. And while Wu Ying had a rough map of the city, if he went in in the middle of the night, trying to dodge soldiers, he wondered if he could find the location. And Wu Ying had to admit, their current orders were not ones he could in good conscience defy. Never mind the eventual, probably much harsher, punishment but also because he had promised to join the war effort. He too had his own honor. No matter what Li Yao thought.

The team stayed still, waiting for the calvary charge to pass them, watching and restraining their auras as best as they could. Thankfully, for this task, the army had provided them all with talismans that concealed their auras. All but Wu Ying, for his control was sufficient for their needs. As such, the rushing Wei cultivators missed their group, charging directly at the siege weapons that continued to attack the city. And if the soldiers noticed them, a few soldiers looking to launch a surprise attack were less important than destroying the siege engines. In truth, Wu Ying couldn't blame them. After all, his team wasn't there to fight the cavalry.

"Here they come!" Li Yao hissed at the group.

She was peeking out the corner of the trenches, staring at another mass of individuals who had left the city after the main charge. Soon, the enemy cultivators split off in different directions to aid the soldiers, moving in small groups. Wu Ying, crouched in the trench, could sense their auras even from here, and he could not help but shake his head. What was it with people and not learning to restrain themselves? Was it a matter of pride?

As they moved forward, barely making a noise, Wu Ying revised his opinion. Of course it was pride.

Still, Wu Ying had to chuckle internally. Their pride made the job easier.

Li Yao gestured at the group, making quick signals to pass on the details she spotted and assigning everyone to their tasks. In short order, the team was ready, weapons drawn and arrows nocked. As Li Yao slowly closed her fingers, the entire group tensed, waiting. When her hand clenched, everyone charged out of the trench. Even Bao Cong jumped out to give himself a better angle of fire.

They caught the group of enemy cultivators semi-unaware. Even if the talismans restrained their auras, they could not do so completely. On the other hand, they must have seemed to the other cultivators like a group of soldiers. Not strong enough to seriously worry about, but enough that their enemy was expecting the attack. What they did not expect was the series of chi-projected attacks, as weapons skills and fist forms gave life to energy projections.

The attacks were so mixed together, even Wu Ying's Woo Petal Bracer's metallic energy was hard to pick out. The surprise attack was somewhat successful, taking down one of the cultivators and seriously injuring two of the others. Together, Wu Ying and his team charged in, targeting the three cultivators left standing and unharmed as they reeled from the attack.

As if it was planned, Wu Ying found himself facing off not against the unharmed enemy but the two injured Sect members who were trying to run away. Rather than waste his time, Wu Ying threw another cut filled with the power of the Woo Petal Bracer, hoping he could finish the battle quickly. His energy field attack was blocked by one, semi-blocked by the other, leaving him to engage them in close combat. A lunge, a quick clatter of blades, a cut down low, then he was in, shoulder checking his opponent into the other. As they stumbled back, he took advantage of the momentary confusion to cut across his first opponent's ankles, hobbling him further.

A sudden thrust of a spear aimed at Wu Ying's face made him dance aside. He circled the pair, parrying the spear strikes while he countered, cheating by sliding his weapon down the spear shaft every chance he could. The attacks shaved off minor slices of wood, but more importantly, they made his opponent leery of committing for fear of getting his fingers sliced off. As the pair clashed, his first opponent pushed himself back to his feet as blood pooled around his ankles.

Realizing he would have to fight them both again soon, Wu Ying decided to risk it. He threw himself forward, and as the spear shot toward him, he twisted his body. He caught the attack high in the chest, just a couple of inches above his heart and to the left, but it glanced off the lamellar plate. His opponents, neither expecting the sudden charge, were caught by surprise as Wu Ying traded attacks.

Unlike his opponent, Wu Ying infused his weapon with his own chi and his sword intent, planting his front foot as he completed Greeting the Sunrise. The attack left his opponent with a new mouth, one that started below his chin and extended all the way to his ear, a mouth that erupted in a spray of blood.

As Wu Ying turned on his next opponent, the man slumped to the side, one hand futilely grasping at the feathers that stood out from below his chest, just under his armpit. It seemed that Bao Cong had beaten Wu Ying to it. It didn't matter to Wu Ying.

He turned to the main battle, ready to help. As always, Tou He was holding his own, but this time, neither party seemed to have the upper hand. However, it seemed Li Yao was the one most struggling of the three, on the backfoot as her opponent conjured swaths of flame that burnt at her ice spear.

Decision made, Wu Ying threw himself into the fight. They had to finish this fast, before the defenders sent help.

***

As the group ran back, their opponents slain, bodies looted of valuables, they grinned at one another. After so many days of boring patrols, the brief encounter had been exhilarating. Even if it had meant the death of others, doing battle was still a rush. The last trebuchet fired its final payload, moments before coming down with a crash as a massive rose petal energy projection smashed into the trebuchet. As he watched, Wu Ying reminded himself that all this glory, all this excitement, came at the expense of lives.

Civilian lives.

War, no matter how glorious, was paved with the blood and bones of commoners.

People like he had been.

And, perhaps, not anymore?

Chapter 19

Later that night, Wu Ying tossed and turned in his bed as sleep continued to elude him. His mind kept turning back to the siege engines, torn and twisted, discarded after their use. He kept seeing faces—of those soldiers who had fallen, the ones who had screamed in the medical tents as their limbs were amputated or their wounds were sewn closed. All around him, the noise of camp packing up resounded. Extra soldiers were on duty tonight to make sure that the army was not attacked in turn, adding to the noise level. The light from the burning city could be seen through his tent flaps, the damage still ongoing.

None of it helped him sleep, even if he normally slept all too easily. Tonight, his mind churned. Too much. He'd seen too much.

Wu Ying rolled off his bed, the cot sagging and buckling a little as the bamboo legs threatened to come apart. He could have gotten something better, but considering they were leaving soon, it had seemed wasteful. Even the tent he had been allocated was small, though larger than any soldier's. He had a cot, a meditation pad, and a location to store his equipment. More than adequate for him. He could have gotten more luxurious furnishings, a larger space perhaps, if he had insisted. Spent his contribution points. But it was a luxury he did not need, a waste of resources and time. Not that he had anything against luxury. He wasn't one of those who railed against it just because he hadn't had it when he was younger. Wu Ying just thought it wasn't appropriate here.

His gaze fixed on the meditation pad, considering if he should train. Part of him, the diligent, stubborn part, said yes. He was not talented, he was not gifted, he was not rich. He had to spend every second, every moment he could training. That was the only way he could progress. Even now, while he had been trying to sleep, his dantian and chi had churned, working through his body subconsciously. A part of him, like breathing. But like breathing, concentrated effort would see better results.

As he considered getting back to work, Wu Ying stared at his hands, noted how they clenched and unclenched, felt the unruly flow of chi within his body, the unbridled and restless energy.

There was no way he could get any real training done. He was too agitated to stop, to wait, the train. He needed to move, needed to be out of this stuffy enclosure, needed noise and sound and movement. Meditating could make the energy calm, himself calm, but he'd have to face those images. Face them again—and he was tired of that. Better to move.

Mind made up, Wu Ying quickly threw on a set of robes, this one plainer and darker than his usual Sect robes. Better to dress like a plain soldier than to wear his Sect robes. He drew too much attention that way. Still, Wu Ying made sure to put on the under armor and his sword, worried that a surprise attack might occur. Better to be ready.

As he exited his tent, Wu Ying glanced up and down the pathway. There were no lights on in any of the other tents nearby, which contained other members of the Sect. He let his gaze linger on the tent that contained Li Yao, debating if he should walk in and talk to her. But she was sleeping. His presence would not be taken well. Also, he could imagine the kind of rumors that would start if he entered an unmarried woman's abode in the middle of the night. Better not to.

Instead, Wu Ying dodged muddy parts of the unpaved path, nodding to the few soldiers who were up. It was well past the middle of the night, and in a few hours, the army would begin its march as the sun rose. The soldiers who were awake and lounging around campfires were up because they too could not sleep. Some would have just come off a watch, some spent their last few hours taking care of their equipment. A few were drinking away their sorrows or nursing injuries that refused to let them rest.

Occasionally, Wu Ying considered joining them. But even if he wasn't dressed in his Sect robes, the gulf between the soldiers and himself as a cultivator was too vast to breach. He was different from them, and his presence would be anything but relaxing. His imposition would be unwanted, and even if they chose not to say anything, he would know. Better to let them enjoy their evening, to spend it in their own company, and rest before their long march.

Strolling through the inner part of the army encampment, Wu Ying found himself in a portion of the encampment he had not visited. Here, a large tent dominated, lights still on, a quipan and other instruments playing to draw in visitors. Like a moth to the flame, Wu Ying joined the slow trickle of curious individuals approaching the tent.

To his surprise, the brightly colored tent's front awning flaps were open, the waiting vestibule glowing and allowing the visitors to enter its welcoming, warm embrace. Not just lamplight, but the occasional spirit lamp was lit, dispersed to ensure there were no shadows here. As the main tent flap was pushed aside, Wu Ying felt a blast of warmth that brought the smells of well-spiced, well-cooked meat, of spilled alcohol and delectable foods within. His stomach rumbled, and hunger joined curiosity in demanding Wu Ying explore.

Once inside the tent proper, Wu Ying was surprised to see that it was actually larger on the inside than he had expected. He let his chi billow out, sensing the ambient flows of energy within, curious to see if it was a formation or a trick of the light. Instead, Wu Ying sensed something else and retracted his aura.

His gaze darted past the cultivators, mercenaries, and soldiers who sat around rough wooden tables, drinking and gambling and talking to the servers and companions. The servers were beautiful men and women sliding in and out of reaching hands, smiling as they deposited food and wine, never staying too long. Wu Ying's gaze tracked across the various servers, surprised that all of them, from serving wench to cooks, were cultivators in the Energy Storage stage at the least, most in the mid-level.

Even more surprising were the working women—and the occasional man—who sat and nuzzled, who laughed at the lewd conversations before they led their temporary companions into another room. These women and men of the night were dressed even more scandalously than the servers, their tops thin—or non-existent—their skin oiled and glistening, sleeves barely hanging on to heaving bosoms, slits on the sides reaching up to their hips, or all too tight pants. It was enough to make Wu Ying blush.

"Move it!" A voice behind Wu Ying woke him from his stupor, making him take a couple steps forward.

Not fast enough for the other, as Wu Ying was pushed slightly aside as the speaker brushed past without another word. Wu Ying's eyes narrowed before he dismissed the provocation. He was no impatient noble, worried about his honor. A little rudeness did not merit a big fuss.

"I'm surprised to see you here," a familiar voice called to Wu Ying on his opposite side.

He turned, spotting Lady Pan, and only then realized that the musicians in the corner were headed by her companion. Yan Qing lounged in the corner, his bow dancing across his erhu.

"Is this yours?" Wu Ying asked.

Lady Pan laughed. "As much as anything can be considered to be owned, it is mine. Now, since we have fought together, I must make sure you have a good time. What can I get you? And don't worry, nothing that happens here will get back to your Sect mates."

"I didn't know what this was," Wu Ying quickly explained, trying to fight down the rising blush and her implications. "I'm not really here for any…"

"Food? Drink? Company?" Lady Pan laughed, placing a hand on Wu Ying's arm and gently guiding him deeper into the tent. Her laugh was so unlike Li Yao's—full-bodied in the same way, but deeper, more seductive. "Come. You've come to visit me, it would be rude for me to let you go without at least a drink. Everything else, you can decide if you will partake of later." As Wu Ying's mouth opened to continue his protests, she added, "Or not."

Forced forward by her gentle but unyielding pressure, Wu Ying traversed the large tent. He was not even surprised to see Bai Hu curled up in one corner with a young lady on his lap, murmuring besotted words into her ear. Deposited in a chair himself, Wu Ying nodded in greeting to the other two occupants of the table. They flicked a glance at Wu Ying and nodded companionably to Lady Pan before they turned back to their own conversation.

The female owner of the tent smiled and gestured to one of the passing waitresses before turning to Wu Ying. "Can't sleep?"

"I didn't realize this was even here," Wu Ying said. "I'm so surprised. It's not what I expect in the middle of an army encampment."

Lady Pan shook her head, clearly amused. "You didn't notice the tents at the edges of the encampment? The ones the common soldiers spend time and coin at?"

"Of course I did. I know about that. But this, this is a little more…"

"Opulent. Professional. Luxurious?" Lady Pan teased, placing her hand on his arm again. He felt the heat of her hand as it traversed the thin silk of his robes. It felt… nice. "Thank you. It's taken me many years to build this."

Wu Ying's eyes narrowed as he considered the lady. She looked young, but so did most cultivators. Once you began cultivating in earnest, especially if you reached the higher stages, aging slowed down significantly. A Body cultivator could expect to live to a hundred, hale and healthy. An Energy Storage cultivator could easily double their lifespan and look young for three quarters of it. As for Core cultivators, they counted their lifespans in thousands of years. As lifespans increased, it was hard to tell the age of others, other than through mannerisms and what they said. He wondered how old Lady Pan really was.

Forty? Fifty? Probably no older, for she was only late high Energy Storage and he got the feeling she was not one to stall there.

"Good. So many of you youngsters, so rude, asking the age of those they just met." Lady Pan turned and took the wine jar from the server before serving herself and Wu Ying. "Come, let's drink."

Wu Ying picked up the cup, raising it to her as well. "What are we drinking to?"

Lips twisted in a smile, she stood and raised her voice. She was not shouting, but every word she said carried through the tent, drawing everyone's attention. "To surviving and taking another step on our path to immortality."

The words brought a roar of approval from the cultivators within the room, drawing shouts even from some of the soldiers themselves. Other soldiers, their heads lowered, looked embarrassed as the cultivators quaffed their drinks and slammed the cups down in approval. The servers spun around, quickly refilling empty cups where tables had no pots of wine or liquor open.

Wu Ying hid his smile while his own cup was promptly refilled by Lady Pan. He lowered his voice as he leaned forward. "You make that toast often?"

"Often enough," Lady Pan said with a slightly smug tone. "It is a good toast. And one we all believe in."

"We all?" Wu Ying asked, glancing around the room. One thing he had noted was the absence of anyone from a sect. At least, by their robes. They could be like him, hiding in plain sight, but he was certain that none of the Verdant Green Waters Sect members were part of this group. Those he knew by sight.

"Independent cultivators. The heretical, the unusual, the ones who do not believe in your straight and narrow path."

"The Sect offers many paths. That's why we have multiple cultivation methods, multiple styles, even Elders who teach different philosophies," Wu Ying said.

222

"You only think you do." When Wu Ying straightened in anger, she shook her head. "Will you listen? Before you judge."

Wu Ying's lips twisted, but eventually he nodded. For a moment, he wondered if she was going to make a pitch for something more dangerous, more heretical. If so, he would need to escape, inform the general. But then he dismissed the notion. Somehow, he did not think that the general, or Elder Pan, would miss something like that in the middle of their own encampment. Fanciful thoughts.

"Good. Your sect, most sects, believe the only way to immortality is by hard work. Hard work in different styles, in different cultivation methods, but hard work. You put in the hours, you train, you draw in chi, and you work at progressing your cultivation. Hundreds, thousands of years perhaps to reach one's goal." Lady Pan spoke softly, her eyes fixed upon Wu Ying's.

He reluctantly nodded, for what she described was true. There was no progress without hard work.

"But why?" When Wu Ying moved to answer, she placed her fingers on his lips briefly, leaving a tingling sensation, a burning warmth that left his heart beating faster. "Why do that? When we have so many examples, so many stories, of those who have achieved immortality without taking that path?"

"You're talking of Lan Cai He and Quan Zhong Li[11]," Wu Ying said.

"Them, and many others. How many have found immortality because of a lucky item, because of their deeds, from of a gift from those above? Fortuitous encounters, peaches of immortality, even the help of other immortals. So many roads, and yet, the sects only choose one."

---

[11] Two of the Eight Immortals in Chinese mythology. Cai He supposedly traveled the world, doing good before ascending after getting drunk, while Zhong Li found a jade vessel that took him as an immortal to the heavens.

"But that's because…" Wu Ying wasn't sure why. He thought about it, sipping on his wine as he did so.

Lady Pan smiled at his furrowed brows while she turned to manage a few other matters her employees drifted over to discuss with her.

As he set down his cup, Wu Ying spoke up. "That kind of immortality—a lot of it isn't true. It isn't… theirs."

"Because they have no dao? Or they find their dao later?" Lady Pan nodded in acknowledgement. "Mostly true. Some though, they find their dao later and become as strong, if not stronger. And really, immortality is immortality."

Wu Ying grimaced but nodded. "Still, you can't control the other options. There is no way to harness destiny and luck."

"True. But are they better?" Lady Pan stood, tapping Wu Ying on his shoulder. "Think about it. Talk to the others. You are young now. You've only just started your journey. Sometimes, the path can be circuitous."

Leaving Wu Ying to think about the matter, Lady Pan went to speak to her other guests. Wu Ying nursed the wine bottle, turning her words over and over in his mind. A different path, a different way to the heavens. In some ways, it was intriguing. Even if intuition told Wu Ying that this was not entirely for him, there was something to what Lady Pan said.

Sometimes, the way ahead was circuitous.

***

It was late in the night, as the sun was beginning to peek over the horizon, when Wu Ying made his goodbyes. He clapped Bai Hu on the shoulder, thanking the talisman master and slipping the talismans he'd purchased into his jacket. If he hurried, he'd make it to the contribution points store before they opened, beating the lines. There was a lot to do still, and if the army was removing itself, Wu Ying had a lot to plan. But if there was more than one way to cultivate, perhaps there was more than one way to steal a manual.

Chapter 20

The next morning, the army withdrew. Preparations for it had taken place all through the night, meaning that the army required only a few hours to get itself together and leave. Not that the entire army left at the same time, for a section of it stayed behind to keep an eye on the city, ensuring they were not attacked while they were moving. Even so, as Wu Ying sat on his horse, watching the divisions march away, he could not help but notice the waste.

Not just of the bodies, which littered the field from the night before. This time around, the army had not bothered to clean up after itself. Nor the various pieces of last night's antics. The corpses that drew incessant wails and cries from those inside the city were just a portion of the waste he saw. For the city still burnt, smoke curling up from the fires that had ravaged the city all through the night. Even with the help of the cultivators within, the army had managed to set on fire a number of the neighborhoods, leaving the city ravaged.

Furthermore, in front of the city walls lay the shattered masonry and the remnants of the siege weaponry. So many trees, so many yards of rope and hundreds of nails left to rot before the city. Every single siege engine, every trebuchet, assault cover, and sky ladder had been destroyed last night—at the cost of lives. All of it, a waste.

Wu Ying turned his head, spotting the nearby hillsides that had seen their fields destroyed, the water left to drain out, the trees that provided shade cut down. Small huts, used for rest, for cooking midday meals, and storing farming implements, had been burnt down.

All destroyed.

Wasted.

Wu Ying shook his head, staring at the remnants of the siege. He did not understand the point of all this, this battle, this war. He understood the Sect leader's rumored dao, but he didn't understand why the king felt the need to expand. His kingdom had food, water, and land. Yet he was forcing his kingdom to fight.

Beside him, Li Yao sat, her thoughts hidden behind an impassive mien. In silence, the pair watched the troops go by, tasked with keeping an eye for enemy cultivators. They were on a hill, overlooking both the city and the army as troops passed them to the south. In a change of pace, Wu Ying's group had been assigned to the northern portion of the encampment.

This was their last task for the army, for they would leave soon after. That discussion had not gone well. But luckily, Chao Kun, in his role as the leader of the cultivators, had intervened, allowing them to continue with their own mission.

As for Li Yao and Wu Ying, things had been strained. As it should be, considering how twice now they had fought over the very same mission. The strain from the disagreements had told on their burgeoning relationship. Neither of them knew how to step back from their positions. How to apologize and forgive. Especially when neither of them thought they were wrong. It was a clash of priorities rather than of morality, for both agreed the other had a point. In such a situation, neither party knew how to approach the subject, so they continued to avoid it. They focused not on their relationship or what there was of it, but on the job at hand.

That was the smart thing to do. It was the responsible thing to do. They weren't the only ones on this mission. Or at least that was what Wu Ying told himself

"Do you have a plan?" Li Yao asked, finally speaking up.

"Yes," Wu Ying replied.

Before Li Yao could ask for further details, the pair of cultivators froze and turned almost in unison. The change in the ambient flow of chi was so great that neither of them could miss it. It was also a highly familiar change in the environmental chi, especially in the sect.

They turned and saw the rigid form of Yin Xue on his horse, his hands down by his sides, his reins dropped and forgotten. Luckily, the animal underneath him had also sensed the change and was turning his head from side to side in curiosity. This was not a bad change; it was, in fact an opportunity. Not just for the man sitting on the horse, but the horse itself. In such close proximity to enlightenment, the change in chi and the world itself could provide the creature an opportunity to progress its own cultivation. And so, man and horse meditated, one upon the glimpse of a universal proof, the other upon the way the world flowed.

Wu Ying shook his head, staring at Yin Xue, and said, "That pig-footed man."

But he said it softly, for even a Six Jade Gates sect member might pause in his attacks when another cultivator faced enlightenment. They all sought these small glimpses of the universal truth, the Dao. They searched and fought for the heavens' benediction on their understanding, their wisdom. To break another's trance, to take away an individual's opportunity to advance, was something only hated enemies and those in the middle of battle might do. As for everyone else, they honored the moment.

Bao Cong got off his horse to take the reins of Yin Xue's service horse. Better to be safe than sorry. Tou He grinned at Yin Xue's unseeing form, happy for the man.

Eventually, the group turned back to the city to watch for cultivators and other threats while the army pulled away. As much as it was a blessing for Yin Xue, they still had a job to do. Soon enough, they would have to move. But for now, Yin Xue could have his small moment of enlightenment.

***

They waited until the last of the army divisions had left. The rearguard traveled slowly, with wide-ranging scouts in place to ensure they were not tracked. As a last parting gift, the general had ordered anything they could not carry be set on fire, including much of the surrounding fields. With the prevailing winds in the morning sending the flames skirting north and west, it would mostly miss the city itself, unless there was a shift in the wind. Even so, the city would likely take action, especially after their most recent experience.

That kind tactic made Wu Ying's lips curl in distaste, as did Tou He's, but neither party protested. After all, stopping the fires would not be a minor transgression in saving lives and disobeying orders. Nothing they said was likely to stop the general. And it meant that the army could pull away before their enemies could sortie from the city. In the end, wars were not won by half measures but by full commitment. Otherwise, one only dragged on the affair, adding pain and suffering in tiny fire ant bites, rather than a single rabid dog's attack.

The group rode along with the rest of the army for a few hours before their time patrolling was over, wherein they rode in to make their final report. They didn't even see the vice-general this time, relegated to reporting to Chao Kun. It was for the better.

As they were riding off—after saying their goodbyes to their temporary friends, including a smirking Lady Pan—they were flagged down by a surprising individual.

"Are you certain you will not change your mind?" Elder Po said to them.

"No, we will not," Wu Ying spoke for the group. He offered the elder a half-smile, an apology of sorts. "If the army is going to be followed by those in the city, if the cultivators inside the city leave too, this will be our best chance."

"Oh, they will follow. We've received word that there are as many cultivators in the approaching reserve army as we have," Elder Po said. "I fear the general's gambit will fail. We cannot risk a fight, not if we are to be outnumbered."

"Won't the general avoid battle against both armies?" Li Yao said. After all, they were only outnumbered if they had to fight the city and the reserve army at the same time.

"Of course he will try. But it's not just the armies we are worried about. We can avoid engaging against the bulk of both armies, but cultivators travel faster than an army. If we are engaged by even a single side, it is likely that the Six Jade Gates sect members will be able to arrive," Elder Po explained. "It's why we need as many of you as possible."

Wu Ying could see why he wanted them to stay. Even if they were not the most powerful, all-talented cultivators, an additional team could make a difference in the fight. Not as much as a Core cultivator, but you never knew. However… "I'm sorry, Elder Po. We have a mission to complete."

The Elder flicked his gaze over Wu Ying's and the others' resolute faces before he broke out into a grin. "Very well. No need to worry. I have no intention of giving up my life yet. This battle will likely not happen anyway. Go. Complete your quest."

Wu Ying bowed from his saddle, taking comfort in the Elder's words, before he gestured the group away. They cut perpendicular to the army's march, moving along the hillside until they reached an enclosed glen. There, Wu Ying gestured for them to pull over near a small copse of trees in the shade of a hill. It would do for now. They would have to wait for the fires to burn out before they could take action. Luckily, their last glimpse had been of the city sortieing, sending cultivators and farmers to put out the fires.

Once everyone was settled, with Bao Cong seated farther up the hill as lookout, Wu Ying found a bare portion of sandy ground and a stick for his presentation.

"Firstly, I'd like to thank everyone for staying." Wu Ying shot a glare at Yin Xue, who had looked as if he might say something. Yin Xue just smirked. Obviously whatever enlightenment he had found, it did not involve being nicer. "As you heard, the plan is to enter the city when the cultivators from the Six Jade Gates Sect are no longer there. While they chase the army, we will enter the city and find what we need."

"And how will we do that?" Li Yao said. "Even if the army is gone, they aren't likely to begin normal commerce. Anyone trying to enter the city will still be under scrutiny."

"That's why we will be sneaking in." While he had been speaking and listening to Li Yao, Wu Ying had been drawing on the ground with the stick. The rough sketch of the city was easy enough to pick out, even if it was just a bunch of lines. "We'll be entering through the docks."

"How?" Tou He asked. "They might reduce the number of guards, but I doubt they'd miss all of us. Never mind our lack of a boat."

Wu Ying grinned, touching his storage ring before he extracted a set of yellow parchment. On closer inspection, the symbols drawn on the papers were familiar to the group, for they had just worn a set of the aura suppression talismans the night before.

"And the boat?" Yin Xue asked.

"That's why we were sent up river today," said Bao Cong. The blacksmith had put it together faster than the others. The choice of them being on the northernmost watch, opposite to where they normally had been stationed. The northernly direction they had left the army, swinging wide and farther north, bringing them upriver. It all set them up so that they could ride away and upriver, circling around the city and getting out of sight easily.

"Exactly," Wu Ying said.

"I'm not a pirate," Yin Xue said, crossing his arms.

Tou He grunted his agreement. Even Li Yao frowned in displeasure at the thought of attacking civilians.

Wu Ying snorted. "What have I ever done to make you think I would do that?"

232

He brought his stick further up the drawing, pointing at a bend he had placed in the drawing. He had to admit though, compared to the rest of the squiggles that made up the river he had drawn, the bend was easy to miss. He had many skills, but cartography obviously was not one of them.

"There's a tight turn farther upriver, one that will force the ships to slow down. At least, as I've been told." Wu Ying's time in Lady Pan's inn had been useful in gaining information from the other cultivators, beyond making his head hurt from doubts about his path of cultivation. "All we have to do is swim to a ship, attach ourselves to it at night, and let it bring us into port. If we make sure to hold our breaths and stay still, with these talismans, we should be able to make our way in without a problem."

Li Yao looked dubious about Wu Ying's plan, but since no one else had a better suggestion, they went over the details of their eventual escapade. In short order, they had the basics of the plan down and rode off, planning to lay low over the next few days while waiting for the army and the opposing cultivators to leave and the fires to burn out.

***

For five days, the group stayed hidden near the banks of the river, waiting for a suitable vessel. During this time, they collected hollow reeds from the shore and prepared them for use. They each stored their prepared reeds in their storage rings for use when they were underneath the ship itself. In addition, Wu Ying and Bao Cong fashioned simple hooked devices that could be driven into the hull of the boat, allowing them to grip and ride the boat to the dock. Wu Ying's greatest concern was that they not strike too hard, creating a breach in the ship they intended to use. As such, in the quiet times while they waited, the group tested their strength, trying to find a balance in force while floating in water.

Among the many variations and improvements were the ropes that Bao Cong tied off in a quick slip knot around each of their bodies. It would allow the group to stay attached to one another such that if one person missed their grip, they could still be dragged along. Thankfully, the pull of the river was so great that it was unlikely the sailors would notice a change even with the addition of the five underwater cultivators.

However, Wu Ying realized a flaw in his plan. If no ship came, they had no way of getting into the port. Worse, they needed one to arrive in the night rather than during the day when their swimming forms would be easy to spot.

He mulled over his options, finally landing on having the group gather bunches of deadwood. If necessary, they would float in under the cover of these branches, going in in small groups and hoping that they would be missed by the guards. Floating deadwood was not uncommon, but five different clumps would likely draw attention if they all arrived too close together.

Wu Ying was growing impatient, concerned they would be caught by the city patrols, when they finally spotted a suitable ship. Even better, the vessel was arriving late in the day. Rather than risk waiting longer, Wu Ying called his friends to get ready.

Together, the group slipped into the water silently, timing it so they entered the fast-flowing river while the ship's watch was looking away. It helped that their river entrance was hidden by low-hanging weeping willows and floating rushes. As quietly as possible, the group swam mostly under water to where the ship would pass. They were all tied together. Tou He, their strongest swimmer, led the pack, with Yin Xue in the back as he was incredibly insufficient. Unlike the others, he had not spent much time in the numerous rivers and lakes that dotted the landscape of the kingdom. Still, the greater strength offered to a cultivator helped offset his lack of technique.

Directly behind his monk friend, Wu Ying noticed that the current was stronger than ever, driving them and the ship forward equally quickly. Wu Ying

234

sped up his strokes, pulling and kicking as best as he could underwater so that they could reach the ship in time. Thankfully, as cultivators, their ability to hold their breath was significantly increased. Their bodies' need for air had reduced—though they were no Nascent Soul cultivators who existed only on the chi of the world. As the ship swept past them, Wu Ying silently cursed as they missed the prow where they had meant to attach themselves.

Tou He struck first, swinging his curved, sharpened hook at the side of the boat. It struck, skipped along barnacles, and dislodged, leaving the monk to flounder as he tried to regain his position. In the meantime, Wu Ying had managed to make his way to the boat's side and strike with his own implement. This too failed to make purchase, the rotten wood beneath tearing apart after a moment of pressure. Wu Ying kicked and twisted as the floating debris swung by him, his loss of momentum dragging him back.

Next up was Li Yao. She was focused, legs beating in rapid rhythm as she kicked her way to the rudder passing by them. As Wu Ying tried his best to catch up, he watched ice form around the body of her hook. She swung, striking deep into the wood near the rudder. In a burst of energy, the hook dug into the wood of the ship and released the collected chi of her attack. It quickly formed a small glacier that adhered to the wood, dragging along Li Yao and the other cultivators. With all four cultivators stuck to her body, her breathing grew strained from the ropes pulling against her waist, catching on her hips, tugging on her arms. She refused to give up, focusing on her chi, expelling ice and cold as she manipulated the glacier to become sleeker, to give better purchase around the bottom of the ship.

Bao Cong, never having lost momentum while trying to attach himself to the ship, swam under the keel and came up and around the other side. Already, Li Yao's ice formation had formed a thin layer around the other side, allowing Bao Cong's chi-infused hook to bury in the wood and hold. With the weight taken off one side of her body, the female cultivator wrapped her hand around the trailing rope and pulled it close. Dragged along by the rope, Wu Ying and Tou He continued to swim, doing their best to catch up. Yin Xue did the same on the other side.

In short order, the group was able to attach themselves to the ship using the crusty-ice for additional purchase. Li Yao was the first to extract her reed, sliding it into the air near the ship to suck down oxygen in greedy mouthfuls. Thankfully, even if it was difficult to draw oxygen from the surface, their strong lungs and the supplementary energy that rushed through their bodies allowed the cultivators to last for hours underneath the water. Of them all, Wu Ying struggled the most, his lower cultivation forcing him to require more air.

Once he had fastened himself properly, he tied himself off to the ship, wrapping his arm around the edge of the rope to ensure that he could continue being dragged along before he focused entirely on conserving energy and drawing down as much air as he could. To his surprise, the flow of energy from his semi-porous aura had improved under the water. Upon further exploration, he realized that it was the increased pressure and the lack of variation in the environmental chi surrounding him that allowed him to improve his circulation methods. Grateful for the additional energy that he used to keep himself alive, Wu Ying focused deep within.

In that way, the group drifted into port and enemy territory.

Chapter 21

Wu Ying lost track of time as he floated and circulated his chi. The struggle to stay conscious as he breathed through the thin reed and circulated his chi caused him to focus only on those two things. To his surprise, he found that this forced concentration pushed his grasp of the aura cultivation exercise even further—so much so that he felt a clear improvement in his ability. A part of him wondered if he had yet achieved the threshold for Minor Achievement. Sometimes, these types of exercises lacked a clear marker. He might not be an Energy Storage cultivator, but none of the others had his cultivation exercise either.

When they finally arrived, Wu Ying found himself slowly floating, the reed clenched between his teeth as he sucked in slow, measured breaths. He didn't notice the change in light or the lack of motion, nor even the hands that detached his death grip on the rope and drew him to the water's surface. It was only when his face broke through the clear air that Wu Ying realized where he was. And that he was being slowly dragged away from the ship to beneath the docks. A hand clamped over his mouth when he opened it, silencing him.

When Wu Ying came fully to his senses, he found Bao Cong holding him tightly, hands around Wu Ying's armpits. Wu Ying gave a nod, acknowledging that he was fully sensible, before the cultivator let go.

He then leaned in, whispering into Wu Ying's ear, "The others have already gone ahead. We need to go. Soon."

Wu Ying nodded, doing his best to reduce the amount of noise and splashes he made as they swam underneath the dock. In the dark of the night, the pair moved to the river's banks, peering around the edges of the dock. A splash next to Wu Ying's face made him jerk, only for him to relax when whatever had been tossed aside sank into the water. In the darkness of the night, whatever it was sank away quickly, though by the smell of the water around them, Wu Ying could guess.

When they reached where water and the bottom of the dock met, they stayed low, bobbing in the water with a hand against the wooden panels. Late as it was, there were few people on the docks beyond the patrolling guards and the dock workers moving back and forth from the single ship that had arrived. Without work to do, most of the dock workers were likely in town, where additional work lay in cleaning up the fires and destroyed buildings.

Inhaling slowly, Wu Ying made sure to extend his senses, checking for cultivators above. When the guards had moved down the dock on their patrol, the pair exited the water smoothly and across the open ground, leaving muddy and wet footprints.

In the shade of a small warehouse, between two alleyways, the pair found the others waiting. Wu Ying moved to go deeper into the narrow alleyway, automatically seeking shadows, only to be held back by Tou He.

"She's changing," the ex-monk said.

Wu Ying blinked and realized that his friends had already removed their sodden clothing and wiped themselves down as best they could. It left them mostly dry, except for their hair. Well, most of them—Wu Ying eyed the shaved head of his friend. Bao Cong was already half naked, redressing while Yin Xue took watch.

"Well?" Bao Cong said to Wu Ying, hopping on one foot as he pulled off his pants.

Wu Ying grunted, realizing that he was still not moving. It seemed his period of intense meditation and oxygen deprivation had slowed him down. He shook his shirt, mentally chiding himself for his failure. He was the leader here. He should be the one telling others what to do. He needed to get his head back into the game.

In short order, Wu Ying was changed like the others. Together, the group headed deeper into the city, dressed in the commoner clothing they'd picked up. The brown and gray, commonplace clothing would hopefully allow them
238

to hide in plain sight. Of course, they were somewhat dirty from their swim, a light aroma from the river water wafting from them. Thankfully, that kind of dirt and aroma might actually help them pull off this disguise.

They hurried into the streets, joining the flow of traffic. As they walked, Wu Ying eyed the throng of peasants, merchants, and the occasional farmer heading for taverns or workshops. The paved stones were worn smooth from the myriad footsteps, while above, the occasional lantern lit up signs and the road itself. Thankfully, for the most part, they were not drawing too much attention. Except...

Scooting close to the pair of noblemen, Wu Ying whispered, "Slouch a little, lower your heads."

To Wu Ying's surprise, both complied. He then moved over to Li Yao, taking her hand and pulling her close.

When she shot him a look, he lowered his voice. "You are too pretty to be alone at night. If they think we are together, you're more invisible."

Li Yao raised an eyebrow, then glanced at the hand Wu Ying held and flushed red. Public displays of affection like hand-holding were generally frowned upon. She released his fingers, making Wu Ying sad, but she didn't stray away from him.

"Don't you have to lead?" Li Yao said softly.

"Yin Xue knows the way," Wu Yang said. "I prefer to be with you anyway."

Li Yao blushed again and stared resolutely ahead. After some time, while the pair continued to watch the city, she spoke. "Thank you. But we should talk about this later. We should have our swords ready for now."

Wu Ying sighed. Li Yao was right. It was not as though they weren't in enemy territory. Not that the commoners around them looked any different from any other city he had visited. Same clothing, same style of hair. Maybe a bit of difference in the coloration of their clothing choices, in the accessories they chose. But even that was so slight it could be a matter of regional variation.

If not for the slightly haunted looks on the occasional faces—the woman who stood in the corner weeping, comforted by her children who looked helplessly alongside her—he would have never known that the city had been under siege. At least this close to the docks, few signs of the battle that had taken place showed. Even food was relatively plentiful, though only the streetside hawkers were present, farmers and fishermen having finished for the day.

The paved road they traveled was wide and straight, an offshoot from the main road that ran toward the center of the city and the magistrate's house. Once, it had been the Wen family residence, but that had been relinquished to the local magistrate. In turn, the family now owned a larger courtyard building next to their former domicile, one staffed and filled with branch member families and those in disgrace from the main family. Thankfully, the cultivators were headed farther north, toward the family tomb and the old city graveyard.

As Wu Ying looked around, he kept an eye out for soldiers and cultivators. But as expected, many of them had left with the army. It meant the city itself was understaffed, especially as some of the soldiers were helping with the reconstruction and clearance of burned buildings. Add to that the need to keep a higher number of soldiers on watch on the walls and those sweeping the countryside, and the city itself was sparse of soldiers on guard duties. The only real concern were the sub-prefectures[12] who would be on the lookout for civil disobedience, but they too would be hard-pressed by the fires.

Too bad the army had no intentions to loop around and attack the city when it was empty. Even if the soldiers were reduced in number, it was unlikely that any significant force could have sneaked by the patrols and done any

---

[12] Equivalent of modern day police or detectives. Sub-prefectures were appointed by prefectures who were appointed by the magistrate. They and imperial censors (who were generally restricted to chasing up corruption in the bureaucracy) were the policing forces of the government. They could be aided by city militia or army personnel, though the amount of help they received from the army varied during the time period.

240

additional damage anyway. And any sufficiently large force would still have to contend with the city wall and the city formations. If not for the relaxation of the formations to allow ships in, they would never have made their way in either.

Wu Ying spotted a young child playing with a small paper fan, the rotors on the fan catching the wind and spinning as she ran back and forth. Having turned to watch the girl, he kept on turning, using the child as an excuse to check on his friends. It was then he realized they were missing one of their members. He stopped, forcing Li Yao to halt as well.

"What's wrong?" she said.

"Tou He." Spinning around on the balls of his feet, knowing that he was making a little bit of a commotion, Wu Ying went on his tiptoes in search of his friend. How hard was it to miss a man in orange robes? Buddhist monks weren't that common.

"There!" Li Yao pointed at a cluster of individuals surrounding Tou He.

The ex-monk had stopped, head bent as he spoke to the group of women and children who had accosted him. Wu Ying stepped toward his friend, but as if he sensed their regard, the monk shook his head slightly while meeting Wu Ying's eyes. Wu Ying hesitated, only to feel an arm land on his own.

"Don't. Dragging him away will cause even more of a commotion," Li Yao said, leaning in to whisper to Wu Ying.

As he watched Tou He lay a hand on a bowed head, a hand held up to his chest in praying position, Wu Ying realized the crowd was asking for comfort. For prayers for lost ones. For... relief. And suddenly, he found himself reluctant to step forward. Even if he could drag his friend away, what right did he have to take away their comfort? It was not as if Tou He's blessings, his regard, was any less effective because he had left the monastery.

Wu Ying offered his friend a nod and turned aside. Tou He knew where they were going. Wu Ying could only hope that Tou He would be able to extract himself and join them in time. Spinning on his heels, Wu Ying hurried after the pair of nobles who had continued down the street, having ignored the commotion. Wu Ying cursed himself, remembering that he'd forgotten to alert them.

At least nothing bad had happened. This time.

***

The remaining members of the party reached the graveyard without further incident. To Wu Ying's surprise, he noticed that guards were patrolling the grounds, even in this time of chaos. As he considered why, Li Yao gestured at them.

"Peach wood," Li Yao pointed out.

Wu Ying's eyes widened in understanding. He had used those weapons before. In fact, he still had a peach wood jian in his inventory. He had purchased the weapon on the off chance he would have to deal with yin-infested monsters.

"Now what?" Bao Cong asked as the group loitered in front of the grass that marked the start of the graveyard proper.

Dotted throughout the graveyard, graves sprouted from the ground, many on the slight rise of the hill that had likely marked this location for burial. The graveyard itself had originally been located a distance away from the city, and even now it was at the edges of the city walls. Only a single neighborhood stood between it and the walls, offering a green—and morbid—oasis in the city. The constantly expanding city had driven the construction of the graveyard's enclosure within the walls of the city, offering protection to the living and dead in equal measure. As for the expanse of greenery, none would gainsay the Wen family their uninterrupted, picturesque views.

It was a pretty sight, and facing the water, Wu Ying could see how the slope of the hill gave the dead a view over the river and the city. At least for those main branch members and the few tertiary branch members who had been in favor before their demise. Those who hadn't been were placed on the opposite side or in dips in the ground where smaller, meaner stones marked their resting places. Still, large and expansive or small and humble, the graves were carefully tended. The tombstones at the top of the hill that they could spot from here were the larger, more ornate, semicircular stone edifices or monuments with large, single-story buildings. He even saw the occasional gilded mausoleum.

"Let me guess, it's the big one," Wu Ying said to Yin Xue. He didn't even wait for the noble to reply, before he frowned at the graveyard guards, thinking.

Before Wu Ying could say anything, Yin Xue walked up the hill, stepping foot onto the graveyard grounds. To Wu Ying's surprise, the moment Yin Xue did so, purple light formed around the perimeter of the grounds, alerting the groundspeople. It was only then, as he felt the shift in chi flows, that Wu Ying realized that there was a formation.

Of course there was a formation.

Yin Xue turned around, looking at the group, and gestured for them to catch up. Not having a better option, the three cultivators fell in step behind Yin Xue.

Wu Ying took two steps, making sure he was just behind Yin Xue before speaking softly. "What are you doing?"

"Getting us in. We don't have time for your hesitation," Yin Xue said. He continued to stroll toward the mausoleum at the top of the hill, ignoring the incoming groundskeepers. He walked with a hand behind his back, acting as if he owned the place.

Wu Ying, on the other hand, looked more nervous, casting glances between the approaching guards. He extended his senses, judging their cultivation levels, and was relieved to note that they were mostly in the mid-stages of Body

Cultivation. On further thought, that made sense. Anyone with any skill would not be relegated to such a task. And the newly risen ghosts or hopping-vampires would be a low enough threat that properly armed groundskeepers could deal with them.

"Honored sir, what brings you to the grounds?" the first groundskeeper to make it to them asked Yin Xue respectfully. He kept shooting glances at the fast fading color of the formation perimeter barrier.

"Why else would I be here?" Yin Xue glared at the groundskeeper, never stopping in his journey up the hill. He occasionally glanced at the tombstones, reading the names of ancestors, but he never broke stride.

"I'm sorry, honored sir. I've just never seen you before at the ceremonies." Again the groundskeeper tried to slow Yin Xue down with conversation. But again, Yin Xue barely shot him a glance as he continued his walk. "And these others are…?"

"My third wife," the Yin Xue said, turning his head and offering his hand to Li Yao. "Who I just took. I want to introduce her to my ancestors. The others are unimportant—a friend and my servant."

The groundskeeper paused, raking his eyes over Li Yao's form. She, in turn, tried to look as demure as possible. She must have succeeded, for the groundskeeper ducked his head and raised his hand to wave off the other approaching guards. Wu Ying let out a small breath of relief, grateful that they would not have to fight these men. They were, after all, doing their job. Not even a morally questionable one. Taking care of the graves, ensuring that no corpses bothered the living, providing food and tending to the ancestors was an honorable job.

"I shall escort you then, honored sir," the groundskeeper said. "I am groundskeeper Han."

"Good." Yin Xue nodded, letting his eyes roam over the graveyard. After a moment, he raised his voice again. "Your men and you have done a good job."

"Oh, not my men. I am only the third groundskeeper. The first died recently. The second is on break, taking the more dangerous shift at night." Still, groundskeeper Han preened at Yin Xue's praise. "It has been difficult, with the war. All that death, all that release of yin chi. It has made the ghosts more restless."

"I can see that." Yin Xue look pointedly at the churned earth around a broken tomb which had been only partly rebuilt.

The pair continued to talk. Forced by social custom to stay back, Wu Ying could only catch brief snatches of the conversation, but it seemed it had turned toward Yin Xue's latest conquest—the beautiful, petite, and demure bride. Li Yao was forced to walk alongside them, a step behind, her head bent as she played her part. Wu Ying could see how she disliked the pretense as her clenched fist grew whiter and tighter.

He only hoped that she could hold her temper until they got what they needed.

"Stop snarling," Bao Cong softly growled the words at Wu Ying.

Wu Ying blanked his face on command, scared that he would give away the game.

Luckily, the walk up the hill was not far, allowing them to arrive at the impressively large mausoleum in short order. The building was nearly the size of Wu Ying's old home in the village, the single-story structure having three wings to it. The double doors sat closed, the gold filigree on the doors failing to hide the glowing enchantments they contained.

Yin Xue turned his head to groundskeeper Han. "My father did not relate much about the opening procedures. He said it was obvious. But now that you are here, perhaps…"

Catching Yin Xue's hint, the groundskeeper smiled. He pointed at a small circular location in the door, stained a light muddy-brown, a marked difference compared to the ornate white marble of the surrounding stone. "You only need to place your hand there to activate the formation. A drop of blood on your hand will be sufficient."

Wu Ying winced, grateful that Yin Xue was with them then. They could probably brute force their way through the formation and the stone doors. Neither looked to be anything more than normal stone and a mortal-tier formation. But that would alert the guards and the groundskeepers.

Complying with the groundskeeper's suggestion, Yin Xue pricked his finger and laid his palm on the circular depression. To his surprise, the stone bubbled and swallowed his hand, leaving him trapped.

Without hesitating, Wu Ying drew his sword and placed it against the groundskeeper's neck. "What is this?"

"Nothing. Nothing! It is normal. If he was not of the blood, if you tried to trick the formation, he would lose his hand." The groundskeeper swallowed, once and then again as Wu Ying's jian pricked his neck, drawing a bead of blood. His eyes flicked sideways to Yin Xue, whose hand continued to be stuck, then to Bao Cong.

"His friends are here," Bao Cong said as he placed his hand on the hilt of his sword.

"Stop it. Stand down, boy. I will be fine," Yin Xue said. He glared at Wu Ying even as the formation that had once been hidden around the mausoleum sparked in a series of colors.

Realizing that he might have given away their disguise, Wu Ying carefully resheathed his sword. Bao Cong continued to leave his hand on his own weapon, while Li Yao, having stepped into the shade of the mausoleum and readied herself to attack, relaxed and stepped out. Luckily, the groundskeeper could not catch sight of the female cultivator as she put away her spear.

246

"No offense is taken, my lord," the groundskeeper replied, wiping surreptitiously at his neck. "It is good that your servant is so loyal."

Wu Ying hid the snarl that now threatened to erupt from his lips, doing as best as he could to project his role of selfless bodyguard rather than enemy cultivator. As abruptly as the light show had begun, the formation surrounding the mausoleum died, leaving the group to watch as Yin Xue extracted his whole hand.

"See? No problem," Yin Xue said.

Even as he finished speaking, the doors ground open, allowing them entry.

Without a word, the group trooped into the ornate interior. Around the marble flooring and stone columns of the mausoleum, two doors led away on either side. A single offering table dominated the main entrance. Directly in front of them and behind the table was the family tablet that detailed the names of the original founder of the family and his immediate family. After that, arrayed behind the main family tablet were smaller stone pieces detailing other ancestors. Most were drawn or carved on stone, detailed, curved ornamentation edging their sides.

"Very nice," Li Yao complimented, which made Yin Xue nod proudly.

Not that Yin Xue had had anything to do with it, Wu Ying thought, but he knew better than to say that.

"Which way?" Wu Ying asked, eyeing both doors even as the front doors ground closed behind them.

Once he was sure the doors were closed, Yin Xue said, "Neither."

Groundskeeper Han on the other side was not important enough to go in, leaving the group alone for the first time since they'd entered the graveyard.

"The entrance is right here." Yin Xue walked around the table and pressed his hand against the small ledge right beneath the second tablet on the right. Again, the light changed, shifting through the colors of the rainbow before the table and the floor it was on rolled aside, revealing a staircase down. "My father told me of this before we left."

Wu Ying's eyes narrowed. "And how was I meant to find the cultivation method if you hadn't come along? Or were injured somewhere along the way? Was I supposed to attack the main family house?"

Yin Xue gave Wu Ying a beatific smile, as if the entire problem was not his. Wu Ying let out a low growl.

"Focus. You can complain after we're out of the city," Bao Cong snapped.

"This isn't over," Wu Ying muttered, but he followed Yin Xue and Bao Cong, who had already ducked down the staircase.

"Later. We have to be alive to have a worry like that. Later," Li Yao consoled him.

Wu Ying grunted in agreement, following the group down the narrow staircase to a room that had lit itself with low-grade demon stones upon their entry. The room was very much smaller, and less ornate, than the one above. However, as Yin Xue walked forward, he had to stop as a shimmering wall appeared before him. Words appeared before their eyes, and Yin Xue read them out loud, since his body blocked some of the calligraphy from those behind.

Only those who are worthy may learn my true cultivation method.
Those who fail shall suffer for their arrogance.
Choose wisely.

Yin Xue's lip curled up when he read the line. He turned sideways, already anticipating Wu Ying's objection. "The test may only be taken by those of the blood."

"And how long is this test going to take?"

"As long as it takes."

Having said his piece, Yin Xue strode forward into the shimmering wall of light and froze in it. Wu Ying gritted his teeth at Yin Xue's arrogance and eyed the formation flags. Perhaps he could break through them?

"Don't bother. You won't be able to do it," Bao Cong told Wu Ying.

"I didn't know you were a formation master," Wu Ying sniped at the blacksmith.

"I'm not. But I can recognize the materials used to make the formation," Bao Cong said as he pointed out the materials to Wu Ying.

White and green jade, peerless levels of quality. Spirit stones from high-tier beasts powered the entire thing, set behind the curtain of power. Other, rarer materials Wu Ying could not recognize at a glance but could feel the chi they emanated. Even if his training was in living things, he could at least recognize the quality.

"So we just wait for him?" Wu Ying said.

"It seems so." Li Yao looked around the small room, eyeing the other tablets arrayed at the other cardinal points. However, they were all protected by formations. Rather than risk being caught, she turned and headed up the stairs.

"Where you going?" Wu Ying asked.

"To see what else we missed."

Bao Cong gave Wu Ying a shrug, shooting a glance at the frozen form of Yin Xue before he trooped off after Li Yao. Given no choice by the bare and protected room, Wu Ying also followed. Who knew? Maybe there was something to be had from the other chambers.

***

There wasn't. The other rooms were annex branches of the main mausoleum, containing ancestral tablets and tables for prayer. Not knowing the names involved, they could not ascertain what the relationships had been, but it was fun to speculate, to make up stories about reasons for the fall and relegation to the wings of each branch family. In truth, at least for Wu Ying, it was all to distract themselves from the worm of worry that grew as more and more time passed.

"Familial relations with pigs," Bao Cong said.

"Ewww. Also, what is with you men and pigs?" Li Yao tried to punch Bao Cong in the arm.

The blacksmith easily evaded the strike while chuckling. "Your turn," Bao Cong called to Wu Ying.

"Leaving the sluice gate open," Wu Ying replied, looking at the main entrance again. The fifth time in just as many minutes.

"I don't think he's getting how this game works," Bao Cong said to Li Yao.

Rather than answer, she shot a worried look at Wu Ying.

Realizing he was making the group concerned, he turned to them and offered them a half–hearted smile. "Sorry. Just…"

"I know. But worrying won't change anything," said Li Yao as she placed her hand on his arm.

"Maybe I should go down and check?" Wu Ying said.

"For the tenth time?" Bao Cong said. "It will take as long as it takes."

Wu Ying could only shrug, shooting another worried glance at the main door that had stayed close all this time. He had no idea what the groundskeepers were doing, what they were thinking. How long did it take to introduce one's new wife to the ancestors? He'd never done it, and his father obviously had never needed to while Wu Ying had been alive. He could only worry.

As he opened his mouth to speak again, to his surprise, a rustle of wind rose from the chamber below. The group hurried over to the main chamber, excited over the change. Even as they did so, a low chime rang out, one that grew louder and louder as they moved.

"You think they can—" Wu Ying said.

"Hear that? Definitely," Bao Cong said.

"Both of you, watch the doors," Wu Ying ordered, hesitation gone.

It seemed their ability to hide what they were doing had ended. It was time to get serious. Wu Ying hurried down the stairs only to see that the formation that once blocked the way had powered down. Not all the way, for he felt how the chi shifted in front of him. But enough that Yin Xue could continue moving, could continue on his way to touch the tablet.

"Yin Xue! What is going on?" Wu Ying shouted.

"Just getting the technique. One moment," Yin Xue said. His hands shifted over the tablet and pulled on it. Surprisingly, his hand did not rip the tablet out of the wall but instead extracted a smaller version of the tablet into his hand. He repeated the action twice more, acquiring the remaining parts of the cultivation manual before he plucked a small jade token from the corner of the shelf. He frowned at the token for a second before he slipped it away and hurried out of the formation.

Yin Xue handed the tablets to Wu Ying, allowing the other cultivator to put them in his storage ring. That action surprised Wu Ying, considering the manual was something Yin Xue had earned. And more so, it was his family technique.

"You're not keeping it?" Wu Ying said.

"No need. I'll get a copy later," Yin Xue replied. "This is just to make sure you have it and that I've done my part in this."

Wu Ying regarded the nobleman and offered a tentative smile. "Thank you. For this. For everything."

"I didn't do it for you. I'm ending my karmic debt." Yin Xue hurried up the staircase, calling down to Wu Ying as he did so. "Are you coming?"

Wu Ying hesitated then shook his head. Karma was weird, and no one—no one not a Buddha themselves—could say what it had in place for them in the future. But if this meant Yin Xue was happy, Wu Ying would not gainsay him.

Upstairs, Wu Ying scrambled through the slowly closing floor, feeling the edge of his shoes nearly get caught. He grunted, shaking his head. For the supposed leader of this group, he seemed to be constantly stuck hurrying up after all his people.

Maybe that said something about him. And his leadership skills.

And maybe it just said something about his companions. Probably the latter.

Chapter 22

"We have a plan?" Bao Cong called as they eyed the still-closed entrance door.

"How do we plan for what we don't know to expect?" Li Yao retorted. "We just have to deal with it when the doors open."

Yin Xue grimaced, opening his mouth to object, but Wu Ying cut them all off. "We know that they are likely waiting for us. To ask questions, at the very least. Yin Xue, try to bluff them. If that fails, or if they try to attack or detain us, we fight. We make a run for the walls. If we have to, we jump."

The group nodded at the quick, curt orders. For their differences, they'd spent a long enough time together that these orders made sense. Except for…

"Tou He?" Li Yao asked.

Wu Ying hesitated, thinking of the ex–monk's predicament, the way he had waved them on. "Probably safer than us right now. He'll meet up with us if he can. We just have to trust in him."

Saying that hurt, but in his own way, Tou He was probably the most suitable individual to travel alone. For one thing, his disguise was not really a disguise. So long as no one stuck any BBQ demon beast sticks before him, he should be fine.

As if he was tired of listening to them talk, Yin Xue strode forward and slapped his hands on the doors. Unlike before, when Wu Ying and the others had tentatively tested it and the door had refused to budge, the doors swung open as if they weighed nothing at all. Another security feature.

What greeted them was what Wu Ying had feared. Seven groundskeepers, all of them holding their weapons, stared at the team. But worse of all, there were four cultivators, two of them dressed in the robes of the Six Jade Gates sect, the other two in colorful, nobleman's silks. They all stood before groundskeeper Han, glaring at Yin Xue as he walked out.

"Which branch member are you? How dare you defy the family's hierarchy? Stealing the cultivation manual when you do not deserve it! We'll kill you, your parents, and all your uncles and brothers for this affront. We will take your sisters and your female relatives and make them our slaves," the leading cultivator, dressed in the robes of the Six Jade Gates sect, shouted at Yin Xue. "Now bow down and kowtow[13] for forgiveness. Or else we will make sure to torture them all before we kill them."

Yin Xue took another step forward, eyebrows creasing as he eyed the group. When he didn't drop to his knees, the cultivators drew their weapons. The subtle signal Yin Xue sent made sure that the team knew not to take action just yet. He wanted them to wait.

Even so, Wu Ying could see that Bao Cong had drawn his bow, even though it was held low to the ground and hidden behind his body.

"My family?" Yin Xue ducked his head then suddenly drew his weapon, sending a shot of sword intent at the cultivators. It was not a powerful attack, spread out in a wide arc as it was, and it caught none of the main cultivators from the Wen family by surprise. But to Wu Ying's surprise, two of the groundskeepers were injured by the surprise attack. "It's the third branch."

Unlike the showboating Yin Xue, the others did not stop to speak. Not when they attacked. Wu Ying drew and struck out, pulling energy from the Brilliant Woo Petal Bracer into his sword strike. Except he kept his attack much tighter, focused on the Wen family member on the far left. Li Yao conjured her spear, sending her chi into the weapon as she thrust forward. The suddenly elongated weapon of conjured ice—formed from around its tip and body—caught her opponent by surprise, shattering against his chi aura and leaving him bloody as he fell back. Bao Cong, rather than targeting the cultivators from the Wen family, shot his arrows at the groundskeepers.

"Don't stop," Wu Ying growled, using quick steps to cover the ground between him and his opponents.

---

[13] Traditional form of submission where the individual kneels and places their head on the ground in supplication. Often, this can be seen when worshipping ancestors and individuals of higher rank, with multiple bows indicating greater significance in rank.

The Wind Steps that he used let him cross the ground at almost a full run, while his sword sent weak attacks of sword intent as he expended his stored chi. It was nowhere as strong as an Energy Stage cultivator's attacks, especially since he was moving so fast, but that wasn't the point. It was meant to keep their opponents on the back foot.

The rush of attacks put the Wen family cultivators on the defensive for a moment, but they weathered the onslaught with ease, falling back but keeping their formation, allowing Wu Ying's team to emerge from the mausoleum. Wu Ying and Yin Xue managed to stay at the forefront of the attack, protected and aided by Li Yao's longer weapon.

As Wu Ying was about to take a step farther, Yin Xue called out a warning. "Stop. Illusionary formation."

When the entire group hesitated, Yin Xue twisted his left hand and thrust forward, talismans appearing and shooting through the space before them, entering the formation itself. The yellow paper talismans seemed to bend as they flew, twisted by the formation, before exploding into pink flames. The flames warped and twisted in space, contained within the formation and marking the outlines of the trap that had been set.

Not to be outdone, Li Yao bounded off, swinging her weapon at one of the unhurt groundskeepers. She cut through his defense, breaking his sword and leaving his torso torn open, ice forming around the edges of his wound and fast expanding across his body.

"This way," she exclaimed, pointing with her spear.

The group rushed after her, taking the momentary lull in battle and the distraction of the failed formation to escape. As they ran, Bao Cong retreated backward, firing his arrows. Each arrow shimmered and replicated itself, making it difficult for the cultivators who had escaped the flames to chase them.

"I said bluff!!" Wu Ying grumbled as they ran.

As they ducked among the graves, alarm bells rang, alerting not just the family members of the Wen household, but the entire city.

Yin Xue muttered as they ran, "Already forgetting who dug the well[14]."

***

Ducking around a carved tombstone, Wu Ying slapped a talisman on the back of the stone. It was the last defensive talisman in the set, and as he glanced around, he saw nods from the remainder of the team. He'd distributed the talismans as they'd run, then the group had split, throwing attacks to slow down their pursuers. Placement confirmed, Wu Ying whispered the activation word and sent a surge of chi into his talisman to activate the formation. It was the same one he had bought to bring the village home safely, but storing seed for spring did no good if you starved in the winter.

As he turned to run, Wu Ying caught the flicker of power that wrapped around the tombstones and the talismans. A wall of power enclosed the area, blocking off the direct route to the group even as they ran. It was not a big diversion, barely fifty feet in length, but it would force the cultivators to choose to destroy the formation or run around it. And destroying the formation would do the one thing they had avoided thus far—destroy the gravestones that anchored the formation.

It was one reason the group had managed to make it so far. The other reason was that the cultivators left behind were of the lowest cultivation level. Most of them were, at best, low Energy Storage stage, with the vast majority in the middle Body Refinement stage.

Wu Ying hopped over the next tombstone, continuing his headlong sprint down the hill as his friends regrouped around him. He kept casting glances

---

[14] Pulled from the proverb about gratitude—"When drinking water, don't forget who dug the well."

backward, mentally reviewing the map he had created of the city. He shouted as he ran, husbanding his breath as best he could.

"We've got three blocks of residential houses before we reach the walls," Wu Ying said. "We should make sure to stay close and don't split up. If you do get lost, we meet at the horses. Get over the walls as far as you can."

Wu Ying felt the lurch in the thread that connected him and the talismans, informing him that their pursuers had managed to break through. He grimaced, casting a glance back, and noticed that they'd managed to add another hundred yards to their lead. Rather than just smash through as he'd expected, their pursuers had somehow managed to disrupt the formation without destroying the tombstones. It was quite possible they had an actual formation master among them, able to discern the issues with the hastily constructed talisman wall. In either case, Wu Ying's group had gained enough distance to put them at the edge of the graveyard. Except...

The ward that had triggered when Yin Xue had first walked onto the graveyard came to life once more. It glowed a deep red, a shimmering wall that enclosed the entire hilltop and surroundings. If they could fly, they'd probably be able to reach the top of the forty-foot formation wall, but even if they'd had good qinggong skills, this was no rough wall to run up. This was pure energy, meaning they'd have to jump directly up to reach the top. Only someone at the Core Cultivation level or maybe the late Energy Storage stage would be able to do that.

"Hun dan!" Li Yao swore as she spotted the impediment. She held her spear down at her side, infusing the spearhead with her chi as she got ready to pierce the formation.

"Bao Cong, keep them busy," Wu Ying ordered, falling in line beside Li Yao. He held his sword down near his hip, sword pointed at the formation as he readied himself. "Yin Xue and I will hit the formation before Li Yao. We'll weaken the formation first. On my mark."

Yin Xue grunted, raising his sword to his forehead and placing a pair of fingers on the edge of the sword. In silence, the pair focused, drawing their power into their weapons before, at Wu Ying's signal, letting out a shout in unison. The bolts of chi and sword intent flew forward as Wu Ying's count bottomed out, striking the rippling wall of the formation and creating a burst of rainbow light. The explosion of energy rippled, making the wall vibrate, but it did not give way.

Li Yao was right behind them. Even as they struck, she planted her feet into the ground as she formed a single line with her weapon, putting all her intent, all her energy into a single focused point. The blade flew between the rapidly moving forms of the pair, so close that Wu Ying felt a deep chill along his back and side as the ice-coated weapon flew by him. The spearhead struck the formation, and for second, it seemed as if the wall would hold. But with a screaming screech, the tip pierced through.

It was enough.

Most formations could fail when too much energy was sent into them. The larger the formation, the weaker they were, as they had to spread their energy across the entire area. Overburdened, the formation was unable to keep its integrity, and lines of energy, freed from their constrained locations by the formation, rippled outward. Like the crumpling of the thinnest metal, the formation released a screeching wail that set hairs on end and teeth on edge. With a burst of light and energy, the formation shattered. Smaller displays of rainbow light and noise erupted from concentrated locations around the graveyard, the anchor points for the formation.

"I think we broke something," Wu Ying said with a slight grin.

With a wave, he directed everyone to run again, calling out to Bao Cong as well. As Wu Ying looked back, he noticed that the area behind them was filled with arrows, their assailants hiding behind tombstones. All but one, his body skewered with a trio of arrows.

For all that, cowering or not, their assailants kept creeping forward, cutting down the distance between them. Once he knew Bao Cong was ready to leave, Wu Ying took off as well. Spotting Yin Xue ducking into an alley, he headed in that direction, only to have his attention drawn to the clatter of footsteps as a group of guards ran out from another street corner. They hesitated for moments, pointing their spears at the cultivators before charging.

"*Gan*[15]! More of them."

***

Yin Xue cut his way through his opponent, his sword catching the man high in the throat and carrying body and head backward as Yin Xue rushed down the narrow alleyway that their opponents blocked. Another guard, hidden behind his shield, was blown back by Li Yao's strike with the butt of her spear, crashing into his friends and knocking them all to the ground. Wu Ying followed her rushing figure, swinging his sword as he ran past the group of fallen enemies, cutting wrists, necks, and ankle tendons to cripple and kill them. Bao Cong, in the back, lurched over their fallen opponents, ducking to snatch up a crossbow that had fallen. He spun, triggered his chi, and released the bolt. The metal within the crossbow head replicated and filled the air behind them with sharp needles of energy.

Their pursuers ducked and covered behind shields. Some of them were too slow to hide, falling to the attack. The attack cost Bao Cong though, as the blacksmith staggered, his face pale as he drew upon his already overdrawn dantian. Wu Ying grabbed the back of Bao Cong's robes, dragging him away from the recovering soldiers, not allowing him to fall.

---

[15] Mandarin equivalent of the f-word.

As Bao Cong let the crossbow drop from his hands, Wu Ying snapped, "Rest. We will need you at the walls."

"But the pursuers…"

"I'll deal with them. Just run!" Wu Ying commanded.

As they ran across the busy street they'd exited into, Wu Ying grabbed at a nearby empty stall, pulling the wooden contraption to the ground behind them. It would offer little impediment to strong cultivators, but they were mostly being chased by the militia and a few soldiers from the army. One advantage of the large number of people chasing them and the narrow alleys they kept ducking into—their pursuers were getting in each other's way.

The three blocks they had to cross turned into seven as they ducked in and out of alleys, backtracking at times rather than take on full platoons. Wu Ying swore more than once, but being at the back of the group, he could only trust that Yin Xue and Li Yao knew what they were doing.

As Wu Ying ran, he heard a shout, one that reached all the way across the blocks to his ears. At the voiceless shout, a chill of premonition ran through him. He turned, never stopping as he pulled Bao Cong along. On one end of the street, strolling forward, his giant sword over his arm, the armored form of the cultivator who had held the wall approached. Wu Ying's eyes grew wide as the man lowered his hand and sword, pointing it straight at Wu Ying.

When he noticed that Wu Ying was looking, he spoke, his voice so loud that it rattled the windows and made the stones on the ground tremble. "You can run. But we'll find you, you little rat."

The loud, almost joyful and insane, voice rang through the streets, chasing Wu Ying and Bao Cong as they ducked into the next alleyway. They pushed through only to find that this one ended not in another street but in a dead-end.

Rather than stop, Li Yao focused her chi in the tip of the spear again and lunged forward. Her attack created a shell of ice around her, one that protected her body as she smashed into the wall and shattered it into pieces. Yin Xue followed her, bouncing past her still form as she recovered to keep running. Another crash, this time of a door being thrust open, echoed toward Wu Ying and Bao Cong. They entered the living room of a peasant house, the front door swinging on one broken hinge as Yin Xue clashed with unseen foes in the street ahead. Wu Ying noted a pair of mortals as he twisted around, intent on throwing another blade strike down the alleyway.

"Get out!" Wu Ying shouted at the civilians, the little girl and her brother screaming. A loud, distressing creak originated from above his head, making Wu Ying glance at the wobbling ceiling. "Now."

Then he had no more time. The first of the guards came rushing in, thrusting with his polearm. Wu Ying blocked, gripped the edge of the weapon behind its sharp knife-head, and pulled, punching the guard of his jian into the man's face. The attack laid out his opponent on the ground, blocking the entrance. The next few moments were a hectic battle as Wu Ying blocked and cut, doing his best to stall the attackers in the entranceway. All the while, dust from the compromised ceiling fell around him.

For all his skill, eventually Wu Ying fell back. One too many spears were shoved at him, forcing Wu Ying to back off. As he did so, he flicked his gaze at the corner where the children had been. Once he noted their absence, he struck upward. He only needed to use a little bit of his chi, focused through his sword intent. Lines of sharp power scored against the ceiling, weakening already compromised joints. His enemies spotted his intentions only seconds before the roof gave way.

Throwing himself backward, Wu Ying tapped the ground with his feet as he floated out the doorway even as the ceiling fell, blocking the entrance Li Yao had created. As the dust and smoke from the collapsed building exploded around him, cloaking his body in the remnants of the home, Wu Ying could only hope that the kids really were out of the house. He had no time to check.

He turned and ran, intent on catching up with his friends before he spotted the city wall. Finally.

There was about thirty feet of clear ground between him and the wall, an area that was fast filling with soldiers. As if they had known where the Green Waters Sect members had planned to go, the army of Wei had sent their men to line the wall. Wu Ying's friends had stopped, resting for a second in an impromptu stand-off. Wu Ying hurried to them, and once they noted his presence, Li Yao offered him a nod.

Together, the group surged forward another ten feet, smashing into the wall of soldiers. They managed to gain a few feet, even against the wall of fighters, before they stalled. The cultivators pushed, inching closer to the staircase that led up the wall. But then the pressure between the attackers stymied their advance, forcing them to hold their ground as they fought desperately to move ahead. Spears lashed out from behind walls of shields, daos cut down and sideways at the cultivators as they fought.

"We can't stay here," Wu Ying snarled, catching another blade high on his own and responding.

His attack drew a line across his opponent's forehead, splashing blood down on his eyes and blinding him. His opponent staggered back, yanked aside and replaced by another, creating a brief moment of respite.

"We're trying!" Li Yao shouted, even as she parried aside three spears with her own.

Yin Xue was much more silent, focused on his own battle. To Wu Ying's surprise, the cultivator had both his jian and a smaller blade, blocking attacks with one blade and striking with the other. It wasn't a style Wu Ying had ever noticed Yin Xue using before, but it seemed highly effective in this crowded situation.

A scream from beside Wu Ying drew his attention, and he saw Bao Cong stagger back, his shoulder pierced by a spear. The cultivator swung his dao, breaking the spear shaft before catching a second that sought his stomach. Even as Bao Cong released a burst of chi that sent backward the soldiers pressing him as the metal in their armor reacted, he paled further. Of them all, the blacksmith had the least amount of skill in melee combat and it was showing.

Once again, Wu Ying cast around in his mind for an option. He had used all the charges in his bracer already—the first time to deal with the cultivators when they came out, the second one to break the formation. None of his other attacks were strong enough to open the way. Li Yao, their strongest fighter, was tired and already taking on one side of their shrinking formation. She'd blown past any blockade that had blocked their way with the liberal use of chi, but strong as she was, all that had an effect. Bao Cong was tired and injured. Only Yin Xue had any real energy left. But he too was fighting multiple opponents. It was unlikely he had anything else to add.

As Wu Ying made up his mind to attempt the breakout himself, hoping to plow all his energy into a Dragon's Breath attack, a familiar armored form appeared in the corner of his vision. A single shout from the cultivator and their opponents retreated, leaving the team surrounded but for the wounded and the corpses that lay strewn around their feet.

"Nowhere to run, little bird," the armored figure said. "I told you so. But be glad, for you will fall before Mo Hei."

"Did he just say that?" Yin Xue said derisively as Mo Hei walked toward them. "Is his ego so big that he needs to announce his name before trying to kill us?"

"I'm more worried about the part where he's trying to kill us than his oratory skills," Bao Cong said. "Maybe you can focus on how we are getting out?"

They had no time to even swear or offer a smart-aleck reply as Mo Hei and the two guards around him approached. If it was only those, Wu Ying could see them winning. But there were also the soldiers surrounding them. And even if their enemies were not particularly gifted cultivators, Wu Ying's group wasn't in their best states. Quantity had a quality of its own, and their enemies had quite the quantity.

"When they close in on us, I'll break us clear," Wu Ying said.

The way Mo Hei and the guards were coming, the ring around them would have to part. In that small gap, Wu Ying hoped he could break through the enclosure, freeing them to run. It would be dangerous, and Wu Ying knew he'd have to stay behind, but it might be the only choice.

"Idiot," Yin Xue snapped, shaking his head. He reached sideways and flicked his hand upward, a glowing jade seal appearing. It was the same one Wu Ying had noticed him take from the tomb. There hadn't been time to discuss what it was, and Wu Ying had doubted Yin Xue would talk of it. Even as he watched, the jade seal doubled in size and doubled again, increasing in form as it floated above the group. "Get in close. The family protective seal isn't something I can control very well."

Even as Yin Xue finished speaking, jade chains shot out from the seal, striking the ground in explosions of dust and stone. Any soldier in the way of the chains was struck and thrown aside, taking others with them. They lay bleeding on the ground, bones crushed, limbs shattered. Even as the soldiers recovered, the jade seal spun, twisting and following the motions of Yin Xue's hands, its chains striking the unlucky standing soldiers.

"What the hells, you couldn't do that earlier?" Bao Cong complained as he finished wrapping up the new injury on his leg, struggling to do so as blood dripped down his arm.

A flick of Yin Xue's hand sent the seal spinning directly toward the wall. The group ran under cover of the spinning chains, protected from those who attempted to close in on them. Mo Hei snarled, breaking into a run and tossing aside his own men as he tried to close the distance.

"We have to hurry. The seal will not last long." Each word was labored, and Wu Ying sensed Yin Xue's chi levels dropping as he manipulated the seal.

Even as they ran, their opponents continued to harass them. Archers at the top of the wall opened fire, no longer worried about hitting their own as commanded by their unit leaders.

The team managed to make it another twenty yards before they slowed again. The pressure from the massed soldiers who had nowhere to go, even under the threat of the spinning chains, meant that Yin Xue had to direct the chains to strike multiple times. Under cover of their wooden shields, soldiers were thrown from side to side before their shields broke, leaving their owners to take the strike on their body. Yet each moment, the jade seal slowed, forcing the group to deal with attackers who crowded around the edges and behind them.

Wu Ying let himself fall back once more, doing his best to keep them back and going so far as to withdraw a second sword to help him block the attacks. He was entirely grateful for the undershirt armor that Elder Lee had made him purchase. If not, he would have already taken at least a couple of serious injuries as he scrambled to shield Bao Cong and the others. As it was, his legs and arms were bleeding freely, from strikes that he had managed to edge away from vitals but not block entirely.

A roar brought Wu Ying's attention to the side as a giant sword swung at him. He crossed his blades in quick order, angling them so that the attack would slide down and hit the guards. Mo Hei's swing smashed into the crossed blades, throwing Wu Ying backward as the momentum of the attack refused to end. He was flung backward, taking a glancing blow from Yin Xue's jade seal chains. A glancing blow from a raised sword dug into the edge of Wu Ying's armor, making him gasp in further pain. Luckily, the soldiers also cushioned his flight, and together, they were sent sprawling and rolling.

Wu Ying stood, shaking his head, ribs aching from where his guard had dug into his chest. The mail might have saved him from cuts, but it did nothing for impact. As he idly cut downward with one sword to deal with another soldier struggling to get up, Wu Ying was shocked to see that his lead weapon had a deep chip in it. Mo Hei's single attack had damaged the sword. Even as Wu Ying marveled, he realized that the jade seal had stopped spinning, its chains retracted.

Another shout as Mo Hei rushed forward, sweeping his weapon down in an overhead cut. Having learned his lesson, Wu Ying ducked to the side and sent a quick stab at his opponent's wrist, at the gap where bracer and gauntlets met. Unfortunately, aiming at a target so small on a moving target was difficult at best.

Impossible in a situation like this.

His blade glanced off Mo Hei's armor, doing no damage before Wu Ying was forced to dance aside and cut with his other weapon at a threatening soldier. Forced to both guard his back and fight the armored cultivator, Wu Ying had no time to help his friends, even as he noted how Mo Hei's team had joined the fight as well, engaging Li Yao and Bao Cong.

Already, Bao Cong was injured again, falling back and waving his hands before him. As Bao Cong's opponent surged forward, he was caught in the sudden spray of tiny metal dust that Bao Cong had dispersed with his chi, blinding his opponent and making them jerk back in surprise. It bought Bao Cong a second to staunch the bleeding in his shoulder.

Wu Ying needed to disengage from his opponent, but he couldn't do so. The larger, stronger cultivator might not be as skilled, but he was certainly stronger and faster than Wu Ying. The extra reach of Mo Hei's long weapon meant Wu Ying could only attack his arms at best, his fingers at other times. Unfortunately, knowing those were likely targets, his opponent had armored his hands and fingers well, leaving Wu Ying's attacks to skitter off in a screech of metal and a shower of sparks.

Rumbling arose from beneath Wu Ying's feet. He didn't know where it was coming from, but he didn't have time to look—until a shout drew his attention. After he had jumped over the latest attack, rolling to come up near a soldier and sinking his blade into the man's groin, Wu Ying looked up. He blinked, spotting a familiar face.

It was Tou He. Riding an ox and leading a small herd behind him. Wu Ying's eyes widened in surprise. Just before the lead ox struck the entangled group of fighters, Tou He jumped off, pulling his staff from his storage ring and swinging it down. Wu Ying's opponent staggered, his helmet dented under the force of the blow before his entire body was caught and thrown as an ox struck him with its shoulder.

All around, the herd slammed into the guards and cultivators. Li Yao jumped up, lightly running across the back of an ox, and struck with her spear at her opponent who had done much the same. It was a marvel of agility and control, as neither party stopped fighting even amidst the rushing animals. As the oxen parted further, Wu Ying ducked and used the bodies of the soldiers as shelter. Even in their fury-driven rush, the herd had no desire to rush through the packed group and instead struck at the edges, at those loitering in the gap between alleyway and wall.

That meant that Wu Ying and the others had a bit of breathing space. Enough so, Wu Ying launched a weakened Dragon's Breath attack at Bao Cong's opponent, who had managed to stagger back into the fight. Between the distraction of his own fight, the oxen, and the over-the-top battle between Li Yao and her opponent, he never saw Wu Ying's attack that crippled his foot. Immediately, Bao Cong stepped back, disengaging. Wu Ying, seeing that Tou He had the rest of the fight in hand, grabbed Bao Cong's arm and dragged him toward the stairs, which were now finally within grasp.

Already, Yin Xue had taken to the stairs, fighting his way up. Unfortunately, he was being hampered by the arrows of the archers above. Thankfully, even the extortions of their unit leader did not make them fire callously, for the group was too packed together to make for easy targets.

"Hurry up," Wu Ying ordered Yin Xue.

Only silence greeted his exhortation. Yin Xue was already fighting, beating aside spears and stabbing at the guards above him. Every few seconds, he ascended another step, ignoring the occasional missed attack or too close arrow.

Wu Ying glanced at Bao Cong, who offered him a nod. He'd already set aside his dao, pulling his bow from storage and fitting an arrow to the string. Propped up against the wall, Bao Cong picked off the guards that continued to harass Tou He and Li Yao.

Wu Ying sprinted up the stairs to join Yin Xue. Just before he reached Yin Xue, he twisted and jumped toward the wall, his feet pushing against the stone edges, and climbed upward with the momentum he had gained. One hand, still clutching a sword, reached upward, fingers just brushing the top of the parapet. Enough to haul him into the sky. As Wu Ying jumped, ascending the wall, he twisted around, swords flicking out on either side.

The Dragon fishes in the Lake.

His first strike took a throat, the second a shoulder. The archers, who had been trying to target his friends, staggered away. But Wu Ying was not done. Upon landing, he twisted on one hand, launching himself at the final archer. A hasty block with his bow broke the weapon but sent Wu Ying's sword aside. As Wu Ying landed on his feet, he twisted and executed Falling rocks in a Rainstorm as he borrowed the momentum of his attacks. The kick sent the archer off the wall, out into the open to crash down amidst his friends and enemies.

"Li Yao! Tou He!" Wu Ying screamed, alerting his friends.

They turned briefly and retreated, trying to reach the stairs. Bao Cong limped up the cleared staircase as Yin Xue reached the top, facing the opposite direction Wu Ying faced. He no longer had time to watch for his friends, for Wu Ying had to deal with the soldiers on the wall. Still, Tou He and Li Yao were close enough to ascend the staircase, blocking off their enemies below.

They'd reached the wall.

Now they'd just have to disengage.

Chapter 23

A quick disengage, a tip cut to draw across his opponent's neck just below the straps of his helmet. It opened a shallow wound, barely an inch deep, but it was more than enough. The veins and arteries that ran across the body were not deep in certain locations, locations that Wu Ying had long learned. The small motion was all it took to end a life and free Wu Ying to regard his friends.

Below, Tou He held the stairs, fighting Mo Hei to a standstill. Staff and sword clashed again and again, neither party gaining an advantage. Tou He was more skilled, able to deflect the weapon and forcing it to crash against the stone with every other attack. But his occasional retaliatory attacks did little against Mo Hei's armored form. Slowly, so slowly, Tou He was being injured, his arms bleeding from missed blocks.

Behind him, Li Yao stabbed her spear into the mass of attackers below, batting aside any cultivator who tried to ascend the staircase in an unconventional manner. Even as Wu Ying watched, another cultivator took a running jump, bouncing off one of his friend's shoulders and leaping to the stairs. Li Yao caught his sword with her spear, edging the attack away before spinning in place and kicking him back into the air.

Bao Cong stood at the top of the stairs, taking his time and firing arrows into the throng. He focused on the few archers, and from the hesitant ways the soldiers moved to pick up fallen archery implements, it was clear that he was more than effective. Even so, his movements had slowed significantly, the wounds he'd acquired slowing him down.

As for Yin Xue, he, like Wu Ying, was free and clear of any dangers as they'd managed to deal with the soldiers on the wall. After moment of debate, Wu Ying handed Yin Xue a bundle of formation flags.

"Get it set up. Outside," Wu Ying ordered Yin Xue, gesturing out of the city.

Wu Ying drew a deep breath, removing something from his storage ring as he turned away from Yin Xue. He could only hope that the man followed his orders, for Wu Ying needed to take care of the other cultivators. He quickly approached Bao Cong.

"Shoot this when it is above the others," Wu Ying said. When Bao Cong nodded, Wu Ying turned to face the stairs. "Li Yao! We'll need your ice."

Not daring to wait any longer, Wu Ying twisted and threw the object. The Flask of Never-Ending Water flew over the group crowded along the stairs, where it was intercepted by a well-placed arrow. The formations, the enchantments in the flask broke, pierced as it was by the arrow. Water contained within the storage space exploded out from the flask, flooding those below.

Li Yao released the last of her chi into the surroundings, freezing the air, crystallizing the water, and creating a sheet of slick ice that covered stairs, armored bodies, and weapons. To aid her, Tou He spun his staff, pulling in the released heat as he churned his own chi. His opponent, drenched in water, froze as he tried to take another step forward. He crashed to the ground as tight joints and slippery stairs took their toll. A single strike by Tou He to the back of Mo Hei's helmet deepened a dent and made the large form twitch before it stilled.

"Run!" Wu Ying ordered the group.

Bao Cong made a face, pulled a pill from his storage ring, and swallowed it, his face flushing with color. Making his bow disappear, the cultivator took a running start and jumped off the wall, following the same path as Yin Xue— who'd left already at Wu Ying's earlier command. In short order, Li Yao and Tou He arrived from below, but to their surprise, Wu Ying was not running. He was instead slapping even more talismans on the ground, all across the wall and in front to the stairs.

When Wu Ying saw them hesitate, he snapped at them, "Move. I've got this."

Thankfully, his friends didn't hesitate any longer and jumped off the edge of the wall. Wu Ying slapped one last talisman onto the ground, extracted a piece of rope from his storage ring, and tossed it over a crenellation on the wall before he jumped, gripping the rope as he let it play out in his hands. The rough rope tore at his hands as he fell, and he was once again thankful that he had gained numerous calluses from his swordplay. Between that and his Body Cultivation, he would not rip up his palms as he descended at speed. Unlike his friends—who had landed and were running for the forests or ducking into the hiding places and trenches the army had created—he could not withstand a full drop. Not without some injury, as he'd learned.

Wu Ying finally dropped onto the ground, and not a moment too soon as screams resounded from above. Wu Ying felt his lips pull apart in a grin, grateful that Bai Hu had been willing to sell him the talismans. The talismans weren't all that destructive, just nerve-racking; more likely to make an individual fall on their face than to kill them. But they bought time, and that was all that mattered.

Once more, Wu Ying ran as fast as he could. But in the corner of his eyes, he saw soldiers on horses exiting the nearest gate, rushing to intercept them. He could only hope that Yin Xue had taken his orders and placed the formation.

***

"Slowly. Slowly," Wu Ying chanted to his friends softly.

The group was crawling forward at a snail's pace, each of them holding onto one of the formation flags as their enemies swirled around them. Deep in a trench that had been dug, created so that the army could narrow the distance, the group moved.

Finding Yin Xue had been simple enough. They'd discussed their options earlier, figured out where and when they would join up again if they were split up, with multiple fallback positions. Yin Xue had set the formation flags around their meeting spot in the ditch they'd chosen, ensuring they would be hidden the moment they entered the ditch. Once everyone was gathered, they began the slow, arduous process of sneaking away.

Unfortunately, their escape had roused the army within, and even if there were still concerns that Wu Ying's group was just another distraction, the soldiers had sent forth a large number of patrols to find them. The patrols now crisscrossed the grounds, searching for them in an ever-expanding circle of horses and cultivators. The soldiers had even loosed spirit animals, scenting dogs that snuffled the ground in search of them. Only the liberal application of talismans and the disposal of certain demon beast cores had ensured their escape from the animals.

With their auras compressed with the talismans they'd purchased, they slowly sneaked away under the illusory formation. Unfortunately, the talismans were running out of power and it would not be long before they were forced into the open. So even if it was dangerous, they were moving the formation.

They had a tense few minutes as groups of cultivators and soldiers streamed through the fields outside the city, intent on finding them. More than once, Wu Ying thought they would be caught, especially when they were forced out of the trenches and were crossing the open ground surrounding the city. Even if they could hide behind the gentle slopes of hills, those same hills allowed their pursuers to appear suddenly and with little warning. Wu Ying stretched his senses to the maximum, doing his best to note when others might be arriving, though all he could really do was rely on the formation.

Nearly an hour later, they'd managed to sneak away to the north. The search parties had spread out so widely that they were no longer within easy shouting distance of one another.

That was when tragedy struck again. The Green Waters Sect cultivators had just crossed another hill when they spotted a returning group of cultivators. Instead of individual horses, the group led a half-dozen additional horses. Their horses.

"Dammit," Wu Ying cursed under his breath.

While they could travel on foot, it would be slow and would require them to spend even more time within the State of Wei. With the alarm sounded and the approaching army, taking too long to get back to Shen was a bad idea. Wu Ying himself could run and keep up with a horse, but he had an advantage that his friends didn't in that he could cultivate while moving. If they ran, his friends would eventually run low on chi. And if they came across enemies while tired…

"We should kill them," Bao Cong said, having already planted his flag in the ground and extracted his bow. He'd strung his weapon as he spoke, hissing softly as his wounds continued to bother him.

"We can find another group and take their horses. We are too close," Li Yao rebutted. "There might be another patrol."

"And if we run, we will get caught. I don't intend to fight an army," Bao Cong snapped. He fitted an arrow to his bow, but rather than fire, he looked at Wu Ying, waiting for his confirmation.

Wu Ying looked at Tou He, who shrugged, then at Yin Xue. The noble returned Wu Ying's gaze placidly, offering no hint of his thoughts. Once more, Wu Ying glanced at the approaching group, surprise flickering within him when he noted a familiar face in the patrol. Perhaps it was destiny. This was the third time he'd met the man.

"We fight." Wu Ying suited action to words, extracting a crossbow from his storage ring.

He loaded it quickly, amused to see Yin Xue copy him. Together, the three archers in the group moved to a position within their formation to fire upon the cultivators. They would have one good shot before they would have to fight the six members of the patrol. It would be best if they managed to finish this fight fast.

Wu Ying glanced at his bracer, making a face as he noted the dull color in the jade, the lack of sheen or pull of power within. It had yet to recharge. Unfortunately, he didn't have the energy to recharge it himself. He would have to finish this fight with his skills alone.

Tension wrapped around the group as they waited for the cultivators to near their hiding spot. When they were within thirty yards, Wu Ying began the silent countdown with his fingers. As he neared the end of the count, Senior Cai, the cultivator in the front—the same one Wu Ying had fought in the night and had met on the road—jerked his head up. He opened his mouth, shouting a warning even as he drew his sword.

Wu Ying's fist clenched, and arrows and bolts shot forward. Unfortunately, their surprise had been ruined. Senior Cai cut Wu Ying's bolt apart before it hit. Bao Cong's attack was much more effective, as it glowed red and plunged directly through the raised arm and lightly formed aura shield of his target. It tore through the armored chest of his opponent, leaving the body to topple to the ground. As for Yin Xue's attack, his left a bloody surface wound on his opponent's arm.

A moment later, Tou He and Li Yao dashed forward. Even if Li Yao was unhappy with the orders, like a good soldier, she committed to the attack fully. With her explosive lunge, petals of ice formed around her spear, containing the majority of what chi she had managed to recoup in the hour they had hidden away. It was a powerful attack, made more effective by its surprise nature. The attack caught two of the cultivators and their horses, throwing them off their steeds onto the ground, ice coating wounds and frosts rimming their bodies. One of the cultivators, too slow to move even his hand to draw his weapon, had his own sword frozen shut.

Tou He, behind Li Yao's explosive attack, launched his own. Unlike Li Yao's flamboyant skill, his was more contained. But each beat, each blocked strike sent sparks from his staff as the fire chi contained within his attacks grew in strength as he rushed his opponent. A missed block, a strike against his opponent's chest, and the tip exploded in flames, throwing his opponent off his mount.

That quickly, two of the opponents were down permanently, another injured.

Wu Ying grinned, for this was going well for them. He rushed forward as he tossed aside the crossbow, drawing his jian as he raced to cut off Senior Cai from escape. He did not have to have worried about that, for the cultivator spurred his horse in a charge directly at Wu Ying.

"You are seeking death! Attacking me. You will not be able to run this time," Senior Cai roared as he turned to charge at Wu Ying.

Close behind Wu Ying, Yin Xue skipped around Wu Ying's slowing down form, turning to target one of the surviving cultivators. It was one that had been blown off his horse by Li Yao, the cultivator having managed to get to his feet. Rather than stay, he'd turned, running at an angle with the intent of fleeing to safety.

Meanwhile, Wu Ying noted how Bao Cong was fumbling, attempting to put another arrow in his bow but failing, as his most recent attack had left him white-faced and exhausted. Stubbornness and endurance could push one only so far, before exhaustion caught up.

A twist of his sword, a lunge, and Yin Xue caught the fleeing cultivator in the hamstring. His blade tore along the unprotected back of the man's legs, depositing him on the ground.

Wu Ying dismissed the man, focusing on the charging equine and its angry rider. As he stared, he realized that he was at a major disadvantage. His opponent wielded a dao and was seated high above on his horse. Wu Ying, on the ground, faced the choice of standing his ground and being run over, or struck as he dodged.

Wu Ying's gaze flicked back and forth between the incoming horse and Senior Cai's raised weapon, before he dropped into a lunging crouch. He formed a small crescent of sword intent, sending it out with some of his chi in fast-flowing flickers of damage and regret.

The poor horse had no defense for its hooves and feet. The attack sliced one then another of its hooves apart, sending it stumbling and falling with a loud neigh. It thrashed on the ground, its screams of pain making Wu Ying's heart ache. The poor animal had done nothing to him, but to survive, he had little choice.

Even as he was getting over his moment of guilt, Wu Ying had to dodge and twist. Rather than go down with the horse, Senior Cai had jumped off the horse, landing with a roll then approaching the distracted Wu Ying as he dealt with the horse. If not for the last moment twist of his body and the armor that lay under his robe, Wu Ying would have been gravely injured. As it was, he felt a bruise forming from his left collarbone to his opposite hip, one that throbbed with every breath as Senior Cai's sword sparked against chainmail and the bruised body beneath.

Rather than let Wu Ying catch his breath or footing, Senior Cai continued to attack at full speed. Each sword cut came at a different angle, chained together in a form that gave Wu Ying barely a moment to block them. Worse, Senior Cai imbued each attack with chi, such that even when Wu Ying blocked an attack, portions of the sword intent cut past his blocks, tearing at his robes and skin. Wounds appeared on Wu Ying's body as the armor he wore beneath his robes was unable to stop all the damage, limited in size as it was.

Forced back, almost losing his footing, Wu Ying let himself drop into a reverse lunge, committing his body to the ground as he sprawled. The Dragon stretches his Tail gave him a moment of respite as the dao attacks whiffed over his head, while his jian slammed into Senior Cai's upper body. The enemy cultivator staggered backward, his expensive and enchanted robes taking the attack without breaking. Even as the cultivator fell backward, his return strike hammered the jian, beating it aside. To Wu Ying's surprise, the accumulated damage shattered the sword, leaving Wu Ying with the stub of his weapon.

Wu Ying groaned, his hands trembling from the attack, fingers spasming. Instinct drove him to close the distance, moving sideways to dodge the attack while he pivoted into a drop step. His hand rose, palm outstretched to catch his opponent's arm as it came around to cut at him. The first portion was part of Dragon catches the Rainbow, but Wu Ying transitioned to his unarmed styles. He stayed close using the Northern Shen's Wind Steps, circling his opponent as he moved, ensuring he was always on his opponent's empty hand. Each second, each moment, he choked up his opponent's strikes with quick, vertical punches—the Fourth Fist of the Mountain Breaking Style. Also known as Raindrops on the Mountain. Each strike kept Senior Cai staggering and twisting, moving to attack him and failing.

But as good as Wu Ying was, so was Senior Cai. A kick that Wu Ying never saw tripped him. Another caught him in the chest, booted feet flexing and imprinting on Wu Ying's armored chest before throwing him back. Wu Ying let himself go into the fall, doing a backflip as he dodged the cuts that followed the strike. He failed to dodge them entirely though, a cut at his thighs forcing him to stumble as he landed.

Pain. But to his surprise, as Wu Ying struggled to his feet, Senior Cai did not follow up. Instead, he clutched his arm, the one Wu Ying had struck again and again. As for his weapon, his sword lay a distance from him, fallen from numbed fingers. Repeated strikes and the sudden motion must have made his hand spasm.

"Having trouble?" Wu Ying taunted, hoping his opponent would get angry. Praying that he would lose his temper.

"You think you can beat me, even unarmed?" Senior Cai snorted. He charged forward, ignoring his own weapon. "Die, you worthless dog."

Objective achieved, Wu Ying stopped his taunting. It was almost pitiful how easy it was to read the man. But Wu Ying had no time to pay attention to that as he focused on his opponent. His lead hand dropped close to his other, his body curled up tight as he raised himself to fight. Then as his opponent neared him, when they were but steps away, Wu Ying pulled on his chi, sent his mind into the storage ring, and extracted another sword. This was a dao, heavy and curved, single-sided but perfect for the cut he unleashed. He shoved all his energy, every inch of his sword intent into the blow as he swung. Senior Cai froze for a moment, surprise taking him for a precious second.

It was not honorable. It was not right. Taunting him to fight, forcing him to commit to the attack without a weapon, only for Wu Ying to use one himself. But it was practical. The attack tore into Senior Cai's body, ripping apart enchanted robes, flesh, skin, and muscle, leaving his opponent sprawled on the ground, his chest split. Not too deep though, for his opponent was stronger, and at the last moment, he had managed to twist aside.

Left untreated, the injury probably would leave him dead. But for now, Senior Cai staggered to his feet, wrapped his fist in power, igniting the very blood of his body and forming smoking tendrils of blood from his chest. The energy wrapped around his fist as he punched. Wu Ying managed to get his dao in front of him, protecting his body, only to be blown away, the sword shattered as it peppered him with hot metal. He flipped over and over until he smashed into the slope of the hill behind, throwing up blood as ribs cracked and his chest compressed. Blood ran from cuts across his face where metal shards had cut him, his entire body feeling singed from the attack. If not for his Reinforced Iron Bones technique, the attack would probably have shattered all his bones.

As if he had used up all of his energy, Senior Cai collapsed onto his face, unmoving. Blood continued to steam from his body, creating a cloud of red around him. Wu Ying struggled to stand and failed, sliding back into the hole his body had created. He stared at the battle that still raged, desperate to get back into the fight and help his friends but unable to do so. At least he had managed to deal with his own opponent.

In the distance, Li Yao had put down another and was holding off her opponent. Tou He was dealing with his own opponent, while Yin Xue edged around the pair. When he saw a chance, Yin Xue darted in, injuring and distracting the metal-clad cultivator. That allowed Tou He to strike as well, but neither of them seemed to be able to injure the man; his body throbbed with the metal chi that wrapped his whole body in protective armor.

Fed up with fighting two opponents at the same time, the cultivator finally snarled. "Do you people have no honor!"

Before anyone could reply, he was struck in the back and shoulder by Tou He, the hit making his head twist to the side. He lurched sideways, and the next second, Yin Xue darted forward and stabbed him in the throat.

"This is war, fool," Yin Xue said, the cut tearing an inch into the throat and leaving blood to bubble around the wound.

Even then, the man refused to fall and lashed out with his axe, narrowly missing Yin Xue.

Grateful to see that matters were in hand, Wu Ying let himself slump to the ground and circulate his chi. As much as he wanted to, rejoining the fight would just hinder his friends. Better to heal and recuperate as fast as he could, because they still had to run. At least their horses—trained from birth to deal with fights around them—had only moved a distance away. Now, all they had to do was finish off their opponents, gather their horses, and flee.

Chapter 24

Cracked ribs jostled as Wu Ying sat upon his plodding horse, sending sharp pains shooting through his torso and stealing his breath. He churned his chi, using the energy within to bolster his bones and help offset the pain and the damage, to patch himself together. But, for all of that, the damage was done and would not heal any time soon. He could only swallow a Blood Cleansing Pill, borrow the vitality it released to help his body fix itself while he rode, and keep an eye on Bao Cong.

Because as injured as Wu Ying was, Bao Cong was more damaged. Pale, with little chi left and the wounds in his leg and shoulder still leaking blood occasionally, the cultivator swayed in his saddle. They had lashed him to his horse to ensure he did not fall while they rode. Still, Wu Ying stayed close, ready to catch the slumping body or grab the reins if necessary. Bao Cong was insensate, his wounds wrapped, a Marrow Opening and Blood Cleansing Pill already swallowed and working their healing magic. Even so, it was debatable if he would survive if they did not stop soon.

But that was, of course, the last thing they could do. After they had finished the battle, they'd ripped the storage rings off the bodies of the enemy cultivators and taken their weapons and horses before leaving. If Wu Ying's group was lucky, they had been the outermost patrol and their presence would not be expected for a while. If not...

If not, they would have another battle to fight. And the truth was, none of them were in a position to do so. Even Yin Xue, who had taken pains to reduce the amount of energy and danger he put himself in, was looking worse for the wear, though he continued to ride at the head of the group. As for Li Yao, the petite cultivator sat on her horse, alert and tense by dint of will. Wu Ying sensed the churning abyss that was her dantian, the way she drew in chi without needing to cultivate—so low was her energy state. Tou He was much in the same boat as Yin Xue—mostly uninjured but tired and forced to ride at the back to keep an eye out for problems.

Wu Ying grunted as another rough step made him wince. As he rode, his mind churned with recriminations. They should have planned better. He should have gotten more—more talismans, more enchanted items. Figured out a better distraction or way to sneak in. He should have expected things to go badly, and he should have planned for them to cause a distraction or split their forces somehow. He should have…

He should not have brought his friends.

As they rode, he faced his guilt over that final fact. He had asked and they had come, but now, their lives were in danger. For him. For his parents and his village. They would not have acted without him asking. And so, their deaths and injuries were his to bear.

As he cast a look at the swaying Bao Cong, at the way Tou He redid the bandage on his arm, Wu Ying mentally chided himself for his selfishness. He'd wanted to save his family, his village—but he had put his friends in danger. Who was he to trade their lives for others?

Then again, he'd asked and they'd chosen to come. And wasn't that too part of the deal between friends? You came when they asked, or sometimes, when they didn't. Because you trusted they'd do the same for you. Just like in the village. When a dike broke, when a fire started in a house, you didn't stop to ask if they would help you when your time came. You acted—because weighing give and take, weighing the benefits and liabilities of aid would just see homes destroyed, animals killed, plants washed away.

And if you did more for one person than they did for you? If they died owing you a debt? Then perhaps that too was fated. The karmic balance would restore itself at some point. In the future, in this life or another, all debts balanced eventually. That was the promise of the Dao, of karma.

A cough from Bao Cong drew Wu Ying's attention and he rode toward him, pulling out a mundane water bottle. He passed it to the man, letting him drink before Wu Ying took a swig as well. It was a pity he'd lost the Never-

Ending Flask, but its sacrifice had given them a few minutes when they had needed to run. Precious time to set up the talismans. To pull away and hide.

As for the flask—it was just goods. And those, those could be repurchased. If they survived.

***

Surprisingly, for all their concern, they made it through the day without issue. They rested for a few hours in the deep of the night, when it was too dark, too dangerous, to ride their horses on earth that might be littered with potholes or staffed by bandits. As usual, with the coming of war, chaos reigned. And while the army had kept bandits back for a time, now that it had gone, they'd creep back in between the coming of one army and the next. Raiding, stealing, and killing before they moved on like the locusts of civilization they were.

The cultivators rested for a few hours in the dark, taking turns sleeping and watching. Wu Ying volunteered to stay awake; his dantian had mostly refilled as they had rode, unlike his friends'. And so while his friends slept or cultivated, he watched over them. Until early morning light filtered in and it was time to go.

Hard tack, dried sausages, jerky, and compressed meal were stuffed into mouths as they rode, switching animals every few hours. Bao Cong looked better, as did most of the others. But that just meant a harder, longer ride today. Speed rather than stealth was their protection now.

For a week, the group rode at a hurried pace. Only twice did they run into additional cultivators. The first time, they'd managed to spot their enemies beforehand and lay low, hiding until the patrol rode off. The second time, they were forced to do battle. Luckily, they were scouts from the Wei army, individuals who were more intent on escaping with their knowledge than standing and fighting the group. After an exchange of blows and the death of one of the Six Jade Gates Sect members, the scouts had broken away. The brief battle saw the laming of a couple of horses, leaving Wu Ying's group with insufficient spares for a proper rotation. As it was, the horses were tired, barely able to keep up the pace the group had set.

"I'll run," Wu Ying volunteered. He'd done it before. It was not pleasant, but he was stronger than he had been. And even if he grew tired, it was nothing that would stop them.

A moment later, Tou He jumped off as his horse as well. "You are not the only one who doesn't fear a little hard work." He laughed, the ex-monk still able to find some humor in their situation.

Whether it was because he was ashamed or because he saw the wisdom in a matter, Yin Xue descended from his stallion as well and stroked the side of his horse's neck. "We will run until the animals have recovered a little."

Together, the three cultivators ran alongside the animals, leading them and their friends on the journey back to the crossing, back to the river, back home.

They ran past numerous fleeing peasants, merchants who flinched and glared at the cultivators. It was clear who they were, especially when on the second day of running, Wu Ying and the others changed back into their Sect robes. There was no point in hiding who, what, they were. Not anymore.

Li after li of paved ground and crushed earth passed beneath their feet under the insistent beat of the horses' hooves. Another animal lost her shoe, growing lame soon after. They left the animal behind, abandoned with a merchant for a few coins, before they took off again. Even as they ran, Wu Ying glanced back to see the merchant pulling hair dye from his pack and beginning the process of mixing it into the mare's body. Wu Ying had no doubt the once-brown horse would be stained black in a few hours.

They kept moving, even as the sun was blotted out by heavily laden clouds. With them, rain and wind arrived, washing out the roads and slowing their pace. It only became more miserable as they grew soaked under their cloaks and their mildly weather-resistant Sect robes.

Bao Cong grew grumpier, the ache in his leg and the constant pounding of rain driving him into sullen silence. Li Yao caught a cold on the second night, her small frame chilled to the bone. Even her improved cultivator constitution could only do so much, especially when so much of her chi was expended during the day while she rode, helping them replenish waning stamina. None of them were particularly energetic, but still, they pushed on.

Late at night, when the group stopped, exhausted and tired, Wu Ying prepared their meals. Pulling from the herbs he had purchased, and some from the ones he had found around the camps, the cultivator cooked new meals and steeped medicine soups, providing them to his friends. He may not be a full-fledged apothecarist, but his studies had given him at least a basic understanding of what would benefit them. It was a waste of herbs, a waste of money, to do it the way he did, but both of those were of little consequence to Wu Ying at this time. They had to escape, and their pursuers, while likely just as inconvenienced by the rain, would also likely be better prepared and provisioned.

All they could do was go on.

They headed north and west until they reached a small fishing village, one that bordered the river separating the two states. By this point, they believed themselves far enough that the passing of coin and the subtle threat of their openly displayed weapons was enough to make a fisherman take them across the river. Even the threat of patrols on the other side, one that shot arrows without hesitation at ships that swung too close, was muted for the fisherman. After all, Wu Ying and his team were immediate threats, unlike the potential threat of patrolling soldiers.

When the team finally landed on the other shore, the group relaxed, a palpable tension fading. For a time, they lingered by the shore, staring at the flowing waters and the border across the misty river. Wu Ying was not sure who began laughing first, but in short order, they were all chuckling and smacking each other on the shoulder as the relief of their escape ran through them.

Eventually, Li Yao sobered and recommended they keep moving. Even if they had outpaced their pursuers, they were still too close to the border. But as they took off at a more sedate pace, a much more relaxed air drifted through the group. They had managed to do it. Now, all Wu Ying had to do was traverse a war-torn country to return the cultivation manual.

As if the heavens itself knew what they had gone through, the rainstorm finally let up, giving them their first glimpse of the sun in days.

***

Two weeks later, a tired and dirty group stumbled into Lord Wen's abode. They'd had to swing wide, taking even more time on their journey back, running into demon beasts and bandits along the way, as they avoided the dueling armies near the border. Luckily, word from the local populace had allowed the group to avoid the armies and their patrols, often for nothing more than the favor of dealing with the latest menace that had been driven to their home.

Lord Wen had been as good as his word, allowing Wu Ying's family and the village to leave. What amused Wu Ying, in a cynical and tired manner, was the way the Lord had already filled the empty houses and fields with refugees from the border. It seemed that the constant fighting and the threat of slavery had driven away even the hardy peasants who had lived in those areas. Wu Ying was sure, if asked by magistrates or pursuers from their former landowners, that all of the new residents of his village—his past village—would swear that they had lived there for ages. It would be a good disguise for them. After all, who kept track of and paid attention to peasants?

And if the armies were close to their new homes, at least their army was between them and the enemy.

Wu Ying was thinking those thoughts while staring at the teacup in his hand. The group waited in the very same room they had first been seen in. Only the quiet announcement of the Lord's presence took his attention away from his cynical thoughts.

"You have it?" Lord Wen said. "Show it to me."

Wu Ying complied. There was no point in dragging this out. He missed the Sect, his bed, and his home. He wanted to make sure his family had settled in—had made it for that matter. This entire journey had been a long diversion from his goal of becoming an immortal cultivator.

Lord Wen stared at the tablets, infusing them with his chi and humming to himself as he read through the text. He studied the documents for long, long minutes. Much longer than he probably needed to to ascertain their validity. Wu Ying was not sure if it was rudeness or that the Lord was used to making others wait. In either case, eventually Lord Wen looked up.

"Good. And my son? You have a copy?" he asked.

"Yes. I made one while we traveled." Yin Xue smiled.

Of them all, the nobleman's son had gained the most from the trip. He had begun training with the new cultivation method, rerouting how his chi moved, how he tapped into the world. At first, his cultivation level had regressed, but in short order, he had cleared his meridians again and even improved his cultivation. He was now in the middle levels of the Energy Storage stage. That left Wu Ying significantly behind all his friends, still stuck at Body Cultivation 12.

"Good. Cultivate well then. Your mother will be happy to hear that." Lord Wen stared at his son for a moment more before he waved Yin Xue outside.

"You should speak with your cousins. Pass on your gathered wisdom. They will be learning this method soon."

Lord Wen glanced at the others, taking in their disheveled appearance, then clapped his hands. In seconds, servants arrived. He directed them to take the others away to wash up, leaving Wu Ying and himself alone.

"Lord?" Wu Ying asked. He did not fear betrayal, not at this point. It would make little sense. Then again, none of this made sense.

"This transaction is over." Lord Wen tapped the manual. "But for what you've done, what you did to my son, I will not forgive you. You will not show yourself before me again. Hinder my son's potential again and I will take further action."

Wu Ying stiffened at the threat. He glared at the nobleman, then he paused as a thought struck him. He regarded the nobleman for a long moment before he said in wonder, "You really believe he could be a true cultivator."

Noblemen sent their children to the Sect to gain power. Influence. And, eventually, to return to the fold. Not even one in a ten thousand cultivators grew a Nascent Soul. Not even one in a million ascended the heavens. Few nobles, few families, would gamble with those odds. At least, not with first sons.

"He has more talent than anyone in the last three generations. He will either be a powerful cultivator, a strength for our clan, or he will be an immortal. If"—Lord Wen fixed Wu Ying with a glare—"others do not get in his way."

Wu Ying shook his head and even found himself smiling as he slapped his hand on the table and stood. "The matter between your son and me was put aside long ago. I do not carry him any longer. Nor he, me. Perhaps you too should set the burden down.[16]"

---

[16] This is a reference to a story about a young and old monk. It basically involves an older monk carrying a young noble lady across muddy ground on his back before he was shoved aside without thanks. The young monk continued complaining about the young woman for a long

Lord Wen continued to glare at Wu Ying, who bowed to the man.

"If you are done, I will join my friends—my Sect mates—in cleaning up. We will be leaving soon," Wu Ying said.

Lord Wen hesitated before he waved the cultivator away. Whatever he wanted to say, he'd decided to keep to himself. All the better, in Wu Ying's opinion. The nobleman had little power over him now.

***

"Did you get what you wanted from your journey?" Elder Lu asked Wu Ying, nearly a month later. He hefted the package of wrapped tobacco leaves, sniffing at the contents and smiling.

"My family and the village have arrived and are settling in," Wu Ying said.

He had just come from visiting them, wanting to see that they had settled in before anything else. The villagers had all arrived footsore and travel weary which was no surprise. That they had complained and were frustrated about their unnecessary trip, having learned that their village was fine was to be expected.

Some were already talking of returning, of claiming back what was theirs. Others had found Wu Ying to talk to him of their needs and the work that had to be done to ensure their new village would be able to sustain itself. Some sought to use his resources. Others to detach themselves from Wu Ying's largesse as quickly as possible. Luckily, good soil and strong bodies meant that setting up the village and producing some food was viable in the short-term. Add in the Sect's never-ending need for supplies and it was likely they would be self-sufficient in a year or two at most.

---

time, until the old monk finally said, "I set the woman down hours ago. Why are you still carrying her?"

Still, the underlying resentment was pronounced and affected Wu Ying as he left the villagers, a reminder that even if he thought he had done the right thing, not everyone agreed. Worse, as the village elder droned on and on about what was required, Wu Ying had felt himself grow bored. Not angry or upset, but bored. Because their needs, their wants were so mundane.

So far from who, what he had been. What he was.

"But did you get what you needed?" Elder Lu asked.

Wu Ying drew a breath and considered the question. Truly considered it. Finally, he smiled at the Elder. "Yes. Yes, I did."

Sometimes, one had to take a long journey, cross many li, and fight a few battles before one could find that what they needed, what was required, was still and had always been where they had started.

Wu Ying was no commoner farmer turned cultivator anymore. He'd had to save his parents, save his village, but not because they were part of his future or even his present. It was because, at the end of the day, he'd had to do so so that he could move forward.

"Good, good. Because Elder Li has been complaining about your absence. You better go see her, after you see your master. She's got a lot of work for you."

Having said his part, Elder Lu closed his eyes and leaned back against the pillar. Around him, the group offered the elder, the gate guardian, a deep bow of respect before they hurried in. Already, the bonds that had held the group together were fraying, parting as they returned to their lives. Even if they had grown close over the last few months, they each had their own goals, their own pursuits. Cultivation, at its heart, was a lonely pursuit.

Wu Ying turned to face the track upward, watching as Li Yao scrambled up the mountain path. During one of the quiet nights on the deck of the boat, they'd finally had time for the conversation that had been burgeoning between them. They'd tried, when the stress and the pressure had come off, to return to what they'd had, to find the tranquility and comfort that had been between them. It had worked sometimes, but mostly, it had been strained. Going back seemed impossible.

The talk had been surprisingly painless, as much as such things were. Somehow, in the midst of all of the hectic scrambling and fighting, their relationship had frayed and ended. In truth, looking back at it, Wu Ying was not even sure why they had gotten together in the first place. Physical attraction. Some innate desire for company. But beyond that, they were friends who knew each other, knew the path that they were walking. But not lovers. Not lifelong, soul companions. Not people who made each other stronger or better, but individuals who had walked along the same path for a time.

Wu Ying was not even sure if they'd stay friends. Of course, they had both assured each other that they wanted to. But the wounds were a little fresh, and even if it had been relatively painless, relatively known, there was still that tinge of doubt, of loss. Even if they had both come to the same conclusion, for the same reasons, it wasn't easy. Better to stay away from the training grounds for a bit, maybe meet with her later. Who knew? At some point, they'd probably be friends again. He still owed her for Yin Xue, for coming.

But for now, their path together was over.

"Get moving. You're blocking my sun." Elder Lu's querulous voice resounded, waking Wu Ying from his musings.

The cultivator offered the elderly gatekeeper another deep bow before he hurried up the familiar pathway. There was still a lot to do, his Master, Fairy Yang, and others to speak with. There was the Assignment Hall to report in, Elder Lee to placate. And of course, it was time to catch up on his cultivation.

Chapter 25

Once again, Wu Ying was seated in the courtyard of his residence. Seated at the table, playing a game of chess[17], were Fairy Yang and Tou He. The scene was similar to the one from months before, when Wu Ying had attempted to break through the Body Cultivation stage. Except this time, the courtyard was lush, filled with grass and vegetable boxes, the herb garden in the corner sprouting and being tended to by Auntie Yee. Of course, Wu Ying did most of the work in caring for the garden, but the watering and occasional trimming was something that even the old servant could do. Most of the contents of those boxes were from herbs and other vegetables that Wu Ying had found on their journey back, now carefully tended and grown. They had been chosen mostly because someone like Auntie Yee could take care of them when Wu Ying was not around. After all, he knew that most of his contribution points would still be gained in the field. That fact Elder Li had been quite clear on when he met her.

It amused Wu Ying, to some extent, the almost negligible effects his departure had had on the sect. Upon Wu Ying's return, his Master had only glanced at him once, stared into his eyes before he offered a simple nod and dismissed him. Fairy Yang had invited Wu Ying and his companions for dinner, where they'd regaled her with their story. But in the end, she too had no comments to offer. In fact, the only person who'd expressed deep interest in his quest had been Elder Li, and that had been entirely because she had sent him with a stack of spirit herb requests.

Of course, she'd been more than disappointed when Wu Ying pointed out that he had no intention on questing immediately because he wanted to break through soon. Still, refilling his dantian and gaining enough chi to commit himself to the breakthrough took weeks. Weeks that had him worked to the

---

[17] Chinese chess, but since you know; they're Chinese, it's chess. :P

bone, often joining the Martial Specialists in search of spirit herbs and digging into ruins. With his increased expertise, the Sect was eager to make use of his skills to exploit known but untouched herbs.

Even if the work had delayed his breakthrough, he could not help but be grateful for the influx of contribution points. He had a debt that had to be paid – to Bao Cong, to the Sect for the villagers needs - and only hard work would see it reduced.

Wu Ying took another deep breath, discarding all of those erroneous thoughts. He was ready to complete his cultivation, to achieve the next level. And he would not fail. Not this time. For he believed he knew why he had failed the last time. It hadn't been a lack of chi. It hadn't been because he wasn't physically ready. It had been because, in a part of his mind, he had not viewed himself as a real cultivator.

It irked Wu Ying that by watching Yin Xue as he progressed through the expedition, he had realized his own mistake. He had been so fixed on the fact that he was a peasant cultivator that he had forgotten that there was no such thing. There were no peasant cultivators. Just cultivators. He had been so fixed on his past, he'd held himself back. Because what peasant could be a real cultivator?

His past, the world he had been born into as a farmer, as a peasant, as a commoner. Those were the bedrocks of his soul, the truth of what he was. It would influence who he was and what he would do. But it was not all that he was now. And it certainly did not dictate the extent of his ambition.

He would become a cultivator. A real one. He would climb the path of immortality, and he would see how far he would get. But his parentage, his background, would not hold him back anymore. He was no peasant. No farmer. He was a cultivator.

Drawing a deep breath, Wu Ying drove the chi in his dantian, sending it at the first Energy Storage meridian as per his cultivation manual. He readied himself for a fight, for the pain that would occur as his chi gushed out, driven by will and intent.

But this time, breaking through was as simple as turning over his hand. It required no effort, just the desire. And though there was no influx of worldly chi, no heavenly sign of approval as he broke through, Wu Ying could not help but admit he felt lighter within.

A smile crept up on Wu Ying's lips as he churned his chi through his body, cleansing the meridian and feeling it fill. He continued drawing in the world's chi, making it his own. And in the meantime, he sat, contented and hopeful.

For he was looking forward to what came next.

The End

Wu Ying will continue his journey to immortality
in book 4 of A Thousand Li: the Second Expedition

Author's Note

With the end of the First War, the book closes on Wu Ying's journey as a Body Cultivator and his first tentative steps into the world of cultivation. Wu Ying has a better idea of what he wants to be, and while there will still be occasional doubts, he's also setting aside mortal concerns.

Book four will be the start of a new arc in Wu Ying's journey, one that sees him traveling out of the Sect more and seeing much more of the world. Along the way, Wu Ying will continue to search for his dao, his own meaning. Continue to follow Wu Ying's adventures in:

- The Second Expedition (Book 4 of A Thousand Li)
  www.starlitpublishing.com/products/the-second-expedition

As always, I've thoroughly enjoyed writing the novel. **If you enjoyed reading it, please do leave a review and rating**. The reviews make a huge difference in sales, which is how I earn a living.

I also host a Facebook Group for all things wuxia, xanxia, and specifically, cultivation novels. We'd love it if you joined us:

- Cultivation Novels
  www.facebook.com/groups/cultivationnovels

For more great information about LitRPG series, check out the Facebook groups:

- GameLit Society
  www.facebook.com/groups/LitRPGsociety
- LitRPG Books
  www.facebook.com/groups/LitRPG.books

About the Author

Tao Wong is an avid fantasy and sci-fi reader who spends his time working and writing in the North of Canada. He's spent way too many years doing martial arts of many forms and, having broken himself too often, now spends his time writing about fantasy worlds.

If you'd like to support Tao directly, he has a Patreon page where previews of all his new books can be found!

- www.patreon.com/taowong

For updates on the series and the author's other books (and special one-shot stories), please visit his website: http://www.mylifemytao.com

Subscribers to Tao's mailing list will receive exclusive access to short stories in A Thousand Li and System Apocalypse universes:

Or visit his Facebook Page: www.facebook.com/taowongauthor/

About the Publisher

Starlit Publishing is wholly owned and operated by Tao Wong. It is a science fiction and fantasy publisher focused on the LitRPG & cultivation genres. Their focus is on promoting new, upcoming authors in the genre whose writing challenges the existing stereotypes while giving a rip-roaring good read.

For more information on Starlit Publishing, visit our website!

www.starlitpublishing.com

You can also join Starlit Publishing's mailing list to learn of new, exciting authors and book releases.

https://starlitpublishing.com/newsletter-signup/

Glossary

Aura Reinforcement Exercise—Cultivation exercise that allows Wu Ying to contain his aura, trapping his chi within himself and making his cultivation more efficient and making him, to most senses, feel like someone of a lower cultivation level.

Blade Energy/Chi—A specific type of energy that is harnessed by cultivators who have gained understanding of their weapon. Can be projected for more damage.

Body Cleansing—First cultivation stage where the cultivator must cleanse their body of the impurities that have accumulated. Has twelve stages.

Cao—Fuck

Catty—Weight measurement. One cattie is roughly equivalent to one and a half pounds or 604 grams. A tael is 1/16th of a catty

Chi (or Qi)—I use the Cantonese pinyin here rather than the more common Mandarin. Chi is life force / energy and it permeates all things in the universe, flowing through living creatures in particular.

Chi Points (a.k.a. Acupuncture Points)—Locations in the body that, when struck, compressed, or otherwise affected, can affect the flow of chi. Traditional acupuncture uses these points in a beneficial manner.

Core formation—Third stage of cultivation. Having gathered sufficient chi, the cultivator must form a "core" of compressed chi. The stages in Core formation purify and harden the core.

Cultivation Exercise—A supplementary exercise that improves an individual's handling of chi within their body. Cultivation exercises are ancillary to cultivation styles.

Cultivation Style—A method to manipulate chi within an individual's body. There are thousands of cultivation exercises, suited for various constitutions, meridians, and bloodlines.

Dark Sects—These are considered 'evil' Sects. Their cultivation methods and daos tap into darker emotions and often include blood and flesh sacrifice and the stealing of chi from others.

Dào—Literally translated, the Way (also spelled Tao). The Dao when capitalized speaks of the universal Dao, the one natural Way or Path. When not capitilized, it denotes a lesser way, a lesser truth.

Dāo—Chinese sabre. Closer to a western cavalry sabre, it is thicker, often single-edged, with a curve at the end where additional thickness allows the weapon to be extra efficient at cutting.

Dantian—There are actually three dantians in the human body. The most commonly referred to one is the lower dantian, located right above the bladder and an inch within the body. The other two are located in the chest and forehead, though they are often less frequently used. The dantian is said to be the center of chi.

Dragon's Breath—Chi projection attack from the Long family style.

Demonic Sects—Demonic Sects draw power not from the chi in the natural world but from the demonic plane. While not necessarily evil or harmful like Dark Sects, many Demonic Sects are hunted by Orthodox Sects due to the damage their presence can cause to the natural order of the world.

Elements—The Chinese traditionally have five elements—Wood, Fire, Earth, Metal, and Water. Within these elements, additional sub-elements may occur (example—air from Chao Kun, ice from Li Yao).

Energy Storage—Second stage of cultivation, where the energy storage circulation meridians are opened. This stage allows cultivators to project their chi, the amount of chi stored and projected depending on level. There are eight levels.

Heretical Sects—Sects practising unorthodox daos or cultivation methods. These heretical sects might not even focus on cultivation in the same manner as 'orthodox' sects.

Huài dàn—Rotten egg

Hún dàn—Bastard

Jian—A straight, double-edged sword. Known in modern times as a "taichi sword." Mostly a thrusting instrument, though it can be used to cut as well.

Li—Roughly half a kilometer per li. Traditional Chinese measurement of distance.

Lord Wen—Father of Yin Xue. The Wen family is a branch family of nobles born in the neighboring state of Wei and that defected.

Long family jian style—A family sword form passed on to Wu Ying. Consists of a lot of cuts, fighting at full measure, and quick changes in direction.

Meridians—In traditional Chinese martial arts and medicine, meridians are how chi flows through the body. In traditional Chinese medicine, there are twelve major meridian flows and eight secondary energy flows. I've used these meridians for the stages in cultivation for the first two stages.

Mountain Breaking Fist—Fist form that Wu Ying gained in the inner sect library. Focused, single, powerful attacks.

Nascent Soul—The fourth and last known stage of cultivation. Cultivators form a new, untouched soul steeped in the dao they had formed. This new soul must ascend to the heavens, facing heavenly tribulation at each step.

Northern Shen Kicking Style—Kicking form that Wu Ying learned at the outer sect library. Both a grappling and kicking style, meant for close combat.

Orthodox Sects—The most common type of Sect. Differentiated from other types by the cultivation type conducted.

Qinggong—Literally "light skill." Comes from baguazhang and is basically wire-fu—running on water, climbing trees, gliding along bamboo, etc.

Iron Reinforced Bones—Defensive, physical cultivation technique that Wu Ying trains in that will increase the strength and defense of his body.

Sect—A grouping of like-minded martial artists or cultivators. Generally, Sects are hierarchical. There are often core, inner, and outer disciples in any Sect, with Sect Elders above them and the Sect patriarch above all.

Six Jades Sect—Rival sect of the Verdant Green Waters, located in the State of Wei.

State of Shen—Location in which the first book is set. Ruled by a king and further ruled locally by lords. The State of Shen is made up of numerous counties ruled over by local lords and administered by magistrates. It is a temperate kingdom with significant rainfall and a large number of rivers connected by canals.

State of Wei—The antagonistic kingdom that borders the State of Shen. The two states are at war.

Tael—System of money. A thousand copper coins equals one tael.

Tai Kor—Elder brother

Verdant Green Waters Sect—Most powerful Sect in the State of Wen. Wu Ying's current Sect.

Printed in Great Britain
by Amazon

31602075R00172